T0124265

BUILDING
CHAMPIONS

BUILDING
CHAMPIONS

Changing Disruptive, Delinquent Teens' Attitudes
and Behaviors to Become Real-Life Champions

John Stephenson

BUILDING CHAMPIONS
CHANGING DISRUPTIVE, DELINQUENT TEENS' ATTITUDES
AND BEHAVIORS TO BECOME REAL-LIFE CHAMPIONS

Copyright © 2019 John Stephenson.

All rights reserved. No part of this book may be used or reproduced by any means, graphic, electronic, or mechanical, including photocopying, recording, taping or by any information storage retrieval system without the written permission of the author except in the case of brief quotations embodied in critical articles and reviews.

This is a work of fiction. All of the characters, names, incidents, organizations, and dialogue in this novel are either the products of the author's imagination or are used fictitiously.

iUniverse books may be ordered through booksellers or by contacting:

iUniverse
1663 Liberty Drive
Bloomington, IN 47403
www.iuniverse.com
1-800-Authors (1-800-288-4677)

Because of the dynamic nature of the Internet, any web addresses or links contained in this book may have changed since publication and may no longer be valid. The views expressed in this work are solely those of the author and do not necessarily reflect the views of the publisher, and the publisher hereby disclaims any responsibility for them.

Any people depicted in stock imagery provided by Getty Images are models, and such images are being used for illustrative purposes only.
Certain stock imagery © Getty Images.

ISBN: 978-1-5320-6630-6 (sc)
ISBN: 978-1-5320-6629-0 (e)

Library of Congress Control Number: 2019900903

Print information available on the last page.

iUniverse rev. date: 01/23/2019

For my family and in memory of Danny, my eldest son, a great guy and amazing Rugby League player, coach, and administrator.

Acknowledgments

I pay tribute to my family for allowing me the time to write this novel—for their patience, understanding, and support in allowing me to complete a paragraph or chapter before I attended to family chores and duties.

Also, I pay tribute to the many hundreds of teenagers I got to know who allowed me into their lives, including me with their fears, thoughts, and confidences. These guys, unwittingly, supplied the random material for this book. Without the interactions and friendship of these guys, this novel would be a book of blank pages. Thanks, fellas; you are all true legends.

Thanks also to the awesome doctors and nursing staff of the hospital where I found myself in August/September 1992, for saving my life and instilling in me the will to go on, which is featured within the first couple of chapters of this novel. Their dedication to my care and recovery was amazing.

Please read on and enjoy the journey of Rocky and his young mates from 1992 to 1998.

Introduction

"Those terrible, delinquent, disruptive teenagers, terrorizing the neighborhood." How many times have you heard that said or even said it yourself? Personally, I cringe when I hear that. And feel embarrassed that I am in the same age group as those who say it. I despise any adult who puts dirt on our young people, who obviously does not understand them or can't be bothered to talk with them (no, I don't mean talking down to them) to understand them and their issues.

I have spent many, many years with young boys in the community, at sporting clubs, in social activities, and in various roles in my employment. I have communicated with thousands of them over the years. I have enjoyed meaningful conversations and fun activities and have listened to their fears, their thoughts, and their concerns. I have been made privy to some of the horrible things to which they have been subjected during their very short lives.

Have you noticed a group of teenage boys in a shopping center, how adults walk around them, seemingly in fear of them? What's wrong with them? They are only a group of people catching up with one another, chatting, just as people do. What do I do? I walk up to them, through the group, and say, "How ya doing, fellas?" or something similar. What happens? They smile at me and answer that they are doing well. They look as if they're thinking, *This one talks to us? How different!* Occasionally, one or two will talk to me with a few more words and ask how I am doing. Next time you see one or more teenagers, they stop for a short conversation.

Ah, it makes you feel so good.

Yep, I have become friends with thousands of teenagers over the years, and I can tell you they are more genuine than a lot of adults.

Why don't you try it? You will be surprised.

This novel, which is set in an industrial township on the east coast of Northern Australia, is based on mostly true, actual snippets of conversation from my interactions with these guys.

The interactions used in this story are from my training young kids on the sports fields up to 1992, my illness and recovery during 1993 and 1994, the experience of assisting teachers at school camps and school-based practical assistance programs with teenage schoolboys during 1995 and 1996, and my adventures when I drove a maxi-taxi from 1997 to 1998.

To this day, I continually talk with young guys, still about their major fears, thoughts, concerns, and issues; I even have fun with them. All it takes is a few discussions with them to show that there are other ways of looking at the issue, to solve their problems or challenges, and to make them feel better within themselves.

I am not a trained counselor, but I've been around for a while and picked up the required attitude, life skills, and knack for communicating with young guys on their level.

I encourage you to read on and experience my life of assisting young guys in achieving their changes in attitude and behavior, to experience their journeys to become respectable, respectful, and content boys and young men, admired in their community.

The Author conducting a disco for High School students

CHAPTER 1

We are the champions of the league!

The cheering from the crowd was almost deafening. The spectators jumped to their feet, still cheering, still yelling, and still clapping. Young Jason picked himself up off the ground and jumped in the air in jubilation; the siren marking full time could hardly be heard in the background.

As Jason threw the ball skyward, his teammates rushed over and ceremoniously hoisted him above their shoulders in celebration. Jason was the captain of the local Thunderbolts Junior Rugby League Football under thirteen team. Once he had the ball, Jason had the amazing ability to duck and weave his way through the opposition and not only make it all the way down the field but score several tries in each match. He was lightning-fast as well; whenever he made a break, no one could catch him, not even the referee.

The joy of the team was infectious, as was the cheering of the crowd of parents who had gathered to watch their twelve-year-old sons play their semifinal football game against the toughest and most successful club in the competition. Jason had just scored the winning points to take them to the final premiership, to be played the following weekend.

Rick Scott was sitting on the sideline with his reserve players on the benches. Rocky, as the boys preferred to call him, was the coach of that under-thirteen team. He beamed with a sense of achievement at the sight of his charges celebrating their win. A warm, fuzzy feeling swept over Rocky as he heard the cheers from the parents and at the sight of his team celebrating what many had said at the beginning of the season was not achievable.

Rocky was a very quiet man in general; he seldom showed excitement or emotion, and most people found it extremely difficult to work out what he was thinking. That day, however, upon realizing what his young team had achieved, he jumped into the air, embraced a couple of parent helpers and the players on the bench, and then raced onto the field to join the lads in their celebrations.

For Rocky, it was a proud moment as he realized that all the hard work had paid off; he'd led the boys through long training sessions and battled to change many of their attitudes and emotional responses. Rocky joined the team, praising and encouraging all of them to recognize their achievement.

"But despite your great win," he told the boys, "your job is not yet complete. You'll have to train hard and listen intently during the coming week's training, so you'll be prepared to accept the challenge of next Saturday's premiership—and win it."

After drinks, a cool-down in the showers, and goodbyes, each boy left on a total high, grinning with confidence. The boys who'd been injured during the game soon forgot their pain as they left for their homes. Some stayed to watch the older age groups play their semifinals, still with their heads in the clouds after their success. Training in the coming week was set for Monday, Wednesday, and Friday after school.

Monday's training consisted of the usual skills with the ball, tackle practice, another run around the oval, and some fitness training. At the end of the session, Rocky allowed the boys to shower and change into their casual clothes and then gathered them around for a discussion over another soft drink or juice. As they finished their talk, they heard a car arrive, tooting its horn. The boys looked over to see a pizza delivery vehicle.

"The committee—your parents and supporters—agreed to reward you with pizza and drinks for a job well done," Rocky told them, "and to encourage you to keep on going for one more week. You'll have to train hard on Wednesday to work off the food you're about to consume to retain your fitness. If training goes well on Wednesday, Friday's training will be light—just a few skills, tactics, and ways to deal with the emotions you might experience with the anticipation of the upcoming match."

Rocky always led from the front during training; he always did the same as the boys. He knew he couldn't expect anyone to do something that he was not prepared to do. Rocky disliked the saying, "Do as I say, not as I do"; he changed it to "Do as I say, just the same as I do."

He always invited comments, thoughts, and opinions from the boys on how things should or could be done. He gave them this chance to offer input, as it encouraged a sense of ownership. This method of dealing with young people always worked for Rocky. If one of the boys said something that didn't make sense to the others, Rocky wouldn't allow the other players to ridicule or criticize the one who'd offered his perspective. He said many times that all young people have thoughts, opinions, and feelings. They should be encouraged to put these thoughts forward, even though they might not always be correct, as their views were the result of what they'd experienced; they would hold on to them until further experiences convinced them otherwise. Because of Rocky's attitude, he always enjoyed the respect and friendship of those who were his age or twenty or thirty years younger or older than him.

All the boys on the team had a great respect for Rocky and enjoyed his company. They enjoyed sharing their good times, their problems and fears, and, in general, having a good time learning about their place in society without being criticized, ridiculed, or spoken down to, as so many adults had a bad habit of doing to young people.

Rocky turned up for training on Wednesday not feeling very well. He had flu-like symptoms—not much energy, a headache, and body pain. The boys soon sensed this and became very concerned. They spent time with Rocky, attempting to make him feel a little better. A couple of parents who had assisted Rocky with training throughout the year took the boys for their skills and fitness training under Rocky's direction, while Rocky watched intently. It pleased Rocky to see his team train so well when other adults were in charge, and he realized that they had succeeded in treating the session seriously by taking instructions from other adults. He knew that the boys had learned more than how to play football; they had also learned responsibility and respect for others who had an interest in helping them achieve a common goal. He felt so proud, even though he felt so ill.

The team talk went well, and it was decided that they were ready to tackle the final on Saturday and probably come up with a win. All understood that winning was not as important as doing their best, putting all that they had learned together, and giving it their best shot; they had the ability to win. Rocky said they had earned the privilege of a light training session on Friday, along with a discussion session on tactics and how to deal with anxiety and fear of what Saturday's match would present to them. After the training session was over, each of the boys came over to Rocky to shake his hand, put his arms around him, or give him a hug and wish him the best for a quick recovery, as well as thank him for helping them with their game.

Rocky returned home, exhausted and suffering severe pain in his head and body. He showered, took a pain reliever, and flopped into bed, wondering what had caused his illness during the most important week of the year. As he lay in bed, he thought about all his players and what winning meant to them. *Which character trait can I develop even further*, he wondered.

Rocky had a very rough and sleepless night, as his condition seemed to worsen. He had severe aches and pains in his head, body, and limbs. As dawn arrived on Thursday, he decided to visit the doctor for assistance in easing the symptoms.

The doctor examined Rocky and concluded that he had a bad case of a kind of bacterial infection, and he prescribed a course of antibiotics.

Rocky decided he'd stay home from work that day. When he got home, he took the first dose of his medication, lay down on the couch, and turned on the television. He soon fell asleep, sleeping several hours until his two young sons arrived home from school. Rocky dragged himself up to attend to their needs, but still felt very weak and in a lot of pain. After dinner, he took another dose of medication and then struggled to the bathroom and then into bed for what he hoped was a better night's sleep.

When Rocky woke on Friday, feeling worse than the previous day, he went again to the doctor, who gave him another prescription for a different, stronger medication. He spent the day in and out of bed, trying to find some relief and comfort, until it was time to go to the football field for training.

As he struggled to get himself out of the car, the boys ran up to him to help him. The lads were very concerned when they saw how sick Rocky was. They helped him to the edge of the field and assisted him in sitting down for their group discussion.

Bill and Mark, two parents who had assisted Rocky in coaching the team throughout the year, got some instructions from Rocky on what the boys were to do during their training run; they took the team to the field and put them through their paces. From time to time, one or two lads would run over to Rocky to make sure that he was okay. As he watched, he began to sweat profusely from his fever, so the boys brought him water whenever he needed it. Rocky managed to find some good comments or praise for the boys as they left the field and sat in a semicircle in front of him.

Rocky ran through some of the tactics that he wanted the boys to think about and invited comments from them to encourage them to concentrate on the task ahead during the final game.

Jason stood up and said, "Rocky, we all want to tell you that we hope you are much better by tomorrow."

Rocky replied, "Yeah, thanks, mate. I hope I'm better tomorrow too so I can get some energy back and celebrate with you all. Just remember everything you've learned this year. Play to enjoy yourselves, and you'll come through as winners. I don't necessarily mean the winners of the game but winners who have achieved so much pleasure from the game, getting to know each other, learning patience, playing as a team, and knowing that you have done the best that you can. Think of someone you want to do it for or some reason why you want to win the game, keep your heads down, and you may end up winning the premiership.

Rocky took a sip of water, wiped his feverish brow, then looked up at the boys and said. "Remember what I've told you all year—if you make a mistake or have a lapse in concentration, get over it and play on. Forget it. Don't let it cause you to lose sight of the goal. I have never yelled at any of you or singled you out for mistakes on the field, and I won't change that now just because you're playing the final."

Rocky was always careful not to ridicule the players' mistakes or yell at them. He knew how to keep their self-esteem as high as possible. If they made mistakes, he knew how to talk about those mistakes in a general context during end of training or game discussions without making the players feel bad about it.

"One more thing," Rocky said. "The team that wins the premiership will earn the privilege of playing the premiers of the competitions from nearby towns in the zone to gain a higher level of experience over the next four weeks. That team will travel to those towns, with overnight stays on three of those weekends." He dismissed the team by saying, "Just do your best, men. Remember everything you've learned, and"—he cupped his hands around his mouth, *"go get 'em, guys!"*

Mike, the vice-captain, who was usually very quiet and reserved, said, "Don't worry, Rocky. We'll kill 'em tomorrow, just to make you feel better."

Rocky had a tear in his eye as he said goodbye to each of the boys with the usual handshake. After he shook hands with Tony, he called him back and said, very quietly and carefully so the others did not hear, "Tony, that's not a handshake. I've told you before how to shake hands. Push your hand forward, man, and grip my hand firmly, like you mean it. That's better. I'll see you tomorrow, buddy."

Rocky and the two parent helpers talked a little about the team and the forthcoming game and then left the grounds.

When Rocky reached his home, he showered and retired for the night. Although he felt very ill, he still thought about the boys' progress since that first day of the season. With enormous pride, he thought, *the team has the guts and determination, and they know how to in the game on Saturday.* He knew they had the required ability, attitude, and stamina. Above all, Rocky realized they had the desire to take the trophy home for the club and the team. As he drifted off to sleep, he hoped the night's sleep and the medication he had taken would help him to feel better for the big game.

Rocky had a very restless night, caused by thoughts of the task his team had ahead of them and the illness that had compromised his health. The symptoms had not eased; if anything, they had worsened. He had lost count of how many times he had woken in a lather of sweat and couldn't cool off. His temperature remained high, and his body sweat profusely.

During one waking period, he noticed an uncomfortable, swollen feeling in his mouth, accompanied by a strange stinging sensation. Little did he know of the major discomfort that was ahead of him. These waking periods continued for the next couple of hours, and his condition seemed worse each time he woke. To ease his symptoms, he took doses of ibuprofen and the antibiotics that had been prescribed for him, but Rocky began to think the medications were causing other complications.

At around half past three in the morning, Rocky woke once again with a very high fever, and the swollen feeling in his mouth seemed to be worse. He tried to sip some water, but it was difficult to do with his swollen lips. He touched his mouth and felt a strange, soft, floppy growth around his lips. In a panic, Rocky staggered to the bathroom to check out his face in the mirror. As he focused on his image, a feeling of horror crept over him. His eyes were puffy and bloodshot—he looked like a very ill, elderly man—but worse than that, clusters of blisters that resembled bunches of grapes were protruding from the inside of his mouth and hanging out toward his jaw.

Rocky realized he could barely speak intelligibly and was having difficulty breathing—his nose was partially blocked, and the mass of blisters in his mouth made it extremely hard to inhale. Rocky woke his wife, Suzie, who called his doctor and explained Rocky's condition. Dr, Clive suggested that he should make a house call, but Suzie's description was so precise that the doctor changed his mind and made some suggestions, including breaking and draining the blisters.

"Bring him to my office at five thirty," the doctor concluded. "That will allow me some time to research these symptoms."

Rocky tried to lie down again, as he was very weak, but lying down, sitting up, or walking around made no difference in his comfort level. Added to his weakness was Rocky's worry and stress about his medical condition. *What's wrong with me?* he wondered. *What caused it? And more important, how am I going to survive it?*

Rocky didn't realize it, but he had forgotten about the task ahead for his young football team.

By five thirty, Rocky was very upset and weak; he had a lot of trouble walking the short distance from his house to the car. From the time they'd called the doctor until now, the blisters had to be broken several times to ease the pressure in his mouth and to keep his airway clear, so he could breathe. As Suzie pulled the car up to the entrance of the doctor's office, the doctor was waiting in the doorway—and he was horrified at what he saw.

Rocky barely had enough strength to get himself out of the car. He made it to his feet but was doubled over and could only manage to shuffle to the entrance. The doctor also noticed the large bunches of blisters attached to the inside of his mouth and hanging out over his bottom lip, almost to his chin.

The doctor helped Rocky to a chair and examined his eyes, mouth, nose, and ears. He checked Rocky's blood pressure and temperature, listened to his lungs, and performed several other tests to ascertain his reflexes, pain threshold, pulse rate, heart rhythm, and oxygen percentage in the blood. The doctor then asked about the blisters—how they felt, if breaking them had eased the discomfort, how quickly they had reappeared, and how Rocky felt in general.

"I am so sorry," the doctor said. "If I had realized your condition was as bad as it is, I would have come over to your house. I'm going to break these blisters for you again, collect some of the fluid, and send it to the pathologist for testing, along with blood and urine. I've examined some medical publications to help determine what's wrong, what the causes could be, and how to heal the illness. I found a reference to a condition called pemphigus vulgaris, which I believe you have, but blisters generally are on the outside of the body, not the inside, as yours are.

"Now, how are we going to treat this? I am not sure? History has shown that administering steroids, the treatment for pemphigus, fixes the condition within twenty-four hours, but only when the blisters grow on the outside of the body.

"I also noted that steroid treatment for a person with the blisters on the inside of the mouth is fatal, in all cases, within a couple of hours. I spoke to a couple of specialists in this field, who advised me to administer the steroid treatment. I am not confident enough to do this, however, as I feel that it will take your life. I'd like to admit you to the hospital, but I'm concerned the hospital staff may be forced or coerced into injecting steroids, which has been used as a treatment for similar symptoms in the past, what I fear would be a lethal dose, which would kill you."

Rocky suddenly remembered his boys and their important game. He wanted to be with them on this important day, and he was sure that they needed him. Rocky convinced the doctor not to send him to hospital yet. He agreed not to exert himself and said he would note any complications he experienced.

"You'll need to eventually give in and go to the hospital within the next twelve to twenty-four hours. I've left a message and details about your condition with a professor friend of mine at a large medical university in the United States. I'm waiting for him to contact me. Don't hesitate to phone me if you have any concerns. Call as soon as you notice any blisters forming on the outside of your body, keep watch between your fingers and toes and other creases of your body, and let me know.

"I am not going to offer any treatment at this stage. Please take care when you break those blisters that you don't allow the area to become infected. Drink plenty of water and eat anything you can—soft foods are probably best, like scrambled eggs. Perhaps you can make an eggnog and drink that if you can."

As Rocky was leaving, Dr. Clive said, "Oh, Rocky, I almost forgot. I'd advise you to stop taking any of the medication in case that's what is causing your symptoms. I'll see you later."

Rocky returned to his home very concerned about what his future might be. Was he going to die? Was it all a terrible dream? Was he ever going to recover? These thoughts crowded into his head. Rocky was not comfortable with his current situation; it was the first time he could not control his destiny. It was very difficult for him to accept his predicament. He slept for a few short periods, waking to break the blisters and clean his face. He wondered how he could be of any assistance to his team of young football players. Little did he know how much effect his mere attendance would have on the boys in the quest to win the grand final.

About an hour before the game was to kick off, Jason's father, Terry, dropped in to see Rocky and to ask how he could assist with the game. Terry had helped Rocky with the coaching throughout the year. Terry worked out of town but had been a great help whenever he was available to assist Rocky.

Terry was extremely shocked at the sight of Rocky standing in front of him. He had no idea that Rocky was so ill. The two men talked about the game and the team and a few tactics that the boys could employ. Rocky asked if Terry could call the shots from the sideline as the coach. Rocky was intent on attending the game, although he realized that his failing health would not allow him to take an active part in the game. However, nothing was going to hold him back from watching his lads tackle the opposition team as they tried to achieve something that a few months ago had seemed impossible. Rocky was going to be there to support them with his presence, if nothing else.

Terry wished Rocky well and a quick recovery. "Don't worry, Rocky. I'll get 'em over the line. They'll win this one too."

"I know, Terry," Rocky said. "I know you can do it. I know they can and will do it. Please tell them for me, 'Hit 'em hard and hit 'em low.' And remind them to play as a team and not just think of themselves as heroes alone but as heroes together. Pass the ball wide and tackle hard—the simple stuff, just as we trained to do all year. No fancy stuff. It has worked all year, so it can work today. And tell them that they can realize their dream if they keep their heads down and think."

Rocky paused to gasp for air and then continued. "Tell Jason as well. He's the captain, and he listens well, and the boys listen to him. He has the ability and attitude to lead and lift his team. You have taught your boy well, Terry. You should be proud of him. Give him a high-five from me, will ya?"

Terry thanked Rocky for his praise. Before he left, he told Rocky, "I can feel a Thunderbolt strike Tyranny Creek today that will cause a lot of damage to the Hawks. Can't wait to see the Hawks' feathers fly as they all come crashing down to earth. Up the mighty Thunderbolts!" He let himself out.

Rocky slowly washed himself and dressed to go to the football field at the Tyranny Creek sports complex. He examined himself in the bathroom mirror and was shocked and embarrassed by what he saw. His mouth was very swollen, and clear fluid dribbled from his mouth. His eyes were very red and inflamed, and small blisters had formed at the corners. His nose also was oozing the same clear fluid. He examined the rest of his body, but no blisters had formed between his fingers or toes or in his underarm or groin areas. He phoned Dr. Clive with an update of his symptoms. Rocky also noted the stinging sensation in his mouth had worsened, and he was experiencing a similar sensation in his nose, eyes, and ears. It was obvious that his condition had deteriorated in the four hours or so since he'd left the doctor, as the infection had spread to other openings of his body.

Dr. Clive advised Rocky not to attend the football match but to stay home and rest.

"I have to watch and support my boys as they play the most important game of their young lives," Rocky insisted. "I also want to witness what could be history being made and to be part of the celebration, just in case they win."

Dr. Clive sighed. "If you're going, make sure you have a towel or two to cover your mouth to ensure that any infection won't invade your body and complicate the condition. I'll visit the grounds. I want to speak with you in person, check your temperature and blood pressure, and examine you before I confer with my associate in the States about any possible treatment."

After ending his phone call, Rocky got himself moving and, with a lot of effort, got into the passenger seat of the car. As Suzie pulled up in the parking lot at the sports complex, Rocky could hear loud cheering from the very large crowd. A team of younger players had just finished their game. He hoped that the younger Thunderbolts had won their game. He couldn't tell by the cheers which team had won. He could hear words spoken across the public-address system, but the cheering was so loud he could not hear any details. He then thought, *the cheering is too loud for the Thunderbolts' supporters.* The opposing team was from a much larger club, so there were probably many more supporters than those for the Thunderbolts. Then he remembered a week earlier when his team won on the siren. The crowd was loud then, so maybe the Thunderbolts' under-eleven team had won.

Either way, it didn't really matter, as Rocky got very excited as the mood of the crowd reached him, and he caught sight of his lads finishing a light warm-up run and returning to the sideline, where Terry was waiting with a handful of parent helpers. The boys sat down to listen to Terry give them some last-minute tips.

Rocky struggled out of the car, a cap on his head and dark sunglasses hiding his eyes. He had a towel over his shoulder and held a corner to cover his mouth. He shuffled over to the boys, who all looked up in horror at the frail man who stood before them. Murmurs rippled through the group;

they were obviously concerned for Rocky. This wasn't the same person that they all knew.

Tom, one of the smaller, quieter boys, jumped to his feet and yelled. "Are you okay? Rocky, what happened to you?" He grabbed a seat for Rocky, so he could join them. As he sat down, the boys raced over to him and showed their concern, some reaching out to grab his hand, put an arm around him, or just stand in silence. Rocky tried to speak but, through emotion and pain, found that he couldn't. Tears welled in his eyes and ran down his cheeks from behind his dark glasses.

Suddenly, the time on siren sounded, and the boys realized that their time was up. They now had to run onto the field and dig deep to find a win. The captain, Jason, yelled out, "Don't you worry, Rocky. We are gunna do this one just for you, sir. That will make you feel better again."

As the boys assembled on the sideline to run onto the field, they began to chant: "Rocky, Rocky, Rocky! We're gunna get that shield just for Rocky, Rocky, Rocky."

The referee spoke to both teams about the rules that he was going to enforce and general instructions about fair play, and then he blew his whistle to indicate play on. The Thunderbolts had the kick-off, and as Jake advanced toward the ball to kick it, Jason saluted Rocky with a special hand gesture that Rocky and the boys had devised among themselves as a signal that all was okay or as a victory salute. The boys and Rocky had, in fact, devised two signals to communicate between the coach and the team when they were on the field. The first was forming a V with the index finger and middle finger of the right hand, with other fingers and thumb clenched, held above the head, with the left arm horizontal to cross the upheld right arm halfway, forming a plus sign. This salute was used to indicate victory or that things were going well. Rocky used this salute to indicate his pleasure or praise to a player or players who did something great, like a pat on the back from a distance, and the team players used it to indicate to Rocky that they were pleased at what they had done on the field, such as a good tackle or good run or scoring points.

The other signal was the right hand held above the head with the middle three fingers hanging down, slightly spread apart. This was to symbolize an M, which stood for mission, which meant that the team had to dig a bit deeper to do better or to remember a tip that they had talked about. It was not to have a negative meaning. Rocky never spoke negatively to or about his team or team members. He always found a positive in everything that a team member had done. The boys hardly ever used the M salute, but they all knew what Rocky meant whenever he used it from the sideline. With these two signals, Rocky and the boys knew what was happening or what should happen to extract the best from the team and, ultimately, achieve their goals and dreams.

The opposition team scored first points, and for a moment, the boys hung their heads a little with a feeling of dejection. They glanced over to Rocky, who was displaying the M signal to get them thinking about what they now had to do. Rocky quickly changed to the V salute, and suddenly, he could see the team lift and sprint back to the center line, heads held high, with a renewed purpose. They obviously remembered what Rocky had told them all year—that what had passed had passed, and they should learn from it and get going.

Both the captain and vice-captain talked calmly to the team to lift them to another level. *It's working*, thought Rocky. He could see the spirit of the team lift as they waited to restart the game. As Jake ran up to kick the ball, Rocky could see several V signals from the boys as they moved as one line to tackle the ball carrier. As the line of players arrived, Jake tackled the opposition player, who coughed up the ball straight into Jason's arms. Jason took four giant steps and planted the ball between the posts to score a try, which added a further 4 points to the score.

The team erupted in jubilation and ran to Jason and Jake to congratulate them on what they had just done. All the boys returned Rocky's and Terry's V salutes as Jake kicked the ball through the goal posts to add a further 2 points. A feeling of pride crept over Rocky as he took his seat.

Although he was very weak and very uncomfortable, it didn't matter for the moment. He was realizing the rewards of the many hours of hard work, sweat, and tears that he had put into getting the lads to where they were that day. The Thunderbolts kicked the ball once again and saw a similar thing happen. This time, Jake kicked slightly to the right of a player who usually fumbled the ball under pressure. Sure enough, as the kid went to catch the ball, he dropped it at Josh's feet, a tall lad who was as strong as an ox. In one motion, Josh stooped down, gathered the ball, held it close to his chest with his left arm, and barged his way through the opposition line, dropping each player he contacted as he went. Josh made a gigantic dive for the line and scored an awesome try to put the Thunderbolts in front. As halftime arrived, the score remained the same, with the Thunderbolts in front. It was a very physical first half with each team advancing to each end of the field. *An even and clean game*, Rocky thought.

As the team left the field, all of them displayed the V salute to Rocky, who returned the salute. He was so happy with the team's performance so far. Terry told them how proud he and Rocky and all the parents were of them but reminded them that they were only halfway there.

"Don't slack off now and lose the way. You have to play as if the other team is in front," Terry said, repeating the words Rocky had told the team at every game. He always told them that if they could convince themselves they were ahead and played hard, more points probably come their way and seal a good win. The lads looked to Rocky, who nodded his approval of what Terry had told them. A couple of the players of the team came over to check on Rocky and reassure him that the team was going to "do it" for him. Rocky signaled the M sign, followed by the V salute to the team as they reentered the field, cheering as they went. Rocky thought they were cheering for themselves, but they were cheering for Rocky—it was Rocky's perseverance and guidance that had gotten them this far.

As the other team kicked off, Dr. Clive arrived to talk to Rocky. "I have spoken to my colleague in the US," he said, "and we have both decided not to treat you with any medication at this stage, although you do seem to be getting worse. Because your symptoms have not appeared externally, you probably don't have pemphigus. The fluid I took this morning is completely sterile; there are no signs of infection or any trace of poison in your system, which indicates that you have a reaction to something. Injecting you with steroids at this stage would be fatal, so I will run more tests when you're in the hospital. I'm surprised you're not in there at this moment."

"I'm not going to the hospital, Clive, if I can help it."

"Make no mistake; you are going to suffer more before you improve. As soon as you can't take it anymore, get yourself to the hospital."

The crowd erupted in wild cheering as the Thunderbolts scored again. Rocky didn't see what had happened, but he leaped to his feet, as he felt that was the try that would secure the win for the boys. They only had a few minutes left to play, and Rocky signaled the V salute, followed by the M signal, to tell the boys that he was very pleased and to remind them that their mission was not yet complete—to keep their cool, play hard, and keep the opposition on the ropes.

As Rocky sat down again, Dr. Clive placed a thermometer in his mouth, connected the blood pressure cuff on his arm, and counted his pulse rate on his right wrist.

"Your temperature is very high, your blood pressure is normal, and your pulse is a little slow. This worries me, considering the excitement here. Your pulse should be quicker than usual. You should be in the hospital—or at least at home, resting."

"I'm better off here," Rocky mumbled, "watching my Thunderbolts, than being at home, not knowing what's was going on at the field. But don't worry, Clive, not much time left before this one will be over. Then I'll go home and rest."

As they said goodbye to each other, Clive insisted that Rocky admit himself to the hospital before the day was over.

As the final siren sounded, the crowd of Thunderbolts' supporters and parents erupted in loud cheering and began stomping the grandstand floor in jubilation. Rocky and Terry and the boys on the reserve bench jumped to their feet and joined in the cheering. Rocky couldn't yell, but he somehow threw his towel skyward to indicate his elation at the magnificent success. The boys were jubilant as well, some jumping in the air, some worshipping the ground, others cartwheeling around the field, and the rest forming a circle and chanting the war-cry song they had devised during the week. Rocky was not aware of the war cry; the lads had put their own words to one of Rocky's favorite tunes, Bon Jovi's "Livin' on a Prayer."

The whole team then joined the circle and chanted the song. Rocky immediately recognized the song and started moving toward the group of boys. The boys noticed Rocky coming toward them, and the chanting circle moved toward him, eventually encircling him. Rocky was so proud; his emotions seemed to explode. He gave each boy a high-five.

As the singing died down, Rocky said, "I am so proud of each one of you. I could not have wished for anything better, both for you and from you. You put into action all that you have learned this year. You worked exceptionally well as a team of heroes, each pulling in the same direction. And that war cry—what else can I say? Well done, fellas."

Rocky sat on the field as his energy dissipated. He had to rest to regain strength to get off the field so that the boys could attend the presentation of the shield. He motioned for the boys to go over to the presentation area.

"We're not going to leave you here alone. We are not going anywhere without you," Jason said.

"I'll be okay," Rocky replied. "I'll get up soon and leave the field."

"We're staying here with you, mate," Tony insisted.

"We're not leaving you here like this," Josh said.

Jason then shouted, "Let's pick Rocky up and carry him over with us."

Seven of the boys carefully stood Rocky on his feet, hoisted him onto their shoulders, and carried him over to the sideline by the presentation area. A very proud feeling swept through Rocky—what fantastic kids to reward their coach in his time of need.

Although he felt elated at his team's win, he also felt sick and weak as his illness took over his body. Rocky realized that he had successfully taught his team members more than how to win a football premiership— much more than that. He had also taught them how to be compassionate, thoughtful, respectful, and respectable young men. They each had certain characteristics, but their thoughtfulness was now on display to the crowd. As the crowd noticed the young team carrying their coach, they once again erupted in wild applause.

Rocky thought, *there aren't many people who experience this level of compassion from a group of boys—boys who eight months ago would have left an "oldie" to suffer on his own.* He knew this experience was the ultimate reward for changing the lives of a handful of young people. He felt fantastic; he only wished his health was better so that he could have celebrated properly with the lads.

As the boys lined up to accept their individual trophies and the team's premiership shield, Rocky thought back over the past year and how much the team members had progressed and grown, not only as players but socially as well. Each one had problems to deal with—bullying from older kids, family issues, attitude problems at school, even getting into trouble with the law. With Rocky's influence, however, each one of them had changed his life for the better. Their attitudes toward life, each other, and their families and friends had vastly improved, and they were much more tolerant of others. *They now respect other people and what is right or wrong,* Rocky thought. The changes in their compassion and their enjoyment of life and what it offered to them had drastically improved.

Rocky realized that his tolerance, persistence, belief, and perseverance had paid off at a time when the boys were entering their teenage years. Now, he tried with all his might to smile as his team accepted their reward for their win. He was so happy. He was smiling on the inside. As the boys were about to leave the dais, Jason asked if he could use the microphone. As he held the mike tightly with both hands, he announced to the crowd, with confidence beyond his years, "I would like to say thanks to all our supporters, parents, and the mighty Thunderbolts football club. We want to especially thank our coach, our leader, our mate, Rocky. Sir"—he looked toward the spot where Rocky sat — "we all appreciate your help this year, so we could win this shield. Thank you very much, Rocky." They all put down their trophies and directed a V salute toward Rocky. "That man over there has taught us all we know about this game. That's why we are the champions—of the league."

Jason tried to continue but had to stop because the crowd cheered wildly, chanting, "Thunderbolts! Thunderbolts!" Jason raised his hand and the noise slowly subsided. "Sir, get your guitar. I have mine, and Nick has his. We have a surprise for you. This time, it's our turn to lead and your turn to join us in song."

The crowd cheered wildly again as the boys left the stage and filed over to the bench where Rocky, Terry, and some of the parents were sitting.

Rocky and the team used to play their guitars and sing at most training sessions. This was part of Rocky's training technique to relax the boys with something other than game tactics and protocols, a kind of bonding session. Rocky would start playing and Jason and Nick would join in, with the rest singing as best they could. They were hardly ever in tune, but that was not the point; they were not training to be great singers, although Rocky remembered that some were pretty good. Jason and Nick played mean guitar for their ages, Nick especially. It never took him long to join in and learn a new tune. Rocky and Nick enjoyed their many jam sessions together after training to a point that Nick felt wronged if they didn't play a tune or two each training day while he waited for his mother to pick him up.

The boys ran over to Rocky and embraced him once again in appreciation and excitement at their fantastic win. Rocky told the boys to go to the shower rooms, freshen themselves up, change, and meet at the shade shelter on the other side of the field, where they could have soft drinks and sausage sizzles as a reward for the way they played the game.

"Don't forget your guitar," said Nick.

"No, mate, I won't. Could you get it from my car after you have your shower?" Rocky asked as he threw his keys to Nick. "It'll take me that long to get to the shade shelter. I seem to have lost energy somewhere and seem so slow."

How great are these kids and the way they have achieved their dream of winning the championship? thought Rocky. Who would have imagined it at the beginning of the season, when a group of sad, wayward boys with defiant attitudes assembled on the field for their first training session? Like most boys of that age, they seemed to have large chips on their shoulders. That needed to be broken down gradually and then rebuilt by someone who cared and who could concentrate on each lad's good points and reshape him into a respectable, intelligent, caring, and confident young man.

The boys settled down to have their drinks and food that had been prepared by some of the mothers. Rocky couldn't manage eating, as his health had deteriorated since Dr. Clive had left. He felt so miserable; some of the boys came to see if he was okay. They could see how sick he was, and they were concerned for him.

"I'll be right, fellas. Can't keep me down for long," Rocky told them. He then called the boys to attention and said, "Listen, fellas, now that you are the Central District Premiers for 1992, you have earned the right to compete against the other district premiers within the Central Division of the state. There are four fixtures, one in each district, over the next four weeks, starting next weekend. You will be traveling by bus for three of those fixtures and staying overnight each time. The other game, naturally, will be a home game. There is no cost to any of you; all costs are covered by the sponsor."

He paused to catch his breath and wipe the dribbles away from his mouth. When he spoke again, it clearly was a struggle. "I will have more information and permission forms and other papers for you on Monday at training." Rocky had to pause once again; he had to sit down before he fell. "I just want to say how proud I am—and all your parents are—of each one of you. Please show your appreciation to Terry for his great help today."

The boys cheered and clapped to show their thanks.

"Well done, men," Rocky said. "You have all made me so happy and proud all year. *Congratulations* for the great win today. Oh, by the way, the next four games are not a competition as such—no points, no competition or overall winners. It's a new concept this year to give you a chance to play against winning teams to give you experience on a higher level than the local competition. Although there won't be a winner's shield, each of you will receive some certificates and other memorabilia to show that you participated." Rocky glanced at Jason, who seemed very fidgety. "Jason, what's wrong?"

"It's time for your surprise, Rocky," Jason said. Tony handed Rocky his guitar, and Jason and Nick reached for their guitars. "We learned this especially for you, Rocky," Jason said. He and Nick started playing the tune to "Livin' on a Prayer" as the rest of the team sang the newly created words. Rocky joined in with his guitar. He missed quite a few notes, but the two boys played a perfect rendition. They went on to play and sing a Queen song, which they had played and sung after games all year, with a small change: "We are the champions—of the league!"

CHAPTER 2

Who stood before him? Was it the gatekeeper, the devil, the Grim Reaper? Maybe it was the Lord himself.

As the players of the Thunderbolts Junior Rugby League Football team left the playing field, each one personally thanked Rocky for his guidance in helping them win the premiership and wished him a full recovery. As they always did, they shook his hand or gave him a hand slap, a high-five, or a one-armed hug.

Rocky also said goodbye to his helpers and accepted their wishes for a speedy recovery. "Don't worry about me," he said, "I'll be okay. I'll beat this, whatever it is."

Rocky's wife, Suzie, helped him to their car and drove him to their home. Rocky washed himself, tried to drink a cool milk drink, and slumped into a lounge chair. He tried to reflect on what he and his young team members had achieved earlier that day. Even though he was very weak and in a lot of pain, he remembered the happy and excited expressions on their faces and felt very satisfied with himself. He had believed in their potential, and his perseverance had helped to extract the best of each one's ability. What made winning the premiership more special was that others had condemned the team at the start of the season, saying there was no hope for them and that they would never win a game, let alone the championship. That gave Rocky the best feeling—that he had taken a group of twelve-year-old boys who were doomed for the scrap heap and helped them to the top of the mountain.

Rocky eventually drifted off to sleep, sitting in his chair. He woke when there was a knock at the door. It was the doctor, who wanted to check on Rocky to see how he was feeling. He also drained the blisters and checked for infection.

"Rocky, you are not getting any better," the doctor said. "It is obvious that the blisters are still only on the inside of your body, still affecting your mucus membranes, so I won't offer any treatment. I have phoned the hospital and told them to expect you this evening. I've left instructions for treatment and the observations that should be followed. I expect the blisters to start forming in your throat, and that will be extremely dangerous, as your throat will be obstructed. When that happens, you will experience more discomfort and may not be able to breathe properly."

He turned to Suzie. "Watch him very closely, and for heaven's sake, get him to hospital soon. I know how stubborn he can be. Please convince him that he must go before it is too late. He will need medical assistance to get over this. The worst is yet to come."

The doctor suggested that Rocky rest and get some sleep, if he could. "You probably won't be able to sleep lying down. If you sleep sitting up, your airway has a better chance of remaining clear and open. I'll be off now. All the best and do keep in touch. I will certainly contact you if any new treatment advice comes from Dr. Golde in the US."

Dr. Clive then let himself out, as Suzie sponged Rocky's forehead, eyes, nose, and mouth. He slipped off into sleep soon after the doctor's departure. He woke many times and finally went to the bedroom to lie down for a while. He still had a very restless time, finding it uncomfortable to lie on his back or side. He eventually found comfort by lying on his side with his head slightly hanging over the side of the bed. Rocky realized his condition was getting serious; he was losing control of his destiny. Rocky wasn't annoyed by much, but not having control of himself was one thing that annoyed him greatly.

By about half past ten that night, Rocky was experiencing a lot of pain in his mouth and throat, and he couldn't breathe too well. He got out of bed and struggled down the hallway to where Suzie and a family friend were sitting, looking very worried, sipping coffee, probably expecting the worse and waiting for the moment that Rocky would give in. Both women seemed very shocked by his appearance. He looked like death warmed up.

Suzie and Rocky decided it was time to go to the hospital. The friend offered to stay at the house with their young sons, who were sleeping. Suzie phoned Dr. Clive, but he said he'd had a couple of glasses of wine and shouldn't drive to the hospital.

"I'll phone ahead and tell the hospital staff that Rocky is coming in," he said.

Suzie got Rocky into the car and began the thirty-minute drive to the hospital.

The journey was a quiet one. Fear and worry crept over Suzie as she thought of what was happening to her soul mate. Rocky, on the other hand, drifted in and out of sleep, although Suzie wondered if he'd lost consciousness. The car pulled up to the emergency department doors, and Suzie ran out to ring the bell, as it was after eleven o'clock and the entrance doors were closed.

A nurse came to the door, and Suzie informed her that she had brought Rocky in to the hospital. "Our doctor said he was going to phone."

The nurse nodded. "The doctor on duty is still on the phone discussing Rocky's condition."

A stretcher was prepared, and Rocky was wheeled into an observation cubical.

As the doctor and nurses gathered around, Rocky opened his eyes and saw the horrified looks on their faces.

"How can someone look so bad and still be living?" one whispered.

"What are the blisters, and where they are coming from?" asked another.

The duty doctor issued several instructions to the nurses regarding treatment options and tests that should be performed. Another doctor came to the cubical, and he asked if the treatment should be injections of steroids.

"No," said the duty doctor, "Dr. Clive instructed that under no circumstance is that to happen."

Suzie screamed out to reinforce the request that steroids should not be administered. Rocky was left in the cubical for what seemed like hours. Occasionally a face would appear to look at Rocky as if he was an alien, but no one spoke. Everyone just looked and prodded and left. It was obvious that no one had ever seen a patient with these symptoms before.

Rocky asked Suzie to get him more pillows so that he could raise himself to assist in his breathing and ease the discomfort. Several samples of blood were taken for testing; his blood pressure, temperature, and pulse rate were recorded, and he was then taken to a bed in one of the hospital wards. Suzie was advised to go home to rest.

"We'll contact you if any changes occur during the night," said a nurse.

Suzie kissed Rocky on the cheek, squeezed his hand, and told him that she loved him. "I'll return as soon as I can in the morning," she promised.

The medical staff attached a drip to Rocky so that he could have nutrition, as it had been almost two days since he had eaten anything of substance. The staff also was concerned about dehydration. The nurses kept a constant watch over him, checking temperature, blood pressure, and pulse rate at half-hour intervals. They kept sponging his forehead and face to keep him cool, as his temperature was increasing rapidly.

Rocky slept for the next few hours but woke several times, especially when the nurses were conducting their observations. As the sun began to rise on Sunday, Suzie and their two sons arrived to see how Rocky was progressing. Rocky could not talk and was so weak he could hardly acknowledge their presence. They didn't stay long; the two boys were distressed to see their dad in such a state.

Soon after his family left, Dr. Clive and the hospital duty doctor came into the ward to see Rocky and talk about his condition. Dr. Clive insisted that no medications or drugs be administered at this stage. Some test results had come back; the fluid from the blisters again was sterile. Sugar was at normal levels, and no infection of the blood was evident; in fact, the test results so far indicated that Rocky was a perfectly healthy guy. This was the confusing part that no one could understand.

While the two doctors were in the room, Dr. Clive phoned Dr. Golde in the States to report on Rocky's condition and confer about the course of action. When he finished his conversation, Dr. Clive told Rocky, "Dr. Golde said you're the first patient in the world to survive this long with these symptoms. He's following your progress very closely to document the findings for further research. Dr. Golde recommends that you transfer to a larger hospital in a larger city to be closer to medical specialists and facilities that may be able to diagnose the illness and formulate a treatment plan to stabilize your condition."

The two doctors agreed with Dr. Golde's advice and decided to wait for other test results to become available. Then they would plan a medical flight the next day to a larger hospital in the capital city. Before Dr. Clive left, he told Rocky, "I'm doing my best to make you as comfortable as possible. I'll phone your wife and talk her through what will be done to help you back to better health."

As the day progressed into night, Rocky's condition deteriorated to the stage where the medical staff were very concerned if Rocky would survive. His mouth now began oozing a clear red- and yellow-streaked thick fluid. Rocky continued to lie on his side with his face hanging over the side of the stack of pillows so that the fluid could flow out of his mouth, preventing it from flowing down his throat and into his lungs. At times, the pillows were removed so that he could lie flat on his side with his face over the side of the bed, allowing more of the fluid to drain away.

The pain in his mouth and throat had intensified to where he could hardly stand it. The doctors said they couldn't administer any painkillers, as they were afraid that he might have a more severe reaction, if that was at all possible. Dr. Clive was contacted, and he advised a form of pain suppressant that could be introduced through the drip, but the duty doctor must stay with him in case his condition deteriorated further.

At about midday, Rocky was moved to intensive care, and the ward was made into an isolated care unit. The doctors believed his condition could be very infectious, even though they had no idea what the cause was. All visitors to the room were required to wear a gown, gloves, mask, and protective glasses.

When Suzie came to visit Rocky, she found the bed in his ward was empty, and the ward staff were disinfecting and sterilizing the bed. She had worked in a hospital as a teenager and remembered that this process meant that the patient had passed away. She stood in the doorway, dropped the bag she was carrying, and screamed.

Her screams startled the medical staff, and a nurse raced up behind her. 'Suzie, Rocky is okay. We had to move him into isolation. I tried to phone you, but your son told me that you had already left. A nurse on the desk was supposed to intercept you when you came in," she said compassionately. "I am so sorry you got such a fright. Come with me, and I will take you to Rocky's bed."

As they arrived at the room, the nurse explained to Suzie that she had to scrub her hands and wear a gown, mask, glasses, and gloves. "It is very important, both for Rocky's and your own health and safety. We are now considering this case as very infectious. You must keep a keen eye on yourself and your children for any symptoms like Rocky's. The doctor will be with you soon. He has other instructions and questions for you." The nurse then left the area.

Suzie stayed a little while, sitting with her husband, who appeared to be asleep but very restless. His mouth was open, and fluid oozed from it. It was a very distressing sight for her, and she had resigned herself to the fact that Rocky could not last much longer. The hospital duty doctor arrived with Dr. Clive just as Rocky woke.

Dr. Clive walked into the room and over to the bed. The other doctor tried to stop him, saying, "You'll need to scrub, gown, and mask up. This is an isolation ward."

"Don't be so stupid," Dr. Clive said in disgust. "He's not suffering from an infectious disease. You cannot catch this. Look at the records. Who is responsible for this?"

"The medical superintendent ordered it. He also wants me to talk to Mrs. Scott and get a list of people with whom Mr. Scott has been in contact since Friday morning."

Clive shook his head. "Gee, Bill, I hope you have several hours and a lot of paper because the places Mr. Scott has been and the people he has been in contact with could number in the thousands."

"No, how can that be? No one can be near that many people when they are so ill."

"You may have read the sports headlines and story in this morning's paper and seen the photo of the Thunderbolts under-thirteen football team and their upset win in the premiership on Saturday. This is the man responsible for that win. Mr. Scott was there in company of all those kids, their parents and supporters, and that entire crowd. Are you going to contact all those people and create a mass hysteria by frightening all those people unnecessarily? Don't be silly; read the reports and charts and think about it. As I said, you cannot catch this." Clive exhaled slowly and said, "Now, we have a patient to treat. Let's get on with it."

They recorded a few observations, and then Clive turned to Suzie. "We were going to transfer Rocky to the major hospital, as I mentioned, but he seems to have gotten worse. I would not advise that he fly, as I am sure he would not survive the flight. I'll contact the hospital and try to arrange for the specialists to fly up here to assess him in this hospital. You look after yourself, and don't forget to contact me if you have any concerns. I'll let you know when the doctors arrive, so you can speak with them. I'll see you later."

Suzie sensed that Dr. Clive was not at all happy with the hospital's having established the isolation ward. As Rocky slipped into a light sleep, Suzie returned to her car to make the journey home, so she would be there when the two boys arrived home from school.

Rocky began to experience extreme difficulty in breathing. It was painful for him to suck air through his mouth and throat; he hadn't been able to breathe through his nose for quite a long time. Each breath required a lot of effort, which caused a lot of pain in his throat. The muscles in his chest and lungs also were very painful, as breathing was no longer an instinct but a conscious effort to inhale. As the pain worsened from the soreness of his lungs and chest muscles, Rocky decided that it was too difficult to keep breathing. He made the decision that he would stop intentionally breathing. He would let nature take control and take him away from his pain and suffering. *After all*, he thought, *I've tried with all my might to overcome this challenge. It's time to let go and drift off in peace.*

When he stopped breathing, Rocky noticed how peaceful it was and how, suddenly, he was pain-free. As he began to slip away, he found himself in the middle of a very bright, silver stream of light. Everything was so calm, and although the beam was very bright, his vision was not blinded by it. He could see very clearly. He noticed, at one end, the weird vision of his two sons with their arms outstretched toward him, both yelling, "Dad, don't leave us! We need you still. We need you to show us the way. We are too small to be without you." A group of other young faces were behind his two young sons.

At the other end of the beam, a man appeared in a flimsy white robe. He could not quite make out who it was. The face was clouded and not very clear. Was it the gatekeeper? Was it the devil? No, he had no horns in his head. It was not the Grim Reaper; he had no scythe. Was it the Lord himself? He wasn't sure. Then Rocky wondered if it could be his father who had passed away twenty years earlier when Rocky had needed him the most, as a teenager? Although Rocky was not sure what was happening, he had no fear. In fact, he felt very comfortable with the presence of this ghostly figure, as if it meant all things good.

Rocky turned back to see what his two boys were doing, but the ghostly figure began to speak, and Rocky quickly turned back to listen to the figure.

"Rocky, do not give in so easily. Take some breaths and live again. Fight hard, just like you have always done in the past. You never give up on a challenge; don't do it now. Your two boys need you to show them the way. You need to show them how to be successful gentlemen, just as you are. Many others will need you too. Many will lose their way, and others will need you to help them, to keep them from running off the rails."

The figure seemed to lose patience, as time was running out. "Go on, Rocky, start breathing, and get on with your life before it's too late."

Rocky started to inhale once again, although it was very difficult and painful. He looked back in the direction of his boys. They appeared to be cheering to see that their father had not given in.

As he glanced toward the other end of the beam, the voice said, "I am happy that you have made the right decision, Rocky. You were not ready to leave your life yet. It is going to be a hard road for you to get back to where you were; it is the biggest battle you will ever have to face, but I know that you will do it.

"You will need to help a lot of young people, as you have been doing. You will be rewarded with a great sense of satisfaction when you change the lives of so many adolescents. You will know by your instincts who needs your help and how you will help them. Your life's purpose is not yet over, but it has changed a little. Go back, learn what is required, and do it. You will need to negotiate many stumbling blocks and obstacles. You will experience much negativity on your journey from those who don't understand or believe as you believe or who don't understand your purpose. Your success will far outweigh the negatives thrown at you. Always think positively, just as you have done in the past. Teach others to be the same. You will have two lives from now on—the one that you have lived for the past forty years and the one that you will start the moment you decide to go back.

"Make sure you live these two lives separately but at the same time, together. That will confuse you for a while, but you will realize in time what I mean by that. You will know how to do this when you get there. Rocky, please go back for the sake of all those young people who need your guidance."

Rocky once again began to breathe as he listened to his guide, and he made the decision not to be weak, not to give in, but to start living again. *After all, as the saying goes, life begins at forty. Let's go back and haunt those on earth for another forty years*, Rocky thought.

Rocky suddenly woke to find himself hanging over the side of the bed. His head and shoulders were hanging down, and large quantities of the reddish-yellow fluid were escaping from his mouth and forming puddles on the floor. He also noticed people gathered around him, a couple of them holding the lower part of his body so that he did not fall out of bed. He didn't know how he had gotten in this position?

Maybe I did it myself while I was unconscious, he thought. *Was there divine intervention?*

Maybe the doctors and nurses had placed him in this position over the edge of the bed because they were aware that his breathing had ceased.

(To this day, Rocky does not know how this happened. He has pain in his left shoulder constantly, which might support the theory that the doctors and nurses damaged the shoulder when they held him over the side of the bed. Rocky does vividly remember the events of the silver beam when he was near death and making the decision to begin breathing again.)

It didn't really matter how it happened; the important thing for Rocky was the fact that he survived that episode and could someday return to his life and family.

As this was unfolding, Suzie had just returned home when she received a phone call from the hospital to return, as Rocky was very low, in and out consciousness, and would probably pass away before the end of the day. Suzie arranged care for her two sons and returned to the hospital. By the time she arrived, Rocky's condition had brightened a little, much to Suzie's relief, but she could see that all was not good long term. Rocky was in no way out of the woods yet.

The doctor had decided to connect a morphine drip that dispensed morphine into Rocky's bloodstream at regular intervals to help relieve the pain in his throat and chest. The mucus membranes inside his body were all affected by the condition. All the internal membranes were being stripped away; all openings were oozing the same smelly fluid that had come through his mouth and nose previously. During the night, Rocky continued to drift in and out of a coma. He also had died on two occasions, as his airways became blocked with the moving of the mucus membranes.

By Tuesday morning, it seemed that the worst was over. Rocky learned that during the night, several friends had called to visit him, not knowing how serious his illness was. These visitors, who were turned away, included a handful of the football team, who found it very hard to understand why they could not see Rocky. How could he be so sick that they could not see him? The nurse was very compassionate and explained that Rocky could not see or talk and that his appearance would probably shock them.

"Just remember Rocky as you know him. It won't be long before he will be back on his feet again. We know he is strong enough to overcome this illness, but it will take some time," she told them. "I'll tell him you came to see him. I know that will make him very happy."

On waking the next day, Rocky noticed that Suzie, Dr. Clive, and at least a half dozen other professional-looking people were in deep discussion in his room. Rocky also noticed that none of them was wearing a gown or mask. *What does that mean?* thought Rocky. *Am I on the mend? By the feeling in my mouth and throat, not likely. Are they going to move me to the larger hospital?*

Dr. Clive noticed that Rocky was awake and moved over closer to Rocky's bed, followed by the other people. Dr. Clive introduced them to him, explaining that they had traveled from the other hospital to assess Rocky's condition and attempt .to formulate a suitable treatment plan. The group of doctors agreed with Dr. Clive that Rocky was so ill that he probably would not have survived the flight. They were all in disbelief that Rocky was still alive.

"No one can possibly survive what this man has gone through and is still suffering from," one said.

"You don't know this man. I have known him for several years now. He always has had the determination to succeed in everything that he does. This, to Rocky, will be no different," Dr. Clive said.

"You know, I cannot work it out. When we were with him yesterday afternoon, he was dead. He was gone for several minutes, and nothing we tried to bring him back seemed to work," the duty doctor said. "All of a sudden, we saw his chest expand and contract a few times, his heart began to beat again, and he was alive. Then he stopped again, for a short time, and then restarted. We could not believe it. Something in his subconscious kicked in, and he got some power from somewhere to overcome the situation."

Dr. Clive said, "You can see from the records and charts that Rocky stopped breathing on two other occasions during the night. As I've said, this bloke has an amazing ability to succeed. If he were conscious, Rocky would have said, 'No one tells me that I can't overcome this. I will succeed.' I have heard him say things like that on many occasions. Sure enough, if Rocky is confronted by an obstacle, he will surely find a way to get around it or get over it and succeed. He is a marvel in that way."

"Yeah, Clive, but this is different. This is a medical condition that no one has control over. You can't beat medical science just like that," the other doctor interjected.

"As I said, you don't know Mr. Scott. You can be sure something happened that we cannot explain that caused him to take control somehow," Dr. Clive said. "I will guarantee that someday Rocky will tell us what happened."

"Do you mean some form of supernatural intervention?"

"Call it what you want. You know as well as I do that sometimes miracles happen in our profession—miracles that cannot be explained medically. Miracles do happen, Doug; I believe that," Clive said. "Anyway, enough of that. We had better get on with it and review the case as we know it. If Mr. Scott has the will to survive, to get over this, and get well again, we must give him every chance."

The group discussed the medical facts in depth and agreed on a course of action. They decided that Clive's treatment was the best course to follow. Clive had refused to administer the steroid treatment, and that most probably had saved Rocky's life, as the handful of sufferers in the past had passed away because of the treatment. They noted the difference between this ailment, where the blisters formed on the inside of the body, and pemphigus vulgaris, where the blisters formed only on the outside. Doug congratulated Clive on his observation of this difference and that Clive had insisted not to use steroids.

"Now what are we going to do?" asked an older doctor with snowy-white scruffy hair and a moustache. "Do we continue with the no-treatment method or try something else?"

Clive answered, "I think that is the best way to go. Although Mr. Scott's condition has deteriorated since I started to treat him, I really expected that."

Tom, the white-haired doctor, said, "I agree, but we need to know what has caused this. We need to make several tests to determine possible causes."

"As you can see, I have tested for sugar levels, blood condition, blood poisoning, and presence of infection. Liver function test results seem to indicate a problem there but that may be because he is so ill. His heart is normal and strong. Where should we go from here?"

Doug suggested, "We should test the liver function again and blood conditions, probably for Ross River virus, glandular fever, Barmah Forest virus, and Dengue Fever."

Tom added, "I would like to contact Steve, the fellow who was treating Mr. Scott for headache and neck pain using acupuncture. I believe Mr. Scott was trying to stop smoking also. Maybe he was having treatment with some form of natural remedies. You know, that rubbish should be banned. Those quacks cause so many problems."

"We are not here to question the practice of alternative medicine or Mr. Scott's use of this practitioner's services," Clive said. "I know Steve very well; a lot of the time these practices help people heal."

"I would like toxicology tests performed, as well as tests for hepatitis, HIV, and AIDS," Doug said.

Clive became visibly agitated. "What are you on about? Mr. Scott is not the type of man to involve himself in activities that cause those types of ailments."

"Clive, I did not suggest that at all," Doug said. "I just think we should cover all possible avenues. I did notice in the records and clinical notes that as well as visiting the acupuncturist—the natural healer—that he recently had returned home from the Gold Coast after being there for a few days at a conference. You never know; someone may have added something to his food or drinks or injected something somehow. I see on your notes, Clive, that Mrs. Scott indicated that Mr. Scott was very successful in his job, earning state and national awards in his profession. You never know; it just takes one or two spiteful or jealous coworkers with their noses out of joint who attempt to fix a 'tall poppy' so that they can get to the top. You all must have seen that at some stage in your careers."

"Jeez, if that happens out there, I am so glad I have lived a sheltered life," Clive said. "That sort of thing only goes on in the movies. Doesn't it?"

As the tensions died down, the decision was made to test for all the ailments that were discussed. The morphine injections were to continue, and the doctors also decided to induce a minor coma to assist Rocky in his recovery. Clive agreed to keep a close eye on Rocky's progress and to confer with the other doctors at least daily to keep them abreast as symptoms changed and which treatment worked, and which didn't.

The doctors then included Suzie in their discussion. They told her of the tests they would perform, the reasons for those tests, the treatment they would give Rocky with inducing the coma, and that they would observe him closely and document all outcomes. Then they'd have a treatment protocol available if it happened again or to someone else in the future.

Suzie asked in a trembling voice, "What has happened to him? What caused it?"

Clive answered, "Just imagine if you cut the top off Rocky's head, flipped the it back like a lid, poured battery acid inside, and put the lid back on."

Doug said, "Clive, that's a bit harsh. You really have a wild imagination."

Clive shook his head. "Think about it, Doug; how else could it be described? Suzie, as I said, if you poured acid inside and put the lid on again, that acid would travel throughout all the insides, stripping away the internal linings, the mucus membranes, and finding its way out of every opening. Yes, I mean every opening, including his behind and his private parts."

Tom then chimed in. "What has to happen now is that all that fluid and damaged linings must leave the body and then rebuild itself. Those mucus membranes will have to regrow. In fact, Rocky will be unique in the fact that all his insides will be reborn. He will have the internal body of a newborn baby."

Clive added, "We won't go into that too much now, Suzie. We will cover that when we get to it. Let's get Rocky over this step first. We are going to put him into a light coma—nothing to worry about—and it will assist his body in recovering at the same time, He won't feel pain while he is in the coma."

Doug said, "From time to time, we will bring him out of the coma for a period so that some body functions can be assessed and because it can be dangerous to be in a coma for extended periods. By the way, we noted that some form of brain damage occurred because of the lack of oxygen during the episodes of nonbreathing. We don't know to what extent yet. That information will come as he recovers."

Clive shook his head. "I told you, Doug, not to mention that at this stage. Don't you think Mrs. Scott has enough to worry about?"

"She has to know," Doug said sternly. "You can't keep it from her; that's dishonest."

"No, Doug. We weren't going to keep it from her. Because we don't know how bad it is and won't know for quite some time, I could not see the point in discussing it with Mrs. Scott today." Clive turned to Suzie and said compassionately, "Don't concern yourself with that now. That's a long way down the track. We must mend Rocky's body first, and then we will look at that. You know how strong Rocky is. You know, and I know that if there *is* any brain damage, he will find a way to overcome it."

Suzie nodded her head in agreement, but tears rolled down her face and fear was in her eyes; her body trembled.

As the doctors left the room, Rocky stirred again and stretched his hand out to Suzie. She moved over to him and grasped his hand tightly. No words were spoken, Rocky could no longer speak, and Suzie could not find any words to say. She was so worried and concerned for their future and Rocky's future.

How will this leave him? she thought. At least he had recognized her and acknowledged her by outstretching his hand.

It was not long before the "vampires," as Suzie thought of them, arrived to collect some blood and other body fluids to send off to pathology. The cruelest one, Suzie thought, was the collection of fluid from the base of his head along the spine. Suzie left as the nurses were settling Rocky for the long sleep. The medication needed to induce the coma had been included in the equipment connected to his chest, where the morphine was administered.

The nurses told Suzie that she should not be alarmed when she visited, as Rocky might be asleep for many hours at a time. When he was awake, he might talk a lot of rubbish that wouldn't make any sense. That would be the side effects of the drugs.

Over the next ten days, Rocky was in his light coma and was not aware of what was going on around him. His condition improved very slowly, but at least it improved. During this time, several people visited Rocky, although he was not aware of their presence. The victorious football team had visited him again, twice. They were admitted to the room so that they could see him. They had some great news to tell him, but Rocky was unconscious during both visits. The nurse told them Rocky was okay; he was just asleep so that he could recover.

Rocky's employers had flown in to visit him to add their support to Rocky and his wife and family. They found it hard to believe that their work colleague could be so ill, with no accident or explanation as the cause.

(His immediate supervisor told Rocky some-time later that he became physically sick by what he had seen.)

By this time, Rocky had lost a lot of weight. His eyes bulged from a very withdrawn face. He had scabby sores and blotches around his mouth, eyes, nose, and ears, and a terrible, rotten stench emanated from his body, like rotting flesh.

By the eleventh day, Rocky's condition had improved, and the doctors decided to bring him out of his coma. This process took almost all day before Rocky regained consciousness completely. He felt the same stinging sensation in his mouth, nose, and eyes. He noticed all the tubes and gadgets connected to various parts of his body to administer nutrition, fluids, and medication and to drain away waste products.

The staff attended to Rocky and his needs for most of the day, trying to make him as comfortable as possible. They were anxious to get him up and mobile, to get his body moving and exercising to regain some core strength. Two of them helped him to the bathroom so that he could have his first shower in almost two weeks. He did not know what day it was or how long he had been in the hospital.

As he looked around the bathroom, he noticed the mirror was covered. He didn't speak, but the nurses noticed he looked at the covers.

"We covered the mirrors in the bathroom and your room, so you can't see yourself," one nurse said. "Your face, especially, is not a pretty sight. It's a good idea to shower with your eyes closed—other parts of your body are just as ugly."

"You'll heal in time," the other nurse said. "None of us has ever seen anything like it before, but the doctors are convinced you will heal."

After showering and drying, Rocky was helped back to his freshly made bed to await the doctor's visit. He needed to hear about all the things that had happened while he was "away."

The doctor came in to explain the test results. "You do not have AIDS, and you tested negative for HIV and hepatitis. You have considerable liver damage; your liver is not functioning properly, which we expected. You have tested positive for Glandular Fever, positive for Ross River Fever, positive to Barmah Forest virus, and negative for the Dengue Fever. Your sugar levels are a little low, but that's okay. Your blood condition is good, with no antibodies or infection present. There were no traces of poisons or drugs in your system."

It was a lot for Rocky to take in, but Dr. Clive advised him not to worry. "What caused it, Clive?" Rocky asked—the first words he had spoken since he woke from his coma.

"We still don't know for sure. It's just one of those things, Rocky. We cannot explain it."

"Clive, that's not good enough; you must have some idea. You can tell me what you think it might be. Even if it turns out to be something else, I won't hold it against you."

"Okay. As I said, we are not sure. We think something has affected your liver and changed it to a state where it is now extremely allergic to penicillin."

"How do you mean, *changed*?" Rocky asked.

"As I said, you have had glandular fever, Ross River fever, and Barmah Forest virus at some point recently—probably not at the same time but sometime over the past four to six months. You probably know that your mother and one of your brothers visited last week, and your mother told me that you were born with a weak liver."

"I forgot about that, Clive."

"It seems that one or some of these viruses has changed some of your liver's functions. And suddenly, we think, you are severely allergic to penicillin. The antibiotic you were taking when you first had the flulike symptoms was penicillin. We are not sure, but we tend to think you were probably suffering from Ross River when they were prescribed for you. Those antibiotics seemed to react with your liver and cause the problem."

"What is it called," Rocky asked, "this illness? Does it have a name?"

"Yes, we put it down to a condition called Stevens-Johnson syndrome. It's very rare. As far as we know, no one—other than you—has ever survived it. You are the first. One good thing, if you can call it good, is that the notes we have collected will be published in medical journals around the world as a possible treatment for the illness."

"Where do we go from here? Will I get better?" Rocky asked.

"I can't see why you won't get better and recover fully from this. Things will be a bit different for you from now on. Your stomach lining has been stripped away and must regrow. Your insides will be the same as those of a newborn baby—that's one thing in your favor; parts of your body will be new again. You will have to watch what you eat and drink for quite a long time, probably years, as your new body parts mature."

"That's a bit scary, Clive. How will I know what's good or bad?"

"You will know that if something causes you pain or discomfort, you shouldn't eat or drink that again for a while. Your body will tell you. Also, you can never take any antibiotics that contain penicillin, and you'll have to watch for food that may become moldy, like breads and cheeses, and watch soils and mulches, as they can have mold in them as they break down. Any contact with these molds or penicillin will almost certainly prove fatal to you.

"Notes have been made on your medical files that if you come to the hospital with similar symptoms, certain treatment can be considered to prevent your having to suffer again. For heaven's sake, Rocky, as soon as you experience a slight swelling or stinging sensation or ulcers in your mouth, get to the hospital immediately, as this treatment must be considered and used before the blisters form. Once the blisters have formed, it will be too late to save you. When you leave the hospital, you will be given a card with your file number on it. If you experience any of the symptoms, get here quickly and present the card. The hospital staff will then see the highlighted emergency information that is on your file.

"Now, I have something else to talk to you about. You have suffered some form of brain damage. While you were sick, you died a few times. Your bloodstream and vital organs were deprived of oxygen for quite a long time. This probably happened the first time, as the other two were reasonably short. It is obvious that your motor skills and your mental state are not affected too much, or you would not have been able to walk to the bathroom or engage in this conversation. Having said that, I don't know what has been affected. Time will tell, as days, weeks, and months pass. You are very lucky; whatever brain damage you have is not noticeable.

"You are very tired, so get some rest. I will call in later today to see you. If anything comes to mind, please let me know, or if you have any questions, ask. If nothing else, it will be good therapy for your mind. See you later."

"Yeah, see you later, Clive—oh, Clive, thanks very much for what you have done. Thanks heaps, mate."

"That's cool, mate," Clive answered as he left the room. "All in a day's work."

Rocky's thoughts suddenly recalled the near-death experience that he vaguely remembered seeing. He wondered if seeing his sons in the light beam was real or his imagination. And that ghostly figure—that stern, solid voice issuing instructions. What had happened? Was it real? *No, that must have been a dream*, he thought. I can't tell anyone about it. *They will think that I am fucked in the head. I will keep that to myself and see if some of it comes true. Then, maybe, I'll talk about it.*

Rocky drifted off to sleep, thinking about what Clive had told him. All this information was a little too much for him to take in. He spent a little time trying to think about what had happened, what was happening, and what was going to happen in the future. *What does the future hold?* Rocky thought. *Can I resume my normal life as I knew it—my job, physical activities, and coaching kids' football? Those kids—how are they doing with their extended competition games? How is my family coping without me?* It seemed that he'd been in hospital for a long time; there was a world out there. All these thoughts raced through his head.

Rocky's thoughts then turned to the months leading up to his illness. He remembered that a week before his fortieth birthday, he'd gone on a drinking binge. He and his wife and some friends were planning a fortieth birthday party, and he'd had quite a few drinks. He was in pain for days afterward from the effects of alcohol. He remembered thinking at the time that something was wrong. He had consumed a similar amount of alcohol many times before over the years and never had suffered any more than the occasional hangover. At the time, he had put it down to alcohol poisoning. Then he remembered that he had not felt his usual self during the month or so prior to that.

Maybe one of those viruses that Clive had spoken about was in his system and had caused his liver to play up. *I must tell Clive that when he calls next time*, Rocky thought. He then remembered not feeling very well after he had spent a long-time gardening and repotting his collection of potted plants. He had a swollen feeling in his mouth, had mouth ulcers, and had felt listless for a few days afterward. He also had suffered with mouth ulcers every month or so for a two- to three-year period before this. Maybe there was a problem for some time, but, as usual, he never followed up with the doctor, telling himself, "It'll be okay; it'll go away soon." *I'd better tell Clive about that as well*, he thought.

The next few days were much the same, drifting between sleeping and being awake, with waking time spent with the many visitors who were shocked at seeing Rocky in such a state. He would get out of bed and spend time walking around the hospital. He wasn't going to let this part of his life get the better of him. He did everything in his power to leave this spell behind him and move on to his new chapter in life.

Several more days passed, and Dr. Clive called to see Rocky. The nurses had to search for him. He had gone for one of his walks, enjoying the fact that he had another chance. When Rocky returned to the room, Clive was waiting for him with Suzie. They were in deep conversation. Rocky came in and sat on the bed.

Suzie hugged Rocky and kissed him on the cheek.

Clive said, "Rocky, I am very pleased with your progress. I am happy to say that you are truly on the mend. Don't get too smart, though; you have a long way until you can say that you're fully recovered." He paused and then said, "There is something that I have to tell you." He paused again, and a look of horror swept over Suzie's face.

"What is it?" she yelled. "Is it bad?"

"No, no," replied Clive, "nothing like that. You may remember that I have been trying to sell the medical practice, as I have accepted a position on the Gold Coast."

"I don't remember that," Rocky said.

"Well, I have sold it," Clive said. "A doctor by the name of Fred Bottomly has bought it. He is from Weipa. He is taking over next week. I will pass all this information over to him, and he will look after you in the future. I will give you my contact phone number so that you can contact me if you need to."

"That's a big kick up the arse, Clive. How am I going to go on without you?" Rocky said, feeling very vulnerable and deserted. "You have done so much for me these past weeks. I will never find another doctor with your professional approach or friendship. I will not be able to put my trust in any other."

"No, Rocky, Fred will be okay. He has a lot of experience in tropical diseases, probably more than I do."

"Yeah, Clive, but …"

"But what, Rocky?" Clive asked.

"It seems that experience didn't matter in my case. Look at what you did and insisted on. You ignored the advice that those doctors with 'experience' suggested. Because you ignored those 'experts,' you saved my life. I really appreciate that. You know that. You mentioned that a person in Weipa died from this because the doctor gave him the wrong treatment. Probably it was this Dr. Bottom or whatever you called him."

"Yes, I know it's hard for you. I am so sorry. I've had it planned for a while, and now I have done it. Don't think that I am deserting you; I am not. This has been planned for a while, and I cannot reverse the deal." Clive said, his tone showing his concern.

"I know, Clive," Rocky said. "I should not sound so selfish. You have done a lot for me, as I said before, and have given me the chance to live. I am sorry for being selfish and so dependent on you."

"No, Rocky, that's understandable. You have been shocked by my announcement. I imagine it feels like being helped out of a hole and placed on a secure surface, and then suddenly, that security is removed, leaving you with nothing to hold onto. I know that you will be okay. After all, you have come this far. You have the mentality to overcome this."

"I hope so," Rocky said. "Yeah, Clive. I'll be right. I have a good family and a great circle of great friends to support me. When do you leave?"

"I will be gone in less than a week. I don't know when you will be going home, but I will see you before I leave. Don't worry; Fred will be around to take care of any issues."

"We will see. I won't have the same faith, though, like the faith I have in your abilities."

"No, Rocky, don't prejudge Fred. You haven't met him yet. When you go home, just phone the office and make an appointment to see him. He will take care of you from then. I'm handing over your case to the doctors in this hospital while you are here. I'll see you soon. Just keep on getting better."

Rocky did not answer.

Suzie consoled Rocky, saying, "Never mind. We all will look after you. You will be okay. The football team is coming up to see you tonight. They have missed you so much. They are doing very well and have some good news for you. They haven't stopped phoning to see how you're doing and to ask when they can see you. Some have been so upset at what has happened, but they are happy now that you are out of the coma."

With all that had happened, Rocky had forgotten about his players, and that made him sad. He sincerely hoped that they were okay. *How are they managing without my guidance and encouraging words?* he thought.

Suzie could see the concern on his face. "What's wrong? You are looking sad."

"It's okay," Rocky said. "I was just feeling sad at losing Clive and that I had forgotten the team."

"That's understandable. The kids are okay; they would realize and understand why you forgot about them. After all, you couldn't have thought about anything. You were in a coma for ten days."

"Ten days!" Rocky shouted. "Have I been out of it for ten days? I had no idea it was that long. What a waste of time."

"No, it was not a waste of time; you had to sleep to recover. Look at you; that sleep time has made you so much better."

Later that afternoon, the football team called in to see their hero, Rocky.

"Hey, Rocky, great to see you!" shouted Jason, rushing over to give Rocky a high-five. "We have missed you, man."

Tony added, "Hey, Rocky, we have won every game so far. We have done it all for you, mate."

"That's fantastic, fellas, good on you. Congratulations. You really are true champions," Rocky replied.

"No, Rocky," Jason said, "we are not the champions. You are the champion. Yeah, sure, we are winning the games. Who put us there? You did, Rocky. You are the champ!"

All the boys simultaneously showed Rocky the V salute and began singing, "You are the champion of the world."

With that, Jason handed Rocky a card, and Tony handed him a glass trophy. The others held up their premiership shield and three other trophies that they had won on their rounds of games so far.

The card had a get-well message from each of the players, and the trophy was etched with Rocky's name, with the message: "To our champ, Rocky. Thanks, from under-thirteen Thunderbolts—1992."

Rocky started crying as the feeling of pride invaded his heart. "You blokes make me so proud. I now know why I have survived this. You may never know what I have gone through, but remember, we did this together, guys. I know that probably seems mixed up and makes no sense. Words are not coming to me."

"Don't worry," Jason answered. "We know what you mean."

The boys started singing to Jason and Nick playing the guitar once again.

"Rocky, you are the champion of *our* world."

CHAPTER 3

No one's going to tell me that I will not be a benefit to society. I'll do it. I'll be right. Just watch me. I'm not going to just sit around and wait to die. There's no future in that!

As the sun set on yet another day, Rocky suddenly found himself alone. His thoughts turned to the events of the day, the walks in the sunshine—simple things that he had not been able to do for so long, things that he had missed doing for what seemed an eternity. He thought of the visits from his wife and family and the encouraging reports from the nurses and doctors, which indicated, at long last, that his health was improving.

He then remembered Dr. Clive telling him that he was moving away and passing his case and care to another doctor who had bought the practice. Rocky thought of his fears in facing the challenges ahead without the familiar face of Dr. Clive. The highlight of Rocky's day had been the visit by most of the under-thirteens Thunderbolts football team. It was so good for Rocky to see the smiles and happiness on each boy's face as they spoke about their experiences and achievements in playing other top-grade teams of the same age. He'd looked at them and at the card and trophy they'd given to him, and he'd been overcome by emotion.

When he looked at the trophy, Rocky felt so appreciative that he had survived the immense pain and discomfort of the past few weeks. It was all worthwhile to come out of this and enjoy life once again.

The next morning brought more visits from medical people—prodding, poking, examining, and the endless questions about what pain was present, what this movement did, what pressing here and there felt like, what bright lights shining in the eyes did. When would it end? Was it because he still looked like an alien? Was it because he shouldn't have survived the ordeal? Whatever the reason, Rocky wished they all would just go away and leave him alone.

Rocky also had visits from friends and acquaintances, which perked him up quite a lot. He escaped his room as often as he could by walking around the hospital and venturing outside in the sunshine and fresh air, with his drips on a stand on wheels in tow. He often questioned the need to be attached to so many drips but always received the same answer: "You need them to keep hydrated, nourished, and pain-free, and the IV medications help you heal. Without them, you would waste away or catch an infection." He had not eaten for over two weeks and had lost more than forty pounds.

With that information in mind, Rocky decided to try eating food and drinking water, so he could get out of this place. It was not that he hated the hospital; in fact, he found the place secure and the staff very kind, compassionate, and helpful, but he needed to be in his own home and surroundings with his family and friends.

After three or four more days, the drips came out and the pain management was handled by tablets and lotions applied to the inside of his mouth. His mouth was where the most pain was centered, as the skin had still not grown back, and food had either a stinging or abrasive effect. At times, Rocky was given juices and other drinks that stung his mouth when the food and fruit acids touched the raw flesh. Overall, he felt he was reaching the stage where he didn't need constant medical attention, but he could not convince the doctors to let him go home. They wanted to see a predetermined level of weight gain and fitness before they would discharge him.

During the night rounds, the doctor and nurse told Rocky that a group of university nursing students would be visiting the hospital the next day for a few days to gain practical knowledge. Rocky agreed to allow a couple of the students attend to him, accompanied by nursing staff.

After his usual visits from nurses the next morning, having his breakfast, and showering and shaving, Rocky settled himself with reading a magazine that a visitor had brought him and listening to the radio. Soon, a nurse, accompanied by one male and two female students, visited. The nurse introduced the students and showed them Rocky's medical records, which at this point resembled a book.

Then the students began asking questions. Rocky thought, *when will this crap ever end?* He became very wary of the male student, he didn't like his attitude. Rocky formed the opinion that the male nurse could be gay. He wished that they all would just piss off, and he wondered what had possessed him to allow these students into his case. After they left, Rocky decided to escape the ward and go for a walk. He needed time to think about how to handle the situation. As he sat in the sunshine, reading his magazine, he noticed the male student seemed to be looking for him. He somehow found a way to break away from the other students and look for him. Rocky moved very quickly, trying to avoid him, and returned to his bed, where he pretended to be asleep. Rocky never discriminated against gays; they could live their unusual lives however they wished, if they never came close to him. Rocky had an unfortunate experience with an older guy when he was quite young, and never came to terms with it.

The more that Rocky tried to accept their lifestyle, the thought of them made him cringe and grit his teeth and made his hair stand on end. The fact that one was in the hospital, getting close to him, caused severe stress to him. All he wanted was to be left alone.

The male student found his way back to the ward; Rocky was aware that he was there. He got the medical records and read them, noisily turning the pages. He made a lot of noise in what seemed to be an attempt to wake up Rocky. Rocky moaned, turned over, and continued to pretend to sleep. The student moved to the other side of his bed, the side that Rocky was facing. He decided to "wake up" and deal with the situation.

"What do you want?" Rocky blurted out, pretending that the student had woken him.

"Just looking at your notes. It is a very interesting case," the male student said.

"What do you mean, interesting?"

"Oh, just the tests, the symptoms, the blisters and wounds, the scars, the treatment and medications, as well as the notes made by the visiting specialists." He then asked several questions about different aspects of the condition, such as where pain was located, and he looked into Rocky's eyes, ears, nose, and mouth.

Rocky felt very uneasy with this student touching him. In fact, he couldn't stand the guy touching him and looking at him.

"Now, it says here that the blisters formed around your anus and on the end of your penis, correct?" the student asked.

"Yes, that's right. You can read very well. They have now healed and formed scars."

"It also says that the opening of your penis actually sealed over while healing. Is it okay now?"

"You can still read good. Yeah, it's okay now—a bit sore still but it seems to work okay."

"Do you mind if I examine you to see how everything has healed?"

"Rack off, you faggot. Yes, I do mind if you look at the scars. Piss off out of here and don't come back, you friggin' creep."

"Mr. Scott, there is no need to upset yourself. I'm sorry if I have offended you," the student said.

"Yeah, sure, mate. You better go now, and if you don't mind, don't come back."

When the student left, the nurse came rushing into Rocky's room, as she'd heard his shouting and swearing. "What's the matter? You seem very distressed. What happened?"

"Oh, just that poofter nursing student. I told him to go away and never come near me again," Rocky said.

"Why? What happened?" the nurse asked.

"He went through my medical records and asked a lot of questions. He looked at my eyes, mouth, ears, and nose, and at my arms and legs and my torso. Then he asked me about the blisters around my pelvic region."

"What upset you, Rocky? Your case is a very interesting and unusual one. He was just trying to find out about it for his studies."

"No. I knew he was a poofter when I first saw him. He wanted to examine my backside and private region. I told him to rack off. No faggot is going to check out by butt and jewels. The creep. I thought they were to be with one of you real nurses anyway. Can you keep him away from me, please? I don't want to see him again."

"Okay, Rocky. Yes, they are supposed to be with a member of the nursing staff at all times. I'll have a word to him."

"When is the doctor coming? I want to get out of here."

"Rocky, you are still not well enough to leave hospital."

"No, read my lips: I'm out of here. When will the doctor be around?" Rocky said, becoming very agitated.

"I haven't heard from the doctor this morning. I'll let him know your concerns and your wish to go home when he arrives, and I will bring him straight here to see you. Now try to settle down and get some rest. It's not much help to you, getting upset like this."

"Okay, I'll wait for the doctor."

As soon as the nurse left the room, Rocky went to his bedside cabinet, got some coins, found a public phone, and called his wife.

"Hello, babe. Can you come and get me and take me home? I want to get out of here—now."

"What's wrong? You sound upset. What has happened?" Suzie asked.

"Oh. There's a faggot nurse here. He wants to examine my jewels and backside. He probably wants to finger my butt too. Wouldn't trust the poofter creep," Rocky told her.

"Hey, settle down. Stop talking like that and stop swearing. You know I don't like those words. I'll be there as soon as I can. Did the doctor say it's okay to go home?"

"No. I haven't seen the doctor yet. I don't care what the doctor says. I'm not staying around here with that creep hanging around."

"All right. See you soon, babe."

When Suzie arrived, Rocky saw her having a deep discussion with the nurse at the nurses' station. Rocky joined Suzie and told her that he would get his gear and bag.

Suzie hugged Rocky and said, "You have to stay, at least until the doctor sees you."

"Now, Rocky," the nurse said, "you really should stay. You aren't well enough to go home yet. Why don't you wait until the doctor arrives, and we will talk to him?"

"No, don't you understand? I am not staying here. I want to go home. If you don't take me home, I'll just walk out and find someone who will take me home. Please yourself!" Rocky began to feel weak and found a chair to sit on.

"Rocky, don't upset yourself," the nurse said. "It's not good for you. You have been here for nearly four weeks, and we have not had an ounce of trouble with you. You have been a model patient—and now this. You really have been spooked, haven't you?"

"I'd better take him home," Suzie said. "Rocky does get determined, and when he does, nothing will change his mind. I'll make sure he is looked after." She turned to Rocky. "You better get your stuff. I'll take you home."

Rocky got up cautiously, and Suzie and he went to collect his belongings. As they walked through the hospital, Rocky said goodbye to the nurses who had looked after him so well over the past four weeks. It was an emotional time for Rocky, as he had gotten to know these people well.

As he signed the papers to release him from the hospital, the nurse advised Rocky and Suzie not to hesitate to call if they had any concerns or questions about Rocky's care. "You should see Dr. Bottomly as soon as you can," she added.

Rocky walked into his home, and it felt unfamiliar. Was it because he had been away for so long, or had his memory failed him? He looked around, searching for something that was familiar to him; he then discovered family photographs. He concentrated on the photos of his wife and his two sons. He knew them; after all, they had visited him in hospital almost daily. He then gazed at the photographs of the football team in their red-and-green jerseys. He then had some sense that he was in the right house.

He walked from room to room, searching for something else to trigger familiar memories. It all seemed like a new learning experience. He then ventured out into the yard and walked through the garden and thought how the trees and plants had grown. Or had they? He wasn't sure. It was a subconscious reaction, suddenly appreciating the simple things that meant so much to a man who had endured so much pain and illness in such a short time.

Suzie followed, concerned with what Rocky was doing. He spoke no words; he just strolled around aimlessly, looking at everything as if it was a major discovery. He then hurried inside as if he feared something. Suzie thought that Rocky must have had a panic attack and needed to find a secure place.

It was a daunting time for Rocky, leaving a safe and secure nest and venturing out into the world again.

Suzie made him an eggnog drink and scrambled eggs, as his mouth, throat, and stomach still had not healed enough to take any other type of food. Rocky struggled to get the food down and eventually succeeded in consuming everything. He got up from the table and sat on the lounge chair to watch some television. Suzie readied the bed in case Rocky wanted to sleep, and she set up a few things in the lounge room to make him as comfortable as possible.

As Suzie walked through the lounge room on her way to the kitchen, she saw Rocky sitting motionless. She rushed over to him and shook him violently, yelling, "Babe! Rocky, are you okay?" He opened his eyes, and she realized he'd been sleeping. "Rocky, you frightened me. Gee, I only left the room for a minute or two, but I thought you were dead."

"Did I go to sleep that easily?" Rocky asked.

"Yes. I've never seen you sleep sitting up."

"Sorry, dear. I can't help it. I was just watching TV. Must have nodded off."

"Well, you better go lie down in bed. You look very pale and weak," Suzie said.

"Yes, I do feel very weak. The trip home must have exhausted me."

"Well, you *are* still supposed to be in hospital, you know. I wish you had stayed there for a few more days."

"Oh, don't you want me here?" Rocky asked.

"Of course I do. I'm just worried that you might get bad again, and something might happen to you."

"Okay, I'm going to lie down now. I'll be okay. I'll get some sleep in my own bed for a change."

When Rocky awoke a few hours later, he opened his eyes to see both of his sons standing beside the bed, looking at him.

"Hi, boys. How are you both doing?" Rocky asked.

"Oh, we're okay. How are you, Dad?" the elder son said.

"Dad, are you okay? You look very thin and old. Are you going to die, Dad?" the younger, eight-year-old asked.

"No, mate. You know your dad. Yeah, I've been sick, and I am still sick, but I'll be okay."

"Okay, boys, we better let your father sleep for a while longer. He will need a lot of sleep, and I'll need a lot of help from you two to make Dad better," Suzie said.

"Yeah, Mum, we'll help," the twelve-year-old said.

Rocky slept for a few more hours, until about seven that evening, and then wandered out into the dining room, where Suzie, the two boys, and a couple of neighbors were seated around the table.

Each visitor asked him how he was and wished him a speedy recovery, and he thanked each of them for their cards, get-well messages, and visits while he was in the hospital. He also thanked them for helping his family through a very sad, demanding, and exhausting time.

Rocky returned to the lounge room to sit in his chair again. He immediately dozed off into an unconscious-like trance.

"See? There he goes again," Suzie said to the visitors. "It's scary how he seems to be asleep while he is sitting up with his eyes half open. You can wave your hands in front of his eyes, and he won't notice. He doesn't even flinch. I better go with him to the doctor, so I can talk to him about it."

The next morning, Rocky and Suzie got ready to visit the doctor.

"Are you ready, babe?" Suzie asked.

"Yeah, I'm ready. Suppose we better get going. I wonder what this new Dr. Bottomly is like."

"Don't know. I've asked a few people, but no one I know has been to see him," Suzie answered. "Rocky, you have your shirt on back to front and inside out, and you left one sock off when you put your shoes on. Come here; I better dress you. You can't go like that." Suzie took off his shirt and putting it on him the right way.

As they entered the consulting room, the doctor said, "Mr. Scott. You should be dead. People don't survive what you have been through!"

Rocky didn't answer. He didn't need to hear that comment as the greeting from a new doctor, of whom he was wary to begin with.

"Oh, I'm sorry. I'm Fred Bottomly. I've been reading Clive's notes and the notes from the hospital. I had a similar case of a twelve-year-old boy in Weipa only a few months ago, but sadly, he didn't make it. He died within a day or so."

"Is this condition fairly common?" Rocky asked.

"No, there have only been a handful of patients since the early 1900s. All male, curiously. You are the first patient to survive. That's why I was surprised to see the details on your medical records that Clive had passed on to me when I took over the practice." Fred said. "Now, tell me, how do you feel?"

"Oh, okay. I am a bit tired all the time. I don't seem to remember much about my past twenty or thirty years. My mouth, throat, and stomach still hurt. I have a lot of pain when I pass water or go to the toilet. My eyes sting, and my vision is not too good—a bit blurry. Otherwise, Doctor, I'm well, thanks."

"Well, you have been gravely ill. It's going to be a long time before you feel well. You will never, ever feel as well as you did before this illness. You will never work again. You should consider cashing in your superannuation and any insurance, leave the workforce, and take your pension."

"Oh, I don't know about that. I'd go crazy if I couldn't go to work," Rocky said. "I don't really want to sit around doing nothing."

"You will find that you won't be able to go back to work. You will always be too tired and weak, and your brain has been damaged. You will be useless to any employer," Fred said. "I need to take more blood for tests and order some scans of your head to see what's going on in there. And you will need to get a medical bracelet in case you are found unconscious or injured and are unable to tell anyone about your medical condition."

"Do you think this is an allergy to penicillin?" Rocky asked.

"Well, everything points to that. We can never be sure without giving you some penicillin to see if you have another reaction. I am sure we don't want to do that, so you must never be exposed to penicillin ever again. Mr. Scott, that also means anything that could contain mold spores, like bread, cheeses, moist clothing, even garden mulch or rotted grass clippings. The bracelet should always be worn as a precaution."

"Where do I get one of those?" Rocky asked.

"Well, I would recommend this one for you, pointing to a picture in a brochure. You can get others from a pharmacy, or you could get the information tattooed on your body. This bracelet in this brochure, as well as the bracelet, has your details and records on a database. The details are engraved on the bracelet along with a phone number and membership. The medical people dial the phone number, quote the membership number, and the operator passes your information to the caller. I will fill the form in for you and sign it, and then you can send it in. It needs to be signed by a doctor to verify that the information is correct. Are there any questions?"

"No, I don't think so," Rocky answered.

"Well, I have one," Suzie said. "Doctor, yesterday and last night Rocky seemed to fall off to sleep while sitting up, but he really wasn't asleep. He was just sitting there, staring ahead, and seemed to be in a trance. His body was motionless, his breathing was very slow and shallow, and his eyes were slightly open, but he did not move. I actually thought that he was dead."

"I don't know what that could be. Maybe these tests and scans might pick something up; otherwise, keep an eye on him, and we can investigate further, if need be."

"And his odor. He seems to have a bad body odor about him," Suzie said.

"That's from all the dead and decaying body cells. His insides have all come away and died. They will decay, and eventually they will pass through his body. That smell will be there for quite a while yet, I expect."

"And his memory. He doesn't seem to remember much; he even forgets how to dress himself properly."

"That's what I meant before. He has suffered brain damage from the lack of oxygen during one or two of his episodes. That, I'm afraid, will never get any better. That's why he'll never work again."

"No one's going to tell me I won't work again," Rocky said. "I'm not going to sit around and wait to die."

"Well, the doctor might be right," Suzie said. "You know that you are not feeling right. You've been through a very serious illness. He should know. He is the doctor."

"No, babe. I'll get back to where I was. I'll be okay. I'll do it; just watch me."

No more was said about the matter; Rocky just thought of how he would beat this situation. He set a goal for himself to get well enough to return to work, however long it took.

Rocky spent the following two weeks mostly asleep but also rebuilding his stamina and healing his severely tortured body. He quite often fell into his now-characteristic sleeplike trance, with his eyes open and fixed straight ahead but never focused on anything. This state worried his family and friends.

Suzie took Rocky to another doctor, who had been the family doctor several years earlier in another town. This doctor had delivered Rocky and Suzie's two sons. Rocky's psychological state had deteriorated somewhat. He felt lost, without the secure feeling he had at the hospital, combined with the feeling of being alone and deserted by Dr. Clive. He needed the help of someone he knew and in whom he had faith and trust.

He also had a lot of trouble remembering many of the simple tasks in life. Dressing himself was rather comical, with clothes inside out or back to front or both, underwear placed on the outside of clothing, shoes on the wrong feet, and mismatched socks. *What does it matter?* he thought. *If it provides entertainment to others, not a problem.* Most of the time he was able to dress himself, so he looked respectable when he went outside the house. There were a couple of occasions, however, when Rocky was discovered wandering the streets near his home, naked. Occasionally, people would find Rocky wandering the streets or sitting in the gutter, but the locals knew him and knew of his medical history, and they would return him to his home.

Once Suzie answered the phone at work and heard, "Suzie, I just saw Rocky driving through town and going around the roundabout three times. He seems to be lost, I pulled him over and took the keys."

"I wondered where he was. I've been trying to phone him at home, but there is no answer. I will come and pick him up. Thanks, Marg."

Suzie made an appointment with the specialist, as well as a week's holiday break in the Sunshine Coast hinterland of Queensland. The specialist found Rocky's case very interesting and challenging. He took scans of his brain, x-rays, and blood tests, which indicated courses of medication needed to open the channels of the brain and nervous system so that messages could get through. This treatment was prescribed for a two-year period but did allow Rocky to slowly return to some form of normal activity.

He had to leave the employment that he had before his illness, as it involved a lot of driving. He obtained alternative employment with a host employer as part of a rehabilitation program. Rocky insisted that he was not going to stop working; he was not going to participate in an invalid-type of activity either. Even though Rocky had a major disruption to his life, everyone knew that if Rocky set his mind to something, that was what would happen.

He had the attitude that he was going to get through, and although it was hard for him, he got through it progressively. The new employment was very close to his home, which allowed him to walk the short distance, as his driver's license was taken from him for medical reasons. He found a lot of enjoyment in walking to work, wearing earphones attached to a Walkman, playing motivational and music tapes. He found it an added pleasure, as the drivers passing on the street tooted, waved, or shouted niceties to him.

Rocky was so pleased to be alive, experiencing the simple things in life. Walking, listening, waving to friends, and thinking positive thoughts all equated to reaching for the goals that he had set himself, slowly but surely. Parts of his recent memories were coming back to him. Each day brought another small piece of his past, putting the small pieces together to form bigger pieces. Discovering those small pieces gave Rocky extreme pleasure that his brain was active—ever so small but still active and capable of remembering.

He was so happy that he decided not to listen to the medical experts and spend the rest of his life vegetating. His decision to fight was the correct one.

By the end of the two-year period, he had been through many harrowing medical experiences and procedures; brain scans; brain-fluid extractions and tests; injections to the head, neck, and spinal column; and medication to rebuild the tricyclics in his brain to allow it to function properly. His driver's license was returned to him, and his rehabilitation was over. Rocky's memory and brain function had recovered enough to allow him to return to his original employment.

His memory of his childhood and early adulthood was still completely missing, but he was confident that he had enough to carry on from where he'd left off. It didn't matter to Rocky that he had no memory of his childhood; all that mattered was that he had some form of his former life back. Anyway, Rocky thought it would be fun to learn about the things that he had forgotten as they came to him or were told to him by others. As far as he was concerned, his goal of returning to his normal life had been realized. Rocky had enough information restored to his memory to resume his occupation as a sales representative for a major Australian paint manufacturing company.

During the following twelve-month period, Rocky regained his work experience, which to allow him to achieve record sales for his employer. Also, during this time, Rocky was encouraged to renew his activities to help young schoolchildren by assisting school sports activities and life skills coaching.

Rocky had attended many sports sessions and school excursions with the young kids. Rocky also assisted the teachers of his younger son at the school class camp. The school had no male teachers on staff, so Rocky was convinced to fill the male supervisory role to provide a balance for the male students.

Several months later, Rocky was approached by the principal and year-seven teachers to assist the female teachers again as a male leader for the year-seven camp. A few parents phoned Rocky, as the principal did again, to encourage him to accept. The parents were reluctant to allow their sons to attend camp unless Rick Scott was a leader at the camp.

One said, "If Rick Scott is not going, my twin boys won't be going because they have a behavior issue, and they need a man like Mr. Scott. He's firm and strict but very fair and caring. Mr. Scott is one of only a few who can handle these boys with respect, gain their respect, and teach them respect."

With these thoughts, Rocky happily accepted the invitation and challenge to attend the six-day camp through Western Queensland. The boys who were tagged as the troublesome boys were very receptive to Rocky's methods of calming them and bringing out the best behavior and attitudes of the "bad guys." After all, everyone was there to learn and enjoy the experience, and Rocky's methods of changing the attitudes of those who were traditionally disruptive allowed everyone to enjoy the experience.

The female teachers who were leading the camp were in awe of Rocky's ability to change the attitudes of the disruptive students, but Rocky told them. "It's just that I talk with them, not down to them. I joke with them, but not about them. And I provide little bits of information for them to think about—things they're interested in. I think that is what works—someone to talk with on their level and listen. I have always been able to gain young boys' respect by those simple things but believe me—you must know how to do it and, above all, be genuine when you talk with them. They sure as hell know when you are not genuine with them."

When the bus returned to school after the six days away from their parents, many of the students brought their mums and dads to talk with Rocky before they said their goodbyes to him. Jim Talbot, the father of the twin boys, also spoke to Rocky about his boys' behavior and experiences. When Rocky and the teachers gave a good report, he asked, "How did you do it? How did you keep them out of trouble, and how did you get them to enjoy themselves so much?"

"Aw, it's easy," Rocky said. "No secrets really. Just talk with them, praise whatever they have achieved, give them a reward for those positive achievements, and give them some examples of how to behave, how to control their anger, how to respect others and be thoughtful and helpful, as well as explaining the consequences for negative behavior. Over the next couple of days, talk with them to see what they remember about their experiences with me—how to gauge what different tones of voice means, and the examples to improve their behavior—and just apply that to yourself. You might learn a lot about your boys, Jim—how to talk with them, how to react and interact with them, how they respond to a certain treatment. You will be surprised. These two guys have great characters. They each have a great sense of humor, sense of responsibility, and a great sense of respect. They know right from wrong. You now have the job of developing that further and allowing them to develop their talents, so they can develop into well-adjusted young men. Jim, I know you can do it, and I know that they can make it happen. If you get stuck or need help, you know where I am; just call me. I only want to see these guys develop and grow so that you and the community can be proud of them." Rocky then addressed the boys. "Now guys, remember all I told you, especially the signs and symbols we used. Tell your dad about the signs we used to communicate. See you later guys, and Jim, I'll see you soon. Enjoy your boys; they really are great young fellas."

After everyone left, the gear was packed away and cleaned up, and they engaged in small talk about the overall success of the camp. Rocky returned to his home with a sense of pride and achievement in providing a great learning experience for thirty-five young people. He was proud to have changed the lives of a handful of guys and—more important—to have helped the parents to realize that their kids could achieve so much just by changing their own attitudes, not necessarily the attitudes of their kids.

The following Monday, Rocky returned to his job of traveling, selling products, and meeting new people. Something was missing, though, as Rocky was not entirely happy with his job and the direction the company was taking. The company had stopped promoting or using current employees from within to fill management positions. They had adopted the method of employing university graduates as managers. Unfortunately, these graduates were either too young, or inexperienced, or both, to take such positions. Rocky could see the company was self-destructing, which annoyed him. Apart from his job, he enjoyed his visits to classrooms to teach life skills to young people, not only how to interact with people and improve their attitudes but to show them craft skills, woodworking skills, art, basic mechanics and bicycle repairs, and various other life skills. Rocky's job, however, didn't fulfill his needs, so he began looking for another job.

Rocky's health was improving. He was slowly weaned off the medication needed for his brain and metabolism. His body was functioning almost perfectly now. He often thought how things had been a few years earlier and the medical experts' prediction that he would never be a benefit to anyone. He thought of the long, difficult journey back to a reasonable quality of life. His loss of memory worried him, but otherwise, all was great. He had made it.

This was proof that no one was going to tell him to give up everything, just to sit around, waiting to die. *No way.*

Rocky persevered with his employment, but still, something was missing, and the company was sliding down-hill very quickly with the inadequate management team. He got sick of his job, so he jumped ship and got a job with a competitor that sold the same type of paint products. He still enjoyed spending quality time with young people, helping them with their sports, music, or learning skills, as well as improving their attitudes. From time to time, teachers and parents asked him to help them with their children's welfare.

This was the field that Rocky thought that he would enjoy as a career, but he learned that he'd need to spend a few years at university to gain a qualification to do this work. He needed to gain a higher level of secondary education before he could qualify for university. He was confident that he could study for these qualifications, but he would need to give up work and therefore his income, something that he could not afford. And at the end of it all, he would only have a piece of paper to show his academic qualifications. His volunteer work with kids had shown him that kids did not show qualified counselors or chaplains much respect at all. They regarded them just the same as other teachers and adults who talked down to them and demanded certain tasks and outcomes. Rocky saw this as people with qualifications directing their talks and tasks by the book, as opposed to using long-time practical life skills.

He made the decision not to travel down the academic path but to help those who wanted help by doing it his own way. *After all*, he thought, *the way I speak with and help young people gets better results than the people with qualifications.*

After a year at his new job, Rocky still felt restless. One day, he needed to use a taxi to get home, as his car had broken down. The taxi driver was the mother of a friend of his elder son. Rocky and the driver spoke about many topics during the journey, including the pleasures of taxi driving. She also told Rocky the requirements for obtaining a taxi license and the duties involved in driving a taxi.

Several weeks later, Rocky began his course to obtain his taxi license and came out the other end as a taxi driver. He obtained part-time work driving taxis while still performing his sales representative job.

He found the taxi job to be very interesting, as he met many new people of all ages with varied interests, problems, or great achievements. Many young men—he guessed most were under thirty—held deep conversations about their life problems and how to overcome their obstacles. These blokes seemed to regard their taxi driver as their social worker, telling him their private secrets. Rocky enjoyed this aspect of the job, but it did open his eyes to the fact that many young men had instability in their lives, which seemed to have begun in their teens.

Rocky's thoughts often turned to his helping kids with behavioral problems. How sad that they didn't have anyone they could trust—no one to show them the way. *Surely there are responsible people to help these kids through their teenage years and set them on the correct path to a respectable, rewarding and responsible life*, he thought. But there was not! There were highly paid politicians and highly qualified teachers and social workers, but none of them had the practical skills—or any desire—to help young people find a better life. Parents, too, seemed not to care; they were too engrossed with their lifestyles to bother with their kids.

As time went on, Rocky was given more shifts on the taxi, and he worked most nights. These shifts often included Friday and Saturday nights, the party and nightclub nights for young people. The times after the clubs closed were the most dangerous but the most interesting. Rocky discovered that angry young men with huge chips on their shoulders, fueled with alcohol and drugs, were the most challenging. Rocky's attitude and the way he spoke with them showed that all taxi drivers were not necessarily grumpy old men with an intolerance for young people. These blokes soon learned that he would listen to them, talk with them, understand them, and help them. Rocky was a driver who was not aggressive or impatient; he was someone they could respect. Someone who encouraged the best from them.

Rocky soon decided to drive a maxi-taxi so that he could carry groups of people. He found an owner who was willing to put Rocky on as a permanent driver for his maxi-taxi. Rocky soon became well known as a driver who always got his fare, and because of the positive attitude he had toward his passengers, they didn't damage the taxi. In a short time, Rocky was convinced to give up his sales job and become a full-time driver for the maxi-taxi, working the afternoon and night shifts—the shifts generally considered to get the most abusive and destructive passengers.

At times, Rocky picked up passengers who started their verbal abuse toward him, yelling at people as they were driven past, fighting and wrestling each other as they were driven to their destination, or started vandalizing and graffitiing the taxi. Rocky merely stopped the taxi and turned the meter off. He got out and opened the passenger door, and he spoke firmly but calmly about what they were doing, asking them to think about why they were behaving so badly. "Why should I tolerate such behavior?" he'd ask. "After all, I'm doing my job, driving you from one place to another." He would get them to understand what they were doing and to see they were only proving how stupid they were.

It worked every time, without exception—and every time they needed a taxi after that, they preferred to travel in Rocky's maxi-taxi.

Groups of teenagers, Rocky found, were the most challenging. So many bitter, angry, drug- and alcohol-affected fourteen-, fifteen- and sixteen-year-old boys were bitter and angry with the world. They drank alcohol and took drugs to try to find something good about their lives. All it seemed to do was make the merry-go-round go faster, making the negatives more pronounced and the positives much harder to achieve.

The boys seemed the worst as opposed to female passengers. They were fine early in the night as they went out. All wore backpacks containing the needs for their addictions and personal items, like their music, change of clothes, and weapons, mainly knives. These items were observed by Rocky many times as they rummaged through the back-packs or taken out for bragging rights. After several hours on the streets, gate-crashing parties, and smashing cars, mailboxes, windows, or street signs—anything and anyone in their paths—it was left to the taxi drivers to drive these gangsters home, at least the ones that the cops didn't catch, and to put up with their disruptive, abusive moods as the effects of the night's alcohol and drugs wore off.

Strangely enough, these bad guys always insisted on Rocky picking them up. The other taxi drivers wondered why and were mostly appreciative to let someone else have them in their taxi. Rocky tried in vain to pass on his techniques to other drivers, but no one had success in taming the gangs of teenage boys or providing a peaceful journey to their homes. The biggest problem the other drivers had, other than the abusive attitudes, loud noise, and damage to the cabs, was obtaining the money for the fare home.

Rocky, however, almost always had more money from the boys than was needed to pay the fare. Normally, a taxi driver would pick up his passengers, turn the meter on, drive the journey, and drop off each one, and the last one left would be responsible for the fare. Most often, the last guy wouldn't have enough cash. He usually bolted, leaving the driver out of pocket. If the driver called the cops, he would wait an hour or so, the boy would be long gone; that was another hour of lost income.

Rocky did it differently. He educated the guys to put their cash in a hat, and by the end of the trip, there would be ample cash to pay the fare—and always an excess.

"It's a simple way of getting your money," Rocky would tell the other drivers. None of them ever tried it, though, so they continually lost income, had stressful arguments, and, quite often, suffered personal injury or vehicle damage for their lack of effort. The teenagers never were dropped off at their homes, so they couldn't be traced by the cops. Rocky, on the other hand, knew where each of them lived because he treated them with respect and earned their trust.

Quite often, Rocky would pick up one of these "bad guys" on his own and drive him to a party or to his home. Each of them knew that when they got into the taxi, they had to tell Rocky how much cash they had. They knew he would stop the meter when the cash level was reached. Other drivers would put the passenger out at this point and make them walk, but not Rocky. He would stop the meter but continue driving to get the passenger to his destination.

"I know that they are safely home and that they aren't angry at being put out and smashing things as they walk the remainder of the journey," Rocky would say when questioned about his methods. "Anyway, I always get a job for the return journey and pick up more cash than I lost by doing it that way." Most drivers would drop their passengers and race back to the city for the next job, while Rocky had a paying fare for his return trip.

Rocky also noticed that when he collected just one or two of these guys, they were totally different than when they were in a larger group. They spoke sensibly, listened intently, and had their own opinions on different subjects. Most of the time, Rocky disagreed with their thoughts or opinions, but who was he to judge? He always held discussions with them and listened to them. They were very open, so much different than they were with other adults.

The difference was Rocky never ridiculed them for their actions or thoughts and never spoke down to them or raised his voice with them. This was why Rocky could communicate with them on a positive level.

CHAPTER 4

You are very angry, frustrated, and neglected. That's why I think you act the way you do. I hate seeing young guys with so much potential, so much to live for, being thrown on the scrap heap with no hope or direction. Let's change that.

During Rocky's shifts over the next few weeks, one group of youngsters was regarded as the most feared of all the gangs. They were nearly always intoxicated and heavily affected by drugs. They were very bitter and angry with the world.

They smashed mailboxes, car headlights and windows, and school and shop windows. They lit fires in garbage cans, broke gates and fences, pulled out trees and shrubs from yards and park gardens, and wrote graffiti on public toilets, walls, and buildings. Heaven help anyone who approached them; they too would find themselves smashed or knifed very quickly.

Rocky knew this by listening to their discussions with each other in his taxi and because other guys and fearful adults he picked up would tell him. When he had one or two of them in his taxi, however, they seemed like model lads, the type of kids you could trust. Rocky decided to tackle the group's behavior and see if he could offer an alternative to get these kids off the streets and out of trouble.

The next time he picked up two of them, he began his mission. It was Saturday afternoon.

"How are you doing, guys?" Rocky asked when they entered his maxi-taxi.

"Aw, good, Rocky. Got wasted last night and smashed a couple nerds who tried to use our skate area," Tony said.

"Yeah, fucked them up good," Decles (the nick name given to Declan) added. "You shoulda seen 'em, Rocky—blood 'n' guts everywhere. Jay 'n' Shayne got 'em big time with some logs of wood. Won't be back for a while, I reckon."

"Why, guys?" Rocky asked. "Why are you doing these things to people and their property? What do you get out of doing it?"

"Dunno, Rocky," Tony said. "They just stuff us up, the scum, always having more than us, more fun than us. That's the place where we skate, and we don't want no rich kid with his fancy clothes and board takin' over our territory."

"Where do you skate?" Rocky asked.

"Down near the council hall and library. There's some sick ramps and rails where we can practice our tricks," Declan answered.

"It's a great place to hide our drinks and smoke our joints and cones," Tony said. "We can see if someone comes from all directions from in there. Even stuff the cops up. They haven't got a chance."

"Yeah, but why? Why do you think you have to drink grog and smoke dope at your age? And why do you feel you have to smash things and fight other guys so much?" Rocky asked.

"They just mess with us all the time," Declan said. "Other guys piss us off with their expensive clothes, skateboards, and new fancy bikes."

"And the oldies always put shit on us. We can't ever talk to them. They always say that we are good for nuthin'. They pick on us all the time. Tell us to do this and that for no reason. All we want is to do the things we want to do without being picked on or bossed around," Tony said. "Why are you asking us this, Rocky? Are you like the rest of 'em?"

"Are you working for the cops, Rocky?" Declan asked.

"No, fellas. I'm not working for the cops. Everything you tell me, or I see stays secret with me. You know that. I don't tell unless something bad happens, like someone gets badly hurt or killed. I'm only asking so I can understand your thoughts and reasons for why you do bad things. I might be able to get you away from crime and save you from jail, that's all. How do you feel the day after all this shit?"

"Sorry, Rocky. Shoulda known you would keep it to yourself. I feel like crap, Rocky. We all do the next day, until we do it again the next night—get pissed and stoned. Takes the bad feelings away," Tony said.

"What can we do to get out of this crap, Rocky? What would you tell us that would make it better?" Declan asked. "I sorta feel like I want to do other things to get my kicks, but don't know what. I want to get a really hot chick for my girlfriend, but they won't even look at me or talk to me."

"Well, Decles, that's the first step. You have just told me what you do doesn't suit you too well. You want to change but don't know how. That's what you are telling me, isn't it?" Rocky asked.

"Yeah," Declan answered.

"Yeah, me too," Tony said. "When I think about it, I am over this bad-guy thing. It doesn't do much for me anymore, but that's what we are used to. And we got no one to talk to who will help us."

"If you guys are serious about this, I am willing to talk it through with you and suggest ways to get out of the hole you are in," Rocky said. "Are you all getting together later tonight? If you think you want to talk, I'll take some time off and chill with those who want to."

"Yeah, I'm in," Tony said.

"Yeah, me too," Declan said. "How will we find you?"

"I'll give you my mobile number. Decles, you can ring me, and I'll work out a time that I can take off. In the meantime, I'll think of a place to take you to talk about it quietly." Rocky handed Declan a piece of paper with his mobile number written on it. "There is no pressure with this, only if you want to try other things to make your lives different. The other guys might not want to try; leave that to them to decide. You can't make someone do things they don't want to do."

"Okay, Rocky, we'll call you. We two will be there, even if the others don't come. I don't give a squirt if they don't. I want a life," Declan said.

"Now, do me a favor. Lighten up on the grog and cones before I pick you up, so you are not too stuffed up to talk and listen. I'm not preaching to you yet about that; I just want you fairly normal, so you can be sensible and think straight."

"OK, Rocky," Tony said. "We'll give you a call later."

After they reached their destination, paid the fare, and got out, Tony said, "Don't go yet. I'm coming around to your door."

Both boys walked around to the driver's window of the maxi-taxi. Tony held his hand out to shake Rocky's hand and said, "Thanks, Rocky, man. You are a great guy. Thanks for wanting to talk to us and wanting to help us."

Declan also shook Rocky's hand and said similar words. Then he said, "I'll see you later, Rocky. Don't let us down now. We get pissed off with guys your age promising things and never doing it. It happens all the time."

"Hey, guys, never fear. When I say I'm going to do something, I make every effort, and I do it. Well, I try my best to do what I say. If I can't, I'll tell you why and make another time. Don't ever think that I will let you down. Never."

"Cool, Rocky. That's magic. See you later, man," Declan said.

As Rocky drove away, he noticed a difference already in the way the two guys walked across the street and toward the shopping center. They walked upright, not with their usual stance of heads bent forward and shoulders stooped. Their steps were more purposeful and springy. Rocky watched them until they went out of sight. A quiet sense of achievement came over Rocky as he realized that merely talking and suggesting a more in-depth talk had made so much difference. They now had to sell the idea to the other guys. Rocky thought that all the guys probably would not buy the idea, but if half of them did, the rest would probably follow in their own time.

The jobs came fast, with large groups of people moving across town to parties, dances, the theater, or out to dinner; it looked to be a big Saturday night. Rocky collected his usual weekend passengers and some others he had not seen before. He also collected the usual groups of teenagers, looking for the perfect party to crash; if they were kicked out of that one, they be on to the next.

What's going on? Rocky thought. *All these teenagers with stuff going on in their heads, and no one caring enough to show them other things in life—things like BMX riding, roller skating, bowling, surfing, athletics, water sports, and many more activities to use their energy and place them in a group or club.*

The kids often gave the excuse that they didn't have the money to buy a bike, roller skates, surfboard, or whatever. Rocky's standard answer was, "Don't worry about that. Go along a few times. Show an interest and be genuine. Someone will have an old bike, or board, or whatever to lend you to use. You don't need the newest or the best when you start off. You can get a part-time job after school or weekends and save some cash to buy your own down the track."

Nearly always, these kids would tell Rocky that he was right—someone had a second or third item that they could use, and most often, they did well in their chosen activities, or at least they enjoyed what they were doing. They also found new friendships with people with the same interests. It was that simple. Just a little bit of interest shown, some direction given, and a life changed. "Not rocket science," Rocky would often say.

After a couple of hours, Rocky's mobile phone rang.

"Hey, Rocky, it's Declan. What we spoke about before—me and the others want to have that talk soon. Can you find the time for us?"

"Yeah, sure, buddy. How about in thirty to forty-five minutes? I'll get these jobs out of the way, and then I'm all yours."

"Sure, man, that will be cool," Declan said.

"Where will you be?" Rocky asked.

"At the bus stop at the shopping center. We've all got our skateboards and bags with us. Is that OK?"

"Sure, mate, that's cool. That will all fit behind the back seat. Have you boys eaten yet? I haven't, and I'm hungry. How about some pizzas and a drink? My treat," Rocky suggested.

"Yeah, we're starved too. We'll put in some money. You don't have to treat," Declan said.

"No, mate, that's cool. Let me treat; you guys can buy next time, if there is a next time," Rocky said. "I'll phone an order through and pick it up at the shopping center when I get you guys."

"Cool, Rocky, see you then," Declan said.

Rocky noticed a difference in Declan's tone and his manner of speaking. *Things might really be on the way up, for him at least,* Rocky thought. *If I can save one guy from the scrap heap, that is a win. If they all change their thoughts and attitudes and accept the challenge, that will be a massive win.* He felt excited at the prospect of developing a group of wayward boys into fine young men with a future and a purpose in life. *Awesome,* Rocky thought.

After finishing with the jobs, he had lined up, Rocky radioed in to the taxi base that he was going for a meal break and some maintenance—this wasn't entirely a lie; he just didn't indicate what sort of maintenance—and drove to the shopping center.

He found twelve guys, sober and unaffected by drugs, quietly chatting and joking among themselves. Rocky noticed how quiet and sensible they were. They were so engrossed in their chat that they didn't notice Rocky walking up to them.

"Hi, guys, how are things hangin'?" Rocky asked.

"Hey, Rocky, cool man," Mitch said.

Tony and Declan raced up to Rocky and walked with him, one each side, with an elbow on each of Rick's shoulders.

"Didn't hear you pull up, Rocky," Declan said. "Sneaking up on us, hey?"

"All us guys want to talk with you, Rocky," Tony said. "I think we all want to do different things."

"OK, fellas, I'll just pick up the pizzas and drinks and be back soon," Rocky said. "Won't be long."

Three or four of them went with Rocky to help carry the food and drinks back to the taxi. As they left, Rocky threw his keys to Mitch and said, "Oi, Mitch! Unlock the back and pack all your bags and boards behind the back seat."

A few minutes later, Rocky and his helpers returned with the food and drinks and put them in the taxi. He told the guys to get in. "Now, there are twelve of you, and this taxi is supposed to carry only eleven, so you see, I too break the law from time to time. We'll just go quietly, and no one will know any different."

"Where are we going, Rocky?" Aiden asked.

"Oh, just across the bridge and down to the waterfront where the jetties are. What do you reckon?"

"Yeah, that's cool," several voices replied in chorus.

"Can you put this CD on for us to listen to?" Aiden asked, passing an INXS CD to the front seat. "Just bought it, Rocky."

"Yeah, sure, buddy," Rocky said. He asked Pieter, who was sitting beside him in the front seat, to put it in the stereo. "Turn it up, if you want, guys. I don't mind INXS, so go for it. Good music never hurt anyone turned up loud."

After the fourth track, the taxi pulled up at one of the picnic shelters in the park near the jetties. Everyone got out and carried the pizzas and drinks to the tables. Rocky opened the windows and doors of the maxi-taxi and left the stereo playing the remaining tracks on the CD.

The group of boys seemed very relaxed and jovial as they ate, drank, sang, and danced to the music.

A couple of the lads pretended to hold a mike as they sang, two others played air guitars, and another played pretend drums. Rocky felt very relaxed and happy that this group of" bad boys" was behaving like normal fifteen-year-olds, enjoying the atmosphere, each other's company, and the company of an "old guy" nearly three times their age. What a transformation from their normal behavior and attitudes. They were always like this when Rocky drove them to their parties or their homes, but it was different to see them relaxing outside the taxi.

"Now, guys, I was talking to Decles and Tony before and asking them what kicks they get out of their present lifestyle. I am not going to preach about how wrong it is or ram it into your heads. You get plenty of that from other people. I am not going to put shit on any of you; you get too much of that now, it seems. I'm just concerned at the direction you fellas are going with your lives, and I might be able to talk it through with you and suggest other things that might help.

"It won't worry me if you don't take notice, but I can see good in all of you. I can see each of you has a great character that is locked in and needs to get out. I know each of you has great potential to enjoy a good life, and I can see you don't know how to do this. I know you are sick and tired of people telling you how bad you are, that you have no future, that you are no-hopers going nowhere—all those negative things people tell you every day. Not me, guys. I never would say that to anyone. You need someone to help you realize the things you're good at, how to use those things, and to help you to live a happy, healthy, and purposeful life. That's what I am going to try with you guys. It won't happen overnight, although already I have seen a difference. I won't tell you how I see that just yet. I'll tell you after we talk. Now, any questions?"

The questions came quickly.

"Why are you interested in what we do?"

"How can you make things better for us?"

"What can we do to change our lives?"

"Why should we listen to you? We don't listen to anyone else.

"Are you going to tell the teachers or the cops about us?"

"Why don't other people like us?"

"Why do other kids have everything, and we have nothing?"

Rick held up his hand. "That's enough for starters. First, why do I want to help you guys? Well, a few years ago I became very ill. I had two boys about your age, but I couldn't help them too much. Luck for me and lucky for them, we had other adults to help them. I won't go into my illness or tell you who my boys are; some of you probably know them. I am very concerned about the trouble you could get into with the way you are going. You are very angry, frustrated, and neglected; that's why I think you act the way you do. I hate to see young guys with so much potential, so much to live for, being left on the side of the track or thrown on the scrap heap with no hope or direction. How can I make things better for you? Well, I can't make things better for you, but I am certain that I can suggest ways for you to make it better for yourselves. What can you do to change your lives? With my help and guidance and with the help of your teachers and other positive people, you will change your life, if you want to."

"I don't have any people in my life that I can talk to," Mitch said. "I got Mum, but she is busy with my younger brothers and sisters; she is always busy. I don't know where my father is. The last time I heard, he was in jail."

"Me too," Josh said. "My old man pissed off a couple of years ago. Don't know where he is and don't care. He was a mean, cruel mongrel to Mum and me."

"Do you have uncles or family friends you can trust?" Rocky said.

"Nah, got no one," Josh said.

"No one in my family," Mitch said. "Don't know where any of my uncles live, and Mum says they are all scum."

"Well, guys, that is so sad," Rocky said. "Every young man needs a father or father figure in his life, a mentor. You can talk to me if you wish. Any of you. I will be here for you if you need help and guidance. I will always keep our conversations private. I've had no training as a counselor, but I have life experiences with my two boys and their mates and in training junior sports teams, interacting with young people, and with my own issues throughout my life."

"I'm glad you are not a counselor. Can't stand them; they talk shit and make no sense," Adam said.

"Yeah, I guess they seem to be like that. I haven't spoken to anyone yet who has faith in counselors. I imagine it's the way they're trained to speak," Rocky said. "Anyway, moving on … why should you listen to me? That's your choice. I'm not saying that I have all the answers. As I said, I have no formal qualifications like those counselors you don't listen to." The group chuckled. "I'll share my thoughts and advice on what might work. Then it's up to you guys. I can't make you listen or force you to do what I say. You gotta want to do it for yourselves, guys.

"Am I going to tell the cops? No, as I told Tony and Declan, I won't tell anyone your secrets. Everything you tell me stays with me, unless you commit a serious crime and then only if I am asked. I hate dobbers, guys. Do we understand each other? As for why other people don't like you, it's probably not that they don't like you; it's that they don't take the time to talk to you on your level, or they don't have the patience to spend time with you to help you along. Or it's possibly because you are very disruptive and bad, mean guys; they don't want to be near you or be seen with you. You don't have to answer me; it's none of my business, but I would say that each of you comes from a family with a couple of siblings and only one parent. I would also say that you probably don't have a father in your life.

"Why do other kids have everything, and you have nothing? Some kids come from rich families where they get everything they want. Believe me, these kids can be very spoiled and selfish, and you will find that they are fake. You wouldn't get on with them too well. In time you will realize there's more to life than having the best bike, biggest TV, best skateboard, or the latest designer clothes. You'll discover you can get great pleasure from finding a job and buying your own things. You will appreciate it so much more.

"That covers the questions. I hope I've answered them well enough that you realize I'm serious when I say that I am here for you. I want to help you change direction and experience a new productive life and continue the right path. Take it or leave it, fellas. Let's enjoy the journey together, hey guys?"

"Thanks, Rocky," Aiden said. "We got some thinking to do and talking to do about this. I don't know where to start."

"Don't let it worry you too much. Just break it down what I have told you bit by bit. Think it over, make notes if you need to, talk it over among yourselves, and catch up with me when you need to, either on your own or as a group. Just give me a call, and I will be there for you, if that's what you want. Declan and Tony have my number. Pass it on to all the guys so that they can contact me when they want. That might do for tonight. I better get back to work and earn some cash. Where do you guys want to go? I'll drop you off. Give me a call when you want to go home, and I will pick you up if you want."

The guys wanted to go back to the shopping center to see what was happening.

"Good night, boys," Rocky said as he pulled up to the shopping center. "Have a great night. Don't get too hung up with what we spoke about tonight. Just think about what you are doing and try to make good choices. It's all about choices, really. We'll get together soon and start your new journey."

"Bloody oath, Rocky. We are going to try and see how we go," Shayne said.

"We are going to chill here for a while and think about everything you said," Pieter added. "Are you really going to be our mate? Are you really going to help us?"

"Yeah, mate, you will soon realize that I mean what I say. I am committed to helping you dudes, if that's what you want," Rocky answered. "Anyway, call me if you want a lift home or a chat."

"See ya, Rocky. Thanks, man, for giving us your time and talking with us," Mitch said as they left the taxi.

"Yeah, see ya, fellas," Rocky said.

The remainder of the shift went well, with some good, well-behaved groups of passengers and no troublesome people, which made the night go very smoothly. And of course, there was Adrian and his girls. Rocky had picked Adrian up earlier in the night and delivered him to the nightclubs.

Adrian got in with his girlfriend and another girl, as usual. Rocky asked Adrian, "How was your night, champ? Have a good one?"

"Yeah, awesome, Rocky," Adrian said, slurring his words. "Had some rums, lots of dancing. Now I'm buggered. Got to go home, chill a while, have some fun with Christy, and get to sleep."

"Don't know about 'fun,'" Christy said. "He is very drunk again."

"Nah, I'll be right. I'm okay," Adrian said.

Adrian got Rocky to turn the music up loud, and Rocky could see his body moving in the semidarkness. Adrian was into his old tricks once again. Adrian was gyrating, swaying, and performing to the music. His weekly strip show was once again in full swing. Adrian performed this ritual most Saturday nights—first the shoes and socks came off, then the shirt, more dancing, then the trousers, then his underwear, until he was fully naked, dancing to the music.

When Rocky pulled up at Adrian's driveway, Adrian paid his fare, gathered his clothes, took Christy's hand, and half fell out of the maxi-taxi. "Bye, Rocky," they both said as they tried to climb the steep driveway. Adrian, still totally nude, dropped some of his clothing, bent down to pick them up, and staggered a few more steps.

"Don't know how he does it," Rocky said to the remaining female passenger.

"Christy gets so embarrassed when he is like that," the girl said. "She also gets so angry with him. She loves him so much, but she can't get him out of his habits. She says that she understands that he works hard all week in the mines and has to relax, let his hair down, and enjoy himself when he gets home, but she really wants to spend quiet time when they are together."

"Yes, it must be a strain. He really is a great young guy, really enjoys himself, but it must be hard for Christy," Rocky said. "It's funny seeing him going through his antics, but I guess she thinks enough is enough."

Rocky arrived at the young lady's home. She paid the remaining fare and left the taxi.

A few more journeys followed, and then Rocky's phone rang. "Hello, this is Rocky." "This is Mitch, Rocky. How ya doin', mate?"

"Not too shabby, champ. How about you?" Rocky asked.

"Awesome, thanks, feeling great. Is it okay that I rang you? Declan and Tony gave me your number."

"Yeah, buddy, that's cool. You know I said to call when you needed," Rocky said.

"Can you pick us up sometime soon?"

"Yep, that's okay. Where are you?"

"At the twenty-four-hour servo on Main Street. We started walking home but decided to call you."

"Okay, matey, hang in there. I will be there soon. I'm just around the corner and I got no one on board now."

Rocky pulled the taxi into the servo where the twelve lads were waiting for him. They had their bags and boards with them and two plastic shopping bags of food and drinks.

"Hi, Rocky," one of them said. "We know the rule about drinks and food in the taxi, but is it okay if we bring these with us? We got some for you too. We wanted to treat you to a drink and an ice cream."

"Yeah, that's okay. I know you guys won't make a mess—that's what the rule is about," Rocky answered. "Jump in. You didn't have to buy for me. How have you guys been? Have a good time?"

"We have had a good, quiet time, just chilling, talking, riding our skateboards, watching all the dickheads who were drunk and stoned. It's weird, really, sitting and watching. Fun, really," Pieter said. "We even had a few great conversations with some people. We didn't realize how different things are when you are clean, with a clear head."

"We even had some chats with some hot chicky babes, Rocky," Shayne added. "They were awesome."

"You really have changed, guys; congratulations. What have you decided? Are you in for a change with your lives?" Rocky asked.

"Yeah, we talked, took notice of what you said, and we want to talk to you some more, if that's okay," Shayne said.

"That's good. You tell me when, and I'll be there," Rocky said. "Where am I taking you?"

"Oh, to my place, Rocky," Pieter said. "We got a big barn that we are making into a chill-out pad where we can chill for a while and camp for the night. We do it fairly often."

"You better tell me where you live. I've dropped some of you off, but I don't remember where you all live."

"Yeah, I'll tell you the way," Pieter said.

"How has your night been, Rocky?" Aiden asked.

"It's been good really, plenty of work, great people, no hassles, just the way I like it. And there was this young guy, Adrian. He is something else."

"What's he do, Rocky?" Josh asked.

"Well, I pick him up early on Saturday nights and take him to town to the nightclubs. Then he calls me when he wants to go home. He jumps in; he is pissed and then begins to dance, taking his clothes off until he is completely nude. Then he dances nude until we get to his place. Real funny. No harm, just enjoying himself."

"Wow, that's wicked," Jay said. "What happens when he gets out?"

"He half falls out, picks up his clothes and shoes, and staggers up his driveway, dropping stuff as he goes."

"That is so cool," Aiden said. "Can we try that too?"

"No, not tonight. There are too many of you," Rocky answered. "You will all fall over into a pile of naked bodies. Not a good look, I'd say."

"Hey, Rocky. Is it okay for a mob of blokes, friends, to get their gear off when they are together and just chill or swim nude?" Aiden asked.

"Yeah, mate, I guess it is okay. Why do you ask?"

"Sometimes we do that. Nothin' gay—no touching or even looking. Don't need to because we are all good mates. We love to do 'nudie runs' or just sit around and talk, listen to music, and tell jokes with nuthin' on. It's so cool. Freedom, hey guys?" Aiden said.

"Yeah, it's real cool. We think it is okay when we are together. It feels really good," Mitch said. "Some people say it is disgusting, bad, or gay."

"I suppose it's okay. I must say I like the freedom of being nude myself but only when I'm by myself or with my wife. I have never gotten my gear off while with other people. Just be sure you are not in a public place or where anyone else can see you; it is against the law to be naked in a public place. It's called indecent exposure, and you can get into serious trouble if you are caught."

"You never know; we might have a nude swim when we get to Piet's place now, hey guys?" Adam said.

"Looks like that's what we are doing soon," Tony said. "I'm starting now. I'm getting my shirt off now."

Rocky laughed at the conversation and at the devious plans they had just thought up. He found his way to Pieter's house under Pieter's instructions, pulled up, and said, "See ya later, guys. Enjoy your swim and the rest of the night."

"See ya, Rocky," Aiden said as he handed Rocky a sock full of coins. "This is for the fare home. I'll get the sock off you next time I see you."

"Fellas, thanks. I didn't even put the meter on," Rocky said. "Just call me when you want another talk. And keep your hands to yourselves when you are in the pool, you deviates." He laughed. "Just gagging with ya."

"Yeah, we will," Pieter said. "Thanks a lot, Rocky, for being so good to us today and tonight. We appreciate it and look forward to changing our lives with your help. Let's have three cheers for Rocky, boys."

The boys let out three cheers as they left the taxi and scurried up the driveway, shedding their clothes as they went.

The next day, Sunday, Rocky's phone rang.

"Rocky, is that you?" the caller asked.

Rick instantly recognized it was one of the twelve guys from last night. "Yes, who's this?"

"It's Aiden, Rocky. We are all wondering if we can see ya today or tonight, so we can ask you some more things we were talking about yesterday."

"Hi, Aiden. I'm just starting work now. Sundays are usually very quiet. I'll just see what's happening, and then I can get you all. Are all of you there? Where are you? When is the best time?"

"Yep, we are all here at the skate ramps," Aiden answered. "Any time. Whatever suits you, man."

"Okay, just keep a lookout for me."

Rocky did a couple of jobs and then sat on the main taxi rank for a while, listening to the small talk with the other drivers. He decided to go around to the skate ramp and get the boys, as he had not progressed in the line of taxis. He pulled up at the skate ramp and watched the youths skateboarding; a couple of the boys noticed that Rocky was waiting. He heard them calling out to each other. They grabbed their bags and boards and bounded toward the taxi.

Pieter opened the tailgate and put his gear behind the back seat. "G'day, Rocky. It's good to see ya." The others followed, putting their gear in the back and climbing aboard. Aiden and Pieter got in the front to sit beside Rocky.

"Hi, guys. Have you had a good time today?" Rocky asked.

They all agreed that they had. Some played football and two worked at the local supermarket, but they had spent an hour or two at the skate park, burning off some energy.

"Where will we go, fellas? You want to have another chat?" Rocky asked.

"Yeah, we want you to tell us more things to make us better kids, so we can be normal," Aiden answered. "We were hoping to go to that picnic shed near the water. It's so cool. We thought we might make that shed our chill-out place where we can chill with you, if that's okay."

"That's a good place; you can base yourselves there. I like that place too. It's so cool beside the water. Not too many people around so you can be yourselves without disturbing anyone. But you must keep your clothes on," Rocky teased, laughing. "At least your shorts, so no one gets offended. How did your chill session and nude swim go?"

"It was wicked, Rocky. It was great lying back with the night air on our bodies under the stars and the moon, chatting about our new lives, talking about the things you told us, skinny-dipping in the pool, jumping around, and wrestling in the moonlight. It was wicked, man. We turned the lights off, so we had some dull light," Mitch said.

The taxi pulled up at the shelter, and the lads jumped out, bounced around a little, skylarking, letting off a bit of energy, and enjoying the fresh air.

"This is awesome this time of year, just before winter. The air is so cool," Adam said as he sat at the table with the other guys.

"What are you going to talk about this afternoon, Rocky?" Haydon asked.

"Let's start with attitudes," Rocky said. "How do you feel if someone comes up to you and says things that indicates that he thinks he's better than you? You get the shits. You feel bad. You even might feel that you are lower class than him or her. What you need to do is ignore the dickheads. You know everyone is the same. Everyone starts life as a baby. They must learn everything. Everyone eats, sleeps, shits, pisses, and dies the same. If you take away the fancy clothes and the money, those people are the same as you. You see, it does not impress you, and certainly does not impress anyone else."

"How should we treat someone like that, Rocky?" Aiden asked.

"Just don't let them see that you notice the high and mighty attitude. Look them in the eye when you talk, and don't react to their attitude. It is hard at first, but it will become easy, and soon they'll realize you haven't reacted to their attitude. Another thing—if they get under your skin, don't get angry and don't bash them; ignore them and walk away. After all, you don't have to be friends with someone who's a jerk. Just be a little friendly and walk away. After a few times, you'll feel much better about it and about yourselves."

"What if someone messes with us and pisses us off?" Tony asked.

"Just ignore the suckers. Think about what hurts physically and what hurts your feelings. If I kicked you in the nuts, cracked a baseball bat over your head, or punched you in the face, those things would hurt. That's physical pain, and you must defend yourself to stop it happening. If I said to you that you were a faggot or a weak prick, that doesn't hurt physically; there is no physical pain, but it does hurt your feelings. You know that what they've said isn't true, so why worry about it? Some people use name-calling to try to get you to react. If you ignore it, it will stop very quickly. They will move on, and guess what, guys? You have won, and you haven't had to lift a finger. No wasted energy on the dickheads. That's anger management.

"Now, Pieter, some rich prick comes into the area where you are skateboarding with your old, battered, scratched, and chipped skateboard, and you are wearing old, torn, worn-out clothes and a cap. He is wearing a new name-brand shirt and shorts and the latest model cap and is riding a new skateboard. How do you feel?"

"Aw, I'd feel really bad, and I would want to extinguish the prick," Pieter answered.

"Why?" Rocky asked.

"Because the prick is just showing off that he has the good gear and thinks he is better than us," Aiden said.

"Why? Can the dickhead skate better than you? Probably not. Does he do the tricks that you can do? Probably not, because he might damage his new board, or he may get hurt. So why is he better than you? He isn't. You are better than him because it doesn't matter if you fall and tear your old clothes. It doesn't matter if you scratch or chip your board because it is already damaged. You can ride better, enjoy trying new tricks, and have so much more fun with your old board because you're not trying to keep it looking like new. Each new mark on your board is like a visual 'trophy,' a reminder of what you tried to perfect. Would you agree? Just stop and think, guys—what does a cap do, other than make you look cool? It keeps the sun off your head, and new or old style doesn't matter. What does your shirt do? Helps protect you from the sun and some injuries. When the rich dude tears his shirt, he cries and goes home with his tail between his legs. You tear your old shirt, and you get up again and keep going. You probably even feel proud, as sometimes tears are like trophies as well; you remember how you did it. Shorts are the same; all they do is cover up and protect your private bits from getting sunburned or injured. I know this is very crude. I'm just trying to break it down to the basics.

"Now your board—an old board allows you to get from one place to another. A new board allows you to do the same. An old board allows you to practice and do tricks, so does a new board. Understand that old or new, they do the same things. So, next time a rich dude comes into the area where you are skating, don't give a stuff about his gear. Watch what he does. If he does a different trick than you, learn to do it better than him, because you know it doesn't matter if you scratch or chip your board or tear your shorts or shirt.

"Any questions about that? There is so much more but that might do about attitudes. If someone does or says something to mess with you, think about it before you react. Now, I've been talking a lot. I'll have a rest, and you guys can talk about what I told you or just chill for a while."

The guys also took the opportunity to rest for a while, some sitting on the seats around the picnic table while others stretched out on the lawn, plying banter with each other, having fun with each other and discussing the things that they all had talked about.

"Right-o guys, back to the talk, if you can take any more of my talking. Any questions?" Rocky asked.

"Rocky, how do we stop being angry and stop wanting to fight and bash everyone?" Declan asked.

"Just like I've been telling you—before you react, get angry, or feel like fighting, stop and think about it. Think to yourself that the idiot who is annoying you wants to get to you. When he gets to you and you react, he has won. He has made you to choose to be angry. If you think about it and ignore the dickhead, you have won. You have chosen not to let him get to you. You have chosen the attitude. It's hard, I know, but you will get used to it, and he will walk away. Don't you walk away; just keep on skateboarding, or talking to your mates, or whatever you are doing, and ignore him.

"Guys, this is heavy stuff. I don't want to keep pushing these words on you all at once, so let's have another break, have another drink, put some more music on, and chill. Any of you blokes who smoke, have one. I'm not encouraging you, but if you feel you need one, go ahead. I'm not going to dob because you're too young. I can't preach anyway because I smoke too. I'm going to have one now." Rocky lit his cigarette.

A few of the lads lit their cigarettes. Aiden chose music by Slipknot, and general discussion took place with Rocky about their interests, hobbies, and sports activities. This allowed Rocky to understand them a little more so that he could apply input later how to occupy their minds and time. Rocky stopped any reference to alcohol or drugs, saying they would discuss it later. Each guy relaxed and spoke about the things they liked to do, the things they hated about school, teachers, adults, or other kids, and eventually, about the lifestyle they had and how they could change things for the better.

Rocky already had noticed a change in most of them. He was very impressed by their change of attitudes regarding the topics already discussed and how they would tackle certain circumstances.

"Right, guys—now let's talk about your bodies, about how your body feels after certain things you do to it," Rocky said. "Everyone enjoys drinking alcohol. You just got to know how much and how often. You gotta learn what it does to you, how it affects your actions, and how it makes you feel afterward and the next day. I'm not going to preach to you about alcohol or drugs. You guys have experienced it repeatedly at such a young age. That's okay. I'm not going to put you down over it or tell anyone you are underage drinkers—that wouldn't prove a thing. You know how drinking, drugs, and smoking affects you and how you feel. If you want a more active lifestyle, you gotta ease up on it or give it away altogether. Just something to think about. No pressure."

The discussion continued about looking after their health and well-being, cleanliness, and better ways to get their kicks.

"Listen, guys, we've spoken about a lot of things tonight. I think we have talked enough about it to give you something to think about," Rocky said. "How about we stop here? Now that I know the direction you guys want to take your lives, I am here, I will help you where I can. I know you can do it if you want. All of you are very intelligent. I am very impressed by how you blokes listened and spoke openly about these things. Remember, everything you have told me about yourselves, your thoughts, and the things you have done stays with me. I'll tell no one. Now let's pack up. I better get back on the road. Where do you want to be dropped off?"

As the taxi loaded with the young guys rolled along, the guys discussed where they would go. They eventually decided to go to Pieter's place, where there was the large barn in the back yard, as was a pool.

"Rocky, we're going to chill in the barn at Pieter's house, talk about what you told us, and have a swim. We won't get pissed or have a joint tonight, so we can talk sensibly and wake up tomorrow and see how much better we feel," Mitch said.

"That's cool, Mitch. I'll drop you off there. If you want, give me a call when you want to go home, and I'll drop you to your houses—no charge, guys."

The gang piled out of the maxi-taxi and each went to the driver's window to shake Rocky's hand, give him high-fives, or put a hand on Rocky's shoulder and tell him how they appreciated what Rocky had told them.

Rocky returned to his job. When he was on a taxi rank, he remained in his taxi. He didn't want to associate with other drivers or become involved in the negative small talk—the whines and moans about how quiet it was, how shit the country or world was, or gossip about other drivers. He spent his time thinking about the young guys and how they had thrown themselves into their new way of life. He thought about what the future held for them as they applied their new information to become respectable citizens. He also decided how he would help them with new activities they could use to occupy their time and energy.

He wondered how these guys could fund any new activity they might decide to pursue. Maybe they could join a BMX club, or mountain-bike riding, or soccer or football. They would need a bike for some activities; others would need just a ball and club shorts and shirt. Then, the penny dropped. He remembered their love of music and that some had pretended to play guitars and drums during a recent talk session. He tried to work out how to fund musical instruments. Maybe they could join a music class at school and start with school instruments.

What about the others who don't want to join in music? Rocky thought. *What about setting goals for themselves? After all, they can't aimlessly travel through life without some direction.* Rocky learned this after he was so ill and tried to get back to a normal life. Setting goals was what got him back on track. *That is the subject we can talk about next*, he decided.

The night shift went very slowly. Rocky was torn between how boring his job was at times like this and how excited he was to help these young boys and their wish to enjoy a new life. He hoped the lads would ring him soon to be picked up. A little while later, Rocky's mobile phone rang.

It was Aiden. "Can you pick us up to take us home? We just want to be with you one last time tonight. We're so happy now that you are in our lives."

"Yeah, that's okay," Rocky said. "Are you ready now?"

"Yes, we are. We've been talking about everything. We want to change our attitudes, like you said, and try to do new things, but we don't know what. We have a plan to make the barn at Pieter's house into our main chill-out zone—make it comfortable so we can chill out and not need to go to places and get bored and get ourselves into trouble. We want you to see the barn, and we want to show you what we are going to do to make it our own."

"Yes, that sounds awesome," Rocky said. "A base where you can spend some time with each other sounds like a good idea. Yes, I would like to see the barn, and I would like to see your plans to make it into your own pad. I'll need to get Pieter's mum's permission to call in."

"She's already said it's okay. We tell our mums everything about you. They're cool about you because they said your influence on us is remarkable. So, can you come in and see our barn and chill with us for a while before we go home? Pieter's mum wants to meet you," Aiden said.

"Okay, buddy, I'll be there soon. See ya then."

Rocky pulled his taxi up outside Pieter's house and walked down the driveway toward the backyard. The boys were bounding and jumping as they approached him. The lads seemed excited to see him and greeted him warmly. He felt welcome and felt good about himself.

After greeting them, Rocky said, "It's great to see you all so happy, sober, and not affected by drugs. I am so proud of all of you and how far you've come in just a few short weeks. This is awesome."

"Come on in," Pieter said, "and see the barn and what we are going to do with it to make it cool."

"I better meet your mum first," Rocky said, "so she knows this 'old guy' is with you, just in case she doesn't want me here."

Pieter went to get him mum and then made the necessary introductions. "Mum, this is Rocky, the guy I told you about who drives the maxi-taxi. He wants to be sure that it is okay with you that he is here. He thinks he's a bit old to be with us. Like I told you, Mum, Rocky is helping us to change our lives to be better kids."

"Pleased to meet you, Rocky. I'm Sally," Pieter's mum said. "Pieter's told me so much about you and what you have told them. I am so pleased that you have taken the time and had an interest in helping my boy and the others to learn right from wrong. It has been so hard; I'm on my own, and no one has been able to get inside his head and make him realize where he has been going wrong or what he should be doing be doing with his life. The other boys' mothers have said the same when I have spoken to them about you. We all thank you very much."

"That's okay, Sally. I just noticed how bad, angry, and destructive these boys were, and I wanted to try to take them to another plane. I could see that they were—are—very level-headed at times, and I was confident that I could make a difference. It's nice to meet you, Sally, and thank you for your kind words." Rocky turned his attention to the boys. "Right-o lads, let's have a look at this chill pad, hey?"

Sally went back in the house, and the lads walked toward the barn. The barn was a timber-walled construction with double timber-plank doors and a single timber door at the front, just like most barns in the backyards of houses built in the 1950s or 1960s—the same size that would take two cars side by side. Each side had two sash-type windows, and the back was a solid wall.

"These double doors don't open anymore," Pieter said, "but that suits us, as we want that to be a wall. Let's go inside, and we will show you what we will be doing." Once inside, Pieter switched the lights on. "Yep, it has lights, as you can see, and power, Rocky."

The barn contained some old furniture and other "junk" that had been stored for quite a few years. There was also a toilet and shower area in the back corner. The rest of the walls were unlined but in very good condition. Behind the barn doors were a couple of old mattresses, where the boys obviously slept when they slept over.

Rocky said, "Hey, lads, this is pretty good as a start-up area where you can chill. Does the toilet and shower work? That would be handy, so you don't have to go upstairs into the house. That's really cool."

"Yeah, they work. We had to clean them up a bit because they hadn't been used much for years. They work now, just got to spend some more time to get them much better. We might work on the walls a bit because they are missing some boards, so you can see in there. No privacy. Not an issue, really; we don't care about seeing each other while showering because we go nude together sometimes. None of us cares, but if we are lucky enough to have some chicky babes sleep over, they won't want to think someone can see them," Pieter said, laughing.

"That's a good thought, fixing the walls up. You just never know what you blue-blooded Aussie guys will get up to as you get older," Rocky said. "What are your plans for this place? Hey, you got a fridge in here," Rocky said, just noticing a fridge in the other back corner. "Does it work?"

"Yeah, it's always been used for parties and barbecues for years. It is old but really works well. Apparently, my dad used it as a drink fridge before he cleared out and disappeared," Pieter said. "We can use it for drinks and food for ourselves now. We actually got bottles of juice and soft drinks in there now."

"Can I ask—where is your dad now, Pieter?" Rocky said. "Don't answer that if it is too personal. None of my business; I was just wondering."

"Nah, it's cool. It is no secret. He disappeared when I was seven. I remember him and Mum having big arguments and fights for a while. He used to hit and bash mum. It was horrible, I remember, but he never hurt us kids. He just disappeared, and she has never heard from him in nearly ten years. She says she doesn't care where he is; she never wants to see him or talk to him, ever. I never want to see him either. Don't care, Rocky. We don't even know if he is alive or dead. Mum doesn't care. She won't even list him as a missing person; he was that much of a bastard and so cruel to her."

Josh chimed in, "Hey, I got something to tell everyone, seeing we are talking about missing dads. Mine is getting out of jail soon. We are scared."

"Is that why you been a bit quiet lately?" Rocky asked. "I was wondering what was on your mind, but I wasn't sure how to ask you. After all, I've only known you for a couple of months."

Tears ran down Josh's cheeks, and he broke into a sob. The other boys seemed horrified at the sight of their mate in such a state, and they moved over to comfort him.

Rocky put his arm around Josh's shoulders and held him tight to help him settle down. "Come on, mate, we got you. We are here for you, whatever you need. When you are ready, just wash your face, settle down, and we can talk about it if you want. No pressure, but buddy, we are here."

Pieter returned with a bucket of water and a small towel, so Josh could wash his face and freshen up. Josh sat down on a small stack of old tires. He looked around at all the concerned faces before him. "I'm sorry, fellas, it has got to me. I am sorry you had to see me cry like that. It was just hearing about Pieter's dad like that. It was too much for me because I've … we … got something happening about my father, and I didn't know how to tell anyone."

"It's really okay for boys or men to cry," Rocky told him. "Don't worry about the saying, 'Big boys don't cry.' That's bullshit, guys; big boys do cry. It's a normal way to express emotions, grief, anything that might affect you. Don't think that you are a crybaby or weak, Josh. It must come out sooner or later. If you are ready and if you want to, we can talk it through. It really must come out; no good storing it up. Let it out, champ; then you will feel better. Or if you want and you trust me, we can talk one on one—whatever you want, man."

Josh said, "Nah, it's okay. I want to tell all of you. I just don't know how because it's so scary and brings up some bad things from when I was a young kid. Can we go somewhere outside and have a drink? I feel like I want to go out beside the pool."

"Yes, we can do that. I'm sure Pieter won't mind. We can talk out there, wherever you feel more comfortable. Do you guys want to drink your drinks? I will get some from the shop tomorrow to replace them." Rocky said.

"Nah," Aiden said, "we have enough in the fridge. It's big bottles so we will have to share. We know each other, we are mates, so it will be cool."

"Now that you have a fridge and a chill pad," Rocky said, "I can restock it sometime."

Pieter said, "You don't have to do that."

"I know, but I'll get some to start you off in your pad."

Shayne grabbed three bottles from the fridge, and they all moved outside so that Josh could talk about his problem.

"Can you sit beside me, please, Rocky?" Josh asked. "I'll feel much better and safer if you sit here with me."

"Yeah, sure, Josh. I'll sit beside you as your support person," Rocky agreed.

"We are here for you too, Josh," Haydon said. "That's what mates do. That's what we do for each other."

As the bottles were passed around and each took a swig, Josh said, "Really, I could do with a strong rum now and a joint or two, but we promised that we're over that. I'll have to tell you with a clear head. Well, my dad is in jail. He murdered two guys when I was three or four over a drug deal that went wrong. He was charged, convicted, and sent to jail for it. I don't know all the details, as my mother doesn't want to talk about it. When I was six or seven, two horrible, ugly blokes and a woman who looked like a witch abducted me, tied me up, put a bag over my head, and took me away. I don't know where because that bag never came off my head." Josh started to cry uncontrollably. Rocky hugged him tightly and tried to control Josh as he swayed and shook violently.

"It's okay, Josh. You're safe with us. Don't continue if you can't, but I think you need to get this out in your own time. No good keeping it inside," Rocky told him. Rocky looked around at the other boys. Each had a look of terror, disbelief, and concern at what they had just heard. Many of them tried to comfort Josh. "Are you guys okay with what you are hearing?" Rocky asked. "This is a major thing. Talk it through, if you are feeling so bad for your mate. It's understandable that you would feel shocked by this." Rocky was equally shocked and had trouble getting his words together. "Now, Josh, leave it there if you don't want to carry on, mate. It's okay."

"No, I will tell you the lot. I gotta say it now since I started, so everyone knows what is happening." Josh took a deep breath and said, "These people locked me up. I did not know where I was, or why they took me away, or what they were going to do with me. They never spoke to me at all. I only heard them talking about me and my sister, my mum, and some money. I also heard them talking about my dad. One day, they put me in a car again, in the boot, with the bag over my head. I was tied up. We drove for a while. I was thrown from side to side because the car was going very fast. When they put the brakes on, I would be thrown forward, then to the back of the boot when they took off again. Then I heard sirens. I found out later that they were going so fast that they skidded sideways and ran off the road as the cops caught up to them. They were going so fast that I went crashing into the front of the boot and hurt my head and shoulders. Then I heard a male voice yell, 'Get out of the car with your hands in the air.'

"I realized it was the cops. Then I heard, 'Get out. I will shoot if I need to.' Then I heard the doors open and someone said, 'Lie face-down on the road, arms behind your backs, or I will shoot.' Then I heard clicking noises, which I was sure were the handcuffs. 'You were doing over eighty miles an hour back there,' the male voice said. 'When we chased you, you increased your speed to over ninety-three miles an hour. Any reason for that?' One of the blokes said, 'We are in a hurry, that's all.'

"I decided to kick, bang, and yell, but I had tape over my mouth. My body, head, arms and legs hurt so bad, but I had to make a noise. I was so frightened. Then the boot opened, and I heard the cop say, 'Why is this child in here? Who is it? What were you going to do with him?' There was no answer. Another cop car turned up, so the road was blocked at each end.

The cop radioed for an ambulance because when I was released the cops saw that I was injured. The cop also radioed for a female cop because they thought a female cop would be better with me. I was taken to hospital and stayed there for a few days, and my mum was brought there by the police, so she could be with me."

Josh paused, asked for a drink. He took a giant gulp; then sighed and began to shake once again. He was still cradled in Rocky's arms, and Josh put both arms around Rocky's neck, as if he was hanging on for dear life. Rocky sponged Josh's face and patted his forehead to console him.

"Sorry guys, sorry you have to hear this," Josh said, "but I have kept this to myself for so long. I needed to talk about it. But the worst is to come. Sorry, fellas, I love you all so much, just like brothers, really."

"Why did they take you away and treat you so bad?" Mitch asked. "That is so bad. I feel so horrible to think that happened to you."

"Well, when my father was sent to jail, people thought that he had a lot of money hidden away or thought that Mum knew where it was. The cops still don't know if Mum knows anything, or if my father contacted them to get me so they could get the money and then give me back," Josh said. "Now, these three people are in jail. They will be let out in a couple of weeks. The cops came around the other night and told Mum that they will be released and that my father is due to get out in about six months. They told us that we must leave town, move a long way from here to a safe house. We have to change our names and not to talk to anyone about it."

Josh began to shake once again. Rocky held him tight and stroked his head and wiped his face again. "I am not supposed to tell you guys—or anyone—but I could not just disappear suddenly without telling you. Please, do not tell anyone this; it must be a secret so that they can't find us and hurt us. You must promise you'll tell no one, please."

Everyone gasped in horror and promised to keep the information to themselves. Then Adam said, "Josh, Rocky, I've heard that having a group hug helps guys feel better when things are bad and when things go good. Do you think we can try it for Josh? I am so sad for him, and I can't imagine what it will be like when he is gone."

"I think that's a good idea. Yes, it does help when times are tough and to celebrate when good things happen," Rocky said. "What do you think, Josh? Are you up for it?"

"That's okay. Sorry, boys, I have to go next week, and I might never see you again," Josh said, crying uncontrollably. "And I will never see you again, Rocky, to listen to your thoughts, your stories, and the help you have given. I want to stay, but because I am only sixteen, I have no choice."

All the boys jumped up. They helped their mate Josh out of Rocky's arms and helped Rocky up; then they formed a circle with Josh and Rocky in the center and wrapped their arms around each other and hugged tightly. This went on for what seemed a couple of minutes before they let go. There was not a dry eye among the group. Everyone found it so very emotional.

Josh let out a loud, long sigh and said, "Fuck, that felt good to get that out. I didn't know how to do that, how to tell you that I must leave. It was worrying me because I could not just leave, but the cops kept telling me not to tell anyone. When Rocky came into our lives, things seemed to be going well, and then this happened. I'd say it would have been much harder if Rocky hadn't come along. Thanks, Rocky, for holding me. I know it might sound queer, but you made it easier. I don't know why, but it did feel good."

"Josh, it isn't queer, not gay, if that's what you mean. At times, everyone needs a male person they can trust, to hold them, to hug them. It was normal. Just like it is normal for mates to express their feelings of love for another male. It is not gay under normal circumstances. It's probably just a need to have a father or older brother figure, a mentor, someone who cares. So, guys, don't hold back if you find a male who is very close to you and you can confide in and talk to him, allowing you to see another aspect or conclude with an issue.

"Let's leave Josh time to recover. That was heavy for us all, but think how heavy that was for Josh. I would suggest we ask no questions. Respect Josh and his family and their privacy. Stay close to him and support him, and we will have a mighty mission before he must leave. I'd say he will not be able to contact any of you for a while, but be sure, we will find a way to keep in contact. I have ideas in my head already, but I won't talk about it yet. I'll talk to Josh first, hey Josh?

"Guys, this has been a full-on sad night so far. I'm thinking that I should stay with you for a while. What do you think? I don't want to pressure you at all, and I don't want to overstay my welcome. I'm here for you if you want; if you don't, I'll go. I will understand."

"Oh, Rocky, you can stay with us. We want you to stay if you can, hey guys?" Aiden asked. "Please stay and chill with us."

All the boys indicated that they didn't want Rocky to leave. "You are part of us, Rocky. We want to spend more time with you and talk with you," Pieter insisted. "What about the taxi? Shouldn't you go back to work?"

"Nah. I will take the taxi back to the base and bring my vehicle back and stay as long as you want. Tonight, you guys are more important than the small amount of cash I could earn. Sunday nights are shit and so boring. And I would be worried about you boys if I sat for long periods, waiting for some dead-shit drunk to come along.

"While I am out, how about I get some pizzas and drinks to help us chill and get over the shocks of tonight?" Rocky walked over to Josh and asked him how he was doing and if he was okay to stay with the rest for a while.

"I'm good, thanks, Rocky. It is a relief now that all that is out. Thanks for caring about me and being there for me to hang onto. It seems strange that I needed you so much, but I'm stoked you were there. Thanks, mate," Josh said, as he hugged Rocky tightly.

Rocky then asked Pieter, "Can you get your mum for me, so I can ask her if it's okay and have a talk with her?"

"Yeah, Rocky, I'll get her for you. Do you want some money for the pizzas?"

"No, mate, thanks. You guys don't get much money. Save your money, hey," Rocky said as Pieter bounded up the stairs to get Sally.

"Oh, Sally, so sorry to disturb you. I was wondering if it is okay if I spend some more time with these boys tonight. They have been through a very hard time. There's no trouble, but one of the boys has a family issue that has upset him.

"Yes, that's okay," Sally said. "What has happened? Who is it?"

"We cannot divulge that information at present. Please trust me on this. I hate to look like I am keeping secrets from you so soon after meeting you. This is for the safety of the boy and his family—they have been told not to tell anyone so that they remain completely safe

Sally said, "I understand. The world is a terrible place at times. I am only relieved that you were with them to help them through and help them understand."

"Thanks, Sally. I am just going to take the taxi back to the base, get some food and drinks for them, and then I will be back. No longer than half an hour, I'd say."

Rocky got into the taxi and drove off, returning in his own vehicle. The boys raced up the driveway when they heard the car arrive.

"Wow, look at that car. That is so wicked, Rocky. Is that your car?" Aiden asked.

"Yes, it is. Didn't you guys know I had this?"

"Nah," Pieter said, "that is so cool. Can we have a look inside?"

"Okay." Rocky opened the sliding door, the front door, and the tailgate. The twelve guys climbed through the car, commented on the interior, the stereo, the TV and DVD player, the plush upholstery, the lighting. They could not believe that an old-people mover, the same as the maxi-taxi, could look so cool. They then walked around it, looking at the paint job, the murals on the sides, the spider-web effect, the color, the shine, the chrome. They were enraptured by what they saw.

"This is so fuckin' wicked," Aiden said. "Look at these seats, the dim lights, the upholstery, the tinted windows, and that wicked sound system."

Rocky climbed into the driver's seat and flicked a couple of switches. As he did, they heard a whirring sound above them. As they looked up, they saw the sunroof slide open.

"Wow, look at that!" Mitch said in awe. "That is awesome!"

"I prefer to call it the 'moon roof,' guys. I designed it to let the moonlight in and so I can see the stars. I love star and moon gazing," Rocky said.

Another switch gradually brightened the lights. He flicked again, and some turned off; then another flick, and they slowly dulled again. Rocky flicked another switch and music surrounded the guys. The volume was turned up; the sound was so unreal.

"Guys, there is a stereo back there as well as this one up here, and there are sockets outside to plug in extra speakers, so the music can be enjoyed outside. The TV and DVD work perfectly with the sound piped through the sound system. That completes the package. It's fully air conditioned. This is my pride and joy. I don't let just anyone in it, but I know you guys will respect it, look after it, and enjoy the ride. Oh, the stereo back there is controlled from up here. I mean I can turn it on and off from here. Okay, let's go," Rocky said, as he kicked the engine into action and drove away.

The guys settled in to enjoy the ride. They asked a lot of questions about Rocky's car. They agreed it was a mean car and they wanted to rebuild and modify cars of their own when they got a bit older. They also wanted Rocky to help and advise them when they did so. Of course, Rocky agreed.

They stopped at the local snack bar, which was well known for its quality pizza's and other food. Each guy ordered and paid for his own food and returned to the Midnight Special for the trip back to Pieter's barn. As they drove up the driveway, they all cheered that they had ridden in such an amazing vehicle.

"That was awesome, Rocky," Aiden said. "I just love it. Is it automatic? I just realized that you didn't change gears while we were driving."

"Yeah, it is a four-speed auto with a push button overdrive for highway cruising. I found that the manual was a bit rough, and I wanted a smoother ride," Rocky said.

"What's this?" Declan asked. "There are limo-type lights up here beside the sliding door and look at the artwork on the name panel."

"Midnight Special," Haydon read. "Is that what it's called? I've never seen a car with a name on it before."

"Yeah, mate. It's called Midnight Special. That's why it is such a dark-blue base color with those murals showing stars and the moon, with the reflection in the water and the silhouette of that dude and chick walking hand in hand on the beach. You will have to see it in the daytime to get the real effect. I'll take you for a drive later if I am taking you guys to your homes."

"Cool. That will be awesome, Rocky. I would love to have a ride in it, but I live here, and I am already home," Pieter said.

"That's okay, buddy. You can ride in it sometime soon. Tell you what—I'll take you when I drop these lads home later and then bring you back home, if that's okay."

"Hell yeah, that'd be prime," Pieter answered. "We better get out back and chill and eat those pizzas while they are hot. I can smell them. They are making me hungry."

The guys chilled, tried to joke among themselves, engaged in discussions about their big weekend and the eventful night and had a swim in the moonlight. They had more talk and a bit of frolicking, trying to change the mood that they were in.

After a fair length of time, Rocky noticed a few of them looked very tired and quiet. "All right, fellas. You guys look like you need a sleep. How about we clean up here, and I will get you all home? You need some sleep to help you get over tonight. Same for me. I am tired and need sleep. I gotta start the early shift tomorrow. Let's climb aboard the Midnight Special, and I'll get you boys home. Pieter, you come too for the drive."

CHAPTER 5

As the sun rose above the water, Mitch's lifeless naked body was lifted from the water onto the jetty. The police had to hold the guys back from getting too close so that they could not see what was happening.

After Rick spent a couple of hours of his Monday morning shift driving late party or nightclub-goers home or workers to their workplaces, the phone rang.

"Hello, this is Rick. What can I do for you?" he said without looking at the screen.

"Hi, Rocky. We were wondering when we could see you again." It was Pieter.

"Hey, buddy. Can I phone ya back? I have passengers on board. I won't be long."

"That's cool. We'll wait for your call."

Rocky delivered his passengers and found a tree to park under; then he dialed Pieter's number. "What's happening, mate?" Rocky said. "Sorry about before. I had to deliver some old fogies to the town hall. I have a little time before I start the school run, so I can talk now."

"That's okay, Rocky. We know you have work to do. We're on our way to school and we were talking about what's been happening. We wanted to know when we can see you again. It's strange, but we really miss ya," Pieter said, as many voices yelled out similar words in the background.

"I've been thinking about you guys and what else I could tell you to maybe make it easier to fill your time and keep you out of trouble and off the streets. I was going to see if you want to have a barbecue get-together before Josh leaves. How is Josh doing after last night?" Rocky asked.

"He's fine, still looking a bit pale and a bit teary-eyed, but we are looking after him and staying close to him, like you said."

"That's terrific, champ. I knew you boys would support him. You are such a tight group of mates. Anyway, I think a barbecue mission might be good on Friday night. I'm off Friday night—actually, every night this week except Saturday night—and I want to have one more talk before Josh leaves; that is, if you guys are up for it. That way, maybe he can use my thoughts or information with any friends he makes at his new school. And I would like to spend some time with all of you, traveling around town in the Midnight Special, just so you can see the sleazy scum who stagger around drunk and getting into fights and pass out drunk in the gutters."

"Wow, that's a busy week, Rocky, fitting those missions in one week," Pieter said. "And that would be wicked, driving around in that awesome car you have. The guys all heard what you said and are keen to do those things with you. Whenever, we are up for it. A barbecue on Friday sounds prime."

"Let's talk tomorrow night. The drive on Thursday night and the barbecue on Friday night? How's that sound?" Rocky said. "So, tomorrow night, do you want to talk at the barn or somewhere else?"

"Can we start at my place? Then maybe we will talk you into taking us for a drive to the waterfront for a mission. What do you think?" Pieter said.

"Yeah, that's cool. I'll contact tomorrow and work out a time. Have a great day at school. Look after yourselves and Josh. See ya tomorrow."

"Yeah, bye, Rocky. Look forward to seeing ya again," Pieter said.

That night, Rocky received a few phone calls from some of the boys, mainly small-talk conversations about their day at school or asking for his thoughts on subjects they had come across. These talks were very relaxed and casual—and very intelligent. A good sign, Rocky realized, as it was obvious that the garbage of the past was being replaced by clear, positive thoughts and actions.

Rocky phoned Pieter later in the morning when he knew the high school kids would be on their morning break. "Hi, mate, just ringing to see what time I should call around for our talk. Is six or six thirty okay?"

"Six o'clock is good, even earlier if you want," Pieter answered. "We're doing good now that we are responsible citizens." He giggled at what he'd said. "We'll be there straight after school and will do our homework until you get here."

"Okay, I'll see ya when I can make it."

Rocky drove the Midnight Special down the driveway of Pieter's house and pulled up in front of the barn. A few guys ran from a table near the pool and a few others bounded from the barn. Rocky got out and greeted each one with high-fives, hugs, or handshakes. The atmosphere was electric and positive. Rocky was not used to being mobbed—but then a past memory came flooding back. He suddenly remembered another portion of his lost memory. He recalled the time with the young boys playing in rugby league, when he experienced the same exuberance of young guys feeling good about themselves and their achievements. Just like old times, he felt so humble at seeing young people achieve good things and show feelings of appreciation.

"Phew, that was awesome—heavy but awesome. I just need to sit a while. That hit me hard."

"Are you okay, Rocky? What's wrong? You look pale," Aiden said.

"Is he sick?" Mitch asked. "I hope he is okay. Let us help you, big guy. Come and sit down." Mitch and Haydon stood on either side of Rocky and helped him to a seat.

"What happened, Rocky?" Pieter asked.

Rocky sipped some water that Declan had brought to him. "Oh, just enjoying your welcome, and then a period from my past came back to me like a lightning bolt."

"Sounds mysterious," Aiden said, confused. The others were equally confused.

"Guys, when I had a serious illness a few years ago, I was in a coma for just over two weeks. I also died, and the lack oxygen made me lose parts of my memory. Every now and then, some of it comes back to me. When you guys were so excited before and every one of you hugged me and gave high-fives, your words made me remember the times when I trained twelve-year-old boys to play and win their games."

"What happened to you back then?" Adam asked.

"Oh, I will tell you the whole story sometime. For now, I am okay. Now, where were we? How's the homework going, lads? I think that getting together to do your assignments and homework is a great idea. I bet you find it much better to bounce ideas and answers off each other than doing it on your own. Do you blokes mind if I look over your shoulders and see what you are doing?" Rocky asked. "I won't be mean or criticize what you are doing. I had to repeat year ten and still didn't get a pass. You guys are already ahead of me in year eleven."

Each lad showed Rocky what he was doing with pride. When Rocky got to Jay, Jay said, "I haven't done my homework or assignments for over six months, but this year I reckon, none of us has. Now, we learn everything we can at school and with our assignments."

They all agreed. They stopped what they were doing, having done enough and said they were nearly finished and would finish it the next afternoon.

"So, Rocky, what do we talk about tonight? What are we going to do?" Pieter asked. "Will we go somewhere and get a feed and come back here? We are all hungry. What do you reckon Rocky?"

"I'd say we go to the snack bar and get a feed and come back here. Then we'll have a talk about what I want to tell you one last time. Then we can drive to the waterfront for a chill session. What do you say, guys?" Rocky said.

Everyone thought it would be the best idea and moved to the Midnight Special and climbed aboard.

"Okay, now it's time for a talk," Rocky said. "I wanted to do this one before Josh has to leave so he can apply my advice, if he wants to, when he makes new friends and a new life. Now … I'd like you boys to think about what you can do with your time to keep yourselves occupied, stay on track, and keep out of trouble. I must congratulate all you fellas for how you have changed direction, listened, and asked questions to get you off the streets and live respectable and responsible lives. I am so proud of all of you. However, you will need to find new activities to occupy your minds and achieve success in whatever you choose. This will make you feel good about yourselves. Any questions so far?"

"What 'things' do you mean, Rocky?" Mitch asked. "What can we do to keep busy?"

"You could volunteer at the Meals on Wheels kitchen or at a senior citizens home to take some oldies for a walk in their wheelchairs. These are ways to help in the community, and if you do those things, you will get lots of satisfaction from helping others. At your stage, though, coming off your 'bad boy' image, you need to do things that interest you and that give you a sense of self-achievement. What do you guys think?"

Most agreed but wondered what and how they would do it.

"I have a paper and pencil," Rocky said. "How about you boys tell me which things you could do—like sports, hobbies, any interests that you have that could fill your time. You say it, and I'll write it. And this is if money was no object."

The boys called out their interests, and Rocky wrote them down:

- Soccer
- Building things
- Skateboarding
- Rugby League
- Work on cars
- BMX
- Mountain bikes
- Go-karts
- AFL
- Hockey
- Learn cooking
- Building an adventure park

"Hey, guys, there is something that I was sure some of you would pick—music. Play music as a rock group," Rocky suggested. "I have noticed that some of you enjoy listening to music, playing air guitar, pretending to play the drums, singing, even dancing."

"Hell, yeah," Aiden blurted out. "I would love to be in a rock band with some of these guys and some dance moves with us. *That would be prime.* I can see us doing that."

"Right, and how would you make that happen?" Rocky asked.

"Well, we would have to get some gear and learn how to play properly," Aiden said.

Pieter said, "Yeah, we have to learn and buy or borrow some instruments and practice a lot."

"That's right. How will you get some gear, learn the instruments, and practice, practice, practice hard until you get there? I know you guys could do it. You have the need, the reason to succeed, and the staying power to get there. Does the school have these classes and the equipment you can use? Could you practice during your lunch breaks? You never know—you might be able to borrow some gear to take home, so you can practice. You already have the barn at Pieter's place if his mum would allow you to play in there and if she can put up with the loud music. I can show you how to reduce the noise by putting egg cartons on the walls that will cut the noise level."

"Yeah," Declan said, "there is a lot of equipment at school, and I'm sure it's not being used. No one plays with that stuff. I don't know why. Maybe we could ask."

"That's possible. Does anyone of you know Mr. Charles? I think he is department head of music as well as his other subjects. I know him. I could give him a call if some of you are interested in going down that track. Or you guys could talk to him if he hasn't been put off by your past behavior," Rocky said. "I can also write a letter to him. Sometimes these things need requests in writing. If you want to play music, just let me know and I will write that letter. As for the other things on the list, some of you can join sporting clubs. If you show genuine interest in a sport or activity, someone will loan you a spare bike or whatever you pick. On the other hand, the ball sports are not that expensive—you need boots, a shirt, and shorts, and away you go.

"Anyway, just something to think about. You know, just because you are a group of twelve doesn't mean you can't have separate activities and come together as a group to relax and chill. I really want to see you guys stay great mates. You've been through heaps together, you trust each other, and you enjoy each other's company. Sadly, you are losing Josh, but you'll always have a place in your hearts for Josh, and I'm sure that he will come back sometime. I think we will leave that subject here. Think about what we have discussed and decide what you want to do as a hobby or sports or interest. How about we have a break for a while. Then we will talk about goals."

"Hey, Rocky, can we go somewhere to chill for a while. We would like to go for a drive in your car again. It is awesome," Haydon said.

"We can go for a drive somewhere," Rocky agreed. "I already prepared my head for that. I had the feeling that you would be up for a drive. Where do you want to go to?"

"Can we go to the shelter shed on the waterfront? If there is no one around, we can chill and listen to music," Pieter said.

"That's a good idea," Aiden said.

"You guys can kick a ball around in the cool evening moonlight, and enjoy each other's company, use up some energy, and get your blood going. You've been sitting still for some time. Like you said, Pieter, we can listen to music, plug the outside speakers in, and turn the volume up. How about you get a couple of drinks from the fridge, and I will call into the supermarket and get some bags of potato chips. Grab a bowl as well, if you have one. Deal, guys?"

"Got 'em," Pieter said. "Let's go. Can we have the moon roof open as we drive, Rocky?"

Soon after they arrived at the park and set up the drinks and chips, Rocky positioned the Midnight Special nearby, plugged the speakers and the subwoofer into the panel under a flap on the side of the vehicle, and powered up the audio system. He put in an INXS CD and turned the volume up. All the guys stopped kicking the ball, faced the vehicle, and stood with blank faces and their mouths open at the quality of sound that they were hearing.

A few of them pretended to play imaginary instruments; others cracked their dance moves.

After about twenty-five minutes, a police car sped toward them, sirens screaming and red and blue lights flashing. The car pulled up near the shelter, and two cops jumped out.

"What's going on here? Turn that noise off!" the cop yelled. "This is a public place, and you can't party here. Drinking alcohol, I suppose. All you blokes line up here."

"Hey, listen, mate," Rocky said. "We're sorry. These boys are letting off some energy. They have just finished their homework, and we've talked about some sports and activities they can use to keep on track."

"We know these delinquents. They are always in trouble. We will have to search them, their bags, you, and your van for alcohol and drugs," he said. "And what is your involvement with them? Are you grooming them for some illegal activity or are you a pervert?" the other cop said.

"Now, listen here, you ignorant cop. Yes, these guys had a history— note, I said *had* a history—but they left that behind them and are well and truly on the road to being decent, level-headed lads. Then you come along with your attitude, harassing them. What's wrong with you, you idiots?" Rocky said. "And calling me a pervert, you creep. How about you be a bit civil. I will be taking it up further with your sergeant. You think you know everything. Get your breath analyzers and test each of them. Then check their bags and pockets and me as well. Then check the car, but I insist you do it without damaging the car. Then, you will give each of them a proper apology. *Have you got that?*"

"That won't be necessary. We won't worry about that," the first cop said.

"No! Don't you understand what I am saying? You come here, harass these guys, accuse them of illegal activities, and accuse me of being a pervert. While you check their breath for alcohol and search them, why don't you ask them about me and about their new lives?" Rocky said.

"We realize we might have made a mistake," the second cop said.

"Listen, you two. Start testing and searching. You are wasting our time, you poor excuses of human beings," Rocky said. "Go on—start your checks."

Each one was breath-tested and searched reluctantly by the cops, as Rocky instructed.

"Well, how did you go?" Rocky asked. "How many arrests are you going to make?"

"All clear," the cop said. "We will be on our way. Just keep the volume down."

"Hang on. How about the apologies? These boys and I were just relaxing, enjoying the cool weather and some music, and you two scream in here and interrupt our night. Apologies, please; you can at least do that. You made such a big mistake. Now!" Rocky yelled.

"Listen, guys, we had some phone calls from a couple of those boats out there, saying there was a mob of teenagers playing loud music, drinking alcohol, and probably smoking drugs. We are very sorry that we were a bit over the top. Sorry, fellas," the first cop said.

"Apologies accepted," Rocky said. "I have both your names and numbers from your badges. I'll be calling into your police station tomorrow and talking to your sergeant about these events. Now, get out of here and let us settle down, and then we will be gone."

As the cops drove away, the lads came over to the table.

"Holy fuck, Rocky, you served them up—really bunted 'em, man," Shayne said. "The pricks. How's the attitude of those pigs, ripping it up us and you too, Rocky. Imagine if we were here without Rocky. We would have been stuffed, the pricks."

The others agreed, saying similar things, some with very colorful language.

"Are you really going to the police station tomorrow?" Pieter asked.

"Fuck oath, guys. It makes me so angry when cops think they are superior and put shit on kids. Well, you're not actually kids anymore, but put shit on young guys, ripping them up the arse like those pricks just did to you fellas. I'm not worried about what they said about me. I've been around a while. I can take it. As well, I want to tell the sergeant about you guys, just for the record—how you have turned over a new leaf and are living a clean, happy life. The real plus will be that I'll use the situation and bleed it for what I can get. I will insist that the police force help us with things you want to do. You see, the cops run the Police Youth Club, and I'm going to ask for assistance with whatever you choose to do and demand financial assistance to get some music gear, or bikes, or whatever you need. I am sure he will do everything in his power, just to stop us from making an official complaint against the cops."

"Hell, Rocky, you never miss an opportunity, do ya? That will be prime," Aiden said.

"Guys, don't worry about the cops again. Those two blokes left with their tails between their legs, and I am sure they will have more to come when the sergeant is finished with them," Rocky said. "The rest of the cops will be tame toward you now as the information flows through the ranks. Right-o, guys, let's get back to the barn and finish our talk session."

Back at the barn, Rocky said, "The last subject, but just as important, is goals, so you can realize your true potential and have a future. All you should do is think what you want to be doing at some time in the future—and where you want to do it. You guys need to set that goal in your heads and work out what you need to get there. Your goals can and will change as you go on but set those goals. To make it more fun, you can write your goal down on a piece of paper, fold it, and put it in a screw-top bottle, a fancy tin, a clay or pottery jar, a pot with a lid, or even a box or something you made at school. Put it in a safe place where you can see it to remind you. You don't need to tell anyone what your goal is; you can keep it secret."

"You can put it in your bedroom or a special place where you can put them all together.

"Pieter, do you think we can find a place in the barn? We like this barn, and it's like a clubhouse. What do you think?" Jay asked.

"Yeah, that's cool. We can build a shelf and put them all up there," Pieter said.

Josh asked, "Can I do one too? I can do two—one to take with me and one to leave on the shelf in case I come back sometime."

"That's a cool idea, Josh. We will look after it for you until we see you again," Pieter said.

With that sorted, Rocky drove the guys to their homes and then went home himself, chuckling about the events of the night with the cops and how the guys coped with the episode.

As arranged, Rocky called at the barn on Thursday night to pick the guys up and take them uptown for a visual lesson on how sleazy the nightlife was around the pubs and on the streets.

After some small talk and a few questions about choices, goals, and sports and other activities, the guys asked about Rocky seeing the police sergeant the day before.

"Yes, that was very interesting," Rocky said. "The sergeant was very apologetic on behalf of his two officers. He tried to explain that they were only doing their jobs. I got a bit angry again, and he soon realized that I was serious about what I was telling him. He then asked if I wanted to lodge an official complaint. Before I gave him my answer, I explained to him that you guys were a bit wild in the past, but that I had spent quality time with you—and still am—and that you fellas have seen the light and turned your lives around. I also told him that we did not appreciate the way those cops accused us of drinking and smoking pot, that I was grooming you boys for something criminal, and that I was a pervert. He understood what I was on about."

"Did you put in an official complaint about those pricks?" Aiden asked.

"After I told him how pissed off we were, I asked him about the youth club and what they could do for you guys. I wasn't going to give him my answer until I got something out of him. He told me that you boys are welcome to join the activities of the youth club. As well, he told me about a scheme that funds activities for young people. So, I said that we needed help with BMX and mountain bikes, as well as some instruments so you can play music."

"Holy hell, yeah, Rocky. Do you think we will get some?" Shayne asked. "That is wicked if we can get some."

"Rocky, how do you do it? How do you know these things? One minute we are being abused and pushed around by the cops, and the next day, you go in to complain and get that," Pieter said. "Stuff me, you are so awesome."

"Thanks, mate," Rocky said. "I only went to him to see what I could get. I try to turn a bad thing into a positive if I can. I had no intention of making a complaint; that only puts you guys through being interviewed, making statements, and putting up with that official crap. You don't want that. I knew that there was funding available from the gambling funds and grants from the government. I only needed a situation that I could use to leverage support. Those dickhead cops provided it. Having said that, you did not deserve to be treated like criminals. Anyway, I got some forms to fill in. Some or all of you will have to be interviewed to sell your case and show why you need the gear, but dudes, I know you can do it. I know you can."

"When do we do that, Rocky? When do we fill in the paperwork? When will we have to talk with them?" Aiden asked.

"We can fill it in now or tomorrow night at the barbecue for Josh. I'll coach you guys on what to say, but I know you can do it," Rocky said. "I don't know if you boys want to do these things—you haven't said what you want to do—but I'd suggest that we go for a full band of instruments and a few bikes. No big loss. Are you in this, guys?"

They all agreed to go for what they could get.

Josh said, "I won't be around when you get this stuff. You guys are so lucky. I wish I could stay." A few tears rolled down his face.

"Hey, buddy, that's so sad. Yes, it's not fair that you'll miss out. I will talk with these guys. Maybe we can send you something if we can find out where you go. I am sure that they will share something with you, hey guys?" Rocky said. "Would a BMX bike or mountain bike suit? Have a think about it and let us know."

They all agreed.

"Now, when will we do the paperwork? Then I can get it back to the sergeant. Now, or when we get back, or do you just want me to just fill it in myself?" Rocky asked.

They all thought that Rocky should do the paperwork for them.

The boys boarded the Midnight Special for their tour of the town after dark. They toured the hotels, the dark alleys, and the parks and saw firsthand what went on with people who were down and out—the scum bashing women; the drunks staggering, slumped, or sleeping in the alleys, bus shelters, or under the bridge; pissing in the gutters, male and female; a couple of filthy-looking females trying to entice drunk, scruffy blokes for sex. They saw it all. Then they saw the other side of life—decent people, young and old, leaving the movie theater or the entertainment center, well dressed, enjoying themselves, holding hands, walking arm in arm, just being clean, decent people who came into town for a night out.

The group traveled to the waterfront to review what they had just observed.

"Okay, guys, what have you seen? What have you learned? I did this, so you can make good decisions, good choices. What you saw happens to people who started off probably just like you were not that long ago, but life got worse for them—always drunk or stoned; probably got women pregnant, split up, probably bashed their partners, abused their kids, probably spent time in and out of jail, and now look at them. Sad to say, they have no life that is happy," Rocky said. "Then you saw the people who made good choices, enjoyed a stable, happy life and can go out respectably. Where do you guys want to be in five or ten years? I know where you want to be. I don't have to ask you, and you don't have to tell me. I am stoked that I know where you are going. So now you must work at it. Don't deviate from the course, and you'll get there."

The guys were all wide eyed and vocal about what they'd seen and adamant about the life they wanted for themselves. They gave heartfelt thanks and hugged Rocky for showing them how different life could be if they made bad choices.

Rocky then the boys home and told them that he would get the food and drinks for the farewell barbecue for Josh the next night.

Friday night arrived, and Rocky drove the Midnight Special up to Piet's barn. The lads greeted him as he arrived.

"We got the barbie fired up, set up the table and got some lighting worked out," Pieter said. "We got some music sorted, and we are also going for a swim. Look at this, Rocky—we got a camera and tripod set up too. Mum borrowed it from her work. We are going to start a photo gallery in the barn, so we can keep track of our adventures."

"That's awesome, a job well done, guys. And that's a great idea to have a photo gallery," Rocky said. "Do you want me to cook while you guys chill? Just spend some time with Josh; it will do you all good."

Rocky and the guys had a great night with good food. They frolicked in the pool, listened to great music, and had all-round great time. They talked about the things they did with Josh, the funny things they did together, and how they were going to miss him. The guys trotted out their goals in a bottle and made a ceremony of placing them on a special shelf in the barn.

As Josh put his clay pot on the shelf, he said, "I got three goals, like three wishes, in there, but I don't want to tell anyone what they are. Can you all look after it for me, please? I will trust you all not to look inside. Can you keep mine safe and secret?"

They all agreed. They decided that they would keep their goals secret as well.

As the night came to an end, Rocky shook Josh's hand and said, "Josh, it was awesome to have met you and spent such positive time with you, buddy. I am so proud at how far you have come since we met, and I consider you as a mate. Please look after yourself and try to remember the things that have helped you. Buddy, I hate goodbyes, but I wish you all the best at your new home."

Josh put his arms around Rocky's shoulders and held on with a tight hug. Tears flowed down Josh's cheeks as well as Rocky's.

"Let me go for a minute, Josh," Rocky said. "I haven't finished yet, mate. I have a gift for you, mate." Rocky handed Josh a box wrapped in gold paper. As Josh opened the box, Rocky said, "I spoke with your mum, and she said it was okay. That phone is for you to use as you wish, but also so the boys and I can talk to you and message you from time to time to keep in touch. The phone plan is in my name to keep your identity secret, and I will pay for it for two years. Just go easy on the costs, so I don't get a big bill each month," Rocky said, laughing. "It is in my name, so you can't be traced. Your mum will tell you her rules about it."

Josh grabbed Rocky again in a hug, sobbing loudly, and he went weak at the knees. Rocky and Mitch half carried him over to a chair and sat him down.

"Rocky, you are awesome. How awesome is that? Thank you," Josh said between sobs. "Can I say that I love you? Don't think that I am gay. I don't know how to describe it. I can only think of love." Josh continued to sob.

"It's cool, man. I know what you mean. It's not gay to hug another male or even tell a guy that you love him. Everyone will know you mean it as a true mate or as a brother. Nothing sexual or gay," Rocky said.

Everyone crowded around Josh and Rocky, shaking hands, hugging, and giving good wishes.

"Now it's our turn, Josh. We dubbed in a couple of dollars each and got this frame for you," Pieter said. "We know it's blank, but Mum will be down soon to take a couple of photos of all of us together. We'll get the film downtown in the morning, get it developed, and get one enlarged to put in the frame."

"Hell yeah," Josh said. "That's awesome dudes. I will hang it in my bedroom, so I see it every morning when I wake up and when I go to bed. At least I will be with you all every night. Thanks, guys."

"Now Josh, wash your face and get ready for the photos to be taken," Pieter said.

Sally came down the stairs, greeted everyone, and instructed how the group should assemble themselves, with Josh at the front. She took five or six photos in several locations and different poses, including one with the Midnight Special in the background. Sally then took Josh aside and hugged him and spoke to him quietly. Sally then said her goodbye to Josh and went back upstairs.

Aiden led the boys in three cheers for Josh and then formed a group hug with tears in their eyes, as well as sharing many jovial comments. The party continued, but Rocky said his goodbyes and hugged Josh one last time. He spoke to him quietly and then left with a heavy heart, feeling very sad.

Several weeks had passed since Josh left. During that time, Rocky picked up the eleven lads in his taxi at least three times a week as they traveled to the skate park and—he now realized—to the bowling alley. They seemed to enjoy that activity immensely. Mainly on a Saturday night, he would drop them off and/or pick them up at the alley. He had also called on them at the barn a few times to spend quality time with them, just chilling or talking with them.

He had also coached them for their interviews with the people associated with the Police Youth Club, so they could obtain funding for their band equipment and a couple of bikes. Rocky had driven them to the interview and back again. A week or so later, he again came to the barn to update them on the success of obtaining the equipment for their activities. A condition was set that they had to use the equipment at any functions that the club had organized, to which they had agreed, and they had to attend a presentation and media event as well.

Five of them had learned to play very decent music, so they eagerly awaited the arrival of the gear. The other six had agreed that they would support the band as "roadies," and they enlisted Rocky's help and his vehicle to transport the gear to any gigs they lined up. Rocky had shown them that the seats in the rear of the Midnight Special were easily removed so it could be a load-carrying vehicle. Three of the support six were also learning to play some of the instruments so that it would be very much a group activity when the instruments eventually arrived.

The boys continued to enjoy their newfound lifestyle, playing their music on the gear borrowed from the school. A few played Rugby League, training two afternoons a week and playing their matches on the weekend. Their love of skateboarding continued, and now, their bowling occupied some of their free time. When Rocky got the message to arrange a time for the boys to receive their new music equipment and bikes, the guys were very excited. They would have real instruments and make good use of their time. When the day arrived, Rocky arranged a maxi-taxi to transport the lads to the Youth Club and used his own vehicle to transport the band gear. He asked a friend to transport the bikes back to Pieter's barn, where the gear was to be used and stored.

After the presentation and media event was over, everyone returned to the barn. The lads were like a family of boys excited on Christmas morning, unpacking the equipment, as they assembled the drum kit, plugged in the guitars, keyboard and speakers into the amplifiers, and tuned the guitars. They were set. Sally and a few of the other mums came to watch and listen to the impromptu jam session. All the boys took turns at playing the instruments; then the five band members belted out a couple of songs with vocals. They were very good, very professional, especially the INXS track that they selected.

Sally announced that they should have a break because she and the other mums had cooked some fish fingers, chips, sausage rolls, and dim sims and had a large barrel of nonalcoholic punch, as well as some of her famous cupcakes and fruit muffins, which everyone enjoyed.

"Rocky, we want to thank you for organizing this gear for us. It is so wicked. Now we can play music and sing," Aiden said.

The rest of the boys also thanked Rocky, as did Sally and the other mums. They also expressed their pride in how the boys had listened to and applied the information that Rocky had given them. Their boys now had positive attitudes in what they had and did.

After a couple more songs, Rocky left the boys to enjoy their new instruments.

The next couple of weeks consisted of much the same routine—playing their music, skateboard riding, bowling, their sports and part-time jobs, and the occasional chill sessions with Rocky at the barn or the picnic shelter at the waterfront. Rocky was content that the guys were doing so well and enjoying a full life, their lifestyles, and their attitudes toward others.

"G'day, Rocky," Adrian said as Rocky picked him up from his home for his usual Saturday night out. "How's life been treating you this week?"

"It's been terrific, mate. I've had a busy week. Plenty of work and a couple of good sessions with the lads with their band practice and a couple of lazy times, talking things through with them, listening to them about their week."

"That's great, mate. How are they doing? I'll have to catch up with them sometime and chill out with them, listen to their music, and give them some encouragement," Adrian said.

As they pulled up to a club, Rocky said, "Have a good night out. I'll see you later."

"Yeah, mate. I'll be by myself tonight. Christy is away, visiting her mum and dad and family. I'll see how I go. See ya later, mate."

Rocky had a very busy night, as a lot of things were happening around town—lots of adults looking for a good night out and young people looking for some action. He wondered what the guys were doing; he hadn't heard from them all night. Usually, on a Saturday night he picked them up at least once to take them somewhere.

Toward the end of the night, Rocky got a phone call from Adrian to pick him up. Adrian jumped in the front seat and told Rocky about the hot chicks that were out, but he insisted that he stayed true to his girlfriend.

As Rocky and Adrian traveled to Adrian's house, Rocky's phone rang. He heard lots of yelling and panicky shouts in the background, Aiden yelled into the phone, distressed, "Rocky, Mitch is missing! We can't find him! We don't know what to do. We can't find him!"

"Hey, mate, settle down. What's happened? Where are you?" Rocky said with a little fear in his voice. He pulled the taxi to the side of the road.

"What's happened, Rocky?" Adrian asked.

"It's the guys. Seems one of them is missing somehow."

"We are at the waterfront, Rocky. Can you come and help us find Mitch? He's in the water somewhere. We can't find him!" Aiden said hysterically. The other guys were also hysterical—Rocky could hear them in the background. "We were jumping off the jetty, and Mitch jumped in but didn't come back up. Please come! Please, Rocky."

"Okay, mate, I'm on my way. Adrian is in the taxi as well. We won't be long. Just make sure the rest of you don't put yourselves in danger," Rocky instructed.

The trip across the bridge onto the waterfront was quiet. Rocky was very stressed, hoping that nothing had happened to Mitch, hoping that he was okay. He couldn't bear to think that something bad had happened to one of the guys. Adrian spoke quietly to Rocky as he drove across the bridge, trying to console him.

As the taxi stopped at the jetty, Adrian and Rocky noticed the guys crying their eyes out, some huddled together, others on the jetty, looking into the water and yelling Mitch's name. It seemed obvious that their mate was not coming back. Fear crept over Rocky. How would they cope with losing Mitch in such a tragic way, after losing Josh a few weeks earlier?

Rocky raced over to the group of boys with Adrian close on his heels. "What happened?

Shayne answered, "We were just chillin' and decided to strip off and dive in the water and have a swim. We did it a couple of times, but when Mitch jumped in, he never came up again."

"How long ago was that, Shayne?" Rocky asked.

"Oh, about twenty-five minutes, maybe half an hour. Not sure."

"What will we do?" Aiden asked. "We can't find him."

"Do you think he's okay, Rocky?" Jay asked.

Adrian answered, "I think we better call the police to report it and see if they can find him."

"We don't know if he will be okay," Rocky said. "If he has been in the water that long, I don't know." Tears now visibly streamed down his face. "Adrian, can you please call the police and maybe an ambulance. The boys may need medical attention and probably me too. I am not handling it too well."

Adrian and Rocky gathered the lads under the picnic shelter to try to settle them down and wait for the police to look for and recover Mitch, hopefully alive.

"Now, guys, if things don't go well, the police will ask you all questions to find out what happened. Just be honest; tell them exactly what happened. This is Adrian, guys, he will help me and help you guys. He is a good guy, so don't be afraid to ask him or tell him anything," Rocky said.

Three police cars and an ambulance arrived very quickly, and the place swarmed with people in uniforms with high-powered lights, searching for Mitch, and checking the timber framework under the jetty in case Mitch was trapped and possibly injured or unconscious.

Two of the police officers and an ambulance officer walked over to the group to ask questions. The ambulance guy checked that the guys were okay and talked to them quietly.

"Will he still be alive?" Haydon asked.

"We can't find that out until we find him," one police officer answered. "We hope so, but considering the time he has been missing, if he is in the water, unfortunately, he possibly has passed away."

"We have called in the police divers to search in the water, but we probably won't be able to dive until the sun comes up. You guys should prepare yourselves for the worst outcome. It doesn't look too good," the sergeant told them.

When they heard that, the boys screamed, howled and groaned loudly at the realization that Mitch probably had perished. Only a miracle could result in a better outcome.

Rocky let out a loud gasp and collapsed, holding his chest. Adrian and two of the boys raced over to him.

"What's wrong?" Adrian asked, trying to comfort him.

Rocky pointed to his chest.

"Hey, need your help over here!" Adrian yelled out to the ambulance guy.

The ambulance guy yelled to his assistant to bring over the oxygen and a defibrillator and give him a hand. They placed a tablet under his tongue, took his shirt off, and connected some pads to the defibrillator and to his chest, arms, and legs. They took his blood pressure and placed the oxygen mask over his mouth and nose. They monitored him for quite a while, as the boys circled him, looking concerned and crying at the sight of their mentor, their mate, in such distress. After what seemed an eternity, the ambulance officers declared that Rocky was okay but suggested that they take him to the hospital for more tests and observation.

"If I'm not in danger," Rocky said, "I'd rather stay with the guys; they need me for support."

"All right, but you should go to your doctor as soon as you can to be checked over," the ambulance officer said.

The search continued for another hour or so, as each lad gave his account of the events that led to Mitch's disappearance. A police officer found a pair of shorts, underpants, shirt, and shoes and socks nearby.

"Those belong to Mitch," one of the boys told the cop. "He took them off—we all did—to dive into the water."

"We strip off all the time before we swim," another said, "so we have dry clothes when we finish swimming."

"Have you boys been drinking alcohol?" the cop asked. Yes, they had.

"Have you boys been smoking cannabis?" Yes, they had.

"Where did you get the alcohol? Who supplied it? Where did you get the cannabis?"

The boys answered these questions in a very honest manner. They then said that a group of older boys, some in their twenties, had approached them when they were sitting in the shelter shed, listening to their music. The older boys forced them to drink and smoke cannabis because they thought that the boys had seem them doing it, and they didn't want the boys to "dob them in." They had gotten drunk or high and had decided to jump off the bridge for fun.

Rocky was shocked by their account, but under the circumstances, he decided not to get angry at their lapse of judgment. Instead, he made himself available to comfort the remaining ten boys and tried to explain how to grieve. It was obvious now that Mitch had lost his life.

As the sun rose, Mitch's lifeless naked body was lifted from the water onto the jetty. The boys saw this and ran toward the jetty, yelling that they had found him and asking if he was okay.

A few of the police stood at the edge of the jetty to prevent them from getting close to the body and attempting to block their view.

The boys fell to the ground, screaming and sobbing loudly, and hugging each other in their shock, grief, and loss.

A police officer explained that they had made some preliminary investigations themselves and with the paramedics, and inspections of the slippery surface on the jetty, they concluded that Mitch had slipped as he jumped and hit his head on the timber edge of the jetty. "Mitch would have been unconscious before he hit the water. He would have drowned without feeling anything."

Mitch's body was put into a body bag, loaded into the undertaker's van, and taken to the morgue. As the guys watched, they asked Adrian and Rocky what would happen next—what did they do at the morgue, where did they keep him, and what happened at the funeral? They all felt sad, but Rocky sat on a log fence with his head in his hands, sobbing quietly, distraught at losing one of his young mates. He remembered Mitch speaking about his future, having fun times with the group, telling jokes and playing jokes on everyone, and now he was gone. *Such a waste,* Rocky thought, *too young to die, and such a silly mistake ended his life.*

Adrian held Rocky's hand and put his other arm around Rocky's shoulder. His favorite taxi driver was someone he could talk to about anything; now it was Adrian's time to support Rocky.

Rocky and Adrian decided to stay with the guys for as long as they wanted them. Everyone got into the taxi, but before they left for their homes, they decided to name the picnic shelter "Mitch's Shed" in his honor. They vowed to visit it regularly, a place where they could gather to remember their mate.

By midmorning, the boys were safely at their homes with their mothers, beginning their long grieving process. Rocky worried how this would affect them in the future. Even though they had lost a mate, they had to find the strength to carry on with their lives. Rocky and Adrian promised that they would be there for them no matter what.

Mitch's funeral was scheduled for the next Friday. During the week between the accident and the funeral, Rocky spent many hours each day or night with the boys, helping them understand grief and answering their questions—why they blamed themselves, what would happen to Mitch at and after the funeral, how he would have felt before he died, and how he would have felt as he died.

"Mitch didn't feel any pain, as when he hit his head, he was knocked unconsciousness," Rocky explained. "Mitch would not want any of you to feel sad or bad. He would want you to continue with a life full of happiness and to remember only the good times you had together."

One night, Rocky said to the boys, "I want you to look to the sky, pick a star, and nominate it as Mitch's star. Then, at any time, any one of you can look up at it and talk to him, smile up at him, and imagine that Mitch is looking down at you, protecting you, and still enjoying being part of the group.

After the funeral, the guys asked Rocky to go with them to Mitch's Shed at the waterfront so that they could spend time remembering their departed mate and try to work out how things had gone so horribly wrong. They spoke to Rocky about their mistake of going back to drinking and smoking drugs and how that mistake had caused Mitch's death.

"It wasn't entirely your fault," Rocky explained. "Those older blokes sort of forced you into it."

"But we outnumbered them," Aiden said. "We could have fought them off. We feel weak at giving in and falling back into our old lives. We couldn't refuse and fight."

"Listen, guys, I am not going to criticize you or tell you how bad you were. You made a mistake. You were easily led by some irresponsible louts into what you did. You all know that you made a very big mistake but learn from it and move on. Keep your heads up. You will survive," Rocky said. "By the way, the cops have arrested those blokes and charged them with eleven counts of supplying alcohol to a minor; eleven counts of supplying a dangerous drug, namely cannabis; and two counts of possession of a drug utensil. The cops also charged them with possessing cannabis and causing a death. They will be locked up for a long time. You guys, you have been cleared of any fault or blame, and that means you won't be charged with consuming alcohol or drugs as minors. Also, the cops discovered that the cannabis those blokes gave you was cut with a cocktail of other drugs.

"I beg of you all—in future, please think before you do something like that that, and think of what could go wrong, so that the events of last weekend aren't repeated. I never, ever want this to happen to any of you. Understand?" Rocky said forcefully, with tears in his eyes and a quiver in his voice. "Sorry, guys, I don't mean to come down on you boys. I am just shattered now. Let's have a quiet time now and talk about your thoughts and fears and about the good times you had with Mitch."

CHAPTER 6

Listen, big fella, you gotta be careful where you put that thing. It's the only one you have, and it's gotta last you for the rest of your life.

The next six months passed with more social activities with the lads, talks about how their lives were progressing in a positive manner, trips in the Midnight Special, and discussions about their musical endeavors, impromptu jam sessions, and how they were coping with Mitch's passing.

One Saturday night, Rocky was about to drop his passengers at their destination when Aiden called, asking Rocky if he could pick him up from home.

"Sure, buddy, give me ten to fifteen," Rocky answered.

Aiden usually called about the same time on a Friday or Saturday night, asking Rocky to pick him up with one or two of his mates to go bowling, to go to a party or the movies, or just to chill out downtown with their skateboards.

Rocky turned the corner onto Aiden's street, where Aiden lived with his mother and a younger brother and sister. In his headlights, Rocky saw Aiden standing on the edge of the street.

"G'day, buddy," Rocky said as Aiden got in the front seat. "How's things?"

"Great, dude," Aiden answered. "Are you having a busy night?"

"Yeah, mate, it's been quite busy. Seems to be a bit of action downtown. Where are the others tonight? Are you going bowling or just downtown?"

"Neither, Rocky. Over to 131 Dunne Street to watch some DVDs."

"Just a quiet night, or is it a party?" Rocky asked.

"Don't know, really. Just one of the girls from year twelve last year invited me. Saw her at the shopping center earlier. She got my number and asked me to come over—on my own. Something about DVDs and games."

"That sounds different," Rocky said.

"Probably be a boring night. Probably call you up soon to take me somewhere else. What time do you finish?" Aiden asked.

"Probably about four in the morning or four thirty—somewhere about then."

After small talk about how Aiden was getting on at school and with his sporting activities and his band, Rocky found the house and pulled up to the curb. He noticed the house was in darkness.

After Aiden paid the fare, he said, "Can you wait till I see if she's home, Rocky? I won't be long. I'll wave if she's home."

"Right-o, mate. If she is, you have a good night."

Aiden got out and walked to the front door, knocked, and waited. The porch light came on, the door opened, and a girl came out. She looked awesome, Rocky noticed—very smooth, tanned skin and long, flowing blonde hair down to her waist. Aiden waved, and Rocky drove away.

The next three to four hours were very busy; there were several functions downtown and a visiting band holding a concert at the theater. It seemed that Rocky was endlessly driving large groups from the suburbs into town. He knew that he was in for a very busy time around midnight and then the usual rush after the nightclubs closed around three in the morning. That night he drove several groups of the younger set—kids he had gotten to know—who were looking for their friends or a party they could crash. A couple of them asked Rocky if he had seen Aiden.

"He's not answering his mobile," one said.

Rocky answered no each time he was asked; he never divulged someone's whereabouts unless that person wished to be found. Although Aiden hadn't said to tell people where he was but also didn't say *not* to tell, Rocky decided to keep Aiden's whereabouts to himself—he *had* said that his host told him to come alone.

As Rocky was stopping for a coffee and a smoke break at two in the morning before his next large booked group, Aiden phoned to pick him up.

"I won't be long," Rocky told him. "I'll be there as soon as I finish my coffee and cigarette."

"Hey, Rocky, nearly forgot. Don't come to the house where you dropped me off. I will be at the twenty-four-hour servo around the corner."

As Rocky pulled up in his taxi, Aiden was waiting with a couple of other lads who Rocky hadn't seen before.

Aiden walked toward the taxi, and the other guys followed. "I told you I'm going home," Aiden said. "You can't come. I'm going home alone." He opened the door and got into the front seat.

"Aiden, how ya doin', mate?" Rocky asked.

"Really awesome, Rocky. How about you? Been busy?" Aiden answered as the taxi moved away.

"Yeah, haven't stopped all night till you called. People everywhere," Rocky answered. "What was that all about back there? Were those guys hassling you?"

"No, not really. Hardly even know them. They wanted me to go downtown or over to my place," Aiden said. "I just want to go home and have a private talk with you on the way."

"That's cool. Have a good night?" Rocky asked.

"Hell, yeah. I am not a virgin anymore, man!" Aiden said with a sense of achievement in his voice.

"The DVDs and games were choice," Aiden said. "Sarah had asked me over to watch DVDs and play games. Hell, man, didn't know she meant porno DVDs and games. Didn't know games could be so good. There were two of them, Rocky—awesome hot chicks too. Halfway through the DVD, I already had a hard-on from watching, and they started slowly undressing themselves. Then they started grabbing my stork and massaging my 'nads through my shorts. I already had my shirt off—you know me; I hardly ever wear my shirt."

Aiden got more excited as he spoke. "Then they put my hands on their breasts and around their groin areas. Then they slowly undid my belt and pulled my pants and boxers off. Then they kissed me all over, Rocky, even down there."

"I don't want to know the details, champ," Rocky said.

"Sorry, Rocky. I can't believe it was so wicked. Been trying for so long to get a chick, but I didn't know what to do if I ever got one. Can't believe I got two at once. First time, Rocky. Can't believe my luck—effen better than batting, Rocky."

Rocky knew his next words might knock the wind out of Aiden's sails, but he said, "I hope you had protection."

"What do ya mean?"

"Hope you used condoms."

"No, why?" Aiden said, "They told me that they are on the pill."

"And you believed them?"

"Yeah, why not?"

"Listen, champ, I don't want to take the enjoyment of the experience away, but mate, you can't always believe them." Rocky shook his head. "Can't believe you didn't use condoms, buddy."

"I didn't have any with me. I didn't know I was going to get lucky, Rocky. I left them at home."

"I don't want to frighten you—well, maybe I do want to frighten you. You know your first sexual encounter could make you the father of not one kid but two kids. You are too young to have that kind of responsibility."

"No, can't be. They told me they are on the pill," Aiden repeated with a hint of fear in his voice.

"And do you want your thing to fall off?"

"What do ya mean?" Aiden asked, grabbing himself in the crotch as if to protect himself.

"You gotta use condoms, mate, not only to protect against pregnancy but also because you can catch diseases."

"What do ya mean, diseases?" Aiden asked.

"Ever heard of sexually transmitted diseases, AIDS, and HIV? All those diseases can be caught by having sex without protection."

"Hell, now you're frightening me, Rocky," Aiden said.

"Well, big fella, sex is good—sex is awesome, mate—but you should be frightened, Aiden. Remember to always carry condoms with you in your wallet or your bag, and use them next time, every time. Remember: carrying condoms and using condoms, equals no kids, no disease."

"OK, Rocky, I'll remember that. Thanks for telling me. I never thought about it like that."

"Because the girls sound experienced, they obviously have been rooted many times before and probably with many boys. That is how these diseases are spread. You gotta be careful, champ. One poke in the wrong chick can stuff your life up forever, mate. Anyway, no more sermons. I don't want to be a party-pooper and make your night seem bad. Just next time—you gotta look after it, man. It's the only one you got. You can't get another one, and you're going to need to use it for the rest of your life."

"Anyway, Rocky, I really enjoyed my night," Aiden said.

"That's awesome, Aiden. Life is full of good stuff like that. I am sorry if I have taken away some of your enjoyment. You just needed to know what can go wrong."

"Yeah, I know that now, Rocky. Thanks a lot, mate. I do know what you mean." Aiden said as they drove up to his front gate.

"I'll see ya later, Aiden," Rocky said, as Aiden reached for his wallet to pay the fare. "No, this one's free. Anyway, I forgot to turn the meter on, and I am not far from my next job. Just please try to remember to look after yourself in the future. Another thing, Aiden—sex is something that should be enjoyed between a man and a woman in love. It really is a shame that young people your age frequently have casual sex, which makes for great feelings and experiences at the time, but they should wait till they are older, when the true meaning can be appreciated. Having said that, unfortunately there is great pressure from peers, the media, and society in general to have sex for the sake of having it. That is why I decided to talk to you about it just now. It is something that fathers usually talk to their boys about, but in your case, you don't have that privilege, through no fault of your own. End of sermon."

"Yeah, thanks, Rocky, I'll remember. See ya later, dude. Shit, my 'nads are sore. What can I do? Is it one of those diseases?"

Rocky smiled and then laughed loudly. "No, buddy, just call them 'lover's balls.' They have had an exhausting exercise session. They will ache for a while, just to remind you of your good time." Rocky laughed again and said, "For hell's sake, don't do what a mate of mine told his younger brother to do after his first sex—to rub arthritic rub into them. He screamed and burned the stuffin' out of his balls for a week or more."

Aiden roared with laughter and grabbed himself as if he was imagining the burning pain on his own 'nads.

"Anyway, bud, you go and have a shower, a drink, and get yourself into bed. Go easy on the dreams, mate. I'll catch you next time. Hey, Aiden, make sure you don't brag to anyone; it really is better to keep it to yourself. You know how everyone talks."

"Yeah, I know. Come to think of it, I remember how all the year twelves last year bragging that they were with Sarah or Alice. That means"—he paused for a few seconds—"that means they have screwed a lot of boys, doesn't it?"

"Yeah, suppose so. Don't worry, mate. Next time I pick you up, we will talk about girls some more, if you want to. In the meantime, find a way to tell the other guys in the gang about the dangers without telling them about your adventure. You never know; you could probably save their lives or a lot of pain and suffering. Make it your mission, man."

Aiden grabbed Rocky's hand and shook it vigorously. He didn't say anything, but his body language showed his gratitude. Aiden held his hand in the air as Rocky drove away.

Later that day, as Rocky was beginning his shift, Aiden called him.

"Are you on your way to work?" Aiden asked.

"Yeah, mate, I am."

"Can you pick us all up around six thirty and take us to Mitch's Shed? And can you take half an hour off? We'll pay ya, man."

"I'm not worried about getting paid, buddy. What's happening?"

"Can't talk now. Can ya, Rocky?"

"Yeah, that's cool, champ. Sounds important. You're not in any trouble, are you?"

"No, no trouble, mate. We need a 'mish,' Rocky. We'll be in the park near Decles." "Cool, buddy. See ya then"

The boys still met at Mitch's Shed quite often to remember their mate, and they still had good times there. They looked after the area, picked up rubbish that other people left after their picnics, and cleaned and washed any graffiti that was frequently scrawled on the posts, beams, and walls.

Mish was a word used by the gang to mean that they were on a mission—something they felt they had to do, a thought they had to put into action. It might be a bike or skateboard stunt. It also could mean a serious activity or "talk fest" to sort out something in their minds.

As Rocky drove his passengers that afternoon, he continually thought about what mish was so important to the guys. He didn't consider Aiden's adventure the night before; he had no idea that the mish was about what Aiden and he had discussed.

Rocky arrived at the collection point, where the ten guys were waiting. They had two coolers with them and a couple of shopping bags.

"What's happening, fellas?" Rocky asked. "I hope you don't have any alcohol in those coolers?"

"No, man, we learned our lesson with drugs and alcohol. You know that, Rocky. After Mitch and the talks, you gave us, we don't do that anymore," Aiden said.

Decles added, "No, Rocky, we know what happens with that shit. We still have a drink, or a smoke sometimes but not like we used to—only one or two."

"That's cool. Sorry to think that."

"We just want a mish with you," Aiden said. "Can you take us to Mitch's Shed? We'll tell you then."

As Rocky drove toward the waterfront, the lads sang, chatted, and joked, as they usually did. Rocky still wondered what this mish was all about.

Aiden and Decles sat in the front with Rocky. Rocky asked, "What did you get up to today, fellas?"

"We were at the BMX track this morning. We had a wicked time, trying new tricks, one-wheel stands and pivots, and racing each other over the jumps," Decles said.

"Hey, Rocky, Pieter can do pivots on the front wheel. He fell off a few times and busted his nuts, but he can do it now. Hey, Piet!" Aiden yelled to Pieter in the back row of seats.

"Piet, how's ya nuts, man?" Declan said. "Busted 'em big time, hey?"

"Yeah, man, still can't walk properly, but I learned to pivot," Pieter yelled back.

"We practiced our songs while the others watched and listened," Aiden said. He leaned over to whisper to Rocky as he rounded the corner toward the park. "I was trying to tell the guys what you told me last night. I can't get them to understand without telling them what happened. Can you tell 'em for me? Like you said, it's important to know. None of them knows about what I told you."

"Do any of them know what happened to you?" Rocky asked, trying to think of a way to start the conversation.

"No, haven't told anyone," Aiden answered. "They just know that you told me about it, but they want to hear it from you."

"Cool, champ, we will have a talk. What's in the coolers?" he asked.

"Just some food and drinks. We got some food to treat you to dinner. You haven't eaten yet, have you?" Aiden asked.

Decles sighed heavily. "Did you just tell him about the food?"

"Yeah, sorry, Decles. I forgot it was a secret. Sorry, man."

The taxi drove up to Mitch's Shed, and the boys went to the picnic table in the shelter. But before they entered the area, they gave the salute they'd devised to honor Mitch.

Rocky was instructed to sit down while they prepared the food for their dinner. They had roasted chicken, sliced ham, prepared salads, bread rolls, paper plates, plastic knives and forks, and even salt and pepper and napkins. They all did their bit to help. Rocky was amazed by the sight of ten teenage boys, bumping into each other while they prepared the spread. He couldn't help but think how these young fellas had changed since he first picked them up about twelve months earlier.

"Rocky," Adam said, "time to sit over here. We thought it was about time we treated you to a feed. Have you got time to stay for a while?"

"Yeah, sure, mate. I had a busy night last night. Tonight, seems very quiet. This is better than sitting on the taxi rank, waiting to get an old drunk from the pubs and arguing about the cost of the fare."

Rocky got up and logged out his taxi so that he wouldn't be bothered by the taxi base pushing jobs on him. "I think I deserve some time out with you blokes. You know, I always make time for you guys whenever I can."

"We all put in some cash and got this stuff from the supermarket. We had to eat, so we wanted to have a feed with you, Rocky. I tried to tell these blokes what you told me last night, but they don't understand and won't listen. Can you tell them so that they will all get the same message?" Aiden said as he opened the other cooler and got out three bottles of soft drink, plastic cups, and some ice. "You guys can pour your own. I'll get Rocky's for him. I know what he likes."

"Jeez, fellas, I don't know what to say. You did this for me. I feel really honored."

Decles replied, "It's cool, old man. You do a lot for us. You have made us change our attitudes, so we can find a better life. We all owe you so much."

"Nah, you don't owe me anything. I only did it because I could see each one of you had a good side, and I wanted to contribute a bit to your lives and get you aimed in the right direction. The reward for me is knowing that you all know right from wrong, good from bad, and that I see you all enjoying good, clean, healthy, and happy lives and making the right choices."

"Yeah, Rocky, we talk a lot about what we used to do and where we would be now if you hadn't told us what to do," Piet added. "What is it you told Aiden about girls last night?"

"Well, I picked Aiden up last night, and we got talking about girlfriends. I told him about a few things that can happen and how to make sure nothing bad happens. I told him how to avoid making mistakes, so he doesn't become a father too young and how to avoid catching diseases."

"Yeah, make sure they are on the pill," Decles said in an authoritative voice.

The all joined in the discussion, sharing how each one thought, or heard, or were told about the subject.

"Wrong. Wrong. Aiden, you haven't said anything yet. Come on, man, speak up."

"Nah, man," Aiden replied. "I tried to tell 'em at band practice, and they all carried on like idiots. I need you to tell 'em; they will listen to you. Hey, you dickheads, listen to Rocky and do what he says."

"I don't know if any of you have been with a chick, and I don't really want to know—that's personal," Rocky said. "While we are talking about it, none of you should ever tell anyone about your love life or sex life in detail. You should never brag about how many you have or who with. That's how gossip starts. You must have heard it." He looked around at every face; they all were focused on him and his every word. "Now, there are a few things you should know. Do you know what a condom is?"

Small talk about condoms began, with some knowing a bit about them and others having never seen one, let alone knowing how to use one.

"I'm not going to show you a condom or tell you how to use one. That's not for me to do. You will talk about it among yourselves later. At least one of you must have one or two with you."

Several boys went to their wallets or bags and got some out and threw them on the table. A couple of the boys took one from the table and looked at it as it they had made a major discovery—which, in fact, they had.

"Anyway, as I was telling Aiden last night, at your age and from now on, you should always carry one or two with you always, just in case you find yourself with a chick and things heat up. You know what I mean. Never, never have sex without one, no matter if the girl tells you she's on the pill. Never believe her unless you form a relationship with her, and you see her take it every day. Otherwise, never believe her. I'm not trying to put down women or girls in general. A lot of them care about their bodies and their futures and won't take any risks. Just like men and boys, most are responsible. Some are not. You cannot tell whether she is telling the truth until you get to know her for a length of time. What I am telling you now is to prevent the girl you have sex with from getting pregnant. One thing you don't want for many years is a baby.

Rocky took a sip from his drink. "That's not the only reason why you should use a condom. Probably more important are the many diseases you can catch from having sex without protection. Some diseases are just uncomfortable for a while and can be cured; most of them can be fatal after a very long, painful illness. What's wrong? Nobody's talking," Rick said as he noticed all the guys looking at him intently, some with their eyes wide, others with their mouths wide open.

"Nothin', Rocky," Adam said.

"Just listening," Nick answered.

"I didn't know any of that, man," Pieter replied.

"I don't want to take away the pleasure of experiencing sex from you guys by frightening you, and believe me, you will learn just how fantastic good sex is. But, fellas, it really is important to know what the risks are and how to protect yourselves from misery or disease. As I said, you don't want to be a father at your age. You have a lot of living to do before you have a baby. Babies cost heaps of money for sixteen to eighteen years at least. The other thing—and this really shocked Aiden—is that you don't want it to fall off by catching a disease."

Groans, moans and grunts were heard from around the table as that thought hit home.

"What are these diseases?" asked Nick.

"Yeah, old man, what are they?" asked Pieter.

"You've probably heard of STDs—sexually transmitted diseases. They've been around for a long time. More recently, we hear about AIDS and HIV, which eventually can kill you," Rocky told them. "You've probably heard of the Grim Reaper—he was used with TV advertising in the 1980s."

"Yeah, I've seen pictures of the Grim Reaper—they're cool. I didn't know what it meant, though," Aiden said.

"Enough of that, guys. I think you get the message. Just wear a condom. Remember: carrying condoms and using condoms equals no kids, no disease. Sex is something that should wait till you are a little older, when it means something more than just getting with a girl. This is something that fathers usually talk about with their sons, but none of you has a father in your life. And with sex thrown in your faces from your peers or in magazines or on TV, you need to know about it in case you find yourself in that situation. Please don't be pressured into it if you do not feel ready for it, just for the sake of doing it. Okay? Let's have a break, guys. I promised Aiden that next time I saw him I would talk to him about how to treat a chick right. I suppose I can tell you all, if you want to hear about it. What do you reckon, Aiden?" Rocky said.

"Yeah, that's cool, Rocky," Aiden answered. "These fellas are my mates. We are a great team together. We all know about each other, so if you tell us all, we'll all know the same things."

"Can I say that we all should know about it so we all have a chance to get hot chicks of our own, one that we can keep? I need a hot chick right now. All this talk about rooting has made me so horny," Haydon, the class clown of the group, said.

Rocky couldn't help himself; he said, "Hey, Haydon, do you have a little discomfort in your shorts? Listen, dude, just grab hold of it with both hands, take it over there in the darkness where we can't see you, and punish it into submission because I doubt you will get a hot chick tonight." Rocky laughed, and the rest of them pissed themselves, laughing. "If you need it that bad, you'd better get it off your chest."

"Nah, it's okay, Rocky. I'll fix it up later. I asked for that, didn't I?" Haydon said.

"Sorry, mate, I couldn't resist that one. Are you cool, Haydon? I just couldn't leave what you said alone without joking about it," Rocky said.

"No, I'm cool, Rocky. We know your sense of humor. That's what makes you so special to us. We talk and joke about those things too, and you say the same things as we do, so it's all cool. Just don't stop your sick jokes; we all love 'em," Haydon replied.

"Let me have more of this awesome food, a drink, and a smoke first," Rocky said as he put more food on his plate. "Put your music on, Aiden, and let's chill for a while." Rocky settled back to eat and drink. "Ah, this is the life, gang. Awesome night, not hot, plenty of stars in the sky, and a group of wicked fellas to enjoy it with. What do you have planned tonight?"

"We are going over to Pieter's mum's place for a jam sesh, a couple of DVDs and CDs, game of pool, probably a swim. Just us, chillin' out for the night. We are going to sleep over, have breakfast, and go to the skate park tomorrow. That's what the bacon and juice is for—a big barbecue breakfast. Piet's mum has eggs and tomatoes," Aiden said.

"No doubt about you guys—you get yourselves organized for a wicked time. It's great that you can think ahead and plan your good times. Bet you weren't like that a year ago."

"Yeah, Rocky, it's because of you, you know. You told us how to be like that; you really showed us the right way to live," Pieter said.

"Yeah, and you listen to us, and we listen to you," Adam said.

"You know, Rocky, wouldn't it be an awesome world if everyone our age had someone like you to care about them, listen to them, and talk to them? The diff is, you join in with us and talk with us, *not* down to us.

We really notice that. You really care, man," Aiden said, as tears welled in his eyes. He gave Rocky a hug and then said, "I don't have a dad—well, I do, but he cleared out years ago. He doesn't even want to know Mum and me and Terry and Justine, but hey, Rocky. I got you, I don't even need the prick. Hey man, are you crying? Come on, old man. Wipe your eyes, you silly old prick."

"Hey, Aiden, well said," said Tony. "I think we all feel like that. Just realized, none of us has a father, or we have fathers who don't want us. Never thought of it before. Yeah, I think we all treat Rocky like what a father should be. Isn't that strange? All of us stick together; none of us has a dad. Mitch had no dad either, you know; that's funny," Haydon said.

"That's probably why I spend time with you, changing your lives around. You all were really lost souls when I first drove you to bowling that night. You were real idiots then, real drop-kicks, but I could see through that, and obviously, at least some of you were searching for someone to guide you. You probably didn't know that was happening. I nearly had you on the right path, and then, that night when Mitch died, you all lost your way again. That's why Mitch, sadly, paid the ultimate price—losing his life." Rocky's voice began to tremble with sadness and emotion. Then I said to myself, 'Don't give up on these kids.' Then I probably became a real bastard sometimes, but you fellas still stayed with it and listened and learned that Mitch's death was for a reason. Thank heavens you guys listened. Look at you now, enjoying your new lives. You all have some direction. You've been out of the police station for six months and have sports, music, jobs, and other interests. That's what makes me feel good. And look what you did tonight—so thoughtful. You put on a meal and invited me. Awesome, guys."

All the lads were wiping their eyes. Some picked up their drinks, and Nick said, "On two, guys: one, two, here's to Rocky, our hero, our champion—the legend."

They clearly had prepared those words to use on this night, as they spoke with meaning and enthusiasm and in chorus.

"Right, thanks, guys, I really appreciate this. Now, do you mind if we leave the talk about girls for another time? I better get back to work and earn some money for the boss and me."

"Group hug!" yelled Aiden. All ten guys and Rocky embraced in a very special and emotional hug.

"Let me help you pack this up, and I'll drive you over to Piet's," Rocky said.

"We'll pay ya, Rocky," Tony said. "We have collected money to pay you for the ride."

"That's cool, Tony. Let's go."

They packed their coolers and bags in the back and climbed aboard.

Rocky climbed into the driver's seat, started the engine, and logged his computer on to the base. As soon as he did, the two-way radio sounded. "Car 47, come in car 47."

He said, "Hell, that sounds like they've been trying to call for a while." He picked up the mike and answered, "Car 47."

"Car 47, is all okay? We've been calling for some time."

"Roger, base. Just had a mish to look after," Rocky said.

"Could you repeat that?"

All the boys roared with laughter. Rocky was still in his "teenage" mode and forgot to change to "adult" mode.

"Sorry, base, I had a problem to deal with. All is okay now; I am back on the road now."

"Roger, 47. I have a few bookings for you. I'll put them through to your screen." "Roger, base," he said and switched back to computer mode. "Anyway, guys, it's been awesome spending time with you tonight. I really appreciate it. Sorry it got a bit heavy there for a while."

"That's cool, mate," Haydon said. "We never miss out on learning something when we are with you."

"Listen, when do you have your break tonight?" Pieter asked.

"Oh, sometime between eleven and one thirty. If it's not busy, maybe nine thirty to ten thirty. Why?"

"Well, man, when you get bored or slack, come over for a while. Mum can make you a coffee or something. Adam's mum and Shayne's mum will be there. Mum says she hasn't seen you for a while. She wants to catch up with you."

"Are you sure, buddy? I don't want to cramp your style."

"Nah, you never cramp our style, does he, guys?" Piet said. "We like having you around us."

"Come on, dude," Aiden said. "Come back and see us later."

"Just might do that. I don't feel like putting up with drunken idiots tonight, especially after spending time with you positive guys. Tell me, have you heard of any parties tonight? I might just stay away from them tonight."

"None that we know of. Haven't heard of any," someone in the back seat answered.

The taxi arrived at Piet's. All got out and unloaded the coolers. They lined up on the footpath, and Aiden handed Rocky a bag of coins. "Here's some money for the ride. There's about forty dollars in there."

"That's too much, buddy. I don't want to take your money."

"We all put in a few dollars. Didn't cost us that much each," Aiden said. "Go on; it's yours. See ya later, boss. Don't forget to come back later."

"Yeah, champ, I'll ring you before I come, just to check if it is still okay with Piet's mum."

"It will be okay, man," Aiden said in a stern voice. "We really want you to come back. We will have the shits if you don't."

"Okay, I'll be back. See you all later. Have a good one, guys. Watch Haydon doesn't get into trouble with his hard-stiff pole," Rocky teased as he drove off.

All the guys cheered wildly, and he honked the horn to acknowledge their enthusiasm.

Over the next three hours or so, Rocky picked up several large groups. Being a maxi-taxi, which carried up to eleven passengers, meant that the fares were almost double that of a normal sedan taxi. While he had some long trips, the passengers were well behaved, which suited Rocky, as he was in a very good mood because of what the gang had done for him earlier. He couldn't help reflecting on the gang and how they had changed so much in a reasonably short time.

During one trip, Rocky thought about five of them who had formed a rock band. They were to compete in a battle of the bands very soon. *It must be coming up in the next week or so*, he thought. "Does anyone know when the rock festival is on?" he asked the passengers on board. He hadn't considered that these passengers were older than those who would be interested in kids playing rock music.

There were a few responses, but one came through louder than the rest. "It's next weekend, driver," a male voice answered.

"Yes, driver, next Saturday afternoon and evening," another said. "Why?"

"Oh, I know a young band who is competing in it. I want to see how they do, and I love seeing young people doing stuff like that and achieving," Rocky answered.

"That's great to hear. Not many of us oldies show an interest in kids like that. I'm one of the promoters. What's the name of the group?"

"Nuver Chanz."

Rocky heard some rustling of papers; then the man said, "Nuver Chanz are pretty good, I hear. My notes here indicate that they have a good chance of going somewhere, or so I am told. Why did they pick a name like that for their group?"

"Long story—they are a group of boys, all without fathers, who lost a mate in a drowning accident a little while ago. Basically, it means that they have had another chance at life, at making something of their lives. It's a shortened version of the words 'another chance.' It means that they are rising from the depths of something that was bad and have the chance to achieve something in their lives, especially at this stage in their lives. It's sad, really; they all reckon they've been called a dog at some stage, probably because of where they were in life's scheme of things, and they were perceived as no-hopers.

"They've come a long way since then and have turned their lives around. They are special to me. Like mates. Better mates to me than any adult I have known. Probably more than mates—more like sons, as if anyone would want to have ten sons the same age as teenagers."

"Driver, that's a great story. I wondered how the band name was pronounced when I saw it on the list. What is your name?" the voice asked.

"Rocky—sorry, that's what the kids call me. It's Rick Scott."

"Rick, when we stop, I will give you my card. I also want to give you some tickets. Entry is worth twenty dollars. I want to give you a free pass and as many as you need for the rest of them. Even for their mums, if they want to go. Heaven knows, they probably deserve a day out and probably want to see their sons play their music."

"That's awesome. I really appreciate that, and I am sure the rest of the boys and their mums will too. Thanks very much."

When the taxi reached the destination, the man who had spoken paid the fare and said, "My name is George Cleator. I am the chairman of the chamber of commerce. We're all here to finalize details for the Youth Rocks Music Fest. Here's a hundred-dollar tip for you. You must be a great bloke to take care of these young people. Also, here are twenty passes. Give me a call by Tuesday or Wednesday if you need more. Can you talk to the boys and their mums? We still haven't selected a group to invite to the banquet afterward. We do this every year; usually it's some sponsor or company or group. I can't see any reason why your group of lads should not be honored this year. Check with their mums, though, because it does involve a large story in the paper, radio interviews, and TV segments. We'll need parental permission because they are under eighteen."

"Thanks a lot, George. I am speechless."

"That's okay, Rick. Can you pick us up about midnight when we are finished?" George asked. "What cab number is this?"

"It's 47, George. I want to thank you very much and for the kids too; that's great. The boys will be ecstatic."

"I think it'll be a great night and great for the kids. And for you, Rick. I can see how proud you are of them."

"It hasn't been easy, George—hard, in fact—but I can tell you it's worth it to see them now and what they have achieved."

Rocky drove off with a sense of pride and excitement. *Can't wait to tell the gang. A hundred-dollar tip. Never had that much ever before. Awesome. Those boys do deserve it, though. They have really made something of their lives.*

The next couple of hours were reasonably busy for Rocky. He put the card that George gave him in his shirt pocket and the twenty passes to the rock band competition in the calico money bag for safekeeping. He pulled over to have a cigarette and a short break and realized that between the time he'd dropped the gang off at Piet's and now, he'd earned him enough cash to cover the period that he was at Mitch's Shed. *And how about the luck of picking up such an important person as George,* he thought. What were the odds that he'd ask the passengers about the rock fest and meet someone connected to it? Very spooky how things fell into place. Someone must be looking down on him and the lads.

As he sat enjoying his smoke, Rocky visualized how thrilled the boys would be when he told them about talking to the promoter of the rock festival and that he had passes for all of them and their mums. Then he thought, *George Cleator—I've heard that name before, but where?* He took the business card from his pocket and read, "George Cleator, Managing Director, Cleator Group of Companies." *Well, stuff me,* he thought. *That's the super-rich dude who owns that big construction and earthmoving company that picks up contracts all over the country.* He remembered reading an article about George and his company. He had won multibillion-dollar contracts to build a new harbor, coal-handling plant, and industrial complex just out of town. No wonder he could afford a hundred-dollar tip. The article also had detailed his life story—where he'd come from and how he defied all his critics when he was younger and earned his first million dollars. It was beginning to gel in Rocky's mind why George had an interest in the gang and why he sponsored youth sports and cultural activities.

CHAPTER 7

What's changed? Nothin' much, just someone who talked things through with them, offered alternatives, and listened to their thoughts and fears. Rocket science? No, I don't think so.

Rocky quickly grabbed his mobile phone and dialed Aiden's number.

"Hi Rocky, are you coming over now?" Aiden asked when he answered the phone.

"Not yet, dude. Still a few bookings to go. I won't be long, though. I can't wait to see you. Got some fantastic news for you guys. It will blow your minds."

"Hell yeah, what is it?" Aiden asked.

"Can't tell you on the phone. I want to tell you all at the same time. Tell the boys to get stuck in and get their music happening and get it perfect. You just wouldn't believe what's going down."

Rocky heard him yell out to the group, "Hey, dudes, it's Rocky. He's got some wicked news to tell us. Said to get stuck into practice." He also heard several voices yelling back to Aiden, wanting to know what the news was. "He won't tell me on the phone. He wants to tell us as a group," Aiden yelled back.

"Give me the effen phone," Piet said as he apparently grabbed the phone from Aiden "Dude, what's happening? What's this wicked news?"

"I want to tell you all together," Rocky repeated, "and your mums too. You won't believe what's going to happen. This stuff is going to blow your minds."

"Come on, mate; tell me now. I won't tell the others. Come on, Rocky," Piet pleaded.

"No, Piet. You know the rules—no secrets from your mates; that's just how we do things. I probably shouldn't have phoned you. I just got excited and had a brain explosion. I will see you all soon. Put Aiden back on."

"Sweet, man, see you soon. Here's Aiden," Piet said with a bit of dejection in his voice.

"Oy, mate," Aiden said, "you want to talk to me?"

"Yeah, I probably should not have told you guys anything about it. I just got some good news for you, and the brain popped, and I let it out without thinking. It's all good for you blokes. Please get a quiet minute or two with Piet. I had to remind him of one of our rules, and I think he might be a bit pissed off with himself. Have a group hug, be patient, and get on with the band practice."

"Cool, man," Aiden replied, "you sound pretty pumped about whatever it is."

"It's awesome. You'll know why when I see you."

"Cool, dude. I'll look after Piet," Aiden replied.

Rocky could always rely on Aiden to calm the group or influence the boys when something important was to be done. He was the steadying influence when the chips were down, or the guys needed motivating. He was a natural.

The boys and Rocky had put together some rules that would assist them in interacting with each other, respecting each other, and looking after each other in certain circumstances. One of these rules was not keeping secrets that affected any of them as friends. They could have personal secrets that did not impact the others but not if something had an impact on the rest of them. Some of them forgot about this rule from time to time, and when one of them did forget, and Rocky reminded them, they really felt it hard. They hated that Rocky had to remind them of the rules. Rocky knew that they were young and that excitement and even enthusiasm took over, and they had a momentary lapse.

When a rule was broken, there was never any yelling, finger-pointing, or rejection from the other lads or Rocky, just a quick reminder, and they quickly got over it. It worked well, and that's contributed more to their progress—to get from where they were to where they are now—than anything else.

Rocky completed his bookings and had a free hour, so he called around to Piet's. He'd made enough money that he didn't feel guilty about taking the taxi off the road for a spell. *What will happen in the next seven days or so is much more than money can buy*, he thought.

He phoned Aiden to say he was coming and that everyone should gather in the barn—the mums too. "Have your music worked out," he said.

"Sweet, man. Just cooking up some chips and fish fingers. We'll have some ready for you too. I'll get you a drink too. Piet's mum has some bourbon. Want a bourbon and Coke?" Aiden asked.

"No, champ. I still have driving to do. Would love one or two, but I can't. Just a Coke in a big glass with plenty of ice would be choice. And I'll have one of Sally's wicked coffees before I get back on the road."

He heard Aiden tell the boys that he was on his way. "He'll have some grub and a Coke as well. Get Sally, Sandra, and Kath here too. Party guys!"

Rocky pulled the taxi into Piet's driveway and flashed the high beams several times onto the barn and tooted the horn several times too. He forgot about the neighbors; too much was going on to worry about that. As it turned out, the neighbors were over also to see what the excitement was all about. Ten excited boys together could be a bit rowdy, and the people who lived next door wanted to be part of the action, whatever it was.

As he logged out his communication console, the group rushed up to the cab, all yelling, "What's going on, dude? What do you want to tell us?"

Rocky got out of the taxi and was surrounded by the boys. It must have looked funny to see the group move as one toward the barn, excited faces beaming and bodies jumping and bobbing along, with Rocky in the center. These kids didn't even know what they were excited about.

As the group entered the barn, the neighbors and Sally, Kath, and Sandra were waiting, seated along the left wall. The barn was a large shed that used to hold three or four cars and a workshop. They had lined it with polystyrene foam sheets for soundproofing, and the walls were covered with posters, stickers, old guitars, skateboards, bike bits, and even favorite worn-out or too-small clothing items. It was junk, but to a group of sixteen-year old boys, it was precious. These things triggered memories for them; these things meant a lot to them. One wall held photos of them doing stunts, playing music, and having fun. There was also a section dedicated to Mitch, with photos taken at his funeral and the wake that Rocky held for them in the park near Mitch's Shed, as well as a section with photos of the guys with Rocky, including photos of Rocky's cars.

"Hey, Rocky," Jay shouted. "Come and look at the photos from today. We printed them just before."

Rocky looked at the photos. "You didn't waste any time with them," he said.

"We had to get them up before you came around. Look at the title— 'Sex Talk.'"

Rocky turned red with embarrassment. "Don't call it that," he said.

"We gotta call it that so we remember about it," Pieter said.

Rocky looked at the mums, a little embarrassed, and said, "They told you about today and what they did? They cooked a great feed and had a lesson about sex and diseases."

Sally answered, "It's okay, Rocky. Thanks for caring about them and their futures. We appreciate your telling them about that subject. They needed to know, but it is so hard for us mothers to talk to them about that stuff. Thanks a million."

"That's cool," Rocky said. "I learned that one of them knew squat about sex, so I wanted to tell them all to save them from problems later."

A look of horror crept over the three mums.

"It's okay, no, none of your boys. It's cool. The boy will be okay. Everyone's okay. It's all learning experiences."

"Thanks, Rocky," Kath said. "We know what you've done for our boys. We were saying before how these kids have changed for the better, and it's all your influence. Thanks for caring. It has been a great help to us, and you can't imagine the worry and stress you have saved us."

"That's all right, Kath," Rocky said. "I just don't like seeing kids harmed or getting into trouble because they don't have the proper information. After all, it's kids like these who will grow up to look after us oldies when we are really old."

"Oy, Rocky," Piet said, "you're not old. Don't talk like that. You're one of us, dude."

"Yeah, I know, Thanks, buddy, for the compliment," he said as Piet handed him a plate of fish fingers and chips and a glass of Coke with ice.

"Let's eat, and you can tell us the news," Aiden suggested. They all gathered around to listen.

"Oh yes—the news!" Rocky said. "Where do I start? So much to tell you."

"Start at the beginning, Rocky!" Haydon said.

"Careful, buddy. I'll embarrass you in front of these other people if you're not careful," he said, and the rest of them laughed.

"Okay, Rocky, you got me again. Sorry," Haydon said.

"It's okay, buddy; only gagging ya. I'll tell it as it happened." Rocky took a sip from his Coke and then said, "When I dropped you guys off here, I had several trips to make. One was a group of people about my age—stuffy business-looking people. As I was driving them to town, one of the songs that you guys play came on the radio, and I suddenly remembered that your rock festival competition was coming up soon.

"Without thinking, I asked if anyone knew when the rock festival was happening, and one bloke answered, 'Next weekend.' Then another bloke said that he was the chairman of the chamber of commerce and that the group in the taxi were the promoters and organizers of the rock fest. They were on their way to a meeting to finalize the arrangements. Now, you know how I tell you never to prejudge people on how they look or how they act? Well, I must admit I did just that and thought that they were stuffy oldies, just like you blokes do sometimes. Anyway, I am happy to admit that I was so wrong, as you are about to find out.

"He asked me who I was and why I wanted to know about the competition. I introduced myself and told him about you guys and that I wanted to see you play at the competition. He asked the band's name and said he'd heard about you guys. You see, guys? Like I tell you so many times, everybody hears about what's happening around town, about the bad guys and the good guys. That's why I talk to you about your behavior, about doing things for people, and about being nice blokes when you are out. People do notice, and people talk."

"That's sweet, Rocky," Piet said, "but we do listen and do the right things, don't we?"

"Yeah, mate, you do. What I am saying is that because you do the right thing, people have noticed—people have talked, and it's all good, Piet. Anyway, back to the news. He said he wanted to do something good for you guys. He didn't mean that he could make you the winners of the competition, but he did give me his card and—wait for it—twenty passes to the festival competition at the theater."

"Hell, that's awesome, man. Really?" Aiden said in disbelief.

"What are the twenty passes for? There are only five in the band," Adam said.

"Well, I am sure the rest of you want to go and watch; after all, you are all one gang, and you all help the band carry their gear and help set up. Anyway, the five band members don't need passes; they will be onstage or backstage."

"Well, why twenty passes? We only need five," Aiden said.

"Hey, I want to be there too, you know," Rocky said.

"Okay, that's six," Aiden said, getting a little impatient.

"All right, I have strung you along enough. He gave me twenty passes and told me to contact him for more if I needed them. He would like to invite all you guys and your mums. He wants your mums to be there to see you play and sing onstage."

The room went quiet and then suddenly, erupted into wild cheering.

Kath said, "Really, Rocky? Are you kidding?"

"No, Kath, I am not joking. This is too serious to joke about. I wouldn't string these guys along like that if it wasn't true. I am a cruel prick sometimes with them but not that cruel. He wants me to talk to you guys and your mums to see if you all want to go."

"Effen awesome," Pieter said.

"Pieter, that's enough with your swearing," Sally demanded.

"Sorry," Piet said, "but Mum, that's effen wicked. Oh, I'm sorry. I can't help it."

"I know, son; it's great, but control yourself, especially in front of Bill and Marg and the kids," Sally said.

Bill and Marg were the next-door neighbors, "It's okay, Sally; we understand. These guys must be beside themselves. And I'm sure Chris and Jeremy have heard that word before, hey Christopher?" Bill said to his thirteen-year-old, with a sense of chastisement in his voice.

Chris cringed and moved behind a couple of the boys, as if to hide from his father.

The guys chuckled and motioned to Chris, indicating that he had been sprung.

Rocky said, "This is a lot to grab hold of but there is more."

"What do you mean, more?" Nick asked.

"This bloke introduced himself to me when he paid the fare. His name is George Cleator. Anyone ever hear of him?"

Most of the guys hadn't, but Sandra said, "I think I've heard of him somewhere."

Bill said, "I know of him, but I won't steal your thunder, Rocky."

"Anyway, I put the card in my pocket, not having a clue who he was, and the passes in my money bag so that they were safe—after all, the tickets are worth four hundred dollars. Then he talked some more."

"There's more?" Aiden interrupted.

"Yeah, champ, there is more."

"Come on, Rocky, you always drag things out," said Adam. The adults smiled and laughed.

"Yeah, I know, I love teasing you fellas. It's fun. He told me that after the show they have a sponsors' banquet and he invites a sports or youth group to attend. He wants to invite you guys and your mums and any supporters to that. He needs to get your parents' permission for you to attend, and we need to count how many there will be. He doesn't care how many; he just needs to know so he can cater for whoever is coming. Are any of you interested?"

"'Course we are interested!" Aiden said.

"Hell yeah," Adam answered. "Oops, sorry, Sally. I forgot."

"Can we all go?" Nick asked. He was always a bit slow.

"That's what Rocky said," Aiden told him. "All of us and our mums."

"Cool," Haydon said. "I didn't know how I was going to save the twenty dollars to see you play."

"What do you mean, permission?" Jacob asked.

"Well, if we go to the after-party, there will be newspaper reporters and photographers, radio, and TV. Because you are all under eighteen, they must have permission from a parent or guardian so that they can print or use it. Something to do about privacy and that you are minors."

"It sucks being a minor. I hate that word. Can't do anything without permission," Piet said.

"That's enough, Pieter. Don't be so cheeky," Sally said.

"Yes, Mum," Piet said, a little impatient.

Rocky said, "Listen, buddy, don't be in such a hurry to get older. Enjoy being a minor while you can. You have plenty of time to be old." Rocky reached into his pocket and grabbed the hundred-dollar note that George had given him. He placed it on the table, saying, "He gave me this as a tip."

"Jeez, what's that? Haven't seen one of those before," Nick said.

"A hundred-dollar note, dickhead," Adam said.

"This George bloke gave you a hundred dollars for nothing?" Haydon said. "He must be rich."

Bill nodded in agreement, looking at Rocky with a huge smile on his face. "He's rich, all right."

"I stopped for a break and a smoke before—that's when I phoned you. I was wondering where I had heard the name before. Then I read the name on the business card." Rocky took the card from his shirt pocket. "I'll read it to you. 'George Cleator, Managing Director, Cleator Group of Companies—Earthmoving, Construction, and Consultants.'"

"Wow," said Tony. "He's that rich man who builds roads, bridges, and shopping centers."

"Yeah, that's him," Bill said.

"Anyway, what do you think? Are you going to be in it?"

"Hell yeah!" the chorus rang out. "Bloody oath."

That seemed to be the standard response to indicate agreement with the guys. Rocky also realized that he said it often as well; he didn't know who learned from whom.

"Anyway, guys," Rocky said, jumping up from his seat, "I think it's time for a group hug, so you can digest all that is going on."

Everyone in the barn joined the guys in a very emotional group hug, including the mums and the neighbors.

"Now, do you have your music sorted? I'm not saying you'll win, but you should practice so you can give it your best shot for the crowd, the judging panel, and the dignitaries who will be at the sponsors' dinner. You just never know where it could lead you. People have told George that you are great and that you have a good chance to win. If you do your best and you don't win, it doesn't matter. You will be competing against bands who have been around for a few years. It'll be a good experience for you anyway."

Aiden picked up the hundred-dollar note and handed it to Rocky.

"Nah, mate," Rocky said. "I want to give it to you guys. I want you to start a pool where you put your money and save it for new equipment or to fund a trip or something. Now, Aiden, you keep it in a safe place, and sometime you blokes work out where to put it and build on it. I suggest a bank account—two signatures along with mine, if you like—or some other adult because you are"—Rocky looked at Pieter—"minors."

The kids roared with laughter to rib Pieter.

"That's okay," Piet said. "I'll get even with you."

"So, have a meeting and sort that out sometime in the next two days or so. Right … the music?" Rocky asked.

Haydon produced a list and said, "Rocky, we got six songs here. We're not sure which ones. Which do you think?"

"Hey, it's not up to me. You gotta choose which ones you enjoy doing, which ones you are comfortable with," Rocky answered. "I reckon you gotta have at least one INXS song—you do INXS wicked, and they seem to be your hero group."

"Okay, let's play 'em and see how we do."

The boys played their short-listed songs and discussed them among themselves and the audience. They chose "Beds Are Burning," "Midnight Oil," and "Never Tear Us Apart" by INXS and "I Still Haven't Found What I'm Looking For" by U2.

"They're some of your favorite songs, Rocky. That's what we'll go with," Haydon announced.

"No, guys, don't pick your music because I like a particular song," he said. "You have all old-school songs. How about something modern, something *today*, as you call it."

"Nah, if it wasn't for you playing your CDs with us, and you talking us into playing music together and forming a band, we wouldn't be doing this. Anyway, those old-school songs from back in the day suit our style better," Aiden said. "It's final; these are the songs we are going with."

"Now, have you thought about what you are going to wear, like a uniform, so that you look similar?" Rocky asked.

"Yeah, we all got black pants or jeans. That's what we will wear," Adam said.

"What about shirts? Are you going to show off your abs and pecs to the crowd and go shirtless?" Rocky asked.

Aiden laughed. "Decles and me wanted to do that, but look at Adam—lily-white and no pecs or abs."

"Don't say that; that's cruel," Rocky said.

"That's cool," Adam said. "I'm used to it."

"No, we thought either a black or white shirt. We wanted to keep it simple, no gimmicks," Aiden said.

"Black is cool, but black might get lost under the stage lights," Rocky suggested. "White might be better. Black is good, especially if you have some sort of fluorescent design on the shirt, but you may not have time to organize it. I would suggest white, and maybe a cap."

"Yeah, we will go with white. I want an open shirt, so I can show my chest, pecs, and abs," Aiden said.

"You poser. Do you think you have the perfect bod?" Rocky said. Aiden did have a muscular body that he worked hard to develop, and he was proud of it and his bronze complexion. "Why don't you choose? Maybe keep it white, a choice of T-shirt or button-down, whatever each is comfortable with. That wouldn't look bad. I think it is good to keep it simple. Sometimes way-out colorful fashion onstage takes the focus away from what you are doing and how you do it. That's great; at the end of the day, you're up there to sell your musical playing and singing ability, not what fashion you wear. Well, except for Aiden"—Rocky smiled to show he was joking—"selling his bod to all the chicky babes, hey Aiden?" Then he asked, "Do you all have white shirts? Black pants will be okay. You should have enough to go around using your supermarket pants. If you don't have a white shirt, the second-hand clothes shops should have some for a couple of bucks. No one needs to know that you got clothes from the thrift shops."

"Rocky, when are you seeing this George bloke?" asked Adam.

"He is ringing me about midnight to take the group back home," Rocky replied. "That's why I have to be back on the job by then. I'll tell him you're keen to go to the banquet next Saturday night. Don't forget to mention it to your mums when you get home tomorrow." He turned to the mothers who were there. "Anyway, mums, do your lads get your permission?"

"Yeah, of course," Sally said. "Couldn't pass that up."

"Yes, certainly," Sandra answered.

"Yes, for sure," Kath said. "It'll be fantastic to see them play and a great experience for the boys to be guests of honor at the dinner."

"I hope you fellas who are supporting the band don't feel left out; you are not. The offer is for all of you. George knows that there's a team of ten. That's what impresses him—that you all stick together and help each other. You fellas deserve it as much as those in the band. You help with the equipment, setups, and being the audience when they practice. I want you to understand that you are just as important as the band," Rocky said. "And of course, all the mums. You boys would not be here if it wasn't for your mums, worrying, cooking your meals, washing your clothes, patching your injuries, dealing with your bad temper tantrums, and even wiping the tears from your eyes when things get tough. Don't ever forget what your mums do for you."

Rocky looked at Sally and asked, "Now, Mum, can I have one of your fantastic coffees? Please, Mum? Please, Mum, please?"

The request for coffee brought the barn down with laughter.

"Mum, I'll help you make the coffee," Piet said. "We'll make one for all the adults and anyone else who wants one."

"Haydon and I will help," Aiden said, and they began to take orders.

A lot of discussion took place about the upcoming band competition and the after-party while everyone settled down to have their coffee or drinks. The boys talked about their song choices and discussed the clothing they would wear onstage. The mothers and the two adult neighbors talked with Rocky about how the kids had grown up over the past six to nine months and how they had turned their lives around.

"Rocky, I would like to thank you very much from my heart for what you have done for these boys, especially since Mitch died," Sally said.

"Yeah, Rocky," Kath said, "these boys have gone through so much sadness, not only Mitch but since their fathers left them stranded with only us mothers to guide them. Every boy needs a man to look up to, to lead them through that minefield called teenage life. It's very hard, isn't it, girls?"

"Sure is," Sandra answered. "You know, the hardest thing is when your partner abandons you, leaving you with the kids. No one, male or female, wants to talk to you, let alone to your kids. Some blokes come along and pretend and use you as an easy ticket into your bed. Other than that, no one wants to know you; no one wants to help."

"Yeah, that's right. They must be frightened, thinking that you are going to trap them or something," Kath said.

"And the females run a mile because they must think that you are going to take their partners. How insecure," Sandra added.

"How do you feel, Rocky? Do you feel threatened or frightened by us women?" Sally asked.

"Yeah, sure do, Sally," Rocky said, trying to keep a straight face. "No, only gagging ya. What is there to be frightened of? All I am trying to do is save these young souls from disaster, help them find the right track, and try to stop them from falling along the way. There are so many obstacles out there these days. I have said many times that I'm glad that I'm not a teenager these days, not like back in the day. I also say over and over that guys like these are going to grow into adults one day, and they are the ones who must look after us oldies, either working to pay taxes to pay us a pension or running the country as politicians in government, or even having a clear and experienced mind to be able to vote. That's very basic but very important."

"That's well said," Bill said. "You are right."

"While we are at it, another thing I hate about adults is their continual putting down of teenagers, calling them idiots and no-hopers or unreliable," Rocky said. "Give the poor kids a chance. Look at these guys. Idiots? No, not now. No-hopers? No, not any more. Unreliable? No, not really. What's changed? Nothing much, just someone who talked things through, offered alternatives, listened to their thoughts and fears. Is this rocket science? No. If only people would talk with them and find out their fears, concerns, and bright spots. Talk like them, within reason. Talk with them, not down to them. Don't criticize them, but listen, and change or teach them the correct attitude. I could go on and on, but I've found that doing these things with them is so rewarding—warm and fuzzy; call it what you want. I can tell you my life with these lads and other kids like them is magical, magnificent. Sorry, I do get carried away. I just feel so good when I see these guys achieving something great almost every day."

"Hey, Rocky, we were talking about a few things over here. We want to ask you what you think," Declan yelled from the other end of the barn.

"Yeah, cool, mate, what have you decided?" Rocky asked, hoping that they had decided a thing or two for themselves as a group. He got up and walked to where they were seated, talking among themselves.

"First, we talked about it, and we want to have Mitch's mum at the rock fest and party next week. What do you think?" Pieter said.

"That's a great idea, guys. That's thoughtful of you to include your mate's mum. That's awesome, fellas. You never stop impressing me lately. I was just talking to your mums about how your attitudes have changed and how thoughtful you all are and how you achieve so much every day. That's a classic example. That suggestion is really a great achievement for you guys, for your mums, and for me. I am so blessed and proud just to witness these things. What's next?"

"We have decided to put the hundred dollars in the bank," Aiden said. "We had trouble deciding whose signatures to use—not that we didn't trust anyone; we trust everyone fully. No one wanted to say that they'd take the responsibility, but we all said we'd take the job if asked. That sounds dumb. Do you know what I mean?"

"Yeah, champ, I know what you are trying to say. I know exactly," Rocky said. "So, have you decided?"

"Yeah, chief, we decided to put each name in a hat and got Chris to draw two out. He drew out Haydon's and Jacob's names," Adam said.

"That's really democratic. Good on ya, guys," Rocky said. "Who have you decided as the adult? Remember—where is Piet? —you are minors."

"Aw, Rocky, do you have to?" asked Pieter.

"Yeah, big fella. I love stirring you. It's fun."

"I'll get you yet," Pieter said.

"Yeah, I know, buddy, but jeez, you gotta be quick," Rocky said. "Oh, sorry, Mum, for swearing," Rocky yelled to Sally, who was sitting on the other side of the barn, as the barn erupted in laughter. "Who did you pick?"

"Oh, don't be so dumb, Rocky. We picked you," Shayne said. "See, Sally? I don't swear … much."

"That's cool. I'd be honored. Is there anything else?" Rocky asked.

"Yep," Haydon said, "we decided how to dress onstage, but some of us will have to talk to our mums first."

"Oh, why's that? What have you decided to do? Is it drastic?" Rocky said.

"We want to do something with our hair instead of wearing caps," Tony said. "We either want to bleach our hair so we are all blond or dye our hair black."

"That's cool, if you all agree. Does that mean the backup five as well as the band?"

"Yeah, we all decided and agreed," Aiden replied.

"Why don't you think about black and use a temporary dye, unless you really want your hair to be permanently black."

"Yeah, that's rad, Rocky. That's a good idea. If someone's mum is not cool with it and doesn't agree on permanent, we can use spray-on and wash it out later," Adam said.

"And we decided to wear black pants and either a white T-shirt or buttoned shirt," Jay said.

"And I can leave mine undone, so I can pump up my chest," Aiden said with a laugh.

"That's wicked, guys. Is that all?"

"Yep, that's it," Aiden replied.

"You know, from where I'm sitting, I feel so proud, watching you all and listening to you all. No raised voices, no arguments, just discussing, deciding, and solving and moving on to the next. Wicked. And I noticed— don't know if the others over here noticed—that each one of you spoke to me about your decisions. That tells me a lot. I am not going to deliver another sermon on how to conduct yourselves. You just did an awesome job. Well done. Anyway, folks, I need to go back to work. I'll phone you as soon as I have dropped George off."

"Hey, Rocky, what time are you finishing in the morning?" Pieter asked.

"Oh, come on, guys. You aren't going out again tonight. You need some sleep. You have a busy week coming up."

"No, dude. We don't want to go out. We'll sleep as soon as you ring. I was going to ask you to come for breakfast on your way home," Pieter said. "You know what we got. That'll be okay, hey, Mum?"

"I'm sorry, Piet," Rocky said. "That would be prime, but are you sure about that? I wasn't going to work much after four, maybe half past."

"Nah, mate, it'll be cool. You know how to get into the barn," Piet said. "Just wake us up."

"No, mate, I don't wake up anybody. I'll be here, but I'll sleep in my car till you get up. I might jump in the pool to freshen up, if you don't mind," Rocky said, "but I'm not into waking you up."

"That's cool, man, but wake me up when you get here. I'll be near the door. We'll have a towel here, and we'll rustle up some shorts for you to wear," Pieter said.

"It's a deal, buddy. Thanks, heaps. Look forward to it. That'll be two meals you guys treated me. Frig, I'm lucky. Sorry, Mum, slipped out," Rocky said to Sally. "Sally, is that cool with you?"

"Yeah, Rocky," Sally answered, "as long as you don't mind sleeping in the barn. You can come up to the house if you want, but can you imagine these boys if you did?"

"Yeah, I don't mind. I'm usually so tired by then. I won't worry where I sleep. Okay, fellas, I'll phone soon. Get some sleep, and I'll see you all at breakfast."

Rocky said goodbye to everyone and told the neighbors how good it was to meet them. He climbed aboard the taxi and drove off to conquer the drunks who were homeward bound by now.

He logged his taxi back into the taxi-base computer system as he turned from the street where Pieter lived. The time was eleven thirty. After a handful of groups of young people, Rocky realized how much he enjoyed the company of young people. All the jobs were for happy, outgoing people who were obviously enjoying themselves.

"Turn the music up, Rocky," most of them would say, knowing that he was into loud music and enjoyed it a lot. They couldn't do that with other taxi drivers; they all seemed grumpy old men compared to Rocky. Also, none of the other drivers could understand how Rocky got on with the younger set, nor did they approve.

Rocky tried several times to help them get on with the kids—how to talk to them and how to treat them. It never worked; all of them had the attitude that they were useless teenagers, no-hopers, losers with bad attitudes, and useless to society—he had heard it all. But they would take teenagers' money. No wonder they had problems; they just could not learn good people skills. Rocky felt so lucky to experience the enjoyment that his regulars gave him by talking with him or their common appreciation for music.

His thoughts then turned to the group of ten young guys. He could not help thinking how much they had changed, their attitudes, their personalities, the respect that they had learned, and the appreciation of good living and the good times in general, without the hang-ups of anger, aggression, and dependency on alcohol or drugs. Yeah, they had the occasional few drinks and pulled the occasional cone or joint, but they now knew how to control it and knew when enough was enough.

He felt so excited for them as he realized what they were about to experience. "Awesome, frigging awesome!" he yelled at the top of his voice as he drove to pick up his next fare.

As he arrived, Rocky's mobile phone rang. It was Pieter.

"I just called to see if you've seen this George fella yet. Some of the guys are falling asleep, and we wondered about it."

"Not yet. He should ring soon. I hope he hasn't forgotten about it or lost my number, but don't worry, bud. I will ring as soon as I drop him off. Gotta go, champ. A bit busy; ring ya soon."

"Cool, man, see ya later," Pieter said.

The passengers for this fare were a couple of adults, some teenagers, and a couple of kids. They told Rocky where they wanted to go and asked how he was and if he had been busy.

He answered, "I'm amazing, thanks, mate. It's been busy, but I've had a couple of breaks."

"Had trouble, have you?" the bloke said. "With the taxi or the passengers?"

"No trouble. Just the opposite. I've had a fantastic night, really. How about you?"

"Hey, is that you, Rocky? Cool, man, I haven't seen you for a few weeks. How ya doing?" one of the teenagers yelled from the rear of the maxi-taxi.

"Who's that?" Rocky said, turning on the interior light so he could see who it was in the rearview mirror. "Hey, buddy, how ya doin', Jason?"

"Driver, do you know Jason?"

Rocky hated being called *driver*. *"Anyone can see that I'm the effen driver. I do have a name,"* Rocky said often. *"But, I suppose, how is anyone to know my name?"*

"Yeah, I pick up him and his mates after roller skating most weekends."

"I hope they behave themselves," the father said.

"Oh, Dad, why do you always say that? Don't you believe me when I say that I don't do anything bad?" Jason said.

"That's enough," the father said.

"Yeah, mate. I have no trouble with them at all—the opposite, really. They are a great bunch of kids," Rocky answered. "I have no trouble with any of them. I just talk, they listen, they talk, I listen, and it is very interesting. The kids have a great knowledge of where they are and where they are going. They only need to talk to someone who wants to listen and show them how to get to where they're going—or actually, where they should be going."

"Jeez, I wish I could get into their heads sometimes. All we get are grunts and one-word answers," the dad said.

"I've heard of this driver," the mum said. "Aren't you the one who spent a lot of time with those kids whose friend drowned down at the jetty?"

"Yeah, that's me," Rocky answered. "Where did you hear about me?"

"At the school snack shop where I help, and at football and soccer games. I don't know. Every mum seems to know of you. Have you seen those boys lately? How are they doing? They are doing quite well at school, they tell me."

"Matter of fact, I saw them twice tonight," Rocky answered. "They are doing so well at school and as responsible young people in the community.

I am so proud of them all. The hate, anger, and aggression have all gone. They now have great attitudes and see where they're going, and they know how to get there. I know they have the guts, attitude, and determination to get there."

"That's great news. They used to be so bad," the dad said.

"Yeah, I'm so happy for them. Classic example of kids behaving really bad changed to adolescents really achieving," Rocky told them. "Actually, they are working on a magnificent project as we speak. They'll achieve their goal. I wouldn't be surprised if they make the papers, radio, and television in the next week or two—for all the right reasons." It was marvelous to have some inside information to base his comments on, without spilling his guts.

As the passengers left the taxi, the father walked around to the driver's window as Jason was saying goodbye to Rocky. The father shook Rocky's hand and thanked him for looking after Jason and his mates.

"That's cool, mate. Just listen to your boys. Talk with them, not down to them. Get involved with their sports and other activities or interests, and you will be rewarded with some great-achieving young men as they grow up. Please, mate, do it for them and for yourself. You too can feel so proud. Young Jason is a great kid. Don't ignore him. Like I said, talk and listen and guide him. Never put shit on him. He will make you so proud. I never want to see Jason in any trouble because you didn't pick him up when he needed help. Got that?"

"Thanks, mate. I didn't know how to get on with them. Their mother and I have been so worried," the father told Rocky. "Hope to see you again soon, driver."

Rocky cringed and thought, *don't call me driver, dickhead.*

As he pulled away, the phone rang. Rocky looked at the screen and saw it was George.

"How have you been traveling?" George asked.

"Been busy. How about you?"

"We're all good. We had a very heavy meeting, but it's all sorted now. Can you pick us up in about ten or fifteen minutes? Just on our last drinks now." "Yeah, that's fine," Rocky said.

Rocky stopped for a cigarette and a cup of coffee and passed on all incoming jobs, so he could be available for George's group. After enjoying break, he traveled to the hall where he had delivered the group earlier. He turned the motor and headlights off and waited till the group came out of the hall. The lights of the hall were turned off, so he switched his headlights on, so they could see where they were walking.

"Hi, Rick," one of the ladies said as she stepped into the taxi. "How are you doing?"

"Fantastic, thank you," Rocky said. He changed his demeanor to a sophisticated one to suit the occasion. "How was your night?"

"Really good, thanks. We have had a heavy time sorting things out, but it is all done now. Now we must put it all into action. I am so tired, though; can't wait to get some sleep."

George waited until everyone got into the taxi, and then he got into the front seat. "How are you, my friend? Have you had a trouble-free night?"

"Yeah, I'm all good. Thanks, George. Yes, it's been a trouble-free night. Mostly young people, enjoying themselves, singing, laughing, joking. It's been a great night. How did your meeting go?" He hoped he didn't sound impatient for some good news, but he couldn't wait to hear it.

"It was a good meeting, Rick. We sorted a lot of things. Oh, please take everyone home before me. Drop me off last so I can pay you."

"Okay. Tell me each address as we go, starting with the closest, please."

"I'll do that," a male voice said, and he gave the first address.

"As I said, we worked everything out. We have good news for you and your young charges. We want them and their mothers and any supporters to be guests of honor at the sponsors' dinner. Have you had a chance to talk with them?" George asked.

"Yes, I have. I hope you don't mind. They are ecstatic about the possibility of attending the dinner. Three of their mums were there also, and they are thrilled and give their permission wholeheartedly," Rocky said.

"That's great. We must get moving on this, so it is all accounted for. We need to know how many and their names, so we can arrange permission documents those who are under eighteen. Maybe you can come to my office on Monday or Tuesday, and we can sort it out properly."

"That's okay. Oh, they wanted me to ask you if the mother of their mate, Mitch, who drowned could come too. I was quite proud when they asked me that. Six months ago, they wouldn't have thought about anything like that."

"That's a great gesture, Rick. You must be so happy and proud of them." "Yes, they do make me feel on top of the world. I can't explain the feeling I get. Every step they take is a giant leap."

Rocky pulled up in front of Frank's house, the last passenger other than George. "Good night, George. Good night, Rick. I'll see you both very soon."

"Yeah, I will give you a call tomorrow about the sequence of appearances onstage. Have a good sleep," George said.

"Yeah, Frank, I'll see you over the next few days, I guess," Rocky said.

The door of the maxi-taxi slid closed, and George told Rocky his address. Then he said, "Now I can talk a bit more candidly, Rick. There are a few things that I should cover with you. Do you know how this rock fest is structured?"

"No, not really," Rocky answered. In fact, he didn't have a clue how it was structured, but he didn't want to sound too dumb.

"Well, you probably know about my business interests and the successes that my company has experienced these past few years."

"Yeah, I've heard a lot about Cleator Enterprises and the building and earthmoving and construction companies," Rocky said, mostly relying on the information on George's business card.

"I am also the chairman of the chamber of commerce. You probably have heard of that group," George said.

"Yes, I've heard your name associated with the chamber of commerce."

"Have you met Bob Watson from the high school? He's the principal."

"I've heard of him, though I haven't met him. I usually have dealings with Tom Charles, one of the deputies, and lately, the music teacher and the manual arts teacher."

"That's right. Bob has spoken of you. It's all coming together now. That's right—you've helped the school with unruly and wayward kids. I remember. He's said he wants to meet with you. He tells me that you volunteer your services."

"That's right," said Rocky.

"Anyway, the high school is involved in this competition as well."

"Oh yeah, that's where the Nuver Chanz got the information on the rock festival."

"Let's put it all together," George said. "The chamber and the high school organize the competition. My company is the major sponsor, along with about ten to fifteen minor sponsors for this show. Now, what usually happens is that minor sponsors donate cash and/or goods and services as prizes, and Cleator Enterprises handles any advertising and promotion and pays for the after-show party."

"Wow, that's fantastic that you do that, George. That must cost you a tidy sum of money."

"Yes, it does, Rick, but like you donate your time to help young people, I get a buzz out of doing this for the kids in the community. The only problem is, I only get to those who are musically minded. You help them continually and daily, it seems, in all aspects of life, assisting them in finding their feet and showing them a path to travel to get them started into adulthood. I have picked music, especially rock music, as in my day, I too played—if I might say so—a mean guitar. You might ask, why young people? Well, probably two reasons. First, when I was a teenager, I was a rebel. I had no father. He ran out when I was quite young and left Mum with five of us to bring up. I went astray, spent time in a home for bad kids, kicked around like something you wouldn't believe. I was told that I wouldn't become anything but a dead shit, a criminal. You name it, I was called it.

"One day, I thought to myself, *everyone has given up on me.* There was no one to look up to, so by myself, I decided to change my life and show all those people who were supposed to guide me and make it in the world. You know, the best thing for me was when I made it, I rubbed their noses in it."

Rocky stopped the taxi and stopped the meter in front of George's home. He let George continue with his story.

"Second" George said, "Mary and I were not able to have children, so this is my small way of coping with that by helping kids."

"Gee, George, that's a sad story but with a great outcome," Rocky said, almost at a loss for words.

"Usually, we have a musical organization, sports club, or youth cultural group as co-benefactors, along with the high school, to share in the profits from the entrance fee, less the theater hire. That usually amounts to about twelve to fourteen thousand dollars, giving the high school around six to seven thousand dollars and the other benefactor the same amount. We do require a legitimate group, though. What I want to do is give you that money to use in your activities with the boys in the community. What do you think?"

"George, I'm stuck for words. That is so generous. What can I say? I am really humbled by your gesture. You know, all that those boys and I have done together hasn't really cost that much. Just a bit of fuel sometimes, picking them up off the streets or maybe carting them somewhere out of trouble. We really could do quite a lot with that. Wow."

"Well, the offer is there, but I must have an answer by five o'clock on Monday. Please think about it, bounce it around for a while, and make your decision. Rick, I really hope you decide to accept the proposal. Don't worry too much about formalizing the group. I can fast-track that for you."

"That's great, George. I just remembered—I passed on that hundred-dollar note you gave me as a tip to the boys to start a fund to buy equipment for their music or some other project. I gave them limited instructions on how to set it up. In no time, they had it set up, ready for the bank on Monday. Gee, it made me feel so good how they diplomatically discussed it and came to a decision."

"What did they decide, Rick?" George asked.

"They decided that I would be a signatory, along with two of them. They put all their names in a hat and got the neighbor's kid to draw out two. They are so mature."

"That's great, isn't it? You must be so proud of them," George said, "Great guidance."

"Yeah, George, I am proud," Rocky said with a lump in his throat. Rocky's mobile phone rang, and he saw it was Pieter. "This is one of them now. I told them I'd phone them after midnight and let them know what your group had decided." Rocky answered the phone. "Hi, Piet, how ya doin', mate?"

"Good, Rocky, have you spoken to that bloke yet?" Pieter asked excitedly, with a touch of impatience.

"I'm with Mr. Cleator now. Listen, hang up and save your credit on your phone. I will phone you straight back, buddy."

"Cool, buddy," Piet said and hung up the phone.

"George, how much can I tell them? I must phone them back. They're tired and want to sleep."

"Rick, tell them everything—no secrets. Tell them how it is. Like I said, you need to get back to me by Monday night, so you must tell them all and discuss it with them. When you phone, can I talk to them, please?" George asked.

"Yeah, sure, George," Rocky said as he dialed Pieter's number.

"Oy, Rocky, what's doin'?" Pieter said as he answered the phone.

"Champ, I am still with Mr. Cleator. I have a lot of stuff to talk to you about, too much to tell you on the phone. Mr. Cleator has given me some good information. It's all good, buddy, much more than we spoke about before. I am so excited, man. Listen, Mr. Cleator would like to talk to one or two of you. Is that cool?"

"Yeah, sure, what should I say?" Piet asked. Then he yelled to the others, "Hey, guys, that Mr. Cleator bloke is with Rocky now, and he wants to talk to some of us."

"Just take it as it comes. You'll think of something to say," Rocky said. "I'm going to pass you over to Mr. Cleator." He passed the phone to George. "This is Pieter."

"Hello, Pieter, how are you tonight?" George asked.

"Hi, Mr. Cleator, we are all doing awesome. We are so excited," Pieter said.

"That's good, Pieter. Are you part of this band? Another Chance—is that what it's called?" George asked. Pieter realized that George got the name wrong, but let it go.

"Yeah, sir, that's us," Pieter said, not wanting to correct the mistake in the name. "There are five of us."

"What do you play, Pieter?" George asked.

"I play rhythm guitar, sir, and I sing some of the songs."

"Has Mr. Scott told you about the arrangements for next Saturday, Pieter?"

"Mr. Scott?" Pieter asked, seeming confused. "Oh, Rocky. Sorry, I forgot Rocky's last name. Yes, sir, he has told us some bits of it. We are so thrilled, Mr. Cleator. Thanks very much."

"You don't have to thank me. It's my pleasure to do this," George said. "Is there another band member I can talk to?"

"Yeah, Mr. Cleator, Aiden is here. I'll hand the phone to him. Goodbye, sir."

George heard Pieter say, "It's Mr. Cleator."

And then, "Hi, sir, this is Aiden."

"Hello, Aiden. How has your night been? I suppose you are tired by now," George said.

"It's been fantastic, sir. We treated Rocky to dinner, and later, he came to talk to us about the band festival and a few other things. We are all at Pieter's and are going to have a sleepover."

"Sounds good, Aiden. You must have a lot of appreciation for Mr. Scott and for his friendship with you guys," George said. "What did Mr. Scott talk to you about?"

"Oh, it's a bit embarrassing, sir. Don't know how to tell you that," Aiden said, sounding nervous. "We love Rocky—not like boy and boy but like older brother and younger brother. That sounds gross, but you know what I mean?"

"Aiden, I know what you mean. It seems you know the difference between loving someone and being in love with someone. I know the love you mean."

Rocky glanced at George with a look of confusion. *What's going on here?* he thought.

"Can you put one of the boys on the phone who is not a member of the Nuver Chanz band, please?" George asked.

"Yes, sir," Aiden said, and he called out, "Guys, Mr. Cleator wants to talk to someone who is not in the band." Tony apparently volunteered, as Aiden then said, "This is Tony, Mr. Cleator. I'll see you next weekend, sir."

"Bye, Aiden," George said.

"Hello, sir, this is Tony."

"Hello, Tony, are you enjoying yourself?"

"Yeah, we are," Tony said. "We've had a good night. The band has been practicing. They sound wicked, Mr. Cleator."

"That's good, Tony. Tell me—how do you feel about some playing music while you and some others are left out?"

"That's okay with us. We don't mind. Some of us can't play music or sing, but we get to listen like in an audience," Tony said. "We are good mates who do everything together as a team. Some play music and sing;

others are good skaters, good at football, or good BMX riders. It doesn't matter much. We stick together."

"Did Mr. Scott teach you that?"

"Yeah, when I think about it, he did. He told us a lot of things. When we started to listen, we saw he was right. He is always right."

"You have a lot of respect for Mr. Scott, do you?"

"Blood oath," Tony said. "Sorry, sir; didn't mean to swear."

"That's okay, Tony. I know what it's like to be excited and forget where you are. It shows great character, son, to say sorry in a situation like that. You will make a good man. You probably are a young man by now, by the sound of you. Now, can you put Pieter back on, please?"

Tony said goodbye and called out, "Pieter, Mr. Cleator wants you again."

"Hi again, Pieter. I just wanted to say good luck to you all. Mr. Scott has some information for you for a proposal I put to him. I want you all to discuss it with Mr. Scott, and he will get back to me on Monday. I won't tell you what it is. Mr. Scott will tell you in due course," George said. "Pieter, you all sound like thorough gentlemen. Please, for your futures, keep it up, but enjoy yourselves. I will see you soon."

"Thank you, Mr. Cleator. Bye," Pieter said.

"Good night, Pieter. Don't hang up. I will hand you back to Mr. Scott."

Rocky took the phone. "Hi, champ."

"Hi, Rocky ... Mr. Scott ..." he said slowly. "What's this information you got for us?"

"It's all good, buddy. Too much to tell you on the phone. You just sleep and have good thoughts and dreams. You never know; they might come true. Listen, it's one in the morning. You all should get some sleep—a big day tomorrow."

"Yeah, we are stuffed, man. Don't forget to come over for breakfast with us," Pieter said.

"I won't forget about our plans, as we planned, I'll just jump in the pool to freshen up and have a sleep until you guys wake up. It will be too early for you when I get there."

"I got a towel and shorts for you, but Rocky, wake me up when you get here, please. I will be closest to the door, and we got a mattress for you too."

"Cool, buddy. Yeah, I'll wake you. I don't really like to wake anyone, but because you insist, I will this time. Otherwise, you will get upset, hey?"

"Sweet. I'll see you then."

"Good night, champ. Get everyone to settle down and sleep," he said. "Bye, mate."

"Yeah, see ya soon, *Mr. Scott*," Pieter said cheekily.

"What a great bunch of fine young men you have developed there. Congratulations, Rick. You've done a great job with them," George said.

"Yeah, I guess I have, when I stop to think about it."

"I'll let you go, Rick. I have some additional thoughts to consider. I'll have more things to propose to you on Monday. If you decide to go ahead with what we discussed, I'd like to see you about midmorning on Monday. I'll pencil ten o'clock into my diary. Can you make it then? I'll call Bob on Monday to give the boys who can make it with you his permission to miss some school for an hour or so. I really hope the boys accept my invitation."

"Thanks, George. I was thinking about this while you were on the phone to them. I won't take any more of your time now, but I'll put it to the boys at breakfast. Oh, I didn't tell you—they insist that I call in for breakfast this morning. That's how thoughtful they are."

"Yeah, a combination of thoughtfulness and a need for you to continue to be a part of their lives. As one of them said, they love you, not in a sexual way but as adult and child. That came across very strongly," George said. "What was it that you talked about with them?"

"Oh, one of them found himself with female company, and things got a bit steamy. I discovered that none of them had much of an idea about protection, pregnancy, or diseases. I spoke to the boy, and he asked me to talk to the rest of them as well. I couldn't believe their ignorance. George, that's what pisses me off about society. All kids that age should know about these issues."

"Yes, it is sad. I may be able to help you there. I need to put some thoughts together tomorrow and talk about it with you on Monday. I'll see you then. While we are at it, here is another hundred-dollar tip for you, although you'll probably pass it on to them. Good night, Rick." George shook his hand and left the cab.

Rocky said, "Good night, George, and thank you very much for everything."

CHAPTER 8

**I just want to know what you're drinking or what
drug you're on so that I can have some fun too!**

Rocky cruised through his jobs for the next three hours or so. His
excitement was obvious to his passengers, and several people couldn't resist
commenting on it. Rocky told most of them that he'd had an amazing
night, shared his taxi with a lot of happy people, and that he "wouldn't be
dead for quids."

At one point, his phone rang; it was Adrian.

"Can you get me?" Adrian asked.

"Sure, champ, where are you?"

"At the nightclub. I'll be down near the fountain so no one else can
push in and take the ride," Adrian said.

"I'll be there in a couple of minutes," Rocky said. "Not far from there,
but across the street. I'm coming from the other direction."

"Cool, mate, I can see ya coming now," Adrian said.

"How ya doin', buddy?" Rocky asked.

"Great, mate. Had a quiet night this time around," Adrian answered.

"Where's the chicks, mate?" Rocky asked.

"Christy didn't want to go out tonight, so it's just me," Adrian said.

"Is that cool?" Rocky asked. "Can't help but ask if you're going to leave your clothes on this time, now that it's only you and me, and you're not in the back."

"Hell. Is that true?" Adrian asked.

"What's that?"

"Do I really take my clothes off?"

'Yeah, you do. It's funny. You pretend to be a stripper. You dance, gyrate, and take your clothes off, one piece at a time."

"No, I don't. Do I?" Adrian asked. "Christy told me that, and I didn't believe her."

"Well, it's true, mate. I guess you don't remember when you do it."

"No, I don't, Rocky. That's bad, doing something like that and not remembering. I'm sorry, man."

"Doesn't worry me. It's just so funny. I just want to know what drink or drug you are on, so I can get some and have fun too. No, I didn't mean it like that; you know what I mean, Adrian. No harm done."

"I only pull one or two cones or joints before I go out, and I do have a lot to drink when I am out. That's why I took it easy tonight," Adrian said.

"That's cool, mate. Really isn't any of my business, and it doesn't offend me, but maybe you should slow down a bit or try another drink. What do you drink?"

"Rum and Coke."

"Maybe you should try scotch, bourbon, or something else. Maybe beer might be better."

"Yeah, probably," Adrian said, "maybe it's the rum. I know rum causes problems with a lot of guys. Some just get happy, and some want to fight.

"Could be. Give it a go."

"I can't drink beer, though. It makes my guts sick," Adrian said.

"Yeah, I can't drink beer; makes me real sick too."

"I'll try that," Adrian said. "Anyway, how's the night been, mate?"

"It's been awesome. I met a couple of great people, spent time with the guys who were with Mitch that night that he drowned, and met a businessman who put forward some plans for me to think about. The guys are competing in the rock fest next Saturday. You should go; it'll be a good night."

"Yeah, I might. I'll take a break from the grog and get back with Christy; might just do that," Adrian said. "What's the band's name?"

"Nuver Chanz," he told him. "I won't be driving next Saturday, though. I have to be there with them."

"That's cool. That might make up my mind. Not to go to the nightclub and have a different night out for a change."

"Good idea, champ," Rocky said. "You'll probably enjoy it," Rocky said.

Adrian got out of the taxi and paid the fare. "Probably see you at the theater. And, mate, thanks for listening and the talk. Makes sense. I will try it. See ya, Rocky."

"Yeah, Adrian, see you next time."

Rocky decided to call it a night. He was close to the base, so he parked the cab, locked up the takings and the cab, collected his car, and drove to Pieter's house.

Rocky quietly walked to the door of the barn, opened the door, and crept in. As he did, he tripped over a body sleeping on the floor, and fell, waking him and the one sleeping next to him.

"Hell man, you frightened the crap out of me!" Pieter said.

"What's happening?" Aiden asked, as he was waking.

"It's Rocky. He tripped over me when he came in," Pieter whispered.

"Hi, Rocky, how's things, man?" Aiden whispered.

"Frig you, Pieter. You did say you would be next to the door, but hell man, how close did you need to be?" Rocky said quietly.

"Sorry, dude. Didn't realize I was that close," Pieter said.

"It's cool, buddy. Sorry to wake you that way."

"That's okay. Are you goin' for a swim?" Aiden asked.

"Yeah, just need the towel and shorts."

"Here they are," Piet said as he got up off the mattress on the floor.

Rocky walked out of the door toward the pool; Pieter and Aiden followed. Pieter had a small coolite box with him.

"What you got there, Piet?" Rocky asked.

"Mum gave me a little bit of bourbon and a bottle of Coke. She said to give you a drink or two. She said that I can have one with you, dude. Is that okay?"

"Well, if Sally said it is okay, it's cool with me."

"Can I have some too?" Aiden asked.

"Rocky, I wouldn't lie to you; you know that," Pieter said defensively.

"Okay, that's cool. What about Aiden? Did she say that he could have some bourbon too?"

"No, she didn't. We didn't ask her. But she won't mind."

"It'll be cool, just one. We don't want to get pissed," Aiden said, "just a drink with you."

"Yeah, okay. Probably no harm," Rocky said. "After all, when I first met you guys, you probably drank a whole bottle each."

Pieter poured the three drinks, handed one to Rocky and one to Aiden, and held his in the air. "Here's to Rocky, the man. Rocky, you are our legend. Cheers."

Aiden raised his glass and said, "Here's to our mate, who looks over us. Here's to you, Rocky."

Rocky raised his glass to meet the other two. "Cheers, fellas. Here's to the next chapter in your wonderful lives. May you all have long and rewarding lives."

"Thanks, buddy. We know while you are around, we will," Pieter said.

"That's right," Aiden said, still half asleep.

"No, fellas, you will break away and go your own ways sooner or later," Rocky said. "You don't want to hang off me all your lives."

"Yes, we will—well, I will. We will be your mates for life, man. You won't get rid of us that easily," Pieter said. "Are you still going to be our mate, aren't ya, Rocky?"

"Yeah sure, but you'll get jobs, girlfriends, and hopefully have kids of your own," Rocky said. "And when you do, I hope you will have learned enough from me so that you will bring your kids up just the same as you guys are now. Spend time with them so that they won't be bad."

"That's scary, man," Aiden said, "but I suppose every year you get older."

"You know what would make my life worthwhile? It's me sitting on the porch of your house, you with a wife and a couple of kids running around, having a few bourbons with you. How awesome would that be? That's why I have spent so much time correcting your attitudes, your anger, the confusion in your fucked-up heads, so that you can have a future, something to live for. You gotta have a fun time at your age but responsibly."

"Yeah, we know. We are thrilled that you're around for us, and you keep talking to us to get the effen demons out of our heads," Pieter said. "We've got it right now, haven't we, Rocky?"

"Yeah, champ. You all have it right. Look at you all—how bad you were, the trouble and fights you got into, always pissed and stoned. Everyone was against you. Now look at you. You got rid of that bad vibe and are living awesome lives. I admire each one of you. And I know something else that you don't know," he teased. "It's going to really show you how having a wickedly good attitude and being able to be responsible and respectful is going to come back and reward you big time."

"Come on, buddy, you big old prick. Stop teasing us. What do you know that we don't?" Aiden said.

"Can't tell ya, big fella. You know the rules. Any info that affects you all, I will tell you when we are all together."

"Well, I'll go and wake the rest of them, so you can tell us," Aiden said.

"No, let them sleep. Be patient. At breakfast I'll tell all of you and your mums who are here."

"Okay, we'll wait," Pieter said. "That bourbon was awesome. Do you think we can have another one?"

"No, we said just one," Rocky said. "What will your mum say? And listen, you are underage, and you all promised me—no alcohol."

"Yeah, I know. Mum won't mind because she knows we're with you, so that's okay. And we haven't had alcohol for months and months. This is different. We are having a quiet drink with our mate, and we are drinking slowly. It does feel different, having a quiet drink while you are having a mission, hey."

"Yeah, I told you that a long time ago—how to drink responsibly with your mates without intending to get pissed off your face. I suppose you want to pull a cone too," he teased.

"Have ya got some? Nah, I don't really want one," Pieter said. "I am over that shit now."

"No, Rocky, we promised ourselves and each other not to go there anymore—for a while, anyway. You know that. You told us that, and look now, we don't need it. We get our highs out of our skateboarding, BMX, and music," Aiden said.

"I don't have any, and I wouldn't give you any if I did. I just threw that in because I know how strongly you feel about it. I am so happy that you answered that way."

"Do you smoke hooch, Rocky?" Pieter asked timidly.

"No, not now champ. Why?"

"Just wondered. I've wanted to ask you that for a long time but didn't know how," Pieter said.

"I've told you to be open with me. You know you'll get an honest answer to anything you ask me," Rocky said. He was going to remind Pieter of another rule about being honest and open but stopped. It would probably upset him if he commented twice in one day about rules, and this question was probably a bit heavy for him. It probably fell in the category of respecting his elders.

"Yeah, I know, but this is a bit different, a bit personal," Pieter said.

"Listen, fellas, I have had it in the past. I haven't had it for a while. As I've said to you, it's not "Do as I say, not as I do," but—"

"Yeah, I know," Pieter interrupted. "Do as I say, the same as I do."

"You got it, man. That means I don't tell you to do something but then do something different myself," Rocky said. "But I do the same as I expect you to do, Anyway, to answer that question about another bourbon, how about we have a dip in the pool and then have another bourbon. Remember no swimming after alcohol—not good." That was a rule Rocky put in place, as that was what contributed to Mitch's death.

"Hell yeah, that's cool," Aiden said, ripping his shirt off and dropping his shorts, leaving his underwear. "Let's go."

"Yeah. I'm going in for a swim with you," Pieter said. "I have some snacks for us with our next bourbon." He undressed to his boxers and dived in.

Rocky removed his shirt, shoes, socks, and long trousers—his uniform at the wore in the taxi—and jumped into the pool.

The three of them quietly swam or floated, disappearing under the water and reappearing on the other side.

"This is awesome, man. It's still dark, only just past five, and it's a wicked night. Look at the stars," Pieter said.

"Let's see if we can find Mitch up there," Aiden said.

"Did you pick a star and name it for Mitch?" Rocky asked. "That's awesome. What a great way to include him in your lives. He will be looking down on you and watching you and guiding you. That's awesome."

"Do you believe in that stuff, Rocky?" Aiden asked.

"Yeah, champ, I do. I'll tell you about my experiences some time, probably over a quiet drink," he said. "You remember I told you that I carked it a few times a few years ago. I haven't told you the whole story yet."

"I remember that, but you kept the rest a secret from us. Remember, no secrets, champ," Pieter said.

"Hey, Piet, it wasn't really a secret; otherwise, I wouldn't tell you now. It was because I was helping you over Mitch's death, and that information would have spooked or upset you at that stage. I'll tell you, as I said, sometime soon."

"Can you tell us now, Rocky?" Pieter said.

"No, we will concentrate on what's happening now, but down the track, when we are all together, chilling out sometime, I will go there."

"That's two things you gotta tell us, Rocky. We never stop learning, do we?" Aiden said.

"Yeah, that's right. You spend your whole life learning things," Rocky said. "What are the two things? One is what I just said. What's the other thing?"

"About girls," Aiden said.

"Oh. That's right. Hell, I am going to be busy, aren't I? Which one is Mitch's star?"

Pieter came over behind him and outstretched his arm from behind his head, aligned at eye level, and pointed to the star. "See it, Rocky? That bright one that's changing colors. See it?"

"Yeah, Piet, I can see it. It's the brightest one in the sky. That's wicked. I am pretty sure that one is Venus."

"I don't care what it is. It's Mitch!" Pieter insisted.

"That's okay, Piet. Don't upset yourself. That's great you picked the brightest one. I was only telling you what I thought it was called. Nothin' wrong with picking a star with a name to remember your good mate. That's cool."

"That's cool, Rocky. Sorry."

The three looked at the star in silence, and each remembered Mitch in their own minds. Aiden and Pieter saluted Mitch's star with the same salute that they used at Mitch's Shed the night before.

"Anyway, fellas, I better get out and dry off. I am stuffed. Better get a bit of shut-eye," Rocky said.

"Yeah, we'll get out too, and I'll get the food and pour the drinks," Pieter said, as they got out of the pool. "Here's a towel for you, old man, and one for you, Aiden. And your shorts, Rocky." He handed a pair of his board shorts to Rocky.

"Thanks, chief," Rocky said and dried himself. "Do you guys mind if I stay in my jocks till they dry before I put the shorts on?" he asked.

"No, that's cool," Pieter said. "It's still dark anyway; no one will see you."

"That's cool," Aiden said. "I'm going to take mine off and go 'free-willy.' Let it breathe for a while."

Piet said, "That's an idea; I will too. Why don't you, Rocky? Go free-willy and give it some space. You should wear boxers, you know; it's much better for you."

"Yeah, I suppose it is. Just used to being old school. I've always worn jocks."

"I'll loan you a pair of mine, and you can try it sometime," Pieter said.

"No, you don't want me polluting your boxers, mate."

"It's cool, dude. Won't worry me. We are all mates. We all share at times. Don't be effed, you silly prick," Piet said.

"Yeah, okay, mate. I'll borrow them if it makes you happy. You don't mind if I go free-willy in your shorts, do you?"

"No, man, that's cool," Piet said as all three dropped their underwear in the darkness, dried themselves, and dressed in the shorts.

"I'll get the snacks, and you pour the drinks, please Rock Daddy. I'll get some ice," Piet said as he crept into the barn to the fridge.

"What's this 'Rock Daddy'?" Rocky asked.

"Aw, something Aiden and I worked out."

"What do ya mean, worked out?"

"You know how I said I wanted you to be my father? Well, that's how we're going to say it when you are our daddy, Rock Daddy," Aiden said.

"You guys are effed. Whatever."

Pieter returned with some ice and a plate of sandwiches made from the food left over from the spread from the night before. As all three sat back enjoying their sandwiches and sipping on their bourbons, Piet said, "I thought you would be hungry when you finished work, so I thought I would make them for us."

"That's very thoughtful of you, Piet," Rocky said. "You will make a good wife for someone someday." He gave Pieter a little push.

"Get effed, Rock Daddy," Pieter said. "I'll get you yet. That makes two I gotta get even with you now."

"That was great, guys. A few quiet drinks, a dip in the pool, some food, and a good chat and a bit of fun. Thanks, guys."

"That's cool. It was awesome being with you," Pieter said.

"Yeah. Cool, Rock Daddy. It was wicked," Aiden said.

"Now, I might lie down. You blokes going back to sleep?"

"Yeah, dude," Pieter said.

"I'm still tired," Aiden said. "Let's go to sleep."

As the three crept toward the barn, Pieter crept up behind Rocky and "dacked" him. "Got ya, Rock Daddy; that's one for me. One to go," Pieter said.

"Fair enough, buddy. I probably deserved that because I've been taking the piss out of you," Rocky said as he pulled the shorts up again.

"You sleep here, chief, between me and Aiden," Pieter said.

"Cool, man. Hope you keep to yourself when you sleep, buddy," he jokingly said to Pieter.

"You never know, Rock Daddy. You might be in for a big surprise," Pieter said." You never know; your luck might change."

"Yeah, Rocky, you don't know Piet. He is all over you when he is asleep. And he's got a whopper! Only joking," Aiden said.

"Got you worried, hey?" Pieter said. "Only joking. I am not into that sort of sex. We play act sometimes, but you are safe."

"That's okay. I knew that anyway; just taking the piss out of you. You played along. That's great trust and friendship."

"Yeah, if we didn't trust you or think you were our mate, you wouldn't be here," Pieter said.

"See ya when we wake up, fellas. Let's get to sleep while it is still dark. Sweet dreams, darlings," Rocky teased.

"Yeah, honey, have a great dream, and to you, Aiden, sweet dreams," Pieter said.

"Yeah, baby. Get effed, you queers," Aiden answered.

After sleeping for three hours, some of the lads began to stir and talk among themselves. "Oy, look—it's Rocky. He did come back. Look at him, sound asleep between Piet and Aiden," one said.

"I wonder if he sorted the things with that fella he was telling us about," Adam said.

"Yeah, he would have. You know Rocky; he always does what he says he is going to do," Decles said. "That's what's different about him. All my life, oldies have said that they are going to do this or that, take me somewhere, do something with me. Never happened. That's what effs me up with oldies."

"Yeah, you're right," Nick said. "He does what he says, never promises something he can't do. I have had the same thing—oldies bullshitting too much, and it hurts when they break their promises."

"He has done a lot for us, when you think about it. I know I owe him a lot, and I don't know how to thank him. It worries me and Mum sometimes," Shayne said.

"Hey, guys, don't wake him; let him sleep. He was rooted when he got here," Aiden said.

"What time did he get here? Were you awake?" Declan asked.

"Yeah. Well, I wasn't, but he tripped over Piet and fell onto me. Frightened the hell out of me," Aiden said. "Shayne, I heard you wondering how you can repay him for what he has done. No need to yet. He told me the other night when I said it. He said that he gets enough reward by seeing us as we are now. He told me it makes him feel good inside and very proud. He also really enjoys our company; don't know why? If you want to repay him, all we gotta do is keep looking ahead, stay out of trouble, and keep our attitudes like they are now. He told me that. But sometime, we will do something for him. We'll probably need to wait till we start work in a proper job or something, if he stays around us. Do you think he will?"

"Yeah, I reckon he will. He is a good mate to us. I think we all enjoy being with him," Declan said.

"I know he will. What he says sounds like he will be for a long time. He told Piet and me a few things that sounds like he will be around for a while. He said what he is going to tell us at breakfast will blow our minds. He is so excited for us, I think," Aiden said.

"What is it? Did he tell you?" Jay asked.

"No, you know him. Rules, man. He can't tell us until we are all together," Aiden said.

Pieter woke, sat up, rubbed his eyes, looked around, and said, "What's happening?"

"Ssshh, don't wake Rocky. Come over here," Aiden said. "Let him sleep. We owe him that much."

"Okay," Pieter said, dragging himself off the mattress. He stepped over Rocky and moved toward the group. He stopped and turned back to cover Rocky below the waist with a towel. "He's chucking a spread, and his nuts are out. All those kidneys and no steak," Piet said. He remembered hearing Rocky say that months before when Haydon had an accident on his skateboard, ripped the crotch out of his shorts, and exposed his jewels—and another time when Tony was under Rocky's car, helping him. "He is free-willy. Dropped his jocks after the swim when they were wet; the three of us went free-willy," Pieter told them, and they laughed quietly at Piet's comments. "Anyway, what's doing? What are you talking about?"

"Just about old man, about how long he might stay mates with us, about paying him back for looking after us, and how he wants us to keep goin' the way we are," Aiden said.

"And Aiden was telling us that he has something to tell us," Jay said.

"I might start the barbecue and start cooking. I heard Mum talking, so they are awake," Pieter said. "Tell me when Rocky wakes up, and I will get a coffee for him."

Piet left the barn with a cooler, Declan grabbed the other one, and all the group followed to help cook and prepare breakfast.

"Hey, whose bourbon? Who's been drinking bourbon?" Haydon asked, suggesting that a few had gone back on their words.

"It's cool, dude. Mum gave me some in the bottle to give Rocky a drink when he came here. Aiden and I had a quiet one with him. It was magic too; had a good talk and a sandwich and a swim. Didn't get pissed, not like we used to."

"Did he really?" Nick said. "He let you drink alcohol?"

"Yeah, it's okay, just one or two, relaxing. It's different, just like he told us when Mitch died," Aiden said. "Piet's mum knew."

"I wish I coulda had a drink with him, you lucky pricks," Nick said.

"You'll get your chance. He said we will have a couple of quiet ones sometime soon, probably after the band fest," Aiden said.

"That's an idea," Piet said. "We should have a barbecue with him and chill out around the pool and have a chat and a drink with him. He would love that, I'd say," Pieter said.

"Let's do it soon. Do you think your mum would let us do it here? Better than in the park where everyone would see us," Haydon said.

"Yeah, she would," Pieter said. "He can show us how to cook something different, just like he used to."

Rocky appeared at the door of the barn and peered around and saw the gang at the barbecue. "How ya doin', dudes. What's cookin'?"

"What's smokin', ya mean," Haydon said. "It's nearly ready, boys."

"That's good; I'm hungry and a coffee would be prime," Rocky said.

"Oh, I'll get you a coffee. Here, Decles, look after this for me while I go upstairs and get the old man a coffee. Won't be long, Rock Daddy," Piet said.

"That's cool, mate; don't rush. We got plenty of time."

"How did you finish up this morning?" Haydon asked.

"Had a fun night, really. Saw lots of the kids who know you, and, stuff me, I got Adrian."

"What's he up to?" Aiden said. Rocky had told them about Adrian's antics from time to time, as he told them a lot of the funny stuff that happened in the taxi.

"I'll tell ya when Piet gets back," Rocky said. "It will kill you; he'll get a kick out of it too."

"Which car you got here, Rocky?" Jacob asked.

"Midnight Special."

"Cool, man. Done anything to it lately?" Jacob asked. Most of the gang loved Rocky's cars, especially Jacob, who loved working on cars and helping him rebuild them.

"Yeah. I put two new stereo heads in it—one in the front and one in the chill-out zone, so you don't have to get over the front to change disks—and better speakers. It sounds awesome. And a few more lights in the chill-out zone."

"Cool. Can we listen to the stereo?" Haydon said.

"Well, you can, but not now; it's a bit early to make that sort of noise."

"What about the Ute? Have you had it back on the road yet?" Jerry asked, "What's it called—something about moods?"

"Moody Blue," Rocky answered. "Just a bit to go. Probably a couple of weeks, and it'll be back on the streets."

"What about a Sandman? Have you found one yet?" Jacob asked.

"Not yet. They are impossible to find, but hey, I'll find one; just watch me." Rocky took a sip of coffee from the mug Pieter offered him. "Thanks, buddy. That's an awesome coffee."

"Pieter's here now. Tell us about Adrian," Jay said.

"Oh, yeah. After I dropped off George, Adrian phoned me to pick him up. I took him uptown earlier in the night. When I got there, he was by himself. Christy and the other chicks weren't there."

"Have they broken up? Poor Adrian," Aiden said.

"I don't know really, maybe for a while until he sorts himself out."

"What do you mean, sorts himself out?" Piet said. "Is he in some sorta trouble?"

"Well, no. When he got in, I asked about the chicks. He said that Christy didn't want to go out with him last night. Then I said that I hoped he'd keep his clothes on because he was sitting in the front, and there were only the two of us. He looked at me, stunned and very pale, and said, 'Do I really strip my clothes off? Christy said that I do, but I didn't believe her. What do I do?' I told him that he stands up and pretends that he's in Man Power or some other strip show and slowly takes his clothes off, and by the time he gets home, he has nothing on. He said he didn't remember any of that and was shocked he did it.

"I told him it was true, and he told me that he only had a couple of drinks and wasn't pissed at all. I asked him what he'd had to drink, and he told me that he had a couple of cones or jays before he left home and had had rum and Coke. I told him that maybe is what makes him lose his mind and suggested that he change to something else because rum does funny things to a lot of guys."

"That's amazing. Do you think it'll work?" Aiden asked.

"Probably, because rum does mess up a lot of guys' heads. Some fight, some just go happy and limp, and some do things that they wouldn't do normally. Anyway, he's going to try that and take it easy. He said next Saturday he wanted to do something different and stay away from the nightclubs, so I suggested he go to the rock fest and see you guys play and sing."

"That's real cool, Rocky. See, guys? Everyone listens to Rocky 'cause he is wise and knows about these things. We might have to call you Yoda or Splinter or something; they are wise guys," Adam said. "Is he going to go?"

"Yeah, he will."

"Talking about clothes," Haydon said, "Pieter covered you up when you were sleeping because you were free-willy, lying on your back with your legs apart, and you had 'kidneys and no steak.'"

Rocky blushed and said sheepishly, "Sorry, Pieter. Thanks, mate."

"It's cool, man. I was going to tickle 'em with a feather but thought I'd better not," Pieter said.

"Wonder you didn't, you prick. You did say you still had one on me."

"Yeah. Shoulda. Forgot about that," Pieter said. "Next time, big guy, I'll get ya. Don't worry."

"I know you will"

"Okay, breakfast is ready. Everyone, come and get it," Pieter announced.

"You did a good job of it, buddy," Rocky said to Pieter, putting his right arm around Pieter's shoulders and hugging him. "You must have had a good teacher, hey?"

"Yeah, sure did. It's not as good as yours, but it's okay."

"Nah, stop putting shit on yourself. You know I don't like hearing anyone putting themselves down." He put his face in Pieter's face. he said. "Okay, buddy?"

"I know, dude; won't do it again."

All the guys sat down with their plates of bacon, eggs, and tomato and a glass of juice and started eating.

"Aren't the mums coming down for breakfast?" Rocky asked.

"No, Mum thought they might leave us alone for a while, so they don't cramp our style," Pieter said. "Really, I think that she doesn't want anyone to see her soon after she wakes up—not a pretty sight, I can tell ya."

"Oh, Piet, that's not nice, buddy," Rocky said. "We might start to talk about the band festival things."

"Yeah, what's the latest?" Aiden asked.

"They want you blokes and your mums to be guests of honor at the banquet after the show."

"Wicked!" the chorus sounded.

"We need to work out how many seats we need at the theater and how many at the dinner. Pieter, can you get some paper and a pen to make notes and use it as a checklist? Thanks, buddy, we will wait for you. He needs the names as well, probably for place cards or name tags."

"What's a place card?" Haydon asked.

"It's a card with your name on it that's put on the table, so you know where to sit," Aiden said.

"He needs a permission letter signed by your mums," Rocky said, "because you are all minors—hey Piet—for media and photos."

"Oh, Rocky, that's stale. Do you have to go on with it?" Pieter said.

"Sorry, champ. Some of you and I need to go to his office at ten o'clock on Monday to meet with him. I'll get back to that soon. Mitch's mum would be welcome at both functions. George thinks that was a great gesture to think of her. Congratulations, guys. After George spoke to three of you, he commented on what a fine bunch of young men you are. Well done, guys. He said he has more thinking to do before Monday; then he'll have more to propose. Don't know what that would be, but it can only be good. He's going to call Mr. Watson on Monday to get permission for some of you to leave school, so you can go to the meeting with me." Rocky got up, saying, "Hang on, guys. I'll be back." He went to his car, and when he returned, he held his closed hand over the middle of the table, then opened it, and dropped the second hundred-dollar note on the table. "He gave me this to add to the other one."

"Wicked," Pieter said. "That's unreal."

"Mr. Watson wants to meet me, apparently," Rocky said. "He must have heard of me from Mr. Charles, I guess. Anyway, I better organize that before next weekend. He told me how the night was organized, which sponsors paid for what, and that he was the major sponsor, paying for advertising, promotion, and the cost of the after-party. Can you imagine? That must cost him many thousands of dollars. Now, the twenty-dollar entry fee to the theater is put together and shared equally between the school and the other club or group who are guests of honor."

"That's us," Pieter said. "We going to get money out of this?"

"Yeah, mate, that's right, but not for each of you. We gotta form a registered group for legal reasons."

"That's cool," Nick said. "How do we get a registered club?"

"We gotta talk about that today, and George will organize the paperwork. He knows people who can quicken the process and have it in place before next Saturday," Rocky said. "Put that on the list, Piet; that's important."

"How much money, man?" Aiden asked.

"George said around twelve to fourteen thousand dollars. That means about six or seven thousand for our share."

"Stuff me," Pieter said. "That's an awesome amount of money. What can we use that for?"

"Sound equipment, maybe a mobile disco, a skate ramp somewhere— something that's for a good purpose that benefits kids just like you. We will talk about that soon; we better have some ideas before we see him tomorrow. Maybe each one of you can put an idea forward later. Write that on the list too, Piet. I told him what I did with the first hundred dollars he gave me and that you sensibly worked out by yourselves what you to do with it. He was so impressed."

Rocky looked around at the wide eyes and open mouths. The boys found it hard to comprehend what was happening.

"Why is he doing all this for us?" Nick asked. "He doesn't even know us."

"No, he doesn't, but he has heard a lot about you from your high school principal, from the community, from people who work for him who know you or have heard of you, and probably his business acquaintances. You never know what people out there know about what goes on. You know, I had a lady passenger last night who knew all about you and me from the snack shop at school and the soccer and rugby league club games. That's why I'm so happy that you listened to me and took upon yourselves to try some of my advice and do the right thing. You should give each other and yourselves a pat on the back."

Rocky applauded them as they patted each other on the back and gave each other high-fives. "You guys have achieved this with your attitudes to life and other people. Time for a group hug. What do you reckon, guys?"

Everyone hugged each other and then ran to the pool and dived in.

After a lot of skylarking and jumping about, several hoisted Rocky above their heads, praised him for achieving all that was happening, and thanked him.

"You are our hero, Rocky. We all thank you for doing this for us," Aiden said.

"No, guys," he said as the boys put him back in the pool. "You did this for yourselves. All I did was suggest ways to get over your angry and depressed states, but you overcame it to lead happy and responsible lives. Didn't I tell you back then that you would have many good times if you succeeded? You guys did it for yourselves. That makes my head swell and my chest explode with pride and satisfaction. *You … have … made … it,*" Rocky said slowly. "Well done. Now, enjoy yourselves for a couple of minutes, and then we'll sort a few things out. We have a lot to do on Pieter's list."

They all high-fived each other and hugged Rocky and frolicked in the water using up some of their energy. After drying off; joking about Aiden, Pieter, and Rocky free-willying; and clearing the plates and washing, drying, and packing away, the group settled down around the table to talk about the items on the list.

"Here, you sit here, Rock Daddy. Here's the list and more paper and a pen for you," Pieter said as Aiden and Jay poured eleven glasses of Coke, one for each.

"No bourbon, Rocky?" Aiden said.

"No mate, alcohol-free. We gotta have clear heads," he said as he lit a smoke. He moved away from the table so as not to blow smoke near them. He thought about the fact that none of them was tempted to ask for a cigarette. All of them had vowed not to smoke as part of their pledges but respected his desire to "mess up his body," as they often reminded him. When he finished his cigarette, he returned to the table and began the discussion.

"First on the list, how many for the theater? Five gang members, me, the mums, and Mitch's mum—that's seventeen. Can you think of anymore?" he asked.

"No, that's about it," Pieter said. "We got twenty so that will be enough."

"Do you think we should invite the neighbors, Pieter?"

"Yeah, that's a good idea, Rocky. They do put up with the noise we make," Pieter said. "I'll ask them later."

"Okay, that's four more—twenty-one—so I will write one more pass on my list. I'll write two more and contact Adrian; he'll want to go, I am sure," Rocky said. "Next, how many for the after-party?"

"Well, ten of us, ten mums, you, Mitch's mum, the four neighbors, and Adrian," Aiden said. "That makes twenty-seven."

"Hell, your math is good buddy," Rocky said. "Go to the top of the class."

"Oh, dude, that's easy math."

"Only gagging, Aiden," he said. "Now, permission letters—can one of you print off ten letters on a computer and get your mums to sign them, giving their permission to have any photos and videos published? One of you gather them and take them to the meeting tomorrow." Rocky thought for a moment and then said, "Bob Watson—I better meet him tomorrow. It might be a good idea for all of you to get to school early tomorrow and see Mr. Watson before school. Tell him who's going to the meeting and that I'm calling in to the school to see him. You can give him my mobile number and tell him that I'll be there about nine thirty, if that suits him."

"Who's going to the meeting, chief?" Pieter asked.

"He only wants about five, not all band members. Don't worry. If you don't go, it's not the end of the world. You will all benefit the same, and its good practice to let some of the group represent all your interests. Want to work that out now?"

"Yeah, let's do it now," Haydon said.

"Yeah, that's cool," Pieter said.

"I reckon the best way is to think about your timetable first. Anyone who has an important class between nine thirty and eleven thirty should stay at school. That's being responsible to yourselves, your teachers, and your school. If we have more than five, we'll decide how to choose after that. What do you think? Put your hands up if you agree."

All boys put their hands up.

"So, who should stay at school for an important class? Put your hands up."

After a bit of thinking and small discussions, Haydon, Adam, Nick, Jay, Declan, and Jacob put their hands up.

"Fantastic work, guys. You're showing a grown-up attitude. That leaves four of you—two band members and two others—so it looks like Aiden, Pieter, Tony, and Shayne will go. I'm sure these four guys will do a great job on your behalf."

At this moment Bill and his family from next door joined the group to join in with what was going on. Bill said that they had heard some loud talking and wanted to see what was causing so much happiness. Marg went upstairs to see the mums, and Rocky invited Bill and the two boys to join them."

"We must organize the group—what we are all about and possibly give ourselves a name. Any thoughts?" Rocky asked.

"Rocky, I think we should use the fund for equipment we need for the band practice, like recording gear and a new amp," Pieter said.

"Yeah, and some lights too," Nick said.

"I think we should get that but some other stuff for our physical activities. I wouldn't mind starting some water sports, and I'd say all these guys would be in that too," Aiden said.

"That's awesome, Aiden. We often talk about kayaking or wind surfing. I forgot about that," Pieter said. "We should think about the whole group, not just music."

"I like the idea of the mobile disco, but that will take heaps of bread," Nick said. "Me and Jay and Jacob wouldn't mind learning to dance so we can back up the band that way."

"Yeah, we can use the skate park and BMX track like we do now. They are already there, but wouldn't it be wicked to have our own? But we don't really need it," Decles said.

"Hey, I think we are getting off the track a bit. Yeah, I say get some of those things, but wouldn't it be prime if we used some to help other kids like us? To help Rocky like he has done for us?" Aiden said.

"That's great, Aiden, that's a great idea," Rocky said. "Okay, I have written down band equipment, amp, lights, recording gear, water sports, mobile disco, dance, helping other kids—that's awesome. You need to have these ideas in your heads in case George asks. How are we going to structure the group?"

"I reckon we start off by electing a leader and a letter-writer. We should have meetings to vote on things, just like the grown-up people do to run clubs or companies," Aiden suggested.

"Sounds good, buddy. Put your hands up if you agree to do it this way."

All hands went skyward.

"Do you want to organize the positions now? Put your hands up if you do."

All hands went up again.

"Okay. Quick lesson on meetings and election of executive."

"What's executive?" Shayne asked, a little confused.

"Executive means president, vice president, secretary, and treasurer and sometimes a patron. You guys probably should have an adult patron because you're fairly young," Rocky said, not wanting to use the word *minor* again.

"What's a patron?" Adam asked.

"Someone who helps the committee or advises them. Their names are used to attract donations and other assistance that may be needed," Rocky answered.

"Like you—are you the patron?" Shayne asked.

"Well, maybe, but you have to nominate me and then all agree."

"Hey, guys, Rocky has to be the patron, or we wouldn't know what to do. Anyway, he already got us that money," Shayne said.

"How much money is involved?" Bill asked, taking in all the conversations.

"Six or seven grand," Pieter said. "How about that? All because of Rocky."

"No, mate, I might have gotten it, but you blokes earned it by taking the lead I gave you and running with it," Rocky said.

"Yeah, suppose so, but without you telling us what to do, we had no chance," Pieter said.

"Okay, let's get the executive sorted," Rocky said. "What we do is call for nominations for each and have an election if there's more than one. Remember, I will be around to help you conduct your meetings and teach you how to do the jobs you get. Don't be afraid; give it your best shots and enjoy the experience. I think, as we are all mates, we won't have a secret ballot, just a show of hands for whoever you vote for. Okay, president—anyone want to be president or nominate anyone?"

"I'll vote Aiden," Pieter said.

"I'll nominate Pieter," Haydon said.

"No, I won't do it. I want Aiden," Pieter said.

"Is there any more?" Rocky asked. "Okay, Pieter, you were nominated. Would you accept if you won an election?"

"Nope, I want Aiden."

"Aiden, would you accept the job of president? I will explain your jobs later, all the jobs."

"Yeah, okay. Thanks, Piet," Aiden said. "I would like to do the job; I got a fair idea what to do."

"Congratulations, Aiden, we now have the president. Now, vice president—he helps the president and takes over if the president is away. Any nominations?"

"Yes, I nominate Pieter," Jacob said.

"I wouldn't mind being vice president," Declan said.

"Okay, two nominations. Pieter, would you do the vice president job?"

"No, Decles would be good; I wouldn't mind being secretary, if no one else wants to do it," Pieter said.

"Decles, seems that you will be vice president. All in favor, raise your hands," Rocky instructed. All hands went into the air.

"Okay, secretary—Pieter's already nominated himself. You know what a secretary does, Piet, don't you?"

"Yeah, writes letters, takes notes," Pieter said. "I like doing that stuff, and I got a computer, so it's okay."

"No others interested? We have a secretary, if all in favor. Sorry, Aiden, you are supposed to run the meeting, as you are the president. Get your arse over here. I'll help you, fellow free-willy."

The group erupted into laughter and cheering at the comment.

"Okay, Rocky, you're a free-willy too, and so is Pieter," Aiden said, "and there are probably a few more too, if I know these guys."

With Rocky's coaching, Aiden said, "Any nominations for treasurer? He handles the money."

"Can I explain?" Rocky said. "Usually the treasurer counts the money, banks it, and pays the bills from it. He signs the checks with at least one other person, and, probably in your case, someone who is an adult."

"Okay, treasurer—anybody?" Aiden asked.

"I reckon Jay would be good at that," Pieter said.

"Hey, Piet, I'm sorry, mate. You should be over here taking notes. I didn't mean to take over your job," Rocky said.

"Cool, Rocky, it's okay. I didn't think about it. You help me through, hey?"

"Yeah, of course, mate."

When Pieter sat next to Rocky, with Aiden on Rocky's other side, Rocky put his left arm around Aiden's shoulders and his right arm around Pieter's shoulders. With a huge grin on his face, he said, "Look at this—the three free-willies together!"

Roars of laughter and cheers rang out from the group. Tony said, "Hold it there; I got my camera. Smile, free-willies, for the photo board." He clicked the camera a couple of times.

"We have Jay nominated for treasurer. Anyone else?" Aiden asked, still laughing. "All in favor?" All hands went up. "Congratulations, Jay. You are the money man," Aiden said, putting his own flare on proceedings. "Now, for patron. Is that what you are called, Rocky?"

"Yeah, patron, but I'm not until I'm nominated and voted for, and then I might not accept."

"Oh, come on, King Willy. You'll do it, won't you?" Decles said.

"Yeah, of course. I would be honored to be your patron, guys."

"All in favor?" Aiden said. "See? I told you so."

"But I reckon we should give Rocky a nickname, like we said when Rocky was asleep," Haydon said. "You know, the name for the wise old man."

"Hey, cut out the 'old' bit, will ya?" Rocky said. "What name is that?"

"Splinter—you know, that wise ol—I mean, wise man from *Star Wars*," Haydon said, "but we will change the spelling to *Splinta*. Just like we spell everything different."

"All in favor?" Aiden asked. "Rocky, you don't mind, do ya?"

"No, champ, whatever you call me doesn't matter. If it means something to you, it's cool with me."

"Splinta, it is," Pieter said.

"You don't write that in the minutes, though, Pieter. You only use correct names in the paperwork for the committee. That's just a fun thing, buddy."

"Cool, Rocky—oh, Splinta," Pieter said.

"Okay, you got Aiden, president; Decles, vice president; Pieter, secretary; Jay, treasurer; and me as patron. That's settled."

Rocky coached Aiden, who then said, "We now have to decide what we are going to be called. Any ideas?"

"Oh, my head hurts," Pieter said. "This is hard."

"What about something about helping teenagers—-however you would say that?" Decles said.

"Yeah, how about changing lives?" Aiden said.

"Or something that means from bad to good?" Nick suggested. "That's what we are really."

"We better ask Patron Splinta to help us; he'll know," Shayne said. "What do you say, Splinta?"

"Trying to think—how about we work out the last part of the name first while I think about it?"

A lot of suggestions were put forward with the group deciding on *Foundation* as the last part.

"Hey, Splinta, what would go with that for a name?" Pieter asked.

"I've been thinking, guys."

"Don't do that, dude; it might hurt," Jacob said.

"Not fair, buddy. Yeah, I'm tired, but I can still think. Has anyone heard the word *metamorphosis* or know what it means?"

Bill said that he had heard of it, and so did one of the mums, who had just joined the boys. The kids all shook their heads.

"Is that a real word, Rocky, or did you make it up?" Aiden asked.

"Yeah, champ, it's a real word," he said. "It means to change something for the better. That sums you blokes up perfectly. What you think? Metamorphosis Foundation?"

Secretary Pieter asked how to spell the word, and Rocky spelled it out for him.

"You may have heard that something is morphed," Rocky said. "That's where it comes from."

"I say we go with that," Aiden said.

"Hey, don't pick it because I said it, guys; you gotta think of things for yourselves."

"No, Rocky, you are Patron Splinta, the wise man; we like it," Declan said.

"I think it is a bit long and hard to say," Haydon said. "What about we shorten it to *Morph* and put something short in front of it to make it diff?"

"What could we use? Would have to be something that says something about us," Aiden said.

"What about Boy-Morph Foundation, or Male-Morph, or Teen-Morph? Something like that?" Pieter suggested.

"Well, Boy or Male means boys only. Even though we are boys now, we might want to have chicks in the club," Haydon said.

"That's a great idea, guys. Teen-Morph sounds good, and it has a ring to it, and it describes you really well," Rocky said

"Okay, all in favor that we are named Teen-Morph Foundation?" Aiden asked. "Hands up if you agree."

Everyone's hands went up, including Rocky's and Bill's and the two other kids as well.

"Okay, men. The other thing is, when someone hears a new word in a title or even a company, people just sit up and take an interest. When I was doing advertising, things were more successful if we had something that drew attention," Rocky said.

"Can we join the Teen-Morph Foundation too, Dad?" Chris asked his father.

"Don't know, son. Depends on these guys. Let them get it up and running, and see what happens with the group," Bill said.

"Why don't we make them honorary members until everything is worked out?" Rocky suggested.

"What does *honorary* mean, Splinta?" Haydon asked.

"It means voluntary, someone without an active duty for the time being. Waiting for full membership, I'm pretty sure," Rocky answered.

"Okay, Chris and Terry, you are in as honorary members. Welcome," Aiden said.

"Okay. Meeting over, guys. You have learned a lot and achieved a lot since yesterday. How are your brains handling it?" Rocky said.

"Brain strain, Splinta," Piet said. "My head hurts. Let's have a swim and then play our songs to clear our heads."

"Hey, thanks, Rock Daddy," Aiden said, "for teaching us that stuff and helping us sort it out. And that money—wow."

"Yeah, thanks, Splinta. How are we going to pay you back?" Haydon said.

"Now, fellas, let's not go there again. The looks and the excitement on your faces is repayment enough. Don't say it again, please. It's all cool," Rocky said.

"Water, guys, into the water!" Pieter yelled. "You two dudes from next door too. You're in this together with us. Get your shirts off and get in. About time you joined in and see how much fun we have."

The swim went well for everyone—a dozen or so bodies jumping, diving, frolicking, and dumping each other; young guys letting off steam after such a heavy session. Rocky realized the balance of play and serious stuff was right. They showed immense interest in learning new life skills, listening to Rocky's stories and advice, and acting the fool with him. This provided them with all the activities they needed. Rocky was one of the boys when he was around them in play mode and as mentor when learning and advice was needed.

If only older people could interact with adolescents the same way, what an awesome world it would be, Rocky thought. *Maybe their idea of helping other kids would be the ideal. My teachings must be rubbing off, as these ten kids are showing unselfish attitudes toward others who might be in the same place as these guys were six to eight months ago.*

They settled down to listen to the three songs the band had selected for the rock fest. The jam session went well. Rocky joined them in a rough version of "Livin' on a Prayer".

Rocky said he needed to go home for a few hours' sleep. "I'll be in the taxi from three till eleven. Not staying out after eleven. If you need me, contact me then; otherwise, I'll see you at school at nine thirty tomorrow and drive you four guys to George's office. If you think of anything, write it down or give me a call. You have done so well. Take it easy today, enjoy yourselves, and above all, *rock on, guys!*" This was a term Rocky used to say goodbye or "see you later."

CHAPTER 9

We think he went to an all-boys school, and he takes it out on boys. He must have been a nerd and got picked on.

Rocky commenced his shift at three o'clock and found that the day had been very quiet. After logging his taxi into the system, he checked for bookings. There were none. Sundays were usually like that. That's why Rocky hated his Sunday shift, but because he drove a maxi-taxi, he couldn't skip the shift. The boss insisted he work the shift in case some good jobs came in. He quite often only got $100.00 in fares. His share was 45 percent, so he worked eight hours on a Sunday for barely $5.50 an hour.

"Jeez, I should find another job. The money sucks," Rocky would tell the other drivers or his family and friends. He never actually looked for another job, as he did enjoy driving and the company of most of his passengers. It was an interesting job, and if he wasn't a taxi driver, those poor kids would be down the drain by now, and he wouldn't have met such a positive person as George Cleator. *Anyway, one of these days I will feel real bunted and throw it in for good, maybe today*, he thought.

He sat in his taxi on the main rank with the other drivers, smoking, chatting about how to fix the country, and seeing the line of taxis in front of him getting shorter ever so slowly. His first job was about an hour and a half after he started his shift. It was a short drive, a drunk who had been in the pub all day, smelled rotten, and continually complained about the cost of beer, the cost of smokes, the cost of taxi fares, the tax he had to pay, and the maintenance he paid to his ex. Rocky just turned off listening to him and wondered why there was so much scum in the world and, at the same time, so many great people. *Maybe blokes like this rubbish were neglected or abused as kids, and this is how they grow up,* Rocky thought. *It's a sad place sometimes.*

On arriving at his destination, the smelly, whining, aggressive scum argued about the fare, saying Rocky took the long way and that he wasn't going to pay.

"Listen, scum, piss off out of this taxi before I punch your lights out, you creep," Rocky said, losing his usual cool attitude. "I am not in any mood for your crap."

"Make me," the passenger said, slurring his words.

The scum had the door open, so Rocky pushed him, and he fell out. Rocky waited, making sure that he was still alive. Then he closed the door and drove off. *It's just not worth the $4.50,* he thought. *But I really should not have pushed him out. I should not have lost it.* He wondered if he should have called the police to remove the drunk from the taxi, but that would have meant waiting for the cops to arrive, giving details, and having him booked for fare evasion. *Nah, not worth it,* Rocky thought. *That would have held me up for another hour or so.*

Still, he thought that he'd better go back, so he turned the taxi around. His conscience got the better of him. When Rocky got to the spot, the scum was not there. He then saw him staggering—one step forward, two sideways, one backward—and falling quite frequently. Rocky drove off and pulled into the nearest rank, which was outside the shopping center in the suburbs, turned the motor off, and sat quietly, wondering why he did this job.

Ten minutes later, Rocky's mobile phone rang. He picked it up and, without checking the screen, said, "Yeah?"

"Is that you, Rick? You don't sound very happy."

"Oh, George, it's you. I'm sorry, mate, just a bit pissed off with this taxi job. Just had a drunken scum, only passenger since three o'clock, and he argued about paying the $4.50 fare."

"Not good, Rick," George said. "You better think about some other job. Your job is something that I couldn't do."

"Yeah, I was thinking about that," Rocky said. "I've decided to look around this week."

"Um, that's interesting," George said.

"Yeah, I suppose it is," Rocky said.

"Rick, I just rang to find out if you saw your lads today," George said.

"Yes, I did this morning. They looked after me very well, got me coffees, drinks, let me sleep for a while, cooked me breakfast. Treated me like a king, George," Rocky said.

"That is terrific. Listen, Rick, I've been talking to Bob Watson—you know, the principal from the high school. You haven't met him, have you?"

"No, but I asked the boys to check on whether I could see him when I pick up tomorrow."

"Oh, that's good. He will look forward to that. Does the group want to go ahead with the proposal I put to you last night?" George asked.

"Yeah, George, they are ecstatic. They cannot believe it. They have had to digest so much, and they have sorted so much too. All is organized," Rocky said enthusiastically. "They have a committee, a proposed name, ideas on how to use the funds, and even ideas to help me to help other kids in trouble. I won't steal their thunder; I'll let them tell you themselves."

"It would be great to hear it from them and see their faces when they do so," George said. "As I said, I spoke to Bob, and he and I have worked out a few things to help him communicate with some kids at the school. I want to talk with you further tomorrow after I meet with the boys. Oh, by the way, how many are you bringing?"

"Four, if that's okay. Two band members and two others."

"Yes. That's fine. Could you come back after you take them back to school? Bob has given his permission for them to leave the school grounds for an hour or two, as long as they're in your company."

"Yeah, George, that's fine, I will make it back

"Rick, you have a devious but marvelous mind. No doubt about that. Everything you do has a purpose to encourage those boys to achieve. That's great. I would have told them not to bother meeting at Bob's office because the permission had been granted."

"All part of character-building, George. All these tasks pieced together help them realize their goals. The cool thing is that they are so innocent they don't realize it."

"You really are amazing." George paused for a moment, as if thinking of another piece of information, and then said, "Okay, Rick, I'll see you about ten tomorrow. I am looking forward to it."

"I'm looking forward to it too, mainly because it gives me a chance to showcase these lads. Whenever I can show people that young people do have thoughts and opinions required to achieve something, I'll grab it with both hands.

No jobs had come in while Rocky was on the phone. He turned the radio up and thought about George's phone call. He wondered what George wanted to talk about in private. He preferred to involve the guys on anything that involved them. *No secrets either way; that's the rules*, Rocky thought. Maybe it had nothing to do with the kids. *Can't think about it anymore.* His head was going around and around, and he couldn't think clearly, so he decided to wait till the next day.

As Rocky listened to the radio, he fell asleep. Ten minutes later, he woke to a loud rumble, a rattling roar, and voices yelling. As he opened his eyes, he noticed in the twilight a group of people on skateboards, skating and jumping and performing tricks and yelling happily. As the mob got closer, he realized it was the gang. They had gone for a skate earlier and decided to take the long way home to see if they crossed paths with Rocky's taxi.

"How ya doin', Rocky?" Pieter said. "Havin' a good shift?"

"Were you asleep, Splinta? What's happening?" Nick asked.

"I've had a shit of a shift—terrible."

"You not happy?" Aiden said, placing his hand on Rocky's shoulder. "What's the matter?"

"Let me out; let's go sit on that brick fence," Rocky said as he opened the door.

"What happened, Rocky? You never sound this bad," Pieter said.

"I started at three, got my first job about four thirty, a drunken scum, stunk like crap, complained, whined the whole time. Then he refused to pay, so I pushed the idiot out and drove off. Haven't had a job since."

"Hell yeah," Shayne said. "Cool. But Rocky, you know, anger management. Don't get aggressive. You know, like you tell us."

"Yeah, I know, champ. You see, this old prick's human too. I let my guard slip, let the scum get the better of me, and it messed with my head."

"Never mind, Splinta; that's cool, as long as you get over it and move on," Jay said, repeating what Rocky had told them on many occasions.

"What are we going to do? We can't leave him like this," Pieter said. "He needs our company and our help. It's our turn to talk to our mate and get him over this. Something is not right with him."

"Yeah, but what can we do?" Aiden said.

"Don't worry, fellas. I appreciate your concerns." Rocky turned to Aiden. Hey, bud, lend me your skateboard. This old fool is going to go for a skate."

"Sure, Rocky, what about the taxi?"

"Stuff the taxi. If the two-way talks, ignore it," Rocky said. "I won't be long, fellas. I'll just go to the end of the street and back. Pick me up if I fall off."

Rocky skated off, stumbled a few times, swore and cursed, and made it to the corner. As he turned, he noticed a couple of the guys were shadowing him a couple of yards behind, as if to form a guard or protection. Rocky stopped and laughed out loud. He yelled out an almighty scream at the top of his voice: *"This is awesome!"*

"Now you know why we love to skate, Rocky. It does make us feel good—wind in our faces and hair, free as a birds" Pieter said.

"What? Don't you think that I can stay upright?" Rocky asked.

"Well, no. Well, yes, we did think that you could do it, but we wanted to be near in case you fell hard," Shayne said.

"Thanks, guys."

"Give us your hands, Rocky. Let's skate in a line. We'll show you how to skate. Don't worry; we won't let you go or let you get hurt," Pieter said.

The four of them—Pieter, Rocky, Shayne, and Jacob—skated in line across the street, with Rocky being pulled along. It was an awesome experience.

"Hey, dudes, what are you up to now?" Rocky asked.

"Don't know. Probably eat something, and chill out at Piet's for a while, and go home, I suppose," Aiden answered. "Why?"

"Feel like a mish, guys?" Rocky asked.

"Yeah, but what?" Pieter said.

"How about we all get into the taxi. I'll get some food, and we can go to Mitch's Shed for a chill-out?"

"Hell yeah," Aiden said. "What do you reckon, guys?"

They all agreed, and Rocky checked on when they needed to be home. "What about the taxi calls, Rocky?" Aiden asked.

"Stuff the taxi. Stuff 'em all. I'm over this effen taxi."

"Hell, you do seem bunted, Rocky," Haydon said.

"Yes, I am, buddy. I'll call in sick. Stuff the lot of them. Right—how about we get some fish and chips or something, some Coke, and go to Mitch's Shed have a feed and a yarn. I'll drop you all off later."

"We'll dub in some cash, Rocky," Aiden said.

"No, man, it's my idea, my buy. It's only money. You fellas treated last night. You gave me that cash for the trip last night when you shouldn't have. I'll use that. It's my turn, okay?"

"Okay, Rocky, you can pay," Pieter said.

"But we must get our gear from Piet's before we go home," Nick said.

"Don't stress, guys. I'll drive you there before I take you home. Just wait here while I drop the taxi and get Midnight Special."

Rocky returned in the Midnight Special about twenty minutes later and the lads all jumped in. "Now, should we get your stuff now or later?"

They all decided to go later. Rocky drove to the fish-and-chips shop and bought a dozen pieces of crumbed and battered fish and heaps of chips, along with a couple bottles of Coke.

"No cups," Rocky said, "but who cares? We're all mates. We can share the bottles around—but no backwash, you guys, especially you, Jacob."

The car pulled alongside Mitch's Shed. All got out, saluted, and went inside. The parcels of food were opened and spread on the paper on the table and the bottles passed on to the next guy.

Rocky spoke about the plans for the following day and the phone conversation he'd had with George earlier. They too wondered why George wanted to see Rocky in private. Some had theories, just as Rocky had. After some discussion about band practice, skating, seeing their mothers about the party after the band competition, the Teen-Morph Foundation they had formed, and the large sum of money they would get, they all climbed aboard the van and went to Piet's. After sorting their clothes, packing their bags, cleaning the barn, and saying goodbye to Piet and his mum, they climbed aboard again, full of laughter and good cheer, and were each dropped off at their homes.

Rocky thanked them for being with him when he needed some good company and saving his sanity by having a great mish.

Aiden was the second to last one left in the van. "Are you going back to work now, Rocky?"

"Hell no. I'm going home now. Like I said, I am over that effen taxi."

"Sorry, man. Settle down," Aiden said.

"Sorry, mate, didn't mean to be abrupt with you. I'm just over it. Listen, like I said before, thanks for being with me tonight when I needed some wicked company. I do feel better now, thanks to all of you guys."

"That's cool. You have been there for us hundreds of times, man. You are always there. It was our turn to talk with you and get you over it," Aiden said, like a man twice his age.

"And thanks for the skate—that was awesome—and the mish. Helped me a lot. See, you guys ask how you will repay me," Rocky said, "but you *just did.*

Aiden got out and said goodbye. "See you tomorrow." He then said to Rocky and Nick, "you two behave now. Don't do anything that I wouldn't do."

"Get ripped; you're just jealous," Rocky said.

"Yeah, eff off. What do you think we are?" Nick asked as he got in the front.

"Only gagging. It's awesome to have mates like you that we can joke like this and mean nuthin' by it. See ya later," Aiden said.

"Yeah, bud, about nine thirty."

Nick said, "Call around on your way to school, and we can ride together."

"Yeah, Nick. See you about eight," Aiden said.

Rocky dropped Nick off at his home and then drove to his own home.

Rocky arrived at Port Vernon High School and went to the administration building, where he signed the visitors' book and told the secretary in the office that he'd come to see Mr. Watson.

"Rocky, you're here," Aiden said. "Always early. Mr. Watson said it was okay to see him at nine thirty."

"Boys, you're not supposed to be here, and you are supposed to be in class," the secretary said. "This is the public area."

"Sorry, miss. Mr. Watson knows that we are here. Rocky has come to see Mr. Watson with us," Nick said. "Sorry."

"Mr. Watson won't be long; he will see you soon, Mr. Scott," she said.

The boys took Rocky to the student waiting area, and they all sat down together. "The others shouldn't be too long," Aiden said.

"Hi, Rocky" said one of the students who also was waiting.

"Oh, hi, Dillon. What's up? You look pissed off," Rocky said.

"I'm in trouble again," Dillon said.

Dillon was another sixteen-year-old who Rocky had contact with from time to time but never gave the impression of being troublesome.

"What do you mean, 'again'?"

"Dunno. Lately I can't do anything right. The teachers give me the shits. One especially. He hates my guts," Dillon said.

"Come on, Dillon, no one could hate you," Rocky said. "What's going on?"

"Every time we have science, Mr. Burke picks on me, and then he gets wild. I say something, and then next day, I get called up here," Dillon said.

"Did this happen on Friday?"

"Yeah, last period."

"What did you say? What happened?"

"I made a mistake, and he fingered me big time. I said, 'Whatever gets your rocks off,' not thinking. He told me to stand outside the room for being rude and disrespectful, so I told him to go and spank the monkey," Dillon said.

Aiden and some of the other students pissed themselves laughing.

"Settle down," Rocky said. "I'm sure you will get into more trouble if you don't stop."

"I don't mean it, Rocky; I didn't even think that he would know what it meant," Dillon said. "Now I am stuffed. I will probably be in detention, or maybe suspended for a week or so."

"Well, you probably shouldn't say those things to most people. If you said that to me, I would have laughed with you, you would have gotten over it, and we would have moved on," Rocky said. "Most adults, especially teachers, don't see the flip side of these things. Teachers must demand a certain level of respect. I guess it is the teacher's job to make sure kids don't say these sorts of things, but they should also have the ability to take a bit of a joke and talk quietly if it offends than, especially in front of other kids. Unfortunately, they don't know any different."

"I know, Rocky. I didn't mean to be rude to him, but he hates me. I forgot I was talking to a teacher; all us kids talk like that to each other all the time," Dillon said. "But he always rips me up the butt."

"Hey, shhh. Don't say those things. Take a couple of deep breaths, think of something good that you have done or want to do, think clearly, and when you go in to see Mr. Watson, don't lose it, man. Keep calm. You will find it won't be that bad. If you don't lose it, you will be back out in no time. You obviously feel sorry; I can tell that. Maybe you can offer to apologize to this teacher. Don't think it is crawling; it's not. It's being diplomatic and making it easy for yourself. Take control."

"Yeah, Rocky, I'll try that," Dillon said.

Pieter, Shayne, and Tony walked in, said hello, and sat down.

Mr. Watson appeared and said, "You must be Mr. Scott. Pleased to meet you. I'm Bob Watson. Come in, and you boys, please come in too." Bob looked at Dillon. "Wait there; I won't be long." He dispatched a couple of others to their classes and told them to come back at lunchtime; some others were also told to wait.

"Sorry, Mr. Scott, it is a busy time after parade. Sorry I'm late."

"Please call me Rick or Rocky."

"I am sorry; I've been meaning to meet you for some time now. Mr. Charles and Mrs. Ruby have told me a lot about you—what you do for our school and what you have done for some of our students. I am very appreciative of that; it does make our jobs a little easier, but more important, it benefits the futures of our students."

"I enjoy helping kids out of whatever hole they find themselves in and try to show them a way forward. We don't always get it right, do we, guys? But we do get there," Rocky said, looking at the boys.

"Are these the four boys going with you to visit Mr. Cleator? I haven't seen these boys or their mates in my office for many months now. Twice in one morning, boys—that must be a record."

"Yes, these guys are coming with me to see Mr. Cleator. He said he contacted you and that you gave permission," Rocky said.

"Yes, yes. That's right. George tells me he is seeing you at ten. I have had several discussions with him over the past three days. These are very exciting times. What do you say about it, Shayne?'

"It's fantastic, sir," Shayne said. "We are all so excited about the band festival and the party afterward and the plans we have with Rocky to carry on looking after other kids."

"I don't know about that. What's happening? What plan to help other kids?" Bob asked.

"Sir, we have accepted Mr. Cleator's invitation to be the bene … Ah, bin … Oh, *benefactor* from the rock festival, and we have already talked about how we are going to use some money on activities to help Rocky help other kids who are like we were," Aiden said.

"That's great. Why don't you drop by sometime with all the boys and tell me about it? Maybe bring Mr. Scott with you," Bob said.

"Okay, sir," Aiden said.

"Well, that's great news. No wonder George is so excited, but he wouldn't tell me. However, Mr. Scott, he has spoken to me about some ideas he has to put to you. That's between Mr. Cleator and you, but I'm sure we will be seeing more of you in the future. Please do drop in sometime. 1 want to pick your brains on how you do it—turning that gang, who were the terror group of the school, into happy, responsible, and respectable role models. They really are our best ambassadors. I should give them a school award at the end of term. I'll make a note of it."

He wrote in his diary and then said, "Anyway, Mr. Scott, congratulations on your achievements in showing these boys a purpose, a reason to come to school, and a future. Well done, sir! Okay, Pieter, Shayne, Tony, and Aiden, good luck with Mr. Cleator. Do yourselves proud, your school proud, and Mr. Scott proud. Please report to me when you get back. Rick … err,

Rocky, thanks for your interest in our students and assisting our school. Have a good meeting with George."

"Thanks, Bob. Thanks for your good words, but these guys did it. I only took the time to care, talk with them, and listen to their fears, their problems, and hang-ups. I told them of certain choices that might get them their goals—that simple. They did it, Bob. Oh, I can't help myself. I saw Dillon out there. I have known him for a while and didn't expect to see him in trouble. I had a brief talk with him while I was waiting. I would be keen to hear how you find his attitude today, if you don't mind."

"Well, if his attitude has changed for the better, that's great," Bob said. "Maybe you can spend some time with him."

"We'll see how he does. Really, all I do is talk about attitudes and choices, with a few jokes thrown in, a little encouragement, some life skills, and a bit of manual activity, if needed—not much else."

"I better let you all go, or you will be late. I'll look forward to talking more soon."

"Sure, Bob. It's been great meeting you, and I would love to speak again soon," Rocky said. "Have a good day."

"I'll try; you too. See you later, boys," Bob said.

"See you, Dillon," Rocky said as they left the office. "Good luck, champ, and remember what we spoke about."

"Yeah. I've been practicing what you said in my head," Dillon said.

"What do you think of Mr. Watson, Rocky?" Aiden asked as they got into the car.

"Oh, he's okay, a typical principal, but he's okay."

"He is good to us now, but he used to rip us up big time," Shayne said.

"Yeah, but you know why. Like I said to you guys way back then, treat people right, and they'll treat you right. Give them respect, and you will get respect. All attitudes and choices—you know it all."

"Yeah, when you said that—attitudes and choices—did you see his face? Were you getting up him, Rocky?" Aiden said.

"No, not really. I just said it because I believe it's true and to jolt people's brains into another gear and give them something to think about. I love to stuff with people's heads and emotions to make 'em realize that guys your age do have feelings, thoughts, and opinions. They just need to be fine-tuned 'cause they may not be correct. You need to be shown, quietly and respectfully, what is right."

"You get bunted, Rocky, don't you?" Pieter said.

"Sorry, guys, yes, I do. I get annoyed at people my age not listening to guys like you. They just have blank minds and stubborn attitudes to guys like you. What's this Mr. Burke like?"

"He's a real prick," Tony said.

"We think he went to an all-boys school, and he takes it out on boys to get even or something," Pieter said. "He hates boys; he must have been a real nerd and got picked on or something."

The car pulled into the Cleator Enterprises car park in front of a very large modern building that seemed to ooze millions of dollars.

"Wow, what a building," Pieter said. "Look at it—like a palace."

"Yeah, it is flash, isn't it? Good on him; he has made it, and he wants to show it. Can't blame him; he told me where he was at sixteen or seventeen. He found a way to change course and make something of his life. Like you guys. I know that's why he is doing what he is for you guys and me. He told me so; I will get him to tell you his story someday."

"Truly. Just imagine, Pieter, if he was like us and then got this. I wish I could do something to get me somewhere like this. That's awesome," Tony said.

"Yeah, mate, you can also make like he has, if you set your mind to it. You gotta remember, like I told you, you can do anything if you really want it, and aim for it, and work very hard at it, and get up every time someone or something knocks your arse over. Yeah, sometimes you can make the lucky breaks and get much more than you imagine, but basically, find what you want in life, and go for it."

"Why aren't you like that guy—you know, rich and very successful?" Aiden said.

"Well, I set different goals. First, wanted to have a happy and productive life—got it; have a good family life—got it; to get over my illness—did it; get back into the community and be productive—done it; help teenagers achieve their life goals—doing it," Rocky said. "I have done that with you guys and a few others before you, but there is more to do yet."

"You haven't told us about your illness yet, Rocky," Pieter said.

"Yes, I know. I have told you briefly, just enough to give examples of how to change, but most of all, don't let any prick tell you that you can't do something. Like something else I've told you many times, do it; if it feels good, keep doing it; if it doesn't, forget it, and try something else."

"Yeah, I remember that," Pieter said, "and it does work, Rocky."

"Yep, sure does, Piet," Rocky said. "Now, before we go in, I want you to think about some basics I taught you way back. Remember, give a firm handshake, just like you mean it. Be polite. Look people in the eye when you talk. And hats, remember. What hat are you going to wear now?"

"The responsible hat," Aiden answered.

"Yep, that's it. Just treat this meeting like a job interview. It isn't, but it will be similar."

As the boys and Rocky approached the main entrance, the door slid open automatically. Inside, the decor was just as lavish as the foyer of a five-star hotel—deep crimson-and-black patterned carpet, very expensive marble and timber coffee tables, surrounded by mahogany lounge chairs covered with rich, deep-red crushed velvet and large pieces of artwork on the wall. Other walls were covered with photos of people, buildings, and bridges that the company had constructed.

Straight ahead was a very large black-and-white marble reception desk, and just to the right was a glass, box thirteen feet by six feet, that held a model of the company's newest project. Rocky looked at the boys and noticed four faces with eyes very wide and mouths open, looking as if they had seen something out of this world. They approached the visitors' section of the reception desk and saw it was attended by a very well-dressed young woman of about twenty-five, with honey-blonde hair, very clear tanned skin, and an awesome smile with very white teeth. In fact, all the women behind the desk were very well dressed, very well groomed, and extremely polite. Not all were as young as the woman in front of them but equally beautiful.

"May I help you?" asked the young lady, whose badge indicated her name was Cindy.

"I'm Rick Scott, here to see Mr. Cleator, please. He is expecting us." The boys were still wide-eyed and stuck like glue close to Rocky.

"Oh yes, Mr. Scott. I will let him know that you are here" Cindy said. She spoke into her phone. "Mr. Cleator, Mr. Scott is here with the four young students from Port Vernon High. Shall I bring them in?" She listened for a moment and then hung up the phone. Smiling at Rick, she said, "Mr. Cleator will be out in a moment or two. My, you must be special."

"Oh, why is that?" Rocky asked.

"Mr. Cleator doesn't usually come out to greet his guests. I have only seen it once before, and that was for the prime minister, when he visited last year." Cindy smiled again. "He won't be long."

"Thank you, Cindy." Rocky took the liberty of using her name. "We'll look at the photos while we wait."

The group moved over to the photo wall, looking at the construction jobs that the company had completed, as well as all sorts of people—dignitaries, people in casual wear, and people in work gear, including helmets and overalls.

"Oh, there you are," George called out. "That's part of our photo gallery."

"How are you, George? This is very impressive," Rocky said.

"Yes, I suppose it is. The whole company is very proud of these photos; they represent the blood, sweat, and tears that my staff have put into their work."

"George, let me introduce the guys to you. This is Tony, Aiden, Shayne, and Pieter. Guys, this is Mr. Cleator." George shook their hands, and Rocky said proudly, "George, these are four of the gang—two band members and two supporters—but all part of a very respectable and responsible group of young achievers."

"Welcome, boys, and to you, Rick. Welcome to Cleator Enterprises. Rick, it's good to see you." George shook Rocky's hand. "Come on in to my office, and we will talk a little."

George's office was a very large room, set up like a living room. The decor was similar to the entrance foyer, with the addition of plush velvet-like cladding on two adjacent walls and the other two walls painted in a rich cream color, with a large TV screen and photos on one wall and more photos on the other painted wall.

In the far-left corner was a very large marble desk and the biggest executive chair imaginable. To the right sat another marble desk, two chairs, a three-seater, two velvet-covered lounge chairs, a very large mahogany table with twelve chairs (obviously a board table), a large timber-and-marble coffee table with several smaller chairs upholstered in the same velvet as the lounge chairs, and, in the other corner, a bar. The lighting was very flash; several down lights illuminated areas to highlight furniture and art objects, and wall wash lights to draw your eyes to paintings or create an ambient atmosphere set at different brightness levels.

"Boys, would you like to sit at the board table or over here at the coffee table?" George asked.

"Can we sit around the coffee table, please? It's really awesome," Pieter said, still in awe.

"I would prefer to sit here too. The other is a bit formal, isn't it?" George said.

As they sat down, George offered coffee for Rick and juice or water for the boys.

"A coffee would be great. Thanks, George," Rocky said.

"Yes, please," the boys answered.

"Melody will get it for you," George said, as he pushed a button on a panel on the wall. "Melody, can you please come in and serve my guests some refreshments." He then pushed other buttons on the panel, and the lighting pattern changed to highlight the coffee table area and dimmed in the other areas of the office. "I love these buttons. I could play with them all day," George said.

Melody came into the room, took the orders, and retreated to the preparation area.

"Now, boys, let's start. I'll give you time to relax. You seem so nervous and in awe. As I told Mr. Scott, I've invited you and your mothers to the sponsors' dinner that I host after the Youth Rocks Music Fest next Saturday. I gave Mr. Scott passes to the festival, as you know, and if you need more, that's okay. Now, at the sponsors' dinner, we'll have all the sponsors in attendance, some civic leaders and dignitaries, representatives from the high school, some of my key personnel from my company, the winning band, the people's choice winner and the runners-up, and a charity, sports or special-interest group. This group is always youth-oriented; after all, the rock festival is all about youth. Don't hesitate if you need to ask questions, boys; just stop me. I do get carried away at times."

The boys nodded but didn't speak.

"After I met Rick in his taxi on the way to the meeting on Saturday night and after heavy discussions with several members of the business community and Mr. Watson, Mr. Charles, and Mrs. Ruby from the high school, and the fact that I have heard a lot about this man"—he pointed to Rocky—"and what he has done for young kids off the streets, mainly you boys, I have been so impressed, and you boys should be proud."

"We are," Aiden said, taking the leader's role.

"And we are so happy that Rocky found us and showed us how things could be better. You know, he was right; things have been better for us since we listened and took notice of him," Shayne said.

"Yeah, if it wasn't for him, we probably would be dead or in jail or something," Pieter said.

"Yes, you are so lucky boys. He has done a lot with you and for you, and by all accounts, you have shown a great attitude toward him, your school, your friends, and the community. Congratulations. Moving on, I asked Mr. Scott to discuss with you my invitation to attend the sponsors' dinner and receive half of the income from ticket sales, as the community beneficiaries. Mr. Scott tells me that you wish to accept my invitation. I am so happy about that. Now, tell me what you have arranged so far. Just take your time. This is not a test. I have a list of things I need to know so I can finalize arrangements. I will ask you as we come to the items. Remember—no pressure. Who will start? I need to know how many for the theater and how many for the function."

"Sir, we have twenty-two people attending the theater and twenty-seven at the dinner," Aiden answered.

"So, you need two more concert passes, and I will arrange twenty-seven tickets for the dinner. Next item, permission letters from your mothers. We need these because you are all minors."

The boys chuckled.

"What's the matter? What's funny?" George asked.

"Aw, just a joke about minors. Rocky has been teasing me every time *minors* is said because I said I hated being a minor who needs permission for everything," Pieter said.

"Don't be in too much of a hurry to grow up, Pieter. You will have plenty of time for that," George said, laughing.

"I have all the permission letters from everyone's mum here," Pieter said, handing over a folder.

"How's that for organization, Rick? You have them on the ball," George said. "Thanks, Pieter."

"Yes. I impressed on them how important it was," Rocky said, surprising even himself with his business-like response.

"Mr. Scott tells me that you have formed a committee and have a name to register so that you can collect the money. That's great. Tell me about your arrangements."

"Rocky helped us run a meeting yesterday morning, and we learned how to elect a committee executive, I think it is called," Aiden said.

"That's good, Aiden. Tony, who are the executive members?" George asked.

"Sir, Aiden was elected president, Declan is the vice president, Pieter is the secretary, and Jacob, who we call Jay, is treasurer," Tony said, reading from Pieter's notes.

"And our mate here is our patron," Shayne said.

"Oh, that's good. You must be honored, Rick," George said.

"Yes, George, I am honored and proud of their ability to follow directions on running meetings and electing office-bearers and the other decisions they made."

"Fantastic. You boys are going to go a long way; I can tell," George said. "Now, what would you do with something like seven thousand dollars?"

"Well, sir," Aiden began, "we thought we would build on it somehow and use it for music equipment, some water sports equipment, maybe build a skate ramp, and use some to help Rocky to help other kids like us."

Pieter added, "We want to help other kids when we get a bit older. We don't really want to move away from Rocky, so the best way is to stay around him and help kids like he helped us."

"That's very admirable, boys. That's like repaying your debt to society for the chance that was given to you. That's great, boys," George said.

"I think it is great too, George. I think you can imagine how I feel about that decision. They have asked many, many times how they can repay me. I tell them that they continually do it, just by their actions, their attitudes, and their thoughtfulness," Rocky said.

"Yes, I agree," George said. "Have you thought about a name for your organization? As I told Mr. Scott, I will look after the paperwork and the legal issues so that you are qualified to accept the money."

"It's called the Teen-Morph Foundation," Tony said.

"How wonderful. That comes from metamorphosis? I haven't heard that word for so long. Did Mr. Scott help you with that name?"

"Yeah," Tony said. "It means teens, changing for the better."

"Yes, it does; how fitting," George said. "I suppose you haven't designed a logo or badge by any chance?"

"Not yet. Haydon and Jay and Nick do art at school, and we were trying to work one out last night," Aiden said. "We don't even have one for the band yet."

"That doesn't matter," George said. "You won't need one yet. I was thinking of having a name badge for each of you. Each badge will have your name. The committee members, will include your position on a second line under your name. The other members, the word director, under your name. After all, you now have a board of directors, the people who start a company or organization become directors. I thought a gold background with black lettering, like this model," George said, showing a colored sketch of a badge. "One of my commercial artists drew it up this morning."

"That's awesome, Mr. Cleator," Shayne said. "Thank you very much."

"Okay, settled. I will have them made up before Friday, so you can wear them on Saturday. Now, be proud of your organization and your badge. Mr. Watson knows all about this, and he said when you get your organization name and your badges, you can wear them as part of your school uniform. I will get two of each, one for school and one for formal occasions. I have your names and your positions, so I will send a copy to my stationery department to have them done. Let's use only first names; we don't need last names."

"Can you do two for Rocky, please, sir?" Aiden asked. "One with his proper name, Roderick Scott, and the other one with 'Rocky,' for when we are mucking about and not at an official place."

"Yes, sure, Aiden, that is as good as done, son. Guys, well done on your mature attitude with all of this," George said. "Thank you for accepting our invitation to the rock festival sponsors' dinner and your input into this meeting. I would love to meet the whole group, preferably before Saturday, so that I can learn more about you."

"George, I will discuss it with the guys, and call you to see if you can fit us in," Rocky said.

"Thanks, Rick. Give me a call to let me know a time. I can shuffle my appointments to suit," George said. "Guys, I will see you in the next few days."

"Sir, as president of Teen-Morph, I would like to thank you on behalf of the guys for your kindness and generosity," Aiden said.

"You have been practicing that, haven't you? You will go a long way, son; that's your first official duty as president, and you are genuinely very proud, aren't you?" George said. "I can tell by the look on Mr. Scott's face that he didn't coach you with that. Very good, Aiden." George shook Aiden's hand.

"Bye for now, fellas,"

"Yes, George, I will be back as soon as I get these heroes back to school."

Rocky went to the reception desk and said goodbye to the women; then he joined the four boys as they left the building.

"Wow, Rocky, isn't this an awesome place?" Aiden said. "And Mr. Cleator is so generous to us. Can't wait to tell the other guys."

"Yeah, he is fantastic to do all this for us, and it's all because of you, Rocky," Pieter said. "Can't wait for the band competition and the party, it's going to be awesome."

"It's all happening guys. Shows you that good things can happen if you do right by people, be positive, and believe in yourselves," Rocky said. "Tony and Shayne, you two aren't saying much. What's up?"

Tony and Shayne usually didn't say much; they were more the listen-and-learn type, where Aiden and Pieter were more the leaders and the talkers.

"Oh, nuthin', Rocky. Just can't get my head around all of this. I am not used to good things coming my way," Tony said. "I just can't believe it is happening."

"You better believe it's true. You're not in the middle of a dream. See? I'll show you," Rocky said.

"I can't believe it either," Shayne said. "It's just too awesome."

"Okay, fellas," Rocky said as they got into the car and put on their seat belts. "It's all true, and it's not only because of me. Sure, I talked with you, I suggested alternatives to you, and I listened to you when the chips were down. I literally cradled you and hugged you when your sorrow was too much for you to bear, and we cried together. But it was you guys, each one of you, who decided to listen and follow my suggestions, listen to my never-ending sermons, and accept my friendship and concern for you that got you here today. You chose to follow and change your attitudes toward other kids, adults, your families, your school, and your lives to get you here. This, guys, is only the start of what's ahead—your futures. It all starts here and now. I can feel it in my gut."

Tears welled in Rocky's eyes as he spoke from deep within his heart. He looked around; everyone had tears in their eyes as the reality of what was then and what was now began to sink in.

Rocky wiped his eyes. "Enough of my preaching. I know you have heard it all before. You must be sick of hearing it by now. Sorry, guys, I do go on, but I can't help it."

"It's cool, big fella. We speak about you talking a lot of times. You know, we love hearing it from you because we know you are not bullshitting. You mean what you say, Rocky," Shayne said. "We all agree on that."

"That's right, Rocky," Aiden said. "We do love it because it reminds us of the past and the present, and now we know we have a future like nothin' else."

"Rocky, one of your fave sayings—and you have a few—is 'Remember the good times with a passion, but never forget the bad times. Learn from them and move on.' We think about that a lot, especially when something goes wrong, and it helps us," Pieter said. "That's what is so good. We do enjoy the good times—the times with you are always good—but like it says, we do go back and think of the bad things, and we see we have learned, and we are going to the future."

"That's effen awesome, guys," Rocky said, with tears flowing down his face. "I am so happy I'm howling. I'm so happy that I have contributed a little bit to your futures."

"A little? Not a little but an effen lot to our futures," Pieter said. "Hey, Rocky, pull over to the park up here. It's time for a group hug. You're crying, I'm crying, we are all effen crying. What the hell is goin' on here? We are supposed to be happy."

Rocky pulled into the park, and they all jumped out. "Hey, guys, we are happy. We are not crying because we're sad. We're crying because we are normal guys who have emotions and feelings. That's good to have emotions and feelings. It is okay to cry. Like I told you, big boys can and do cry. Don't ever be ashamed. Okay, group hug," Rocky said, as they all hugged together and threw their hands in the air. "The future," he said.

They all got back into the car and continued back to the school; no one said a word. Suddenly, the song "I Still Haven't Found What I'm Lookin' For" played on the stereo. Shayne, who was sitting in the front, reached over and turned the volume up very loud, and they all sang along with the song. When it was over, Shayne returned the volume to where it was.

"That was insane. That stereo is wicked; it's effen awesome," Tony said. "I know we have picked the right song for the competition with that one."

"Yeah, man, that stereo is wicked," Pieter said as they pulled into the school car park.

"Before you go, Aiden, Pieter, do you have your mobiles with you?" Rocky asked.

They both indicated that they did.

"Can you get the other guys together and tell them what happened today? I'll text both of you after I have seen George again. It seems I'll have more to tell you," Rocky said, realizing that the rule about telling all the guys at the same time could be broken this time. He wanted to get the news to them as soon as possible and couldn't wait to get them together.

"What do you think he wants you for?" Aiden asked.

"Don't know, mate," Rocky said. "It must be important."

"I hope it is good, Rocky. Can't think what else good can happen to us. Must be good for you. Hope it is something wicked for you," Pieter said.

"I'll see. I will let you know the next step in the life of the Teen-Morph Foundation and Nuver Chanz after I talk to George. Have an awesome day, and remember, rock on, brothers," Rocky said.

"Rock on, bro," they replied.

Rocky drove back to George's office, still wondering what was next. What else could George put to him?

CHAPTER 10

✧ ‹‹ ‹› ≫ ≫› ⋘ ⋘› ⋙› ⋙› ⋙› ⋙› ⋙› ⋙› ⋘ ⋘ ⋘ ≫ ≫ ✧

**Please let me say—you really are a legend, a
champion, to help those downtrodden and
forgotten teenage boys become champions.**

"Welcome back, Rick," George said. "Please sit down."

The atmosphere seemed a bit more formal than his last visit just thirty minutes earlier.

"Thanks, George, what did you think of the lads? Aren't they great?" Rocky said, trying to get the conversation off on a good note.

"Yes, Rick, but they are better than great; they are absolutely terrific," George said enthusiastically. "I can see why you are so proud of them and, equally, why they absolutely admire you and love being near you. They just had a glow about them, an aura that didn't stop glowing. Now, Rick, I want to talk to you about a few things that I hope will interest you. I don't really know where to start. I am really in awe of you and respect you immensely as a human being, a man, and a mentor. I'll give it a go and see where we find ourselves.

"I have known of you for quite some time. Some of my business acquaintances have spoken highly of you and your achievements; some of my employees either know of you or know you. One of them helped you coach that winning football team four or so years back. Your team of 'no-hopers' beat the team that my nephew played in—in that grand final.

"Bob and John from the high school speak highly of you also, even though you hadn't actually met Bob until this morning. He's been aware of you and your volunteer role. I am sorry I didn't seek you out earlier; we wouldn't find ourselves in such a hurry as we are now. However, the pressure is off a little as you looked ahead and helped the boys organize their group. I must admit I was very impressed with them and your guidance. There was nothing that I needed that wasn't available from those boys."

"Oh, George, the guys organized themselves. I merely planted the seed and gave them pointers, and they picked up the ball and ran with it," Rocky said.

"I hope you don't mind my mentioning this, but I understand that a few years ago you were seriously ill and almost lost your life and that you battled all odds to get over it."

"Yeah, that's right. It was a difficult time for me and my family, but I kept my eye on the ball and constantly made myself have positive thoughts and goals, and the bonus for me was that I got back into the workforce and defied the so-called experts who said that I would not be any good to anyone and that I would never work again. George, no one tells Rocky that he can't do it; he will prove you wrong every time."

"I can see that, and I admire that attitude, Rick. Now to continue— and once again, I apologize for bringing this up—but I have also heard that since then, and with your wife's illness, medical bills piled up, mortgage got behind, you refinanced twice, and you still found yourself financially embarrassed to the point that you have sold your house to repay your debts."

"Yes, that's right," Rocky said. "You really have done your homework, haven't you?"

"Rick, sorry if this upsets you. Please forgive me. I do find this hard to talk about with you, as I found out about it from others, rather than you, but I have a plan for you, which I will save till later in this conversation.

I also sense that you are not really happy in your job as a taxi driver. I understand that you enjoy some aspects, but at the end of the day, a person has to be entirely happy in their work."

"Yes, that's right. I do enjoy most of the passengers, but the eighty hours or so that I must put in for so little return is a strain, and with Suzie not being able to work, it's also a strain on the available cash. She is in a wheelchair, you know. Some of the proceeds from the sale of the house, I hope, will fund the surgery that she needs to, hopefully, allow her to walk again. Last night, when you phoned, I was probably at my lowest. I had started work at three that afternoon and got my first fare at about four thirty. He was drunk, scum, a proper drop-kick; he refused to pay the fare—a mere $4.50 or something like that—so I pushed him out of the taxi and drove off. I am not proud of that; if one of the boys did something like that, I would be a bit disappointed."

"What did you do next?" George asked.

"I went to a different rank and sat for the next job," Rocky said. "Then you phoned. After that, I dozed off and woke up to rattling, scraping noises and a bit of skylarking. I woke in a fright as a handful of faces peered in the window, yelling my name. It was the guys on their way home; they had decided to detour to see if they could find me. We had a yarn and decided that we would go to the park that they frequent, and I treated them to fish and chips for dinner. Aiden loaned me his skate-board, so I went for a skate, with two of them shadowing me as if they were my protectors. It must have looked funny, but hell, it was just what I needed to clear my head."

"That's a story, Rick," George said. "Fantastic. Back to what I was saying—you have overcome a severe illness, engineered your life to attempt to overcome financial hardship, are still working to make a quid, trying to look after your family issues, and have found time to help children out of a hole and place them on the summit of a mountain. Please let me say you really are a legend—a champion—to help those downtrodden and forgotten teenage boys become champions."

"The boys call me that, a legend. I only do what I feel I need to do to assist others," Rocky said.

"What I would like to do, Rick, is this: I have a large parcel of land at the mouth of Coachman's Creek, fronting the creek and the ocean, that was used as a caravan park and camp for construction workers when we were building the coal-loading plant and container wharfs on the harbor several years ago. It's been idle for a couple of years now. We have a well-equipped workshop there, where some of my maintenance staff work on repairs to equipment and office furniture and so on. It also has a few cabins, the amenities block, several other buildings and sheds, and a jetty that was used to ferry workers and equipment to the harbor construction site. As I said, except for some of our maintenance workers, it stands idle. I don't want to sell it, but it is deteriorating and is vandalized on a continual basis. Now, what I would like to happen is this: you live on the site and become the caretaker of it."

Rocky attempted to respond, but George said, "Wait till I finish, Rick, please. I need to tell you all. Now, as well as caretaker, I would like you to work for me at that site as the permanent maintenance foreman, maintaining equipment and so on that would be taken there for repairs. I know your work background, and I know that you are well qualified. What I envisage is that other maintenance people who work for me will still use the workshop, and you could instruct, assist, and teach the younger staff on site. I know it will work because you have the amazing ability and patience to help young people. You do it every day without trying."

"That's …" Rocky tried to say.

George put his hand up to stop him. "I am not finished yet. There is much more, Rick. As well as that, I would like you to continue with your work with your kids, and what I got from your kids is that they want to help you help other kids. I think that this area would be great for them too. It is a very large area, a lot of wide-open spaces, and some buildings and shelters that would be ideal for your work with developing skills with boys. I had planned to develop the site down the track as a youth center, but I think that you are better suited to doing this for me and that this plan has more merit. The place is overgrown, but I would imagine they would love to clear it, develop their own ideas into actions, and produce an area of their own to be proud of. I will insist that any construction on the site meets building standards and obtain council approvals. Our people— architects, plant operators, builders—would be enlisted to do all of that. Bob also wants to be involved, to the point of asking for your assistance in taking groups with their teachers for practical experiences. You will be free to use your time as you see fit—work, personal, mentoring, and the high school. Now, what do you think, Rick? I'm excited. What about you?"

"George, I feel so excited and, at the same time, so humbled by your offer and plans. I am a little lost for words, but I have this vision of many kids developing life skills that they would never have had the opportunity to experience, ever in their lives. George, it's fantastic. I will have to digest it, talk to my family, and think it through. Thank you very much. I am so appreciative of your gesture. I am going to say yes right now. I am sure everyone in my life will agree."

"Fantastic," George said. He held his hand out to shake Rocky's hand. "Welcome to the team at Cleator's."

"Thanks, George. Thanks heaps."

"Oh, I didn't tell you—the wage will be between $45,000 and $50,000 per year, holidays, all the usual. Rent and electricity are free, and a Ute is supplied. No, let's make it a round $50,000—just made that decision, no matter what the accountant says. Also, I neglected to tell you that we have mountains of leftover building materials from our constructions that the boys can use for their projects. I never throw anything away. Recycle it, and teach kids to recycle, Rick. When you get to a stage of clearing some of the site, we will transfer it over for you, sort it, and stack it for your use. Maybe locate an area adjacent to the park site outside the fence. I own all that land over there, so if ever you need more land, let me know. Here are the keys. Please look it over. The cabins will need some attention, but I'll organize a foreman and some apprentices to renovate wherever you wish to live and make it comfortable for you and your family."

"I am lost for words, George. This is very generous of you."

"You are welcome, Rick. I have wanted to develop that site as a youth center for some time but didn't know how to go about it. If it's kept like it is now, instead of some giant building, and with you running it, that's the way to go. And I need to invest some cash into the community. When I met you the other night, I knew that this was the best thing I could do for our future adults."

"Can I give the park a name, George?" Rocky asked.

"Sure, what are you thinking?" George asked.

"I would like to name it simply Teen-Morph Youth Center, with the subheading, 'Changing Our Youth's Lives for the Better!'—with some mention of Cleator Enterprises, as the supporters."

"That's okay by me," George said. "I thought you would want to do something like that. Now, take the keys. They are your set. Visit the site with your boys, let them look around and dream their dreams. Think about it and get back to me with their views. Now, Rick, if you would excuse me, I have another meeting."

Rocky got up from his chair, saying, "Thank you sincerely, and on behalf of the Teen-Morphs, thank you."

"I'll talk with you soon," George said as they shook hands. As Rocky turned to leave the room, George said, "Oh, I forgot—you probably realized that my talk with the boys on the phone on Saturday night and earlier today was like a job interview with them. Please be assured that if any of them want a job with us, they are straight in."

"Thanks, George, thanks again. See you soon."

Rocky left the building and texted a message to Pieter and Aiden that he wanted to see the group as soon as they were available for an important mish and to text back a suitable time. The message came back: "At school when school gets out." Rocky spent the next two hours at his home, trying to comprehend all that was put to him.

Rocky was waiting for the boys outside the school in the Midnight Special. As each one raced up to his van, they wanted to know what was happening, what the urgent mish was all about.

"I'll tell you when we get going," he told each one of them. They all piled in, there were enough seats for six of them, and the other four got into the chill-out zone and were told to sit quietly without attracting attention to themselves. If he was more organized, he would have fitted the other seats in the rear to accommodate them legally.

As he drove, he informed them of the points that George had spoken about, but he didn't tell them where they were going; that was to be the surprise. They were excited by what Rocky had told them and at the same time in a state of shock and disbelief.

As they approached the waterfront, they asked where he was taking them and why. He ignored their questions until he pulled up at the very large metal gate and seven-foot–high fence surrounding the property.

"You can't go here," Pieter said. "This place is a security area, Rocky. Why are we here?"

Rocky's face was highlighted by a very wide smile. As he fumbled to find the keys that he placed in the console, he said, "Who says we can't go here? These keys say that I can." He found the key to the gate, handed it to Aiden, who was sitting in the front seat, and said, "Open the gate, buddy."

"What's going down, Rocky? We can't go in there," Aiden insisted.

"It's cool, fellas. Listen to me, guys. Welcome to … Teen-Morph headquarters. Go on, open the gate, and then get back in the car."

Aiden unlocked the gate, swung it open, and the boys yelled, *"Awesome!"*

Aiden got in the car, and Pieter said, "What do you mean, Teen-Morph headquarters?"

"It's now known as Teen-Morph Youth Center. It's ours, fellas, and I will explain more when we drive in," Rocky said.

The car rounded the first bend in the road around the very large workshop and past a couple of cabins. Rocky yelled, "Effen awesome! Look at that. Eff me. I always wanted to live in one of those."

"What do you mean?" Jacob said.

"Are you going to live here, Rocky?"

"Yeah, dude. This is where I am going to live and work," he said.

"Are you going to work for Mr. Cleator?" Shayne asked.

"That's right, champ. He has offered me a job."

They got out of the car and wandered around as Rocky told them the full story. His new job, the things that could be done here, how he and the group could use it as their base to teach and rescue other boys, and how school groups could come and visit.

"Do you want to live in railway carriages, Rocky?" Pieter asked.

"Yeah, mate, all my life I have dreamed of living in railway carriages. This blows my head," Rocky said.

"Will we be able to live here sometimes, Rocky?" Haydon asked. "That would be wicked."

"Are we able to plan and build things and work in the workshop?" Tony asked.

"Yeah, fellas, the whole lot is ours to use. Everything. We need to clean it up and rebuild a few things, anything we want. You now have a creek, a beach, a jetty for your water sports activities, space for a skate park, plenty of bush for tracks, and plenty of buildings that you can rebuild so that you can live in on weekends and holidays. Look at that area over there—what sort of stage could you use that for? You can have concerts, anything you want."

"When can we start?" Pieter asked.

"As soon as you want, but we better wait until after the rock fest is over. You can start thinking of what to plan and what to do. You know, you now have entered the most amazing stage of your lives. You all have earned this, just by a few of you talking to George on the phone the other night and this morning in his office. You have a committee in place now, and the rest are directors of the Teen-Morph Foundation. You are now also directors of the Teen-Morph Youth Center. How about that? Oh, George also said all of you automatically qualify for a job at Cleator Enterprises if you ever want one. How about that?

"Anyway, I gotta go to work tonight for a boring Monday night again, and you blokes better get home. Your mums will be worried. Did any of you contact your mums before you came with me?" Rocky asked.

Each answered that he had. They left the site, Pieter locked the gate, and Rocky delivered each to their homes, and then drove home to get ready for work.

Rocky picked up the taxi on time to start his shift. He asked some other drivers how the Sunday night had turned out. He discovered that it was the quietest Sunday in a long time. Rocky didn't feel so bad at not finishing his shift. He wondered how this shift was going to go, as Monday's were traditionally quieter than Sundays.

Rocky's thoughts turned to what changes he should make to his roster. He usually had Wednesday or Thursday off, so he thought that he'd better work it out and tell the taxi owner what changes to his roster that he required.

Rocky dialed Aiden's number.

"Hi, Rocky, what's doing?"

"Hi, Mr. President," Rocky said to Aiden. "I'm great. How about you?"

"Awesome. Still havin' trouble believin' today—the last few days, really. It's unbelievable."

"Yeah, it is a lot to take in, isn't it? It really is the best outcome, a great opportunity. I think it will be fantastic when we get it up and working," Rocky said. "Listen, bud, I rang to find out what we need to do and what we need to organize this week, leading up to Saturday. I am going to phone the boss to get the roster changed so that I can be there Saturday night. I can't concentrate on things; I am so excited about everything that is happening."

"I don't really know, Rocky. I guess it's all done; we just gotta practice our songs and try on the clothes we'll be wearing. I see that dress code is 'smart casual' for the party, so I suppose the band stays in the clothes that we wear onstage." Aiden said.

"Smart casual can mean jeans and a short-sleeved or long-sleeved shirt, and shoes, or you can dress up a bit. So, your jeans or black trousers and white shirts would be okay. You could wear a buttoned shirt over the top of your T-shirts if you wanted to."

"What are you wearing, Rocky?"

"Haven't thought about it yet. I will find something in my wardrobe that should do."

"Can you catch up with us on Friday night for a couple of hours? We need to do a few things with you."

"Well, I don't know how busy it might be on Friday night. Can't really tell yet. Tell you what; I might change to day shift on Friday, so I can have Friday night off."

"Cool, that's awesome. We might go to Piet's barn and have a mish. What do you reckon? A barbecue, a swim, a jam session, then just chill out?" Aiden said.

"Yeah, sounds wicked. You tell me a time, and I'll be there, buddy. Sounds wicked."

"I'll talk with the boys tomorrow at school, and we will work it out. Just the usual—a couple of dollars each for food be okay?" Aiden asked.

"Yeah, sure, let me know if you want me to get the stuff. I can do it during day shift if you like. If anything else comes up, ring me, and if I get something from George, I'll ring you."

"Sweet man. I'll see you then."

"Yeah mate, see ya. Stay cool," Rocky said.

Rocky then phoned the taxi owner and put to him the changes to the roster that he required to allow him to be at Piet's barn on Friday night and be at the theater on Saturday afternoon and night. The changes were okay with the boss, as was usually the case if he needed time off.

The next few days passed very quickly, with some contact with George to finalize some arrangements regarding the Teen-Morph Foundation and between Rocky and the guys discussing minor issues, so everything would fall into place. George had notified him that the name badges were ready for collection on Friday. Rocky accepted the proposal when George presented it: "I am going to say yes right now. I am sure everyone in my life will agree." Rocky had contacted the boys to put some thoughts on paper so that he could help them prepare a speech for the dinner. He also made notes for his speech in case he needed one. Arrangements were made for a small party at Piet's barn on Friday night. Everything seemed set by the time Friday came around.

On Friday morning, Rocky called to George's office to collect the name badges. They were awesome. They had a gold background with black printing, with the words *Teen-Morph Foundation* on the top line, the person's name on the second line, and their position on the bottom line—two of each, as George suggested, one for school and one for formal occasions.

"I have made a few changes, Rick. I hope you and the lads don't mind. You will notice I have changed the word *president* to *chairman*. It sounds more professional, and I left the surnames off except with yours."

"Yeah, that's great. I think that chairman does sound better than president, and I agree that surnames are better left off. We don't usually identify surnames of kids, and the school is the same," Rocky said.

"Now," George said, as he pulled another box from his drawer, "I took the liberty of doing this." He removed the lid, and Rocky saw another set of badges, more awesome than the first set. They too were rectangular, maroon in color, with gold lettering with black shadowing on the right side and bottom of each letter. The wording was the same layout; the top line read *Teen-Morph Youth Center* and the bottom line read Foundation *Director*, instead of the position held. Rocky's was slightly different; it was like the others except it also had a gold border, and the bottom line read *Chief Executive Officer.* There were also two sets for each person.

"That's terrific, George. They are so elaborate; the coloring is perfect and very professional-looking. What else can I say? Thank you for getting those made for the boys. They'll be thrilled and very proud to wear them. I can see them now—ten feet tall, chests out, so proud."

After a few smaller issues were discussed. Rocky told George that he hadn't yet told his boss of his intended change of employment; he was waiting until after the weekend.

"There's no great hurry," George said. "The accommodation has to be refurbished and a few other items have to be fixed. The boys can start using the site, though, and start planning as soon as they wish."

Rocky left George's office with the precious parcels under his arm.

Rocky continued his shift with a beaming smile, happiness in his voice and actions, and a spring in his step. His passengers noticed this and commented. Rocky's answer was the same to all of them: "Something great is happening, and the whole town will hear about it in the next week or two. You won't miss the good news—just wait and see."

Rocky also found time to buy some meat, salads, bread rolls, and drinks for the leisure party at Piet's barn later that night. The boys and Rocky did this type of thing often; everyone always put in cash to cover costs so that Rocky was not out of pocket, the same as they always paid the taxi fare whenever they took a ride somewhere. They realized that that was part of being responsible and that every activity came with a cost. That was part of Rocky's teachings. They never expected to get something with value for nothing.

Rocky put the food items in one cooler and the drinks in another so that they would be cold by nightfall. After finishing his shift, he changed vehicles, went home, showered, and drove over to Pieter's barn.

The boys were waiting for him. He got out of his car, removed the two coolers, and walked toward the boys. He put the coolers down, and the boys gathered around him, giving him high-fives and hugs as he moved among them. "Group hug!" one of them said. The group hug lasted for a long time, and then questions came from all directions.

"Hang on, guys. Let's settle down a bit. I will tell you all that I know as time goes on."

Suddenly, seven of the mums appeared from the house, including Ellen, Mitch's mum.

"Hi, Ellen, how are you doing?" Rocky asked.

"I'm pretty good, Rocky," Ellen said. "Still miss Mitch; just taking it one day at a time. It's good to see you, and isn't it good news about the boys doing so well?"

"Yeah, it's great. They deserve it, though, and they have well and truly earned it."

"I am so honored that Mitch's mates thought of me and asked if I could go to the concert tomorrow. Thank you too, Rocky, for following it through," Ellen said.

"That's okay, Ellen; I was so proud when they asked me. They really are compassionate and thoughtful, you know."

"Now, I want to treat you to a drink or two. How about a bourbon and Coke?" Ellen said.

"Oh yes, that would be nice, Ellen," Rocky said.

"And I wondered if the boys could join us adults for a drink as well, if that's okay," Ellen said.

"Well, I don't know about that," Rocky said, as he looked around at the boys, their faces appearing to plead with him. "It's not really for me to say. What do their mums say? I don't want to encourage them to drink until they are a bit older, although I did tell them that we would have a few quiet drinks one night as a treat for doing so well."

"Oh, they all give their permission," Ellen said, with the mums nodding, "but they all agreed to see what you thought about it. After all, it was you who taught them that it was wrong and that they didn't need alcohol in their lives. By the way, they knew nothing of this until I asked you now."

"Well, I think it's okay. Just one or two sensible drinks wouldn't cause any harm. Let's say it is teaching them that alcohol in moderation is acceptable in some circumstances, if it's controlled and in a relaxed, clear environment, and they have their parents' permission. After all, they have a lot to celebrate. Their minds must be racing with all the excitement; they probably haven't slept too much all week either.

"Yeah, you did say that Rocky," Aiden said. "Can we do that tonight? Please, Rocky, it would top off what we have planned."

"What have you planned, Aiden? Nothing stupid, I hope."

"Oh no, just a barbecue, some music, a swim, a chat—that's all," Aiden said, though he never was good at hiding the truth.

"I can tell something is going on, Aiden," Rocky said. "Come on, out with it."

"No, that's all, Rocky, truly,' Pieter said.

"How about we have one drink now, then the barbecue, a swim, some music, a chat, and finish with another drink or two over listening to music or a chat. That way, your drinks will be paced. It will teach you responsible drinking, I suppose, but legally, you are too young. It is probably accepted at someone's house with parents, instead of sneaking it on the streets like you used to."

The guys and the mums agreed with the plan. Pieter and Tony poured the drinks, handed them around, and settled in to enjoy their drinks. The barbecue was lit, and Pieter, Aiden, Jacob, and Tony helped Rocky prepare the food and cook the steaks and sausages. Each boy placed five dollars or more in the traditional tin that was used to pay for their barbecue or snacks or whatever needed cash. In no time, Pieter said, "Okay, guys and mums, food is ready. Come and get it."

As they ate, they discussed the week's events in detail and, at the same time, allow the mums to learn exactly what was happening with their sons. Everything seemed to be in place—the name, the committee, the bank account, the songs that the band was going to play, notes for their speech, transport to and from the theater, what everyone was going to wear, and their hair color and style. Everyone was satisfied that everything was in place.

"What are you going to wear, Splinta?" Haydon asked. "Have you got that sorted?"

"No, I haven't had time. I'll find something," Rocky said. "I haven't sorted my speech yet either. I'll help you guys write yours, and then I'll try to write mine."

"Hey, Rocky, can a few of us share the speech. We talked about it the other day, and a few of us want to talk as well," Aiden said.

"Yeah, I'm sure that will be cool; that's a great idea" Rocky said. "We will sort it out after the swim, if you like."

Everyone cleaned up after the barbecue, and a couple of the mums commented on the boys' willingness to jump in and how clean and tidy they had become. The mums also commented that their dress sense had changed. Although still teen fashion, they had tidied their appearance quite a bit and were conscious of it, right down to their deodorant, body spray, and hairstyles.

"Time for a swim, guys!" Pieter yelled.

Everyone removed their shoes, socks, and shirts and dived in. The pool seemed to boil with eleven guys swimming, diving, jumping, throwing each other into the air, and generally mucking about, and enjoying themselves. One by one, the guys left the pool, dried off, and lounged around until their shorts dried, as the mums decided to enter the pool for a much quieter swim.

The band began setting up to play their songs for the band competition.

"While you set up, I've got something for all of you. I'll just go to the car and bring it back; won't be long," Rocky said.

As he entered the barn, he noticed the corner was cordoned off with some old hessian draped over a rough timber frame. "What's in there? What's it for?" Rocky asked.

"Oh, it's our change room, Rock Daddy. We are going to try on our band clothes, and the others have a sort of uniform too. We are all going to change to show you," Aiden said. "No, Rocky, don't go in there." Aiden's voice had a hint of panic.

"Don't be stupid, guys. I am not that stupid. You guys never wanted to change in a change room before. You usually just strip off your clothes and change anywhere; it has never worried you before. You were never that modest," Rocky said. "And why can't I go in there?"

"Um … err … ah, we don't want you to see our clothes until later," Aiden stammered.

"No, you guys are bullshitting me; I can tell. All right, I'll play your game; I'll wait." Rocky then said, "I've got something to give you guys." He placed the boxes on the table, peeking into one to see which badges it contained. He opened the first box as he said, "Gather around, guys; look at this."

"Holy hell!"

"Awesome!"

"Stuff me, look at that!"

"Wicked!"

"Cool!"

Many other similar comments were heard from the boys.

Rocky handed the badges around and said, "You will notice that the word president has been changed to chairman. George said that term is more professional and used in this modern business world, and I agree with him."

"Can we show our mums?" Pieter asked.

"Yeah, sure, but wait till I show you this other box," Rocky said. He opened the second box, and the boys erupted into wild applause as they realized what the box contained. Their faces showed their excitement, their pride, and their appreciation as they picked up the badges to look closer at the wording and lavish-looking color.

"Now can we show our mums?" Pieter asked.

"Yeah, call them to the edge of the pool and show them," Rocky said.

They rushed out of the barn to the pool, yelling as they went. The mums showed their enthusiasm at seeing the badges and their sons' excitement.

"Why don't we get our mums to pin the badges on us when we change into our uniforms?" Tony suggested.

"That's awesome," Jay yelled, "like a badge ceremony."

"That's a great idea," Rocky said. "That would be a great gesture. I'm sure your mums would be honored. What do you say, ladies?" All indicated their approval. Rocky asked, "What about the four whose mums aren't here? They will feel left out and a bit disappointed."

"Oh, they are coming later. They had to go to a meeting, but they'll be here soon," Jacob said.

"That's cool; that's what we will do," Rocky said.

"What about you, Rocky? Who's going to pin yours?" Decles asked.

"What about Ellen?" one of the mums suggested. "I am sure she would love to do that; then she won't be left out."

"Yes, Rocky, I would be honored to pin your badges on your shirt. In honor of Mitch. I'm sure that he would be thrilled. I know he is with these boys in spirit all the time. He is watching."

"I would be honored too, Ellen," Rocky said.

"Look, there's Mitch now," Aiden said, pointing to his star. "Look, he's winking red, yellow, white, orange—look at him; he approves."

"That's set," Rocky said.

They all went back into the barn and put the badges back in the boxes.

The band played and sang their three songs to near perfection. The quality of music was tops, and the mild dance moves of the band members was also very good—not overdone, just right. The other five danced just like they were on stage, the dance moves choreographed very well and executed perfectly.

"You guys are doing very well. You play and dance just like the pros, and you enjoy yourselves so much. That's fantastic," Rocky said.

"Wish we had a light show, Rocky," Tony said. "It would make it so good."

"Don't worry, Tony; that's coming. You will have that at the youth center soon enough," Rocky said.

"Yeah, can't wait Rocky. Do you think that we can do the stage area first, after the clean up?" Pieter asked.

"I don't see why not, but remember, all these things have to be voted on at your meetings. You can't just go and do it without your committee's approval."

"Oh yeah, forgot about that," Pieter said.

"Don't worry. I will show you how to do these meetings, get quotes, apply for donations and grants, and so forth, to keep everything above board."

There was a bit of movement outside the barn, as the other four mums arrived and the mums in the pool got out. The four boys whose mums had just arrived brought them into the barn to show them the badges and explained their plan for a badge-pinning ceremony. All the mums then moved to the house, leaving the guys to their plans and activities.

"Now, Rocky, time for a dress rehearsal. Before we do, we gotta dye our hair black. We are going permanent black—our mums got it for us— and we are going to remove the hair from our chests and backs and snail trails—well, those of us who have any. And you, Rock Daddy, we are going to give you a makeover," Aiden said.

"Oh, rack off, what do you mean a makeover?" Rocky asked.

"We are going to dye your hair and your moustache black, and you are going to lose your body hair too, Rock Daddy," Pieter said.

"Bullshit. Why?" he asked, shocked.

"Because we can. You have said that you wished that you weren't so hairy, so, we want to do it for you. You said that sort of thing was okay when we asked you about it a couple of months ago," Pieter said.

"Yeah, I know. I do clipper it myself, but guys, are you sure you want to do this for me?"

"Why wouldn't we?" Aiden said.

"No, just do it for yourselves. You don't want to do that for an old guy like me."

"No, it's cool Rocky. You're one of us; anyway, when we asked about removing or waxing hair on our chests, backs, cracks, and down below, you said that it was our bodies, and we could do what we wanted with our bodies as long as there was no danger. Rocky, we have done it before."

"Are you guys going gay on me? What's going on with you guys?" Rocky said.

"No, you told us it wasn't gay then, so it can't be gay now," Jay said.

"No back, crack, and sack wax for me, thanks, guys," Rocky said. "I'll leave it to you fellas."

"No, man, we're not doing our cracks or nuts this time, just our backs and chests and snail trails. And we are doing yours too, man; you can't disagree. It's happening, man," Decles said. "We want to do it for you, dude, as part of the makeover."

"Well, okay, talk about 'Queer Eye for the Straight Guy,'" Rocky said, "but only my front and back, fellas. I'm the straight guy. Who's the queer eye?"

Laughter filled the barn as the guys rubbed black dye into each other's hair and Rocky's hair and moustache. Rocky had quite a lot of gray hair, so there was no harm in letting them dye his hair.

Rocky commented, "Are you guys embarrassed by my graying hair?"

"No, we just want to make yours the same as ours, so you feel more like a member of our group. Anyway, it does make you look younger, if I may say so," Tony said. "That's okay, isn't it?"

"Yeah, fellas, it's okay. Listen, I do appreciate it, but I wasn't prepared for it. You sprang it on me. I knew something was going on, you little pricks."

The guys kept busy, dying hair, washing the dye out, and shampooing hair.

Rocky said, "I must admit it looks wicked, all with black hair. It does make some of you look different, but you look the same as each other."

The hair removal cream was next to come out. The basins and buckets were emptied of the black water from the hair dye and refilled with clean water. The towels used to dry everyone's hair were hung over the pool fence, and new ones were produced.

"Jeez, who's going to wash all those towels, fellas?" Rocky asked.

"We all brought two, and we'll take our two home to be washed," Adam answered. "It's no big deal."

Each took their turn to have the hair removal cream applied and then removed and sponged down and dried. Then it came to Rocky's turn. As a couple of them applied the cream and removed the hair, Aiden said, "You really are a hairy prick, man. You look like an ape."

"Oh, get ripped, you little prick; that's not fair."

"Look, he's got so much hair; he's even got it on his shoulders," Adam said.

"Yeah, I know. It does piss me off, but I guess it's all gone now," Rocky said.

"Now, our hair," Pieter said, as the hair removal was completed, and basins and buckets were emptied.

"What do you mean, *our hair*? You've dyed your hair and taken off what you don't want," Rocky said.

"We need to gel and style our hair, so we look the same. You too, Rocky."

Hair gel and fudge was applied to each guy's hair and then fluffed and teased until loose curls were formed into a messy but a controlled appearance. Aiden and Pieter did Rocky's hair, and Pieter said, "We better do yours for you tomorrow before we go to the concert. You won't be able to do it properly."

"Whatever you say, chief," Rocky said, giving up on objecting to what was happening to him and resigning himself to his fate. These guys were in control, and when they were in control, nothing was going to convince them otherwise.

"Now to change into our clothes for photos and badges," Aiden said.

Each boy took a turn in the "change cubical" and emerged wearing the clothes they had chosen for the concert. The band members wore their black boots or shoes, black jeans or work trousers, and a white T-shirt or buttoned shirt. They added a red scarf around their necks, which was printed with small black and white skulls. With their jet-black curly, scruffy hair, they really did look very flash. The red scarf against the white shirt and black trousers looked stunning.

The other five guys had similar black footwear, medium-blue denim jeans, a red or maroon T-shirt or buttoned shirt, and a white scarf with red and black skulls printed on them. They too looked smart.

Aiden and Jacob disappeared behind the hessian cubical while Pieter and Decles covered Rocky's eyes. Rocky was told to stay still and play the game.

"We aren't going to do anything to you, dude, but I should nipple crimp you to pay you back for the other day," Tony said.

"I should dack you, Rocky. I still owe you one," Pieter said. "But I won't."

"We have another surprise for you, Rocky. We just want to say thanks to you for everything you have done for us," Pieter said. "Keep those eyes closed," he said, with a hint of chastisement in his voice.

"Don't look till we tell you," Decles said. "Come out, guys."

Aiden and Jacob came out of the cubical and stood before Rocky. Aiden was holding a deep blue shirt made from a shiny fabric, embossed with a small swirl pattern, as well as a black tie with a small print of skulls in red and white. Jacob was holding a pair of medium-blue denim jeans, a black studded belt, and a pair of black suede boots and a pair of dark-blue socks.

"Open your eyes, Rocky," Aiden and Jacob said in chorus. "This is what you are wearing tomorrow night."

"Oh, hell no," Rocky said in shock, "I can't accept that from you guys." Tears welled in his eyes. "What in the hell are you fellas doing to me? You can't afford this." Rocky sat down, almost crying at what the boys had done for him.

"Do you like it, Rocky?" Aiden asked.

"Yeah, dude, I do. I really appreciate it, but you can't give me that." Rocky was almost a blubbering mess.

"Yes, we can, and we are!" Shayne said.

"Where did you get the money? That must have cost you guys hundreds."

"Well, we had a meeting with Mr. Watson and Mrs. Ruby on Tuesday, and we told them that we wanted to do something for you. We discussed it for a while and then Mr. Watson called the student council to his office, and they discussed it. We all decided that we wanted to get you some new clothes to wear to the concert to show our appreciation. Mr. Watson told the student council a little bit about what was happening, about the plans, without telling them what it was. He told the council that the school and the students would benefit greatly from it, and he suggested the student council have a uniform-free day so that we could raise some money to get some clothes for you. They also told us to get the scarves from the money and the change could go to the foundation," Aiden said.

"That's awesome, guys," Rocky said. "And I really do appreciate this. I wasn't upset before, just tears of happiness. Group hug, hey?"

Aiden said, "They raised $754.20 from the uniform-free day, and the clothes and the scarves cost $427.80. Our treasurer Jay has the receipts and $326.40 ready to bank."

"Come on, Splinta, try 'em on. We want to see what you look like," Jerry said impatiently.

Rocky removed his shorts, leaving his jocks. He had no shirt, as he was showing his newly acquired hairless body. "No change cubical for this old guy. I don't have to hide behind the hessian." He put on his shirt, then his jeans and belt, his tie, shoes, and socks and paraded so all could see his new clothes. Aiden then threw Rocky a new pair of boxers, saying, "Forgot these, Rock Daddy; they're special boxers for under jeans that I got for you."

"Well, I'm not going to strip off to put them on now. I will promise to wear them tomorrow, just for you. Thanks, champ," Rocky said. "How do I look?"

Aiden and Pieter straightened up his tie, straightened his belt, and pouched his shirt, just like two boys fussing over their father in much the same way Rocky's sons had done several times in the past.

"I don't know, you old man. You don't know how to dress yourself properly, do you?" Aiden said.

"You look awesome," Jay said.

"I could almost kiss you, you look so wicked," Nick said.

"Yeah, Nick, I thought you were the gay one. Good on ya," Rocky said, "Nah. Only gagging ya, buddy."

"I'll get our mums to come and see us all dressed up, and they can give us the badges," Pieter said. "Can a couple of you come with me? Mum has been baking, and she told me to tell her when we were ready for coffee or drinks and cakes and biscuits."

A couple went off to help Pieter while the rest chatted about the concert and the dinner that was coming up the next day. They discussed the format of two songs in the first round and then the last song in the next round; what sort of food might be at the dinner; the presentation; the paper, radio, and television reporters and how they should answer questions; and how excited they were about the youth center.

The mothers came into the barn, followed by Pieter, Jay, Jerry, and Shayne, who carried the coffeepots, milk, sugar, mugs, drinks, and the cakes and biscuits. Pieter and Adam poured the coffees, Shayne poured the soft drinks, and Jay laid out the cakes and biscuits. Each lad served his mother, while Rocky served Ellen. Then each lad served himself and joined the mums.

Refreshments finished, Rocky and Aiden laid out the badges in rows on the table, so it was easy for the mothers to find. Pieter and Nick set up the video camera and digital camera on tripods so that the proceedings could be recorded. The video camera was focused on a certain spot and set to be operated by remote; the digital camera could be operated by the boys in turn after they had their badges pinned.

When the badge ceremony was over, the mums returned to the house as the guys settled into working out their speeches. A couple of boys wanted to make a short speech as well as Aiden, who was making a speech as chairman. Rocky spent time with each of them, helping them to convert their thoughts into words on paper that could be spoken. The task of writing the speeches didn't take long, as each one had notes, and the others helped compile the thoughts.

"Now, we are finished," Pieter said. "Time for a drink, Rocky."

"Yeah, I guess it is," Rocky said. "I think we have earned it, guys. It's been a busy but awesome night."

"Me and Haydon are the barmen," Adam said. "I'll get the bourbon, and Haydon will set up the glasses."

"I'll see if our mums want to join us," Pieter said, running upstairs to the house.

Adam and Haydon served the drinks to the guys, and they settled down beside the pool for a quiet drink and a chat.

"Naw, they don't want to come down; they are already drinking, a bit pissed, actually," Pieter said as he returned from the house.

"Cheers, fellas," Rocky said, raising his glass. "Here's to a wicked and successful night tomorrow."

The boys followed the action with similar wishes of their own. The guys started chatting about the past week, the past six months, and the six months before that. They reminisced about their bad days; their low time, when they lost Mitch to the ocean, and their mate, Josh, who had to leave town to keep safe; and their achievements of the past six months. At times, it was very emotional, and at other times the discussions were very lighthearted and jovial.

Rocky let them continue, as it was good therapy for them to talk about their experiences. Pieter returned to the barn and got the CD player and put on an INXS CD. "Just for old-school days, hey, Rock Daddy?" Pieter said. The guys began singing along with the songs, while a few, who still had some remaining energy, broke into dance routines.

"You guys really are keen on dance, aren't you?" Rocky said. "I can't help noticing the rhythm and moves."

"We told you that we wanted to learn to dance," Jacob said.

"Well, I might consider some way of getting help to teach you guys," Rocky said. "Now that we have a relationship with the school, there must be someone there who can help."

"Now that we have a base to call our own to practice without disturbing anyone, how about we plan a musical and dance show, put it on, and charge admission? What do you reckon?" Declan said.

"That would be awesome," most said.

"We will probably need extra kids to make up a good number of performers. You guys and someone who knows about these things can take the auditions," Rocky said. "Leave it with me, and I will make some inquiries in the next couple of weeks."

Drinks finished, the guys stripped off to their boxers or jocks, and jumped into the pool. Rocky and a couple of others were happy to float around on float boards, while the rest of them jumped, swam, and dived, still using energy that Rocky couldn't believe they had in them.

"There's Mitch, guys," Pieter yelled, pointing to Mitch's star. "Look at him; he is still winking at us, changing colors."

"Awesome," Aiden said. "He's so happy for us. Hell, I wish he was still here. He belongs here with us."

"Yeah, but I know he is here. We just can't see him, that's all," Nick said.

Eventually, everyone finished swimming and left the pool, toweled off, and dressed.

"Well, guys, I better call it a night. I'm so rooted, and it's a big day tomorrow," Rocky said. "Does anyone want a lift home?"

Everyone had arrangements, most going home with their mothers and the rest catching taxis with their mums.

Rocky and the boys went upstairs to say goodbye to everyone, and then they returned to the barn.

"Rocky, do you want to get dressed here tomorrow?" Pieter asked. "We are all sleeping here after our night out. Do you want to stay here with us tomorrow night?"

"Oh, not sure, dude," Rocky said. "I probably should get dressed here, so you guys don't get up me if I don't get it right. I don't know about a sleepover; you blokes don't want this old guy here spoiling your night."

"Hell yeah, we do," Aiden said. "Don't we, guys?"

All yelled their approval. Pieter said, "Shut up about being the old guy, Rocky. You're not effen old; you are one of us." He thumped Rocky's shoulder lightly with his fist, reinforcing each word as he said, "You are one of us. We have noticed that age is a number. Mates don't think about numbers. Just mates enjoying the same interests and having fun, learning from each other as we go. So, man, all of us are sleeping here—and if you are here, we can have another bourbon."

"Oy, Piet, don't make a habit of this drinking, mate," Rocky said. "It's not really the right thing to do."

"Yeah, we won't make a habit of it. We just want a couple when we get back just to celebrate whatever happens and to unwind and look back over the night."

"Hey, listen, how are we getting there? We better organize it," Rocky said.

"What about a maxi-taxi?" Aiden suggested.

"Yeah, that's a plan. I'd better book them," Rocky said. "What time? Who's traveling?"

"The band has to be there about two. The concert starts at three," Aiden said.

"Do you other guys want to go at the same time as the band? I want to be there with the band guys at two," Rocky said.

The non-band guys indicated they too would go at the same time.

"That's settled. I'll book one for 1:40, then. What about the mums? Do they want to go in a maxi-taxi?" Rocky asked.

"I'll go see what they are doing. You know women—they wouldn't have a clue," Pieter said.

Pieter and Jay went to find out. Rocky and a couple others decided to take the instruments to the theater at about ten thirty the next morning.

"No, they will make their own taxi bookings," Jay said when he returned. "They don't want to go like us peasants in a maxi-taxi. They will organize three or four sedan taxis themselves."

"Cool," Rocky said. "I'll think about the sleepover."

"Nuthin' to think about, Rocky; you will be here," Pieter said, "even if I have to let the air out of your tires."

"Okay, then, if you put it that way," Rocky said. "All right, guys, I will see you in the morning."

"Group hug before you go, Rocky," Haydon said.

Rocky climbed into his car, said his goodbyes, and drove off into the darkness to make his way home.

CHAPTER 11

**Thank you for everything that you have taught
me and done for me and for being a wicked
mate to me. I really wish you were my dad.**

Rocky arrived at Piet's barn around ten and loaded the band's equipment into his vehicle with the help of the band members, Pieter, Aiden, Adam, Haydon, and Declan. Once loaded, they drove to the theater to unload and arrange the equipment so that the backstage people could move it onto the stage and then take it off again when they were finished.

They were met by the stage manager and his assistant at the stage rear dock. "My, you fellas are keen, right on time. You are the first ones here," the stage manager said. "Which group are you?"

"Yeah, we are real keen," Decles said. "We're the Nuver Chanz."

"Well, boys, you might as well set up first. You're the fifth group to appear, but that doesn't matter. Looking at my list, you are coded green; I'll explain that soon. Let me check the spelling. I've got here *N-U-V-E-R C-H-A-N-Z*. Is that right?" the stage manager asked. "I wondered how to pronounce when I saw it."

"Yeah, that's right," Aiden answered.

"Now, I mentioned that you are fifth to appear; the first four groups well perform their two music items, then you will perform two of your songs, and then there will be two other groups after you. Then we have an interval of about twenty minutes or so and start the cycle again, with your final song," the stage manager said.

"Jeez, that will keep the stage and props people busy," Rocky said.

"Well, yes it will, but the way we do it, it's very easy. The curtain closes briefly, and the boys move gear off. Then the next group's gear is moved on. It usually only takes ninety seconds to two minutes. That's why we have color codes," the stage manager said. "Let's get your equipment onto the stage, and we will get you to position it where you will need it. We don't need your amps; you will use the ones that are already set up."

"Wow, this is awesome," Adam said as the guys walked to the front of the stage. "This is awesome."

"Rad," said Haydon. "Look at those amps and speakers and the lights."

"You haven't played onstage before?" the assistant asked.

"No, man," Haydon said. "We haven't even seen a live concert, only on TV and DVDs."

"I don't think any of them has seen a live show or been onstage," Rocky said. "That's why the excitement. Are you going to record this competition on video or DVD?"

"Yes, we have recorded everyone for the past eleven or twelve years," the assistant said. "It's much easier now with this new technology, using DVDs. Before we had to use videotapes."

"Can I buy a copy?" Rocky asked.

"Nah, mate, you can't buy one. I will give you a copy as long as it's never played in public or broadcast—and you don't tell anyone," the stage manager said.

"That's cool. Thanks for that."

"Are you guys satisfied that your equipment is where you want it?" the assistant asked.

"Yep, that's it," Aiden said.

"As for green"—the manager sifted through seven large envelopes—"here it is. Now, lead and vocals." He found the two symbols on green sticky paper. "That's right; you are vocals as well."

Aiden answered, "Yeah, that's right."

"You will need a mike as well," he said, as the assistant got a mike and placed it in front of Aiden. He stuck the two symbols to the floor and used green half-inch tape to mark his spot. He then plugged his guitar and mike into a panel that was connected to one of the huge amps.

"Okay, mate," the manager said, "strum your guitar and sing or speak until I signal to stop." He signaled to the control platform above the stage.

Aiden played his guitar and sang a few lines; then the manager signaled to stop.

"That's wicked," Aiden said. "That is so insane. I have only heard about and seen fold-back speakers on DVDs. That is so awesome!"

The manager and his assistant and Rocky chuckled to themselves as Rocky put his arm around Aiden's neck and hugged him a little. Aiden had a smile from ear to ear and said, "Can I play some more?"

"Not yet, mate. You'll play together when this is done," the manager said. "Be patient, young man."

They moved their attention to Pieter and said, "You too need a mike for vocals," the manager said, getting the stickers with rhythm and vocals. He stuck them to the floor and outlined them with green tape.

Each in turn had the stickers and green lines stuck to the floor, plugged into the amp system, and sound tested.

"Now, fellas, it's time to play your three songs. You don't have to play them in the order that you have nominated," the manager said. "We also need to test the lights, and the lighting guys will need to work out a sequence and document it, so be patient if we ask you to start again."

The guys played their first song, "Beds Are Burning," and the manager said, "You did that one really well, fellas. The sound and lighting guys are happy, so onto the next one."

The Nuver Chanz played and sang "I Still Haven't Found What I'm Lookin' For," and the manager said again, "You guys really do a good job, especially considering that you haven't performed on a stage before." He checked with the sound and lighting guys, and they asked if they could play it again; they wanted to include a few sound and lighting effects, as they had never had to mix that song before.

The guys played it again, and when they finished, a couple of the stage guys voiced their approval and commented how awesome it sounded and looked to them.

"That's good, guys. I'm happy too, and I'm happy at how easy you are to get along with. That's good. It makes our job so much easier," the stage manager said. "Now, when you are ready, your last song, "Never Tear Us Apart.""

The guys played their last song to perfection, as they usually did. The sound and lighting guys were happy, and the assistant manager said, "You guys do Michael Hutchence and the boys proud. I closed my eyes, and the sound coming from that group sounded the same as INXS. And you"—he pointed to Aiden— "look very much like Michael with your baby face, your hairstyle, and your open shirt. Well done."

Aiden blushed and then took his posing stance, pushing his face forward like Michael did, and flashed his pecks and abs, opening yet another button.

"Yeah, that's it; just like that. If you do that onstage this afternoon, you will kill 'em, lad."

The rest slow clapped and cheered Aiden, to which he responded with a bow.

"Now, do you have any questions?" the manager asked.

There were no questions, just five excited, thrilled faces attached to bodies bounding onstage, high-fiving and congratulating each other. The excitement was catching, as Rocky and the manager went over to congratulate the boys.

"You need to be here at two for any last-minute instructions and adjustments. I will see you then," the manager said, and the stage people quickly but carefully moved the equipment into the wings into an area bounded by wide green tape.

"You see, the stage guys are practicing their bit, and they put your gear into the green area so that nothing is lost or forgotten," the assistant said.

Everyone exchanged pleasantries, and the guys boarded the Midnight Special to return to Piet's barn.

"Jeez, that was awesome, Rocky," Aiden said. "I won't forget that in a hurry. I am stoked that you talked us into forming the Nuver Chanz and entering this competition. Thanks, man."

The other four agreed, all showing excitement.

"Jeez, I'm glad we got there first. How long is it going to take the rest of them to get through that. I had no idea it was so professional," Rocky said. "Still, better that way, at least you get to use your own instruments, and you don't have to set it up yourselves."

"Hey, Rocky, thanks, man, for getting our arses off the streets, our fucked heads out of the shit, and persisting with us. We are so stoked we met you, man. Hell, where would we be without you?" Haydon said as he started to howl and cry. The emotion and realization of what they had just done began to sink in.

"Hey, buddy, it's okay. That's what mates are for. Stuff me, if I hadn't done what I could for you guys—heck, you got me lost for words, mate." Rocky composed himself. "Listen, you guys, I am just a human being who sees potential in young guys, just a person who can't stand by and ignore young guys in trouble. I just gotta do my bit and try to give young fellas like you a helping hand up. If a young guy listens and accepts that help, I have succeeded in saving that guy. If he doesn't, that's his choice—too bad, yes; it does tear my guts out, but I have tried.

"You guys, at fifteen or sixteen, were those guys who needed my help. You had a choice, and you chose to try things my way; that's good. Look at you; you have made it—and how. I must admit you have done a whole lot better than I ever imagined. That's what makes me feel so wicked inside. The only disappointment I have is that there are a whole lot more young guys out there who need a helping hand, and there is no one for them. That's where I know that you guys want to help. Some of these guys can be saved through Teen-Morph. Heck, I talk a lot, but guys, you are all so *fucking awesome*! Now you pricks have me blubbering."

Rocky looked around; everyone was crying. "Hey, guys, wipe your eyes. I'm going to turn up here and stop at the youth center, and we are going to have one big group hug, just to share the love, okay?"

"Yeah, cool, Rocky, a group hug is what the doctor ordered," Haydon said.

"And we might just sit for a while and take it all in. Okay, Rocky?" Aiden asked.

"Yeah, that's cool. Can't stay long, though. Gotta get ready and be on time for the taxi."

The Midnight Special pulled up to the locked gate, and Aiden jumped out with the keys, unlocked the padlock and chain, and threw the gates open. Midnight Special then drove up to the railway carriages and stopped. Everyone got out and looked around once again.

"Where's the beach from here, Rocky?" Aiden said. "Let's go and check out the beach. It must be awesome. Is it our private beach?"

"I think it's that way," Rocky said. "There must be a track somewhere."

The guys moved in the direction of where he thought the beach was, looking for a track.

"This might be it. It looks like it was a track," Declan said, pointing at a very overgrown track that led in the direction of where Rocky thought the beach was.

"Each of you grab a stick, a pole, or a lump of steel, just in case of snakes or if we need to beat some scrub away from the path," Rocky said. Rocky's biggest fear was snakes; anything else in this world didn't bother him, but snakes—he hated them.

"That's right, Rocky," Aiden said, "you hate snakes. I have seen you. You flogged the stuffin' out of that one at the park that day. The fire in your eyes. The sweat. Never seen anyone sweat so much. That poor snake. I think it copped a hundred whacks. I remember it frightened me, seeing you flog it to death. It ended up in four or five pieces. You went psycho. I thought at the time, better not stir Rocky too much. You just lost it big time."

"Oh, piss off. I didn't scare you that much," Rocky said. "I could never treat any of you guys like that. No matter what you do, I would never do anything like that. I just *hate snakes*."

"Yeah, I know that now, Rocky," Pieter said. "I know that you would never harm us, but we didn't know you that well back then."

"Yeah, I guess so," he said.

The guys came to the end of the overgrown path and came upon a high fence with a locked gate; a secluded, sandy beach was on the other side. Aiden located the key—the same key that unlocked the main gate—unlocked it and ventured through to the beach. The sand was almost pure white, and the water was crystal-clear with waves rippling ashore. The beach was lined with natural bush, with a few grassy areas that were overgrown with long grass and a couple of neglected shelters with tables and stools. The sand sloped slightly toward the water, with no visible rocks. Some washed-up logs and driftwood littered the high-water mark.

"Wow, look at this," Haydon said. "This is insane. I don't think anyone has been here for a long time."

"This is awesome," Declan said. "Is this our beach, Rocky? Do you think?"

"It looks like it, mate. Looks like there has been no one here for a while. How wicked is this?" Rocky said. "You can never actually own a beach, usually only land above the high-water mark. We probably can't stop anyone else using it but seeing it's at the park's back door with no other way of getting here, you could say it is almost ours."

"What do you mean, no other way of getting here?" Pieter asked.

"If you look that way, the land comes to that high, rough, rocky outcrop. It would be very hard getting over that, and the creek is the other way, so really, you would need a boat to get here if you didn't come through that gate."

The guys sat on a log that had washed up onto the beach and gazed over the ocean, taking in the moment. The looks on their faces said it all.

"Hey, guys, we didn't have our group hug. Let's have a group hug," Declan said.

All six guys huddled in a group, very quiet, all thinking how lucky they were to be in an area so isolated—a world of their own.

During the group hug, some of the boys let their emotions out. Rocky told them that the events of the past week had been very demanding on them.

"Listen, fellas, I want you all to stop for a while and just think about what's been happening. A lot has happened over the past week or so. No one could ever imagine that so much could happen in such a short time. I want you to think about how you are handling this. If it gets to you, like it just got to Haydon, don't be embarrassed. It's only natural, especially for guys so young. If you have trouble dealing with it, talk about it. Talk to me, talk to your mums, talk among yourselves. I know it is a lot to take in for guys your age."

"Yeah, sure, Rocky," Adam said. "We've been talking about it this week."

"It's cool, man. We look out for each other all the time. We talk about things all the time, and we are always here for each other, just like you are always here for us," Declan said.

"I would dearly love you to experience something that my mates and I used to do when we were sixteen or so—an old-school beach party. We will have to organize it when the band competition is over, and you settle down."

"That'd be cool," Pieter said. "We can pitch a tent and camp here too."

"That's an idea," Rocky said. "We'll do it soon."

"I'm in," Aiden said.

"Me too," the others said.

"I think a brush cutter and a mower should be the first things on your list," Rocky said. "Look at those picnic areas—need a bit of a trim."

"Just like your back last night, hey, Rocky?" Declan said. "That was a bit overgrown dude. Don't let it get like that again, Rocky."

"Get rooted," Rocky said. "That can be your job, hey, dude?"

"Yeah, that's okay. I'll do it for you," Declan said.

"Thanks, champ, for being concerned."

"It's cool," Declan said.

"I think I better get you guys back to the barn, so we'll be on time," Rocky said.

"Yeah, I suppose so. I don't want to leave here; this is so wicked," Aiden said.

"Ah, it is," Rocky said, "but who is going live here, fellas? Me!"

"Ah, not fair. I might move in too, Rocky. Can I come and live here too?" Adam asked.

"We'll have to look at cabins and see what has to be done. What about your mum? She needs you with her. That's your family, bud, but we will organize weekends and some nights through the week. We gotta work all that out—all of us," Rocky said.

The guys got back in the car and drove to Piet's barn.

"You guys get ready, find the other dudes, and get them here by one. I'll be back soon to get ready and catch the taxi to the theater," Rocky said.

"Are you coming back here to get dressed so we can make sure your shirt and jeans are right and your hair is done right, hey, Rocky?" Pieter said.

"Yeah, sure. You make it sound like organizing the father of the groom at a wedding."

"I suppose it does. Hey, will you be my father at my wedding?" Pieter asked.

"Don't know. I'd be honored, but you might get to know your father by then. That's for him to do, Piet." Rocky said. "Anyway, you gotta find the right girl, fall in love, and commit to her first. That's years away, Piet, I hope. Don't rush it; you got a lot of living to do and growing up to do first, mate."

"Oh, Rocky, forgot," said Aiden. "Can we have that girl talk tonight when we get back from the party?"

"We'll see. You might be too tired for that. Do you think you are going to be swamped by teeny-boppers and rock chicks after tonight?"

"That would be cool. We would love to have chicks hanging off us. That sounds prime," Declan said.

"Hey, guys, don't think you are that good. It's windy outside; the tickets might fly off," Rocky said.

"What do ya mean?" Adam asked, a little confused.

"Oh, an old saying, buddy," Rocky said, giving a quick explanation. "Okay, guys, gotta go. Stay cool. Remember, no pressure. Contact the other guys, and make sure they are here on time." Rocky left to go home to wash and change for the big event.

Midnight Special pulled into Piet's driveway. Rocky jumped out and unloaded a couple of coolers and a sealed carton.

"What ya got there?" one of the guys asked.

"Just some supplies for our mish," Rocky answered. "Never worry; the Rocky looks after you. You'll have to wait till much later."

"Are we going to have a mish, Rocky? What mish are we going to do?" another guy asked.

"Yeah, dudes, we are going to mish, but no peeking till we get back."

"Oh, come on, Rocky," Pieter insisted.

"No, wait till later. Now, time to get ready. Are we all here?" Rocky asked.

"Nearly. Adam's on his way; he won't be long," Pieter said.

"Let's get ready, guys," Rocky said. They all went into the barn to get ready for their big night.

"Oy, gotcha," Aiden said to Pieter as he pulled Pieter's shorts down around his ankles.

"Ah, you free-willy dude," Haydon said to Pieter, as Pieter shuffled around the barn, totally nude except for his shorts around his ankles, his hands behind his head.

Then it started. Three or four more guys did the same.

Fun-loving guys letting off steam, Rocky thought, letting them go. *Young guys, not hurting anyone, without inhibitions or hang-ups.*

"Come on, Rocky, get yours off. We just wanna be free. It feels awesome," Aiden said, as the nude exhibitionists pranced around, with the others rolling around the floor, laughing at the nude parade. At least they were happy and not stressed over the upcoming concert and night out. Or was it their way of overcoming the stress of what was coming? Adam walked through the door to the barn, saw what was going on, and said, "Holy hell, what's happening, dudes?"

"Just hangin' free," Piet said. "Try it. It's awesome."

"Nah, I'm right, but we better get dressed for the concert," Adam said.

While this was happening, Rocky started changing into his clothes, including the cool boxers that Aiden bought him. As he pulled his boxers on, Pieter moved behind Rocky, grabbed his boxers, and gave him a wedgie. "Gotcha! I owed ya that; we're even."

"Yeah, you got me. I guess I had that coming," Rocky said.

As the laughter and ruckus died down, several others joined him and changed into their band or supporter's clothes and encouraged the other guys to get into theirs. Pieter and Aiden went to Rocky and arranged his clothes, centered his belt buckle, and straightened his tie, like two sons making sure their father was dressed so as not to embarrass them in public.

"There you are, man; that looks sweet, Rocky," Aiden said. "Now for your hair."

"Rocky, just wet your hair, and I'll put the gel in and do yours for you as soon as I do Pieter's and he does mine," Aiden said.

"Okay, boss," Rocky said. He thought to himself, *how great to see the guys straightening each other's clothes and doing each other's hair.* Only well-adjusted guys who were great mates would do that for each other or allow another guy to get that close to them to allow that to be done. Rocky too considered each of them to be great mates, so he allowed them to adjust his clothes, straighten his belt and tie, and gel and style his hair.

Aiden applied the gel to Rocky's hair, combed, fluffed, and teased it until it was untidy in a tidy fashion, with small curls and ringlets. Pieter also put in his contribution for what they thought was the desired result.

Pieter held a mirror in front of Rocky's face and asked, "How's that, dude? Isn't it wicked? Now, don't touch it; let it set, and don't mess it up."

"If you say so. I can't really see it all, but if you fellas say it's cool—well then, I guess it's cool. You guys are the ones who have to look at it, so if you like, I like. Now, we better put on the badges, hey, guys?"

Pieter went to get the two boxes. Each boy got their respective badges and attached them to their shirts. Rocky laughed at the sight—some put badges on the left side, some on the right, and most at all angles.

"Right, guys; let's decide where these badges are to be worn. Look at each other and realize the mess that has been created."

"How will we wear them, Rocky?" Adam asked.

"You guys decide which one is to go on top, and I will show you where they should go," he said.

Some decided that gold should go on top, others wanted maroon on top.

"Take a vote. Before you do, each of you speak about why you think the color you picked should go on top," Rocky said. "When you decide, let me know."

More talking and discussions took place; then the vote decided that maroon would go on top as that, they decided, was the most important.

"Can you guys give me the honor of pinning your badges on each of you?" Rocky asked. "Then one of you can pin mine on me."

"That's sweet, man," Aiden said. "Can I do yours, dude? I would love to do yours for you. Anyone object?"

No one objected. Rocky proceeded to pin each one's badges to the left side of his chest, maroon on top, with about half an inch in between. He stepped back each time to ensure each boy's badges were straight and in the right place. As he finished, he shook each one's hand and told him how proud and excited he was for them.

Aiden then pinned Rocky's badges to his left chest. He hugged Rocky very tightly and said, "Rock Daddy, thank you for everything that you have taught me and done for me and for being a wicked mate to me. I really wish that you were my father. I just think what the prick who is my father is missing out on."

Tears rolled down Rocky's face, and he struggled to say, "That's cool, champ. I am extremely proud to have done those things for you and all these other guys. Aiden, you are like a son to me. You and Pieter have become very close to me. That's cool; don't get me wrong. If that's how you feel, okay by me, buddy, but I prefer to think I am a great mate and probably like an older brother to you guys. No one can replace your father, no matter how bad he seems. You never know; he may contact you someday and come back into your life, and you could end up being the best of mates."

"No, Rock Daddy, I will never do that, not after what he has done to Mum and us kids. No, man, never," Aiden said.

"Sorry, man, didn't want you to get upset. If you want, Aiden, I will take the part of your dad. After all, that's what I have been doing, I guess," Rocky said. "Okay, man?"

"Yeah, I'm okay, Rocky. I just hate thinking about him, and I really enjoy our father-and-son talks," Aiden said, as tears rolled down his cheeks.

"Oy, buddy, don't upset yourself. I will always be there for you, at least for however long you want me, no matter what. I'm not going anywhere in a hurry," Rocky said. "Now wipe your eyes and compose yourself. We are all happy here. These are good times, and as long as I am breathing and kicking, there will be many more good times to come." Rocky reached over and gave Aiden another hug.

"Okay, guys, get your arses over here and spend your private time with Rocky before the taxi gets here. Tell him how much you love him; we all said it, how much we love him," Aiden said.

Each boy, in turn, shook Rocky's hand or hugged him and had a similar discussion to Aiden's. Pieter was the last guy to talk to Rocky, and as he walked away, Rocky said, "Hell, guys, that was heavy. Awesome, but heavy. I appreciate everything each one of you said to me. You know the pride, happiness, and emotions that you have for me? I have ten times that pride, happiness, and emotions, 'cause, I love each one of you as one of my own, and I have a great appreciation for the lives that you lead. Uninhibited, unashamed, and purposeful lives. Good on ya, guys, for making this old guy so proud and happy. You do not know what you guys have done for me.

"I have never really told you what happened to me a few years ago, what it did to me. Unknown to you guys, you have taught me a lot, letting me realize things that I have forgotten. I am stuffing this up but seeing that you asked me to stay here tonight, I have a plan. I am going to tell you all about it so that you can see what you have done for me, what you all mean to me."

"I thought we were going to have a talk about treating girls like ladies," Aiden said.

"Yeah, champ, we are, and then I will tell you my story," Rocky said, "over some food and a drink or two."

"Oh, cool man," Adam said. "We are going to have some drinks."

"I got permission from your mothers for some sensible celebrations," Rocky told them, "but guys, my rules still stand. This is special, and I consider you are grown up enough, sensible enough, to have a couple of quiet drinks. I know none of you will disappoint me and be silly. I just know it."

The journey to the theater was very quiet. Some discussion about the concert and the dinner took place, but it was obvious that nerves were taking hold. Rocky sat in the back seat so that he could observe if any of the boys had an adverse reaction. Aiden and Pieter sat on either side of Rocky. Lately, both these boys had stuck like glue to him. Maybe it was nerves and butterflies; maybe it was just that they felt safe with Rocky or appreciated his company. Whatever the reason, it was harmless. He was there for all of them, whatever their thoughts or reasons.

Aiden commented that his hands were sweating, and Pieter replied that his were too.

"That's normal when nerves and anxiety set in," Rocky told them. "Just to take a couple of slow, deep breaths and think about something else that's good in your lives," The cab arrived at the theater, Rocky paid the fare, and the guys and Rocky made their way to the rear entrance to enter the stage area.

They were met by the stage manager, George, their school principal, and a handful of local business people.

"Welcome, Rick," George said, shaking Rocky's hand firmly. "How have you been?"

"Pretty good, thanks, George. A bit busy, but I've been doing well. How about you?" Rocky asked.

"I've been extremely busy too, but it's all in place for a very good concert and night. Whatever is forgotten won't matter. It will fall into place," George said. "These young men scrub up well, don't they? Can I meet them all? My apologies for not getting time during the week to have that meeting with the entire group. Time just got away from us."

"Oy, guys," Rocky called, "can you come over here? Mr. Cleator would like to meet you all." Rocky said to George, "The guys in white shirts are the Nuver Chanz, and the red shirts are the rest of the gang, the rest of Teen Morph."

"Well, they do look clean-cut and smart," George said, "but I don't see any of those I met the other day. What's happened?"

"Oh, they probably look different when dressed the same and out of school uniforms, in different surroundings, or even their wide eyes and broad grins because of the dramatic life-changing experiences of the past ten days or so," Rocky answered, not letting on that their hair had been dyed jet-black and gelled and styled almost identically.

"Okay, guys, gather around, and I'll introduce each of you to Mr. Cleator," Rocky said. After each introduction, George had a very short discussion with each of them.

When the introductions were finished, George said, "I would like to welcome you all to my fold. I treat all my workers and staff just like a very large family. Although you boys don't work for me, I welcome you to my company's family. I feel very privileged to meet you all, and I know you can step up and help your friend and mentor, Mr. Scott, to continue his fantastic work with young guys in need. Rick has mentioned Teen Morph, and I must say those badges sit so well on your proud chests. Although I didn't know any of you when you needed the guidance and helping hand of a very patient and proud man, I have heard all about you.

"I would, with your permission, call you 'Young Guns.' Congratulations, Young Guns, on your maturity, your achievements, and your great attitudes toward responsibility, respect, and having a pleasant character. You are fantastic ambassadors to the local community and to people your own age.

Good on you, guys. Now, before we start the concert, a photographer will take some photos—not formal photos as such, just casual. We would like some individual photos, photos of the group, photos of the band, photos of the support group, and some of each of you with Mr. Scott. If you would come this way, we will begin the photo session."

The group moved to the right side of the stage, where the photographer had set up his cameras and lighting with a few different backdrops and props. There was a stool, a couple of different chairs, two ladders, an old wooden stump, a partial wall with a window, several different-sized boxes to stand on, and a few other unusual objects. The photo session progressed well; although the excitement level was high, the guys relaxed completely and had their photos taken in several poses using combinations of the props. Rocky thought the poses using the ladders looked the best; he looked forward to seeing the photographs.

"Now, don't go, fellas," George said. "We aren't quite finished. Bill, can you get those cartons out now?"

A fellow who was obviously Bill wheeled three cardboard cartons onto the stage from behind the left wing and placed them on the floor in front George.

"This is Bill Turner, one of my company's family that I spoke about. He is involved with our social group of people, and he has something for you all. Over to you, Bill," George said.

"Thanks, George," Bill began. "As George said, we have a social club at Cleator's, and we raise money for social activities for all of the staff. However, we put a percentage into a separate fund to donate to worthwhile activities or clubs. Some of our staff are either related to some of you, or know of you through acquaintances, or have children who go to school with you. Doesn't matter how, but each of you is known by somebody at Cleator's. So, the social club has decided unanimously to honor you guys."

Bill began to open the boxes, and George and Bill removed the contents. The two men revealed twelve new skateboards, which they lined up along the floor. "We want to present to each of you—including you, Rick—a skateboard to keep. Each one has your name along with the word *metamorphosis* on one end of the deck. On the other end is the company's logo and the words "Cleator Young Guns." If you would like to come forward as your name is called, please accept your skateboard and move over to the photographer for one more photo. Thanks, guys," Bill said.

At first, all the boys were dumbstruck. Then words like *mental, awesome, cool,* and *wicked* came from them.

"I did say one is for you, Mr. Scott," said Bill, "but I didn't tell you that there is a twelfth one for you to use in the best way you see fit—maybe to give as a prize or for a very important supporter. You will decide sometime. Congratulations, Young Guns. May your youth remain with you for a very long time."

"We better move away so the final preparations for the band fest can happen," George said. "Good luck, fellas, both for this afternoon and for your future endeavors. I will see you all soon. I really do want to get to know you much better over a chat."

The boys thanked George and Bill and shook their hands as they left the stage. Some of the guys helped the photographer pack up his equipment and assisted him in moving it to where he was setting it up to photograph the bands during the competition.

"Thanks, fellas," the photographer said. "What a pleasant and helpful bunch of boys you are. Here, take a couple of my business cards. I would love to be your official photographer if I could—no charge. When you have an activity, let me know, and I will be there. If you need private photos of yourselves or your families, let me know. It would be my pleasure. I will see you when you're onstage and then later, at the dinner. Yeah, more photos. Can't have too many, you know."

The boys moved off stage and presented themselves to the stage manager, seeking any last-minute instructions. The manager went over a few points with them and told them they could sit on any of the groups of chairs set out backstage or that they could walk around outside and get some fresh air. He also advised them not to miss their call to prepare for their performance, as it was important not to hold up the program.

They elected to take a small stroll to the front of the theater so that they could see who was arriving to attend the concert and to wait for their mothers. Each carried their newly acquired skateboard. Pieter and Aiden carried Rocky's and the extra skateboard. The boys chatted with excitement with some of the younger people who arrived, while Rocky chatted to other people and some of the business dignitaries who he knew or who wanted to meet him. Rocky never missed an opportunity to talk with influential people. He knew that at some point, there usually were benefits to be gained—cash or assistance for youth projects.

Adrian, the nude taxi passenger, also came up to talk with Rocky and wished the guys the best for their big night out. As the cabs arrived that were carrying their mothers and Piet's neighbors, the boys went into hysteria. They embraced their mothers, showing great pride and excitement, talking quickly, trying to tell them as much as possible, and showing off their new skateboards. The photographer was nearby and did not miss an opportunity to take several photographs of the boys with their mothers. A couple of guys with TV cameras came up to Rocky and asked him if this was the group of boys who had formed the youth foundation with Cleator Enterprises. When Rocky answered that it was, they began to roll their cameras and tried in vain to get an interview with the boys.

"Instant celebs," Rocky said to one of the mums. "Isn't it fantastic? I think I better interrupt and tell these guys to arrange a formal interview later, after the concert."

Rocky spoke to a couple of the interviewers, suggesting he would organize the guys for a group interview after the rock competition. They agreed that would be the better option. Always the worried protector, Rocky was a little concerned with how the boys would cope with their instant celebrity status. One of the ladies who worked at the theater offered a storage room to store the skateboards, so the guys took the boards with her and locked them up in the secure room; then they returned to the foyer, where the band members hugged their mums and Mitch's mum, said their goodbyes, and accepted their wishes of good luck.

"Do you guys want me backstage with you?" Rocky asked.

"Nah, Rocky, we'll be right. You and the other guys go in and enjoy the show with our mums," Aiden said.

"Yeah, Rocky, we're cool," Piet said.

"All right. We'll walk back with you and then go in for the show," Rocky said. The group walked around the back of the theater to the backstage entrance. "Best of luck, guys. Kill 'em with your charm and talent, and more important, enjoy the experience." The group went into a group hug. "Rock on, dudes," Rocky said.

He and the others walked away, leaving the five band guys to enter the backstage area. Rocky could not help the feeling of sadness; it was the same feeling he'd had on his sons' first day of school. He'd felt that he had to be with them to hold their hands and support them. *Lighten up, old man*, he thought. *They are strong enough to experience their first public appearance without you in their pockets.*

The guys walked to the front of the theater with Rocky. Several of the festival organizers met the five lads and Adrian and Rocky as they entered the theater. After a short chat, they made their way to their seats in the same area where the mums and neighbors were already seated.

"Oh, sorry, Adrian, I haven't told you, have I?" Rocky said. "Guys, just stay here. I need to call George and organize a place for Adrian at the dinner. Adrian, come with me. I'll explain what has happened. Guys, you were talking before about your after-party at Piet's barn—is Adrian invited to that too?" "Hell yeah!" Jay said. "He is a part of us, really. He was there with you for us that night."

"Okay, Adrian, let's be quick," Rocky said, and they hurried toward the exit.

Rocky briefly explained the dinner after the concert, the youth foundation, and the youth center to Adrian and asked if he wanted to join the guys after the concert.

"Hell yeah," Adrian answered. "Sounds awesome. Are you sure, Rocky? I don't want to intrude?"

"You won't be intruding. I'm sorry I didn't think of you earlier. You are part of this; it was you who helped me calm these guys when Mitch died. We would be honored if you'd join us. Shit, man, I need you to keep them under control, especially if they are successful. Can you imagine how hyped-up they will be? I am so excited for them. They deserve some good vibes at last. After the dinner, we're going back to Piet's barn for a chill-out and a sleepover. You must join in, if you want. Piet won't mind; in fact, I know he would love to see you again."

"Yeah, I'll be in that. Christy is not coming out again, so hell yeah, I'm in," Adrian said.

"What's going on with your lady? Are things a bit rocky with you two?" "Yeah, a bit. I think my being away all week and her hanging out with her girlfriends—I don't know—I think that they're getting into her head. I'm not worried too much. If that's the way it is, too bad. I got plenty of time, and there are other chicks who want to go out with me. It's all cool."

"That's a shame, but like you said, you got plenty of time. Sometimes these things happen to test you, to show you if you are with the right one. Things happen for a reason. Hang in there," Rocky said, putting his arm around Adrian's shoulders.

The compares for the band competition were Dave and Fran, the breakfast show hosts from the local radio station.

"Ladies and gentlemen, welcome to the 1998 Youth Rocks Music Fest," the announcement began. "Please welcome the master of ceremonies, Mr. George Cleator."

The crowd erupted in applause as the curtains opened, music blasted from the surround-sound system, and a pinpoint spotlight highlighted a lectern with George standing behind it.

George gave a short speech, welcoming the audience, listing the bands that were competing, and announcing that there was a special group of people in the audience and that more details would be released later.

Another group of spotlights highlighted Rocky, the five remaining guys, and their mums, as George said, "Please welcome Mr. Rick Scott and his group of young guns, called the Teen-Morph Foundation, or as I like to call them, the Cleator Young Guns, along with their mothers. Welcome ladies. The group is not complete. Another five of them are competitors today; they're called Nuver Chanz. Please make them welcome."

The audience erupted with wild applause once again as Rocky and the guys stood to acknowledge their applause and to bow to George. The spotlights crisscrossed the audience in unison with their applause.

"Now, as I said, more details will be released later today about this great man and the group of young men who make up the Cleator Young Guns, and some exciting news about other developments in fostering great outcomes for this town's adolescents. However, without further hesitation, let the show begin. Over to our announcers, who will introduce the judges and then the bands as they move onstage."

More applause from the audience; then music filled the theater. As each group was called onstage, the announcer spoke briefly about them and introduced them to the audience. As the fifth group were about to be announced, the announcer said, "Band number five—Nuver Chanz." The crowd erupted as they realized that they were the band that George had mentioned earlier.

"These boys are the youngest group in the competition. Only been playing seriously for three or four months, and people, wait till you hear them. They sound like they have been playing and singing for years."

The boys walked toward the front of the stage to be introduced, and the announcer said, "I won't tell you their story, although it is an exceptional one. I am sure that over the coming days, weeks, months, and years that you will hear a lot more about these guys and the half dozen or so up there in the audience."

The spotlights came on to highlight the group in the audience as they stood once again. Loud applause erupted once again from the audience. They didn't really know why; they just applauded.

"You deserve it, guys," the announcer said. "We have Aiden, lead guitar and vocals; Pieter on rhythm and vocals; Haydon, drums—and is he one mean drummer; Adam on bass guitar; and Declan on keyboard and trumpet. Good luck, guys. Now, ladies and gentlemen, please give it up for Nuver Chanz."

After the applause died down, the announcers continued with the introductions. Then the announcer outlined the format for the afternoon. "Each band will perform and sing two songs in the first round and then come back to perform a third song in the second round. The judges will judge each group on each song on various criteria, like appearance, sound, lyric clarity, professionalism onstage, and a few other criteria. Points will be awarded, and the group with the most points, naturally, will be declared the winner of Youth Rocks Music Fest 1998. The group with the second highest points will be given the Encouragement Award. The third award is not judged by the judges onstage but by you, the audience. You need to cheer and applaud and yell your praises for the band or bands that you prefer. We have pickups positioned around the theater to record and measure your approval it in the control room for volume and length of time above a set decibel level, so if you like a group's performance, make a noise at the appropriate time."

The announcer announced the first group to perform and then the next three competitors' performances in turn. The atmosphere was electric, as nothing could beat watching and listening to live music. The guys were beside themselves, taking in the live performances, the antics of each band onstage, and the atmosphere in general.

"Now, will you please welcome back to the stage, Nuver Chanz," the announcer said as the stage lit up to highlight the five boys. The audience roared with wild applause. "The boys have chosen to play 'Beds Are Burning,' made famous by Midnight Oil, and 'Never Tear Us Apart' by INXS. When you are ready, guys," the announcer said.

The lads started playing the first few bars and the applause began. The boys weren't fazed; they played on.

"That sounds awesome," Jay said. "Sounds so much better than in the shed."

As they finished the first song, the crowd went wild. The noise from the audience was by far the loudest and longest. The mums were ecstatic, cheering, jumping, and clapping, almost appearing to lead the rest of the audience. As the noise settled, Nuver Chanz began their version of "Never Tear Us Apart," one of their favorite tracks from their idol band INXS. It too was performed very well, which was rewarded by the applause from the audience. As the noise settled again, the announcer suggested that Michael and the boys from INXS would be very proud if they heard that version. "Thanks, boys," the announcer said as Nuver Chanz bowed and left the stage amid wild applause once again.

The round finished after the next two groups performed their songs, and the announcer said there would be a twenty-minute intermission, and then the next round would commence.

The boys, Rocky, and the mums moved out of the theater to have a cigarette, for those who smoked, or a drink or chips. Rocky and the boys decided to wait till after the concert to get a drink, and they moved over to the edge near some bushes so Rocky could have a cigarette.

"We've told you before you should give that shit away," Jacob said. "It's no good for you, you know."

"Yeah, I know, buddy. I'm sorry, but I really need this one," Rocky said.

The five guys from the band ran up to the group and jumped and hugged the rest, talking about their experience and how wicked it felt up onstage. The others told the band guys how awesome they sounded and looked onstage.

Adrian walked up to the group carrying a small container with cans of soda for the boys and ice-cold cans of bourbon and cola for Rocky and for himself.

"Thanks, mate, that's wicked. Thanks for treating them with drinks," Rocky said.

"That's cool," Adrian said. "That was awesome, guys." He threw himself at them.

"Hey, Adrian, how ya doin', dude?" Aiden said.

"Good, mate, you too?" Adrian responded,

"Sweet, man. We had a wicked time," Aiden said. "It's been an awesome week or two."

"Yeah, so I hear," Adrian said. "Rocky's been telling me a bit about you guys. Good on ya's."

"You haven't heard the rest yet," Rocky said, as Adrian lit a cigarette and insisted Rocky take one from his packet.

"Hey, guys, I have arranged for Adrian to join us at the dinner, and he probably will come to Piet's barn for a chill later," Rocky said. "Just like old school."

"Yeah, that'll be sweet. Adrian, we want to catch up with you and see what's been happening," Pieter said, "but you gotta keep your clothes on!"

Adrian blushed and said sheepishly, "Did you tell these guys?"

"Yeah, a couple of them," Rocky answered.

"That's cool," Adrian replied.

"No, Adrian, you can get your gear off. We all will and go skinny-dipping," Piet said. "We just got to convince old man, here, to join us. He is a bit shy about getting his clothes off when we are around."

"Hey, cool. That's a great idea. Why don't we?" Aiden said.

"You better check with Sally first, Piet," Rocky said. "You better see if it is cool with her."

"It'll be okay. We do it all the time. You know us, Rocky, not frightened of getting our gear off. No harm," Pieter said.

"Yeah, I guess I have noticed that a few times, like this afternoon in the barn at dressing time."

Adrian asked what had happened, so the boys explained the antics they got up to earlier.

The bell rang, and a voice announced, "Five minutes to part two of this afternoon's competition. Please take your seats."

"Good luck, guys. We will be with you when you appear onstage again. You're doing well," Rocky said as the band members broke away and walked toward the backstage entrance. The rest entered the theater. "Thanks, Adrian, for the drinks," Rocky said as he once again put his arm around Adrian's shoulder. "The guys appreciated that."

"Cool, Rocky, the least I could do. It's great to catch up with them and see how great they are doing. They were real drop-kicks six months or so ago. Now look at them, on top of the world. I'm a bit jealous. I wasn't doing that well when I was that age. Hell, they are enjoying an awesome life, thanks to you, old man," Adrian said, putting his arm around Rocky's shoulders. "Congratulations, Mr. Rick Scott."

"Thanks, Adrian," Rocky said.

The second part of the show commenced, this time with the announcer onstage. It was one of the hosts from a local radio show. Rocky thought he recognized the voice. He was the male host on a breakfast show. A spotlight lit up his female counterpart, and they went into some of the familiar chitchat routines they used on their show, which entertained the audience. He then said, "Welcome to part two of the rock festival for 1998. Before we begin, I have some announcements to make. We have an area down here that is vacant between the edge of the stage and the first row of seats. This area, people, can be used to dance, or you can simply come down and be closer to the action. It is not big enough for all of you, but if you are sensible and don't overcrowd the area, everyone will be safe. Okay, on with the show," he said and then announced the first group once again.

Each band in turn, played their final songs. Then it came to Nuver Chanz to play and sing their final song.

"Please, welcome Nuver Chanz to our stage once again. Aiden, Pieter, Haydon, Adam, and Declan—welcome. Nuver Chanz, ladies and gentlemen, with the U2 classic 'I Still Haven't Found What I'm Lookin' For.' Take it away, boys."

"Before we start," Aiden began nervously, "we would like to honor two people with this song."

"The first," Pieter said, "is our mate, Mitch, who died six months ago. We know you are out there, mate. This is for you."

Haydon came to Piet's microphone and said, "And the other guy this song is for is Rocky, our great mate. If he hadn't been around for us, we wouldn't be here doing this."

"And we probably wouldn't be alive either. Thanks, Rocky," Pieter said as the spotlight came on to highlight Rocky in the audience.

"Please listen to the words," Piet said, "and I hope we can do it good for you, and you can hear the words. 'I Still Haven't Found What I'm Looking For'—here we go." The audience applauded and chanted.

The boys performed an almost-perfect version of the song, and people in the theater seemed to be visibly concentrating on the words and swaying and dancing to the rhythms and beats. As they finished, all stood up and gave a great ovation to Nuver Chanz and applauded and chanted loud and long. As the boys left the stage, they bowed to the audience and used the V salute to indicate to Rocky and the other guys that they felt good about their performance.

The female host said, "Did you see that hand gesture? What does it mean? Is that part of their act, I wonder?"

"I don't know," the male host said. "I have seen a lot of hand gestures from our young people, but I haven't seen that one. I must find out what that means." He tried to imitate it but got it wrong.

The last two bands performed their last songs to the very appreciative audience, and then it came time to announce the winners.

George Cleator and Bob Watson came onto the stage with Dave and Fran, the radio hosts, to announce the winners.

"That was a fantastic display. Our local youth obviously possess great talent," George said. "Congratulations and thanks to the wonderful girls and boys and men and women for entertaining us today. Bob, as the principal of the local high school, you must have known each one of them at some stage."

"Yes, George, I have known all of them, and one group is still at our school. Congratulations to all of you for your display of enthusiasm and professionalism that you've shown us today," Bob said.

"Now, I have the pleasure of announcing the winner," Fran said. "I have the envelope here. I must thank the judges. They had a very difficult task today. I am told that there are just two points separating first and second place. So, here we go." Fran opened the envelope. "The winner of Youth Rocks Music Fest 1998—or, as Mr. George Cleator likes to call it, Young Guns Rock Festival—is … 2B2S, the group made up of Zane, Celeste, Byron, and Jo, brothers and sisters combination. Congratulations to 2B2S. Come and accept your prize of two thousand dollars, sponsored by Eric's Electrical, Vision, and Sound and presented by Mr. Eric Hudson, managing director. Let's hear it for 2B2S."

Dave then said, "The second-place band, our Encouragement Award, coming just two points behind out of a possible hundred points, is … Nuver Chanz. Congratulations, guys." The audience roared their approval with loud applause. "This prize of one thousand dollars is sponsored by Hot Shots FM Radio and will be presented by Mr. George Cleator, managing director of Cleator Enterprises, the owners of Hot Shots FM and chairman of the chamber of commerce. Let's give it up for Nuver Chanz, five young guys, barely sixteen, who have only been performing together for three to four months—Aiden, Pieter, Haydon, Adam, and Declan." As the applause died down, Dave said, "Tell me, guys, that hand gesture you gave at your last performance—what was it?" He placed the microphone in front of Aiden and Pieter.

Aiden made the traditional V signal. "This?"

"Yeah, what's does it mean? I haven't seen that one before," Dave said.

"Don't know if I'm allowed to tell," Aiden said. He looked toward where Rocky was sitting. "I can't see him. Should I tell everyone?" Aiden asked, looking at the rest of Nuver Chanz.

The spotlight shone where Rocky was sitting.

"Can I tell 'em Rocky?" Aiden asked.

Rocky stood and showed the V sign, indicating that it was okay. The crowd roared with laughter as Rocky regained his seat.

"Cool, well, it is a sign we use to indicate a victory or that something that we have done that feels good to us or to show we approve of what was done," Aiden said proudly. "It's just something we do among ourselves."

"Can I do it?" Dave asked.

"Yeah, sure. Just do it right, though," Aiden said.

"Show us how it's done," Dave said.

"Form a V with the first two fingers on your right hand, with your thumb and other fingers curled into your palm," Aiden said, demonstrating, with the other four guys doing the same. "Now, your left arm is held above your head horizontally like this," Aiden said, again demonstrating. "Now hold your right arm, with the V fingers in place, above your head, in front of your left arm to form a plus sign, with the V upward like this," Aiden said, showing the signal.

"Like this?" Dave asked. "Is that right?"

"Yeah, that's it. Man, you're doing well," Aiden said.

Dave laughed at Aiden's cheekiness, and the audience laughed with him. "I like this cool guy," he said to the audience, shaking Aiden's hand. "You're one cool dude, Aiden. Thanks for showing us that. Does it work?"

"It works for us. Not worried what others think," Aiden said. "You gotta have some positive thoughts in your life; that's one of ours. See, V on top for victory and the two arms forming a plus sign. Plus means positive."

"That's awesome, man. I like that attitude," Dave said. "No wonder you guys are going places. Good on you all. Okay, moving on, thanks, guys. Nuver Chanz, ladies and gentlemen, our Encouragement Award winners.

"Aren't they cool dudes?" Fran said. "Boy, have they got a future with the attitudes they have. Now … People's Choice Award. You guys in the audience picked this one, with the sensors around the theater measuring your applause in the control room. Sponsored by Channel 8 television and presented by Mr. Bob Watson, principal of Port Vernon High School, the People's Choice Youth Rocks Music Fest 1998 is … Nuver Chanz. Good on ya, guys."

The crowd once again erupted with applause and chanting while the band moved forward to be presented with the trophy and a $1,000 check. The other five guys ran down to the mosh pit area in front of the stage, yelling their congratulations and praise to their mates.

"You know these guys?" Fran said.

"Yeah, they are the other guys from our gang," Pieter said. "They're our mates and the guys who help with our equipment. They gotta put up with us, listening to our practice." "Come on up here, guys, with your mates," Fran said. "Mr. Watson is going to present you with your prize."

"Congratulations, boys, well done. It gives me great pleasure to present this to these boys. These are the ones I mentioned before who still attend school. I am so proud of them. They were—I know they won't mind my telling you this—they were the worst behaved kids on the block not that long ago. They have achieved so much, not only through their musical skills and consistent perseverance, but also with the fantastic help from their mate and mentor, Mr. Rick Scott. I know their families, their school, and the community at large want to thank Mr. Scott for his efforts in taking these ten lost souls and showing them another journey. Thank you, Rick. George Cleator touched on some new initiatives earlier. I won't steal his thunder, but as principal of Port Vernon High, we are fully supportive of the program that he intends to implement with Mr. Scott and these ten lads, and we will be a big part of expanding it to assist all of our young people."

"Thank you, Mr. Watson," Fran said. "Is that what these badges are all about? I've just noticed that all of you have them. Did you notice them, Dave?"

"Yes, Fran, I was going to ask about those badges. Maybe one of you can tell us about them."

Aiden said, "The gold one says, 'Teen-Morph Foundation', a fund that us guys and Rocky ... err, Mr. Scott has set up to fund equipment and activities for young kids in trouble."

"That's amazing. Ten sixteen-year-olds caring for kids their own age. Fantastic!" Dave said.

Pieter said, "The maroon badge says, 'Teen-Morph Youth Center'. I don't know what we can say about it, but it will be this awesome youth center with activities for teenagers. We haven't worked out details yet. We have a lot of work to do to get it up and running. We only decided about it last week."

"That's just amazing, fellas. Congratulations on your two wins with Nuver Chanz and your ventures with young kids. Tell you what—can you play and sing your last song by U2? I'm sure it will be okay with the stage people," Dave said, looking around for approval.

The band's gear was brought back onstage very quickly, and the band members took their positions as the others moved away to leave the stage.

"No, guys, you can stay with your mates and enjoy the moment," Dave said.

"Before we start, can I ask a question?" Pieter said.

"Yeah, sure, Pieter," Dave answered. "What do you want to ask?"

"Can we have Rocky up here with us too, and Adrian, if that is cool?"

"Why not? You obviously appreciate what Rocky has done for you. Come on up, Rocky," Dave said.

"Who is Adrian?" Fran asked.

"Oh, he was with Rocky when Mitch went missing in the water. He helped us then, when we didn't know what to do to find Mitch," Aiden said in a slightly depressed voice. "He is a legend too, just like Rocky."

"Well, Adrian, I'm sure it would be okay," Fran said.

"Yeah, come on up here, Adrian," Dave said.

Both Rocky and Adrian joined the guys onstage and immediately formed a group hug.

"Look at that, ladies and gentlemen. Have you ever seen such a sight? Those boys sure know how to show their excitement, appreciation, and enthusiasm. That's fantastic, guys," Dave said as the crowd erupted into loud applause once more.

"Okay, ladies and gentlemen, Nuver Chanz with the U2 hit 'I Still Haven't Found What I'm Lookin' For,'" Fran said.

Nuver Chanz performed their song to perfection. There was hardly a dry eye in the theater. The other five guys and Adrian broke into a dance to accompany the band, with Adrian displaying his tremendous dance skills. Rocky thought how well the boys had conducted themselves, and he was impressed with their professionalism in speaking to an audience, how they had thrown themselves into their music, and how the other boys displayed their support of the band on their night.

As they finished, wild applause again filled the theater. Dave called Rocky over to the mike and asked, "Rocky ... Mr. Scott ... how does that make you feel?"

"Awesome, mate," Rocky said. "I feel just great. What more could I or anyone else wish for? These boys never cease to amaze me. Thanks, guys, for listening to an older man who cared. I am at a loss for words. These guys just make me swell up with pride, and you, Adrian—hell, you can dance. I forgot about your dance abilities. I have heard a lot about your dancing, but I had never seen it. You got a job coming up. These guys have a wish to dance like you wouldn't believe, and I know that when they have an idea or a plan, they break down all barriers to get it, and then they make it happen."

"You are proud of these guys, aren't you?" Fran asked.

"You betcha, Fran. Everyone wrote these guys off to the scrap heap. I couldn't watch that happen 'cause at that time I had gotten to know them. They didn't fool me with their tough, buff, brazen front. I could see through the smoke screen, and with a little bit of work and a lot of talking and encouragement, here we are, these mighty young men. Good on ya, guys. Yes, I am proud. I didn't force any of them to change their attitudes, but they did! They chose to become the successes that they are today. Also, thank you very much, guys, for allowing me into your inner lives, and boy, did we get very deep at times. Thanks, guys, and congratulations."

"Thanks, Rocky, for those words," Dave said. "Good luck in your future endeavors. I have some inside information on what is to be announced later tonight, but I can't say too much about it here. Please give a rousing round of applause to Mr. Rick Scott, Adrian, the Nuver Chanz, and the Cleator Young Guns—oops, I probably wasn't allowed to say Young Guns, but now that you know, watch out for them over the coming week or so."

The audience applauded loudly as the band guys went backstage and the other guys, Adrian, and Rocky returned to their seats.

"Now, we haven't forgotten about the other bands. We wish to thank them as well as the sponsors, the backstage team, front of house, and the lighting and sound guys up there for their contributions, and, above all— without them there would be no competition—the bands. Well done to all of you. To finish the show, 2B2S, the winners of Youth Speaks 1998 will perform one of their winning songs. Please welcome them back—2B2S," Dave said.

When 2B2S finished their song, the announcer said, "Ladies and gentlemen, please stand and show your appreciation for our bands." He went on to introduce each band as they came back onstage.

The lights in the theater came on, and the audience filed out to the front of the theater. Rocky and the guys, with Adrian and the mums, moved to the side near the shrubs, where they were at intermission. Rocky said, "Hell, I need a smoke," as he lit a cigarette and offered one to Adrian and the mums who smoked. "Wasn't that a wild show and an awesome result for the boys?" Rocky said.

There was agreement all around from the guys and the mothers. People came up to meet Rocky and his crew, along with Nuver Chanz, who had joined them. People spoke to Rocky about the guys and spoke to the guys, congratulating them on their lifestyle and their achievements. Several reporters asked Rocky for interviews and photographs.

"It might be better if we have the interviews now and get them out of the way," Rocky said, calling the guys over as a group. They held the interviews and posed for photographs and TV cameras.

After the interviews and photographs were finished, they continued chatting with their mums and each other.

"That's awesome, Rocky. Can I really be a part of it when I am home?"

"Yeah, sure, mate, you are a part of it. The guys know you, appreciate what you have done for them, and all of them have a lot admiration for you. Of course, you are part of it. I would be disappointed if you weren't. I'll need someone like you between their age and my age. You are in," Rocky said. "I'll arrange for badges for you too, to make it official. Think about what title should be on your badges, and we will talk about it." Rocky shook Adrian's hand. Then he called out to the guys, "Adrian wants to join the team and help us plan and build the youth center. What do you say? Should we let him in?"

"Hell yeah, he's one of us. He knows us, our story. He's gotta be in," Aiden said. "Hands up, guys, if you agree."

All ten hands went skyward indicating that all wanted Adrian to be on the Teen-Morph Foundation team.

"Thanks, guys," Adrian said. "I am honored to be your mate. I work away most weeks, so I will only be around on weekends, though. Okay?"

"That's cool; we go to school on weekdays anyway and hope to find a job in a couple of years, so we are same," Pieter said.

George came over to talk to the guys and said everyone he had spoken to had sung high praises. He spoke to each of them in a very jovial manner and shook each one's hand. He then turned to Adrian and said, "You must tell me about yourself sometime. You sound like a very good friend to Rick and the boys. I heard about you while you were onstage. Pleased to meet you, Adrian," George said as they shook hands. "Good on you for assisting

Rick to help these boys find their friend. Very admirable. Most people just turn their backs and walk away. Fine character. I'll get to know you in due course and look forward to seeing you inside."

"Thanks, Mr. Cleator, for your comments. Pleased to meet you too."

"Call me George, please. No formalities here."

"Okay, George, I look forward to speaking to you soon."

"Rick, if Adrian is part of the foundation, we better get him the badges. I'll make a note of it, and we will sort it out next week. Don't forget about my job offer," George said.

"Oh, sorry, George, I wish to accept. I hadn't formally gotten back to you," Rocky said.

"Well, I knew that you were going to accept by the way the boys spoke and the things that they have said. Congratulations. Glad to have you on board. Make your way inside when you are ready. We have a few extra places because we had some set aside for each of the winning bands. Because Nuver Chanz took out two categories, we have a few left over. You can spread out a bit if you wish; I will leave that to you fellas," George said. "I'll see you all inside. Hi, mums, welcome. Some fine sons you have here." He continued to speak briefly to the mothers before disappearing through the function room doors.

CHAPTER 12

Remember the good times with a passion, but never forget the bad times. Learn from them and move on.

"We better get inside," Rocky suggested. "Why don't each of you accompany your mum inside, and Adrian and I will accompany Ellen."

The boys went to their mums and told them that they were ready to accompany them to their table. "Rocky and Adrian will accompany you inside, Mrs. Harvey," Aiden told Ellen.

"How about we let Mitch's mum and Rocky and Adrian in first, hey, guys?" Pieter said, "Then we will follow. Is that okay, Mrs. Harvey?"

"Yes, Pieter, that's fine," Ellen said. "I'd be honored to be escorted by these fine gentlemen."

Once inside, the guys seemed like fish out of water. They obviously had never been present at a formal occasion. Their eyes were open wide, looking around the room at the decorations, the lighting, the small stage, the dance floor, and the neatly set tables. It all seemed too much to take in.

"Wow, this is awesome," Adam said. "Look at that screen. What's that for?"

"Probably some pictures, maybe some video footage of the concert," Adrian said.

"Did they video the concert?" Jacob asked.

"Oh, I forgot to tell you. Yes, they did video the concert, and they are giving us a copy."

Each boy found the place cards for their mums and made sure that they were comfortable. Then they looked for their table. "There are two tables—one for all of us and one for Nuver Chanz," Nick said. "Which one will the band sit at?"

"I think we might all sit at the group table, and any of you can sit over there when you need to spread out a bit," Rocky suggested.

The guys decided to sit at the group table for the time being. They found their place cards and sat down.

"Still can't believe this is happening," Pieter said, still looking around at the way the room was set up and decorated.

The waiters placed a few jugs of water with ice and juice on the table and proceeded to pour drinks for the guys. Then, several plates of different types of bread and spreading dips were placed in the center. It seemed obvious that the guys wanted to eat some, but none of them was game enough to be the first.

"Here, guys, I'll show you," Rocky said, picking up a piece of bread and spreading it with one of the dips. Immediately, all copied the process, and suddenly, the ice was broken. From that point, all the guys relaxed, as they realized that the food placed on the table was to be eaten.

"Guys, you better look at the menu in front of you and pick what you would like to eat," Rocky said. "There are two entrees to pick from and three main courses. Work out what you want so we don't hold up the waiters too much."

After several questions, asking what this is or what that is, the boys had worked out what meal they preferred.

"Now, guys, did you notice the dance floor?" Adrian asked. "When the time comes, you should get up and have a dance."

"Hey, Adrian, they are all oldies," Jay said. "There aren't any hot chicks. What's going on?"

"Well, who are you going to dance with?" Rocky said, laughing at Jay's observation.

"You guys better pick one to dance with and be prepared to get up and ask," Adrian said, also laughing.

"There isn't anyone that I would dance with," Haydon said, still looking around for his perfect partner.

"Oh, come on, guys; get with the program," Adrian said. "You are missing the point. There is a perfect partner for each of you, and the one left, Rocky and I will fight over," Adrian said, giving Rocky a nudge with his shoulder.

"Come on, guys, wake up. If you haven't got a partner, you will have to dance with Rocky and me, and I hope it is a slow song," Adrian said, pissing himself laughing.

"Oh, you mean our mums?" Nick said.

"Oh, that's a cool idea, man. I'd love to dance with my mum," Pieter said. "Much better than getting an offer from one of those oldies."

"And I am sure your mothers would love to dance with their sons," Adrian continued.

"Good evening, ladies and gentlemen, I am George Cleator, chairman of the chamber of commerce. Welcome to the 1998 Youth Rocks Music Fest reception. Please enjoy your evening. I would like to sincerely thank and welcome our 1998 sponsors, as without your support, this event would not be possible. Welcome also to the winning band, 2B2S, and their partners and supporters. Congratulations on your win earlier today. Welcome also to the Encouragement Award winners, who also won the People's Choice Award, Nuver Chanz. You will notice that they are not sitting at the band table at the moment, as they are here also representing a larger group of young men, a youth support group called Teen-Morph Foundation. Earlier today, these boys were named the Cleator Young Guns by the Cleator Enterprises Social Club. Congratulations, boys. More on the Young Guns later. Welcome also, table eight. These lovely ladies are the proud mothers of these boys. Congratulations, ladies, on having such fine young men as your sons. Now, Mr. Scott, welcome to you as well. I won't say any more of Mr. Scott until later. Finally, welcome to Mr. Adrian Cooper, who has also played a part in the lives of these fellows. Welcome to you, Adrian. Now please enjoy your meal and enjoy the evening. I will be back for more speaking after the entrees. While we are enjoying our entrees, photographs and video footage of today's proceedings will be shown on the large screen near the stage."

Entrees were served. The guys enjoyed the food and drinks that were served but could not understand that it was not their meal. *This is a great learning curve for these guys*, Rocky thought. *The experiences will stay with them for a long time to come.* They were maturing and growing up so fast. Each boy, from time to time, visited his mother's table to check on his mum or tell her how awesome the night was. George also called to table eight to talk to the ladies, and then moved on to table nine, the table where the Young Guns were seated, for a chat.

As the entree plates were cleared away, George moved from his table to the lectern. "That was a great entree, wasn't it? Thank you to the caterers. Now, where do I start? First, I would like to inform you, per tradition, that the profits from today's concert are divided equally between the high school and another group, a sports club, a target organization in need of funds, a church, a youth group, an organization with its focus on young people and their activities. This year, the high school will receive their check for half the profits, but the other half, it has been decided, will go to the Teen-Morph Foundation. I imagine not many, if any, of you have heard of this group before tonight. It is a very new but a very important group, whose aim is to help young people, our future adults, who find themselves in trouble or at risk. This group was borne of one man's concern and courage for the well-being of a group of boys who were lost to society. These boys were well on their way to a decent future under the guidance of this man, when suddenly, tragedy struck. This man was there for these guys, offering a shoulder to cry on, comfort, compassion, hope and a shining light, showing them a path to follow. He took them out of the depths of depression and despair to, what they are today, yeah, that's okay guys, you can stand up, where was I? From out of the depths to what you see here tonight, this group of fine young men, who still hold the sadness of losing their friend, have moved on to enjoy their lives, their achievements, each other's friendships, love for their families, and love for their mentor and friend, Mr. Roderick Scott.

"Stand up, Rick; you too, Adrian. This is the man who has mentored and nurtured these boys and showed and coached them on a better path. Both these men were there when Mitchell Harvey was lost in the water, and they tried to help them find Mitchell. They comforted them when Mitchell's lifeless body was pulled up onto the jetty that night. The chamber of commerce congratulates you boys in changing your attitudes toward life and the community and your school and your family—a truly worthwhile recipient of the money.

"You will hear more about this group in the coming weeks and months. These boys are adamant that they will help other boys at risk and emulate Mr. Scott's help and friendship that he has given to them. They have wonderful plans for the cash, like outdoor sports facilities, water sport opportunities, and of course, music activities. We wish them well.

"Now, for the next announcement—and you can sit down, guys—I have had a dream for a long time of developing a center for youth activities. I have a parcel of land that was used by the construction arm of Cleator Enterprises as a caravan park and workers camp for those who built the harbor loading plant and container wharf some years back. I considered selling it a few times but, luckily, I decided to hang onto it. It gives me great pleasure to announce that I am handing it over to these boys at table nine. They have decided to accept it and have decided to call it Teen-Morph Youth Center. Mr. Scott will be residing onsite and is moving to my payroll so that he can manage it more efficiently. Mr. Adrian Cooper, who is also at table nine, will be assisting Mr. Scott from time to time, when his busy schedule permits. This center is also making its facilities available to the students and staff of the high school and other youth-support agencies. So, would you please join me in congratulating Mr. Scott and his young men and toasting the success of their venture. Thank you.

"The main meal will now be served and during the meal, we'll show more still photos and some video footage of our youngsters achieving, courtesy of the Port Vernon High School. You will also notice that there are images of sports groups and some taken earlier today of those fine guys at table nine. After our meal, we will invite Mr. Scott to the lectern. Be warned that he does get emotional about his cause and will probably not hold back. Please enjoy your meal."

During the main meal, the guys enjoyed watching the vision and sound on the screen and more footage of the rock fest. Aiden came to Rocky and asked him, "Rocky, when do we say our speeches? When you go up or before or after?"

"I forgot to tell George that you wanted to speak. I'll ask him now. When would you prefer?"

"When you do, if that's okay."

"Okay, won't be long," Rocky said. He got up and went to talk to George.

"How's things going, Rick? Are you and the boys enjoying yourselves?" George asked.

"Yes, George, they are having a ball, as I am," Rocky said.

"Sorry I haven't been able to get over to visit your table yet. I will get over soon," George said.

"That's okay. You've been a busy man. George, three of the guys would like to address the people here tonight. I was supposed to see you earlier, but I forgot. They would like to come up onstage when I do," Rick said.

"Yeah, sure, Rick, that would be great," George answered.

"Thanks, George," Rick said. "By the way, this is a fantastic night that you have organized. The boys are beside themselves; they appreciate your hospitality very much."

"That's good, Rick. Yes, it has come together very nicely," George said. "I'll be calling you up soon, if that's okay. You decide who goes first, you or the boys."

Rocky returned to the table but stopped at the mothers' table on his way to see how the mums were enjoying the night and seeing their sons enjoying their first formal night out.

He told the guys that it was okay to speak and come up onstage when Rocky went up. "I'll speak first, and then you three boys will have your turn. Okay?" They agreed.

"Ladies and gentlemen," George's voice boomed over the public-address system, "would you please welcome the man responsible for rescuing these ten young people from sure disaster, the patron of the Teen-Morph Foundation and the group leader of the Teen-Morph Youth Center, Mr. Roderick Scott. Three of those guys will accompany Mr. Scott to also share some of their thoughts with us. Make them welcome—the Teen-Morph Foundation."

After the long and loud applause settled, Rick stepped forward to the lectern, placed his papers on top, and moved the microphone closer to his face. "Good evening, ladies and gentlemen. Thank you, George, for your introductions earlier, your comments, and for inviting us to tonight's function. Thank you also to the sponsors of this afternoon's rock festival, the chamber of commerce, and the high school for placing your trust in these ten great guys to wisely manage the money you have given them. Also, I would like to acknowledge those lovely eleven ladies at table eight. They are the proud mothers of these lads. Yes, there are eleven; you see, Ellen Harvey is there also. Ellen is the mum of Mitch, who sadly and tragically lost his life about six months ago. These boys have never forgotten their mate Mitch; these mates came to me, asking if Ellen could attend the concert today and tonight's function."

Applause erupted throughout the function room. When it died down, Rick said, "Thank you for applauding their thoughtfulness. So, thanks to you Ellen, for accepting the boys' invitation and attending tonight. I would like to introduce three of the lads up here with me. This is Aiden, the chairman of the foundation. That's Pieter, who is secretary, and Jacob, a founding member. They wish to speak to you.

"Now, where do I start? I have permission from these boys and their mothers to talk about their private lives, as it may help others understand the troubles faced by our young people. I met them twelve months ago— they were barely fifteen—when I picked them up in my taxi after their street-crime sprees or wild parties they had crashed. They were always drunk or stoned, or both, very abusive and disruptive, the type of boys that adults would push away and label them as no-hopers, deadbeats, disruptive teenagers—you know what I mean. However, instead of doing that, I talked to them calmly but with purpose, and I listened to them, both as a group and individually. I just explained to them that what they were doing was not tough, that they weren't heroes but just making idiots of themselves, wasting their lives and opportunities. They came to realize that other kids and adults hated them because of their attitudes; that was why they continually found themselves in fights. I know 'hate' is a very strong word, but it is the only word that applies.

"These boys also were in trouble with the law continually because they would tip rubbish bins over, set fire to mailboxes, smash lights on parked cars, bend street signs, smash windows—the list is endless." The three boys onstage, heads hanging down, nodded in agreement. "As I got to know them better, they began to talk more and listen to what I was telling them about changing their attitudes, leaving behind the drunkenness and drug-taking, and managing their anger; in short, how they could substitute other activities to change their life's direction. The best way I found was to show them the likely outcome if they continued on the track they were on, what they could expect their lives to be at twenty-five or thirty-five—a life of misery, in and out of jail, men who could not find a decent partner, who did not have the pleasure of a functional family. That was not a good life to have. The examples were there, in the news, the papers, on television shows, and on the streets and in the pubs. Just explaining where they were headed and where they could go was all that was needed to plant the seed to success.

"At last, it seemed, they had found someone they could talk to about their problems, their fears, their thoughts, and their opinions. Their vocabulary and communication skills changed from grunts and one-word answers to full-on, in-depth conversations. They still went on the occasional drinking binges and to drug parties but less often, and they didn't get nearly as affected. Things were going well until one Saturday night, they found themselves at a party near the waterfront. They went to the wharf. That night will stay in our minds and hearts forever. That's the night that I got the hysterical phone call from one of the guys that they couldn't find Mitch. They needed help. Adrian Cooper was a passenger in my taxi at the time, and he willingly agreed to help me to help these guys in their time of need.

"We won't go into any details, but Mitch's lifeless body was found a few hours later as the sun's first rays appeared over the ocean. From that moment, I realized that the task for me had gotten much more important. I spent several weeks talking to the guys, comforting them, helping them understand death and grief, listening to them, and offering them a helping hand to get them over this tragedy and their sorrow. I would like to tell you that all these guys have made it. They decided to accept my help once again and change their attitudes to life and become responsible young people.

"Folks, all I have done is recognize a problem, talk it through with them on their level, listen to them with genuine interest, offer support and care for their emotions, and offer to be their mentor—take it or leave it. They accepted, and slowly, we moved away from the alcohol and drugs by showing them other ways of getting their kicks and managed to get rid of the anger, hate, and destruction and violence. They don't drink alcohol, except on special occasions and with responsible adults in controlled circumstances; don't do drugs; don't smoke; don't destroy things; don't fight; and don't ridicule or criticize others. Sound boring? Ask these guys." Rocky turned to the three guys onstage. "Do you find life boring?"

The boys shook their heads.

"Sorry, guys, for leaving you standing there while I rave on. I won't be long. Anyway, just like old school, you are used to me preaching, aren't you?"

The boys nodded and smiled.

"They do enjoy life, do help others, and do take care of each other, and they take care of me at times. They do love their mothers and their families. They have become responsible, respectful, respectable, caring, and well-adjusted young people in the community, instead of where they were headed, probably seriously injured, dead, or in jail. That is why they have been rewarded with the responsibility of managing the Teen-Morph Youth Center and developing the site that George spoke about earlier. I told them several times that good things come to people who do good things. Thanks, George and the chamber of commerce, for allowing my prediction to come true. When I told these guys that good things would come, I never imagined it would be ever that good.

"My message to each adult and parent is to listen to your kids with genuine interest; talk with them, not down to them; and help them. Although they may want you to think they know everything, they don't— they can't, unless and until they are taught positive life skills. Recently, I had to tell these guys about preventing pregnancy and diseases—not one of them had any idea. You can't blame them or their mothers. It's extremely difficult for a mother to sit her sixteen-year-old son down and talk to him about this subject. Another thing—never, never promise anything unless you can deliver. They feel that as a loss of trust.

"There is an obvious neglect of our young males in our society. I am not against women's liberation, far from it, but since more emphasis has been placed on"—Rick made air quotes with his fingers— "'women can do anything,' young males in our communities have been neglected. The sooner the authorities recognize this, the better off we will be. For one reason or another—and it's none of our business why—a lot of families don't have a father in the home. Others have a father living in the same house, but they do not know him.

"These guys, sadly, have the need to look on me as their father figure. Have you ever tried to act as a father to ten teenagers, all the same age?" Rick joked. "It's not as bad as it sounds. I'll let you in on a secret—the clothes I'm wearing organized by these guys. They ensured my shirt was right, my tie was straight, my belt straight, and my hair done. That, people, is what fathers and sons do. Thanks, guys, I do appreciate you dressing me this afternoon and fussing over me to make sure that I looked perfect.

"Now, folks, just ponder this question: What are their dads missing out on tonight? Not one of these ten guys have his father with him to experience the pride of seeing his son achieve what these boys have tonight, today, in the past couple of weeks, and in the past six months. We approach another stage in their lives, where they finish school, find employment, find a partner, and settle with their own children. I only hope the cycle has been broken with these guys. I know it has been; they have told me so.

"I would like to finish by saying how proud I am of these guys, their achievements, and their attitudes. Yes, they do ride skateboards; yes, they do wear strange or different-looking clothing and hairstyles; yes, they do wear their shorts below their hips; yes, they do some random, fun, daring, and sometimes dangerous stuff, but yes, above all that, they do live happy, rewarding, and respectable lives. I know that the life ahead for these guys is awesome. Don't judge our young. Don't put them down. Don't walk all over them and then walk away. Give them a chance and be patient. They will come back and reward your efforts big time.

"Now that these boys have become the fine young men that they are at such an early age, they want to do the same to help other kids achieve the same kind of life that they enjoy. This was their decision. I know that my, Adrian's, and these guys' job will be a little easier because teenagers talking to teenagers is easier, as they take more notice of their peers who have experienced the good times. Thank you all for your support. I apologize if this speech has been a bit long; I had some messages that I had to get across. The boys and I are going to take this opportunity that we have been given by the throat and kick goals. Hey, guys?"

The boys at table nine jumped and yelled and applauded Rocky's speech and indicated that they were ready for the challenge.

"Before I go, I want to tell you a saying that I have told these guys many times, which helped them get through: 'Remember the good times with a passion, but never forget the bad times. Learn from these experiences and move on.' Now, over to these three awesome guys.

The people in the auditorium gave Rick a standing ovation.

Aiden took to the lectern. "Good evening, ladies and gentlemen. My name is Aiden, and I am chairman of the Teen-Morph Foundation. I just want to say how proud I am to have met this guy, our mate, our mentor, the legend, who took the time to care about us. Rocky is right when he said we were headed for the dump, the scrap heap. I am so glad he came along when we were lost. We had no one we could trust with our secrets, our feelings, and the things that made our heads stuff up. Also, Rocky said about our fathers, where are they? I know I probably shouldn't say this in public, but Rocky always says that we should say what we are thinking, that we should talk about it, so we can decide. Well, now I don't care where my dad is. I don't even know my dad; he pissed off before I started school. That's why I asked Rocky the other day—and again today—if he could be my dad. Now, Rocky, I have said it, and now that I have told the world, it feels good that I said it, and I know you will talk to me about it later.

"Anyway, thank you, Rocky, for helping me—us—and giving us opportunities that we could accept or leave. You are a good mate, and you really do abide by another saying. Remember? 'Do as I say, just the same as I do.' You're spot on. You are our champion, man, forever. Thanks also to Mr. Cleator for having us here and letting us use his park to build our dreams on. As was said before, we are all committed to helping Rocky help other kids. You probably don't know, but there are hundreds out there who are going the wrong way.

"Before I go, thank you, Mum, for trying to look after me when I thought I didn't need looking after. I was wrong. But you know that, and thanks to the other mums. You know what I mean. Also, Mrs. Harvey, I know Mitch is still around, and I know how much you love him. We are glad you came tonight because this guy belongs to Mitch as much as he belongs to us." Aiden gave Rocky a hug. "Thank you."

Aiden gave the audience a bow, then pushed his arms skywards as the audience clapped showing their appreciation for a heart-felt speech. As Pieter moved toward the microphone, the two boys crossed paths and gave each other a 'high five' as they did. Pieter approached the microphone and gave the audience the now traditional V sign, as the audience clapped to acknowledge Pieter's arrival to the microphone.

"Hi, I am Pieter, and I am the secretary. I just want to thank everyone here and especially Mr. Cleator and Mr. Watson. Mr. Watson, I know we were proper idiots before we woke up to ourselves. Thank you for believing in us. Mr. Cleator, thank you for today and tonight and for letting us have the money for our projects and for the caravan park so we can build our dream and help other kids. Rocky, thanks, buddy, you legend. Thanks for talking and listening and being our mate. We have had some sad and bad times, but we have had some wicked times too. You join with us when we are having fun, muck around when we muck around, show us how to do things like make things and fix things, give us ideas for things that we can do, and just talk when we need to talk."

Then Pieter shouted, "*I just feel so awesome!* And I didn't need a drink. I didn't need some dope. I didn't need to smash things or smash someone's head in. We just play our music, ride our skateboards and BMX bikes, surf, and do good things. Wow, what a buzz our lives are now! Seriously, thank you, Rocky. You are a legend; you are our champ. And thanks to our mums. You are all so cool. Sorry for the stress and worries we put you through, but hey, that's all gone now. We'll show you."

Pieter turned to face Rocky, George, and the compares in turn and bowed to each of them, to show his appreciation. He then returned to the microphone to welcome Jacob to the microphone. As he returned to his position at the side of the stage, he performed a cart wheel, showing his enthusiasm and excitement.

The crowd once again erupted in loud applause in appreciation of hearing Pieter speak so well of his mentor and his life changes, and his antics on stage.

As Jacob made his way to the microphone, he raised his arms seemingly to hush the crowd, as well as, to show his jubilation.

"Good evening, I'm Jacob. I want to thank everyone who organized the rock festival and this dinner tonight. Thanks also to Mr. Cleator for what he has done for Rocky and us. Now we can do the things that we have dreamed about and, at the same time, help other kids. I have said to Rocky and a lot of other people that everyone in grade ten and eleven needs someone like him. We are so lucky that he stopped and cared about us and showed us how life could and should be. Thanks, mate. Thanks too for our mothers. Like Pieter said, all that bad stuff is gone, and we know right from wrong. None of us ever wants to go back to that. It's over.

"Rocky, from all of us, thanks, champ, for what you do for us. We will remember it always. I feel so good; this is awesome. I thought I would be nervous and scared, but with Rocky beside me, I can do anything." Jacob shook Rocky's hand and hugged him.

"Thanks, Rick; thanks, boys," George said. "Aren't they amazing? Good luck, guys. Enjoy the rest of your lives. I know you will find what you are looking for, but I have a sneaking suspicion that you already have. Champion, legend—what wonderful words to describe Mr. Rick Scott, and that came from each of those boys. Good on you, guys. Congratulations. Moving on, we will have dessert, tea, and coffee, and then we will invite everyone onto the dance floor to be entertained with live music from last year's winners."

As desserts were served, several of the guys commented on how cool, how awesome, or how wicked the night and the food was.

"If this is what it's like to go out for dinner, you got me," Nick said. He had never experienced eating out.

"I'm so full," Jay said. "This food is really good."

Rocky was so happy that he was able to witness yet another experience in their lives. "Life is full of new experiences, guys. I am so happy I have been with you on your first night out in society. Let's hope this is the first of many good nights out for you."

The music started, and the guys were eager to get up on the dance floor.

"Go for it, guys. Ask your mothers if they would like to dance, and I'll ask Ellen," Rocky said. "What about you, Adrian?"

"Well, why don't we all get up and move from partner to partner? That way, none of us guys will be left out for too long. We all can take turns dancing solo," Adrian said.

After the guys thought about it for a short time, working through the idea in their heads, they agreed that was a cool idea.

"I'll show you how to ask a lady for a dance, guys; just watch and listen," Adrian said.

All twelve got up in unison and moved toward table eight.

"Ladies, all of us guys would like the pleasure of this dance," Adrian said politely. "These guys want to start off dancing with their mothers. Mrs. Harvey, Rocky would like to start the dance off with you. Then we will move to the next lady in a clockwise direction."

The ladies eagerly and excitedly accepted. They hadn't danced for years, and none of them had ever had the opportunity of dancing with their sons.

"We will change partners on my signal," Adrian said.

The group moved onto the dance floor, forming a circle—mothers with their sons, Rick with Ellen—with Adrian dancing his professional moves in the center. Adrian let the mums dance with their sons for a song or two before he signaled to change partners. Each spell after the first change was much shorter than the first, and eventually each guy had a turn with each lady and in the middle by himself. Adrian kept a keen eye on each of the guys, rating them secretly on their movement styles and skills, rating them with the view of instructing them on dance movements and techniques. The dance floor became very crowded, so the guys and ladies returned to their tables, so the rest of the people could enjoy their dance.

"As soon as the next bracket starts, we will be back, girls, so we can get up before the rest of them. We will do that again," Adrian instructed. "But this time we will do the change-partner thing and then we will do the conga line. These guys probably don't know the conga. We might even ask the band for the chicken dance before the night is over."

"What's the conga, Adrian?" Pieter asked.

"It's a line made up of people on the dance floor that moves, dancing, around the dance floor, and if it works properly, it eventually ends up with everyone on the dance floor joining on to the end of the line. I'll lead, then Rocky and Ellen, then one guy, his mum, the next guy, his mum, and so on," Adrian said

"And what's the chicken dance?" Haydon asked.

"Well, I won't tell you that. You'll have to wait and see how it's done. Rocky and I and your mums will know. Then I'll expect you guys to join in."

The band started to play, and the guys, Adrian, and Rocky rushed to table eight to get the ladies up again. The same procedure took place but in counter-clockwise direction. As each guy completed the round and ended up with his own mum, Adrian said, "Let's go," and he broke away from the circle in front of Rocky. The conga line began its weaving trail through the other dancers. As the end of the line passed each couple, they joined the line. It took nearly two songs for the line to complete, with everyone in the auditorium joining in. Adrian took the line around the dance floor, weaving around and between tables, out the entrance, once around the portico, back inside, around the room, and back to the dance floor. As it reached the dance floor, it stopped, and as if on cue, everyone yelled and applauded and stomped, so loud that the music could not be heard.

The music stopped. Everyone looked toward the stage where the band was playing and saw George standing in front of the band at the microphone.

"Adrian, come up here, son," George said. "That was a terrific effort. Come on; come up here." Adrian sheepishly walked toward the stage. As he climbed the three steps onto the stage, George said, "Adrian Cooper, that was amazing. In all my years I have never witnessed a conga line so long and have never seen a conga line consume every single person in a hall like that. And your dance skills—you are terrific."

"Oh, thanks, George. Thank you very much," Adrian said. "I have never seen everyone join in either. That was awesome. Thank you, everyone, for joining in. And congratulations and thanks to this band, 'cause their music rocks. It makes it easier if there's good music to dance to."

That comment attracted immediate applause from the audience, most of whom were still on the dance floor.

"Where did you learn to dance like that, Adrian?" George asked. "You dance so well."

"Well, I've been dancing since I was five or six. I was professionally taught. I actually just got my dance instructor's diploma a few weeks ago," Adrian said.

"Why haven't we heard about this in the news or the papers?" George asked.

"I keep my dancing to myself—until now. You all know about it now. I have been what you might call a 'closet dancer.' I always got teased and bashed, called a sissy, even called gay because I wanted to dance, mainly at high school. It was tough, but I am so happy that I didn't let them get to me, and I kept going. Yeah, that's about it, really," Adrian said. "Although nowadays, guys dancing professionally is much more accepted."

"Well, good on you, Adrian," George said. "Good luck with your future dancing. Maybe we will see your name in lights or on billboards, in a starring role in a musical in the future."

"Yeah, I hope so," Adrian said, "maybe sooner than you think. You see, some of those guys over there already asked me to teach them, although they didn't know my level or that I was trained. They want to put on a musical and dance show in conjunction with the high school. Although it's only early days, they want to use your park as the venue—that is one of their plans."

"That's great," George said. "Ladies and gentlemen, you heard it here first. Please show your appreciation for Adrian Cooper." As the applause died down, George asked Adrian, "Would you perform a dance routine for us later in the evening?"

"Yeah, sure, I'm up for it. I will have to put something together in my mind and talk to the band, but yeah, sure," Adrian said. "But before that, we would like to do the chicken dance in the next bracket if we can. The guys have never seen it, and I would like them to see it and learn it."

"I'm sure the band could accommodate that. What do you say, guys?" George said as he turned around to the band. They indicated their approval. "Well, that's organized. See you then."

"Thanks, George," Adrian said. He left the stage and returned to the group.

"Okay, folks, a short break and then back to the band for their last bracket of the night, including the chicken dance and a dance routine from Adrian," George said.

Everyone returned to their tables to enjoy another drink. Rocky said, "You didn't tell me you got your diploma. I knew you danced, but I didn't realize that you had formal instruction. Congratulations, buddy. Good on ya."

"That was awesome, man," Aiden said. "That was real mental." All the guys agreed with Aiden, giving similar comments.

"What song will you get them to play?" Pieter asked.

"I have a dance routine in mind, but I will have to put music to it," Adrian said. "I'll work it out with the band." Adrian walked over to the band and spoke to them, working out what music they could play and sing for him as he danced. After several minutes, Adrian returned to the table. "That's sorted. We got some music."

"What are you dancing to?" Pieter asked.

"I'll keep that a surprise until the dance starts. We won't even announce the song; we'll just get into it. Dancers never announce their music before they perform their routines," Adrian said.

"Oh, come on, dude; you can tell us," Jay said.

"No, that's it. No announcement, no telling." Adrian was adamant.

The music started for the final bracket, and the guys and mothers got up to dance, this time not partnering but each dancing solo in a group. After the third song, the band played the chicken-dance song. Adrian and the mums started dancing the chicken dance, showing the guys how it was done. One by one, the guys joined in, enjoying the newfound skill. After the chicken dance, the group returned to their tables to rest and to let Adrian prepare mentally for his routine.

After two more songs, the front man of the band announced that the next song was for Adrian's dance display and that everyone should clear the dance floor. Adrian had removed his shoes and socks and had applied a rubber band to each cuff of his jeans to hold them tight to his ankles. As he got up from his place at the table, he removed his shirt, revealing a tanned, muscular, trim torso. He tied a bandana around his head and moved toward the center of the dance floor. He posed like a statue, slightly bent over, as if in thought. The muscles in his shoulders and neck were pumped up and flexed. His six-pack resembled that of the famed Fabio. He stayed still until the first bar of his chosen music sounded. Rocky remembered seeing similar stances in the back of his taxi when Adrian stripped while performing dance movements. The penny dropped. *He was going through his dance routines and didn't know it. Or did he?* Rocky thought. *Maybe he did know and wasn't ashamed of taking his clothes off in front of an audience.* Rocky made a mental note to find out later.

The band began to play. As soon as the first notes of the song sounded, Rocky recognized it as the Billy Idol hit "Rebel Yell." As he recognized it, Rocky jumped up from his seat, stood tall with his right arm extended skyward and his index finger pointed, and yelled, "Oh yeah, bring it on!" He then realized where he was and what he had done, and he sat down very sheepishly. The guys laughed.

As the music played, Adrian launched into his dance. Everyone was in awe of Adrian's movements. Adrian did very well, especially for someone who hadn't rehearsed the routine. As the music came to the guitar riff and drum solo halfway through the song, Adrian's moves seemed to become more definite and in perfect harmony with the beats. Rocky couldn't help thinking how more awesome it would be if it was accompanied by a lighting sequence.

As the music finished, Adrian's routine took him to the floor, where he lay motionless as the audience erupted into applause. Adrian stayed on the floor until the applause subsided. Once quiet, he got to his feet, bowed to the crowd, and then threw himself across the floor to table nine. The guys all stood and clapped wildly once again, and all gave him a high-five.

"That was awesome, man," Rocky said, and the boys echoed his words. "How fantastic would that be with good strobe lighting and a good lighting pattern?"

"Yeah, Rocky, it would be wicked with good lighting," Adrian said.

"You guys should learn to play that track," Rocky said. "How good was that drum solo, Haydon?"

"Yeah, cool. I would love to play that tune. We must get hold of a sound track and give it a go," Haydon said.

Rocky felt a hand on his shoulder and turned around to see George, who placed his other hand on Adrian's shoulder. "Can I talk to you two? Adrian, Rick, we want to see if Adrian would be prepared to judge an impromptu dance competition?"

"When? Now?" Adrian asked.

"Yes. A couple of the chamber members would like to see that tune played again and invite anyone to get up and dance to it. If you would, I'd like Adrian and you to judge it, Rick. I've already spoken to the band.

The sponsors are prepared to put up some prizes. There is already a stereo system, some sporting goods vouchers, some clothes vouchers, surf wear, jewelry, and backpacks. What do you think?"

"What do you say, Adrian?" Rocky asked. "I don't know if I would be qualified to judge dancing."

"Yeah, I'm in. That's a wicked idea. You probably won't get any of the people from the other tables, so it would be only these guys," Adrian said. "What do you say guys? Are you in?"

They all excitedly answered yes; they were very keen.

"Well, George, it is a yes all round," Rocky said. "When do you want to do it?"

"Let's say after the next three tunes. I'll okay it with the band." George went over to the band and spoke to them; then he signaled with a thumbs-up.

As the third song finished, George grabbed the microphone and announced. "We have a surprise for you. We've decided to have a dance competition." The formal tone in George's voice was gone. "Adrian and Rick are going to be the judges. The song that Adrian danced to, because it was so groovy, will be played again. There are many prizes available, so anyone who wishes to compete, please make your way to the dance floor. Bare feet and bare chests are permitted."

A small table and two chairs were hurriedly put on one corner of the stage for the judges.

"Are you ready?" the lead singer asked. "Okay, here we go."

All the guys and the 2B2S members assembled on the floor and began their dance routines, some with shirts removed. Most had their shoes removed. The dance competition was underway. All the dancers put on a very good display of their favorite moves; all took it seriously and concentrated hard, obviously attempting their best.

Once again, the guitar and drum solo produced the best movements. As they finished, the remaining audience applauded the dancers, appreciating their moves and their enthusiastic participation.

George moved over to the judges' table to speak to Adrian and Rocky. "Don't be too hung up on your decision. It's meant to be a bit of fun and entertainment but do pick a winner. We had seventeen competitors on the floor. A stereo system worth about eight hundred dollars is first prize, and we have managed to rustle up sixteen other prizes, mainly vouchers at local stores. So, after you pick a winner, we will distribute the rest of the vouchers to the others."

Adrian and Rocky decided on the winner and told George who it was. George then went to the microphone.

"People, we have a winner. As well, we have sixteen second prizes, so no one misses out. Without any further suspense, the winner is … one of those guys over there," George teased. After the laughter died down, he said, "Sorry, the winner is Haydon. Come on up, Haydon. Congratulations. You obviously like to dance, son. You are the drummer in the Nuver Chanz too. Good on you. Here is your voucher for the stereo. If you go into Eric's Sight, Sound, and Electrical on Monday, Eric will give you your stereo. Good one, Haydon."

George then said, "I have sixteen vouchers for all sixteen other contestants donated by various business sponsors who are here tonight. The values range from $100 to $150, so I think, to be fair, I will shuffle them and hand one to each of you. Well done, guys and gals. You really entertained everyone. And I thank you Adrian and Rocky for being the judges on short notice."

George handed the vouchers around and then returned to the microphone. "We'll have two or three tunes from the band; then that will be the end of the night. Thank you all for attending. Thanks to our valued sponsors and our contestants from today's rock festival. A special thanks to the Young Guns from Teen-Morph and their mothers. We hope you enjoyed your day and night, ladies, and enjoyed seeing your boys attend their first formal night out. And not forgetting Mr. Rick Scott and his newly acquired sidekick, Mr. Adrian Cooper. Thanks, Adrian, for your dance display. I hope you go a long way with those skills, and son, I hope to catch up with you soon. I hope I haven't forgotten anyone; my apologies if I have. Have a safe journey to your homes, and I hope to see you all again on the last Saturday in March next year for—I hope—just as much fun. Thank you. On with the music. Oh, I forgot—thank you to our great entertainers for the night, last year's Youth Rocks Music Fest winners, Wild Theme. Thanks, guys. Now, let the music begin one more time. Good night."

As the music continued, Rocky went to table eight to find out how many taxis were required. They all thanked Rick for the night and for all that he had done for their boys. The mums would go to their own homes, but Piet's mum would be staying with one of the other mums for the night so that the boys and Rocky could be alone. Rocky returned to the table, phoned the taxi company, and booked the taxis for the ladies and a maxi-taxi for the guys. As the guys were leaving, they were directed to the store room to collect their skateboards.

After the function was over, the group waited outside for their taxis, with the mums talking to the boys and hugging them and straightening their clothes and hair, like loving mums do. They said their goodbyes as the taxis pulled up. One of the drivers yelled to Rick that the maxi-taxi wouldn't be long. All taxis were busy, but as soon as one was available, it would jump the queue.

Pieter walked up to Rocky and said, "Mum said you got something to tell me. What is it?"

"Your mum told me that she isn't coming home tonight; she's staying at someone's mum's house, so she can get some sleep and so you guys can have a good time."

"Cool, that's wicked." Pieter said, bouncing around and giving the other three high-fives. "Hey, dudes, we got the place to ourselves tonight."

The guys all had reactions similar to Pieter's. They were in for a great chill session when they got to Piet's barn. Rocky and Adrian suddenly realized they had the responsibility, as the adults, of ensuring that the boys behaved responsibly.

"They will be cool," Adrian said. "We'll be okay. We can join in with whatever they get up to. They know how to behave."

"Yeah, I know, mate. Don't know why I thought otherwise. They do know how to be responsible and sensible," Rocky said. "I have been saying that all night."

CHAPTER 13

No, Rock Daddy, you are the champ. You did it for us. You showed us. You gave us the reason to live.

The taxi arrived at Piet's carrying the precious cargo of the newly crowned Cleator Young Guns. The entire group of the Teen-Morph Foundation got out, and their leader, their mentor, their Rock Daddy paid the driver. The guys went to the barn, with most removing their shirts before the entrance. Once inside, shoes, socks, and jeans were off, and board shorts or cargo shorts were pulled on. Pieter threw a pair of board shorts to Adrian, and Aiden had a pair for Rocky.

"Come on, you two. Chill out. Change and be more comfortable," Aiden said. "Come on, get it all off." He clapped slowly, as if it were a strip show. The rest joined in the slow clap as Adrian and Rocky removed their ties, shirts, shoes, socks, and jeans and replaced their jeans with the shorts the boys loaned them.

"How awesome was tonight?" Rocky asked.

The guys all yelled their agreement, excitement, and enthusiasm for the experience they had enjoyed.

"Oi, Rocky, we really want to thank you, man; you legend. Thanks for having faith in us and believing in us," Jay said. "Without you man, we would not be doing these awesome things, going to that awesome party and have that park for ourselves to do things we like to do. All of us have said to each other over the past couple of weeks and again tonight how awesome it is to have a wicked mate, or big bro, or Rock Daddy like you to help us

Some of the other guys said similar things to Rocky and Adrian, showing their appreciation for their new life experiences.

"That's cool, guys, that you feel like that. How do you think I feel, seeing you guys loving your lives like you do? Now, as promised, let's crack a bottle or two. I am not going to lecture about responsible drinking. You all know what's going down, but please don't disappoint me guys," Rocky said.

"Yeah, sure, Splinta. We know," Piet said. "Where are they? What did you get, Rocky?"

"Just the usual—bourbon, rum, and I also got a bottle of port and a bottle of rum liqueur, just so we can play 'old guys' later."

"What do you mean, 'play old guys'?" Aiden asked.

"Oh, just so we can sip it slowly, straight in a shot glass and ice, just like older guys do after their night is over."

"What's this 'Splinta,' Rocky?" Adrian asked.

"The guys named me that after the wise guy in *Star Trek*."

"'Cause he's the wise old guy," Aiden said.

"And 'Rock Daddy'?" Adrian asked.

"Aiden and Pieter named me that."

"Yeah, the Rock part comes from his name, Rocky," Aiden said.

Pieter butted in with "And because he rocks, man—rocks in our world, anyway."

Aiden said, "And the Daddy part is because we told him a few times that Piet and I want him to be our dad."

"That's cool, guys," Adrian said.

"I explained to them that no matter what, no one except their fathers can be their fathers, but I am honored to be their father figure, especially because it means so much to them. That goes for all you guys. If you look to me to be your father figure, that's cool with me. Whatever rocks your boat

"Yeah, it does look awesome," Adrian said, "Can't wait to see the video footage of it. I hope that video guy got it all."

The guys talked about their experiences of the day and night while slowly drinking their chosen drink. They had fun recalling the concert and the function afterward. The food that Rocky had brought earlier was prepared and consumed; then they had another drink and more chatting and chilling out.

"Hey, Rocky, remember you going to tell us about how to treat girls properly. How about now?" Pieter asked.

"Yeah, come on, Splinta," Haydon said. "We might need to know because we might score some groupies after today."

"Oh, come on, get your hand off it. Groupies? Who do you think you are?" Rocky asked, laughing.

"Yeah, we'll have chicks chasing us, now we're famous," Aiden said.

"Okay, guys, Adrian might give me a hand, hey, Adrian?" Rocky said. "Yeah, sure, mate," Adrian said. "If I can. Haven't been doing that well with Christy lately."

"I had to tell them how not to get a girl pregnant and about connies and about diseases. I told them then that I would give them a few hints on making girls feel important and on how to treat them so that they will stay around," Rocky said. "Okay, guys, the first thing is to treat them better than you want to be treated. Never talk about what you do together with anyone, even if it is only a pash."

"Yeah, that's right. Don't tell anyone; don't even tell your mates any details," Adrian added. "It's cool to say that you went out with so-and-so, but that's it—no details. Treat it as personal, 'cause, like, you don't want others talking and gossiping about you, and they don't want everyone talking about them. When you do, the story grows with each person who is told. That person adds more to the story, and suddenly, your girl is upset and walks out on you.

"The only time you talk is when there is a problem, and you want advice, and then you only talk to someone you can trust to give you the right advice and who won't tell anyone else. Just the same as you have been able to talk to the man, Rocky, about things in the past, he'll give you the best advice, and your personal situation will go no further."

"Guys, you will find the same goes for Adrian," Rocky said. "If you got a problem, you can go to him too. He's been there, done that, and he will help and keep it to himself. And you probably could go to one of your mates as well; any of these guys here can be trusted. Next, don't form a relationship with just any girl, unless you have the need to get your rocks off, but remember the rules—no connies, no sex. They will tell everyone about your relationship, probably even rate you—how good or bad you were, how big or small you are, and compare you with their last guy or next guy. Not worth dropping your daks for that crap, fellas."

"And that's where you get diseases," Adrian said. "You don't want to poke it in where every other guy in town has been."

Everyone collapsed with laughter as the message sank in.

"You will get one-night-stands now and again—every guy aims to nail one or two strays every now and then—but you will realize that these are not the same as when you are with a chick that you have fallen in love with or think that you love," Rocky said.

"Yeah, that's right, shagging a stray is nothing like a chick that you really like and have taken some time to get to know and fall in love with," Adrian added. "And don't be the town guy slut either because if you pork everything that spreads her legs at you, you will get a name, and no decent chick will have anything to do with you."

"When you find the right chick, you will know it because she will be all you think about. Not so much thinking of sex with her but a feeling that you want to be near or with her all the time. You will always imagine that you can smell her scent and feel like she is with you even when you are apart. You will dream about her and the things that you have done together and want to do together. You will dream of romantic things you can do for her and with her. Yeah, guys, sex is a part of it but probably not the most important part of being in love," Rocky said.

"Is that what they mean when someone says, 'he's in love' when you can't talk to them or get their attention?" Jacob asked.

"That's right, dude," Adrian said. "It's an awesome feeling. Nobody or nothin' can get into your head when love hits you."

"The other thing is that you gotta do nice things for them. Give them a flower, some chocolates, some jewelry if it's real serious. But you gotta mean it. Cook her a feed, go for a walk on the beach, hand in hand. A midnight walk is awesome, especially on the beach. There is not much better," Rocky said. "But, guys, the right chicks will want to do good things for you too. Let 'em, guys; believe me."

"Yeah, mine loves to squeeze my pimples. I hate it, but she loves doing it. She says it will make me look better without pimples. And removing my body hair from my back, chest, and things," Adrian said.

"What do you mean, 'things'?" Pieter asked. "Do you mean crack and nuts?"

"Yeah, sure. She loves trimming my cheeks and 'nads. I love it too," Adrian said. "Nothing better than a smooth baby bum and smooth shiny balls."

"See, Rocky, I told you that's okay to do that," Aiden said, "when we stripped your chest and back last night."

"Yeah, I know. Remember I told you it was okay, that it's your body. If you don't damage or harm your body, anything is okay," Rocky said.

"Anyway, I was going to say most chicks go nuts over a smooth back, crack, and sack," Adrian said.

"Moving on ... nice things," Rocky said. "If you do nice things for a chick, give her nice things and accept nice things from her, your love life will get better and better. Do romantic things, like plan a sunrise breakfast or a sunset dinner at the beach, in the park, wherever. She will love you forever. If things turn a bit bad for some reason, talk about it. Find a way to get over the problem. If she is the one you want to be with, do something to rekindle the fire, guys."

"Hey, Adrian, where's your chick?" Piet asked.

"Oh, she's out with the girls or at home, I suppose."

"What? Are you fighting or something?" Aiden asked.

"Ah, not really. She just wants a break for a while. I did some things that she didn't like, and I didn't realize it," Adrian said, turning to Rocky with a smile. "Rocky knows what I am saying. Yeah, guys, I stuffed up, but Rocky—your mate, my mate—talked me through it, and it will be cool."

"What did you do, man?" Haydon asked.

"Well, better let Rocky tell you, I suppose. He knows more about it than me. I didn't believe it, but he saw it, so it must be true," Adrian said. "It's cool, Rocky, nothing for me to be ashamed of. It's funny, actually. Anyway, I'm among mates, so we can share our stories."

"All right, guys. Pour another drink each and one for Adrian and me, and I will tell you the Adrian story. Yes, it is funny, Adrian. Good that you see it that way, and you are not hung up or embarrassed by it, buddy," Rocky said. "Listen, dude, when you were dancing tonight—actually, before you started to dance—you took off your shirt, shoes, and socks. I thought suddenly, that is obviously part of your dance prep or routine. I wondered if that was why you used to strip off in the back of the taxi."

"Don't know, Rocky. Really don't know. Probably is, you know, because I was always pissed and stoned and felt good, like I feel wicked when I dance. Probably the brain kicked in, and I just did it, week after week, it seems."

"Christy is getting over it, isn't she? You will be cool," Rocky said.

"Yeah, I think so. I think she will be okay. I'm just staying low, trying to do the right thing, say the right things. Not much else I can do, I guess," Adrian said. "Actually, I might pinch your idea and plan a sunrise breakfast or something like that. Like starting over, I suppose, because I really love her, Rocky, and I don't want to lose her."

"Talking about doing things right, have you phoned her yet to tell her where you are?" Rocky asked.

"No, I haven't," Adrian said.

"Well, listen, ring her, and tell her how the guys went. Tell her that you had a great night, but it was a shame that she decided not to join you because you missed her, and she would have enjoyed the night. Tell her that you are with me and the guys, just going over the day's and night's activities and planning a few things with the youth center. Got an idea—I'll lend you the keys to the park. Take her there tomorrow if you want. Look around, walk along the beach, just the two of you; even take a picnic lunch. Try it, buddy, nothin' to lose," Rocky said.

"Yeah, I will. Won't be long. I'll go outside, if that's cool," Adrian said.

"Yeah sure, mate, go for it. I'll wait till you get back before I tell the guys about your strip show, eh?" Rocky said, laughing.

Adrian got his drink from Adam and went outside.

Cheers, guys, here's to more awesome times together for the future." He raised his glass of bourbon and Coke, with the guys doing the same.

"Hell, can that dude dance," Declan said. "That was awesome tonight. Wish I could dance like that."

"Yeah. He is so wicked. Hope he can teach us some of that. He is so good," Haydon said.

"I know he will love to teach you guys," Rocky said. "Why don't you ask him when he gets back in."

Adrian reentered the barn with a look of satisfaction on his face.

"How'd ya go, champ?" Rocky asked.

"Good. Christy's cool. She's having a good time with the girls. She said to congratulate you guys. She is even taking up the offer of a picnic and walk along the beach. Thanks, old man. You really are a legend. Cheers."

"Hey, Adrian, we guys want to tell you how wicked you dance and wondered if you can teach us some moves," Decles asked.

"Thanks, guys. That's cool. Yes, I would love to teach you to dance and choreography, sound, and lighting, if you are up for it."

"Adrian, I didn't realize that you were professionally taught or that you actually danced. You really hid that one, champ," Rocky said.

"Yeah, like I said, I used to get the crap flogged out of me at school when the boys found out. I was called a sissy, a faggot, spat on, hit and kicked in the nuts, pants pulled down, legs kicked out from under me— you name it, I had it done or said to me and more," Adrian said. "But I'm glad that I wasn't a soft cock, that I had the balls to keep on going because I've made it, man, and that feels totally wicked."

"Hell yeah, you got a way with words, buddy," Rocky said. "Hasn't he, fellas?"

"Rocky, Adrian, what's this story?" Nick asked.

"Well, how do I start? You sure you want me to tell 'em, Adrian?" Rocky asked. "A couple of them already know."

"Yeah, I'm not worried. Nothin' wrong with it. Now that I know that I did it, I'd do it again but pick my audience next time. You mentioned that you thought it might be subconsciously something to do with my dance training. I think it is, and I might even incorporate it in a dance routine someday. Nothing sexual, nothing gay about it, just a vision of art in motion. I'm not ashamed of my body or ashamed of nudity. Let's face it; every guys got the same, except mine's got no hair, and every chick has seen them before."

"That's a cool way of thinking, bud," Rocky said. "Yeah, at the end of the day, all guys have the same. Anyway, let's get into this tale. I used to pick Adrian up in the taxi, as you guys know, on Saturday nights and take him to town where, most times, he met up with Christy and her friends. At the end of the night, I'd pick them up and take them home. Adrian and Christy would get out at his house, and then whoever was left, I would take them to their homes." "Yeah, so? What's so bad about that?" Nick asked.

"Nothin'," Rocky said.

"Come on, Rock Daddy," Aiden said. "Stop teasing them."

"We always had the music up loud, like we do with you guys, and this guy Adrian, here, used to stand up in the back and dance. As he danced, he took his clothes off, one piece at a time. Shoes, socks, tie if he had one, shirt, singlet if he had one, belt, trousers, and yes, his boxers or jocks. Then he would dance naked. Now guys, he always did it respectfully, if that's what it is called. Never thrust himself at anyone who was in the taxi; just Adrian, dancing around with nothing on. When he got to his house, he and Christy gathered his clothes. Adrian would get out, still totally nude, dance around the street and then up the driveway. Now that I think of it, Christy was never happy when you did that. She would curse you and yell at you all the way up that driveway, and stuff me, that driveway was steep. I used to think that if you ever fell over, you would gravel rash that poor thing of yours really bad."

"No, man, never fell over until I got into the bedroom. Wondered why I never got lucky. Now I know why," Adrian said.

"But hear this, guys, Adrian never knew he was doing it. He didn't believe Christy when she told him. He had to ask me if it was true. He and I have spoken about it, and he is trying to do some things differently to see if he can overcome his lapses of memory," Rocky concluded.

"That's wicked, dude," Nick said. "I'm the same. I like to strip off sometimes. I think we all do. We have done it lots—run around naked when we are getting changed or go for a swim. It's cool."

"Yeah, we do," Aiden said. "Never worried about it at all."

"Maybe your chick doesn't like it," Piet said.

"Probably. She doesn't mind when we are at home alone. Probably gets embarrassed when other people are around," Adrian said.

Jacob said, "We planned a nude swim tonight, hey boys. Still up for it?" All the guys nodded.

"You too, Rocky. You gotta get yours off, and you too, Adrian," Piet said.

"Ah, I don't think so," Rocky said. "It really isn't right—an old prick like me swimming with young guys in the nude or swimming in the nude in front of you guys."

"Get off it, Rocky. You're one of us. Don't be embarrassed. There is nuthin' wrong with it. We are your mates and you are ours. You join in; you are one of us. I know you got nuthin' against being nude. It's natural. We've all seen you nude, and you have seen us with nuthin' on. Nuthin' wrong with it. Normal guys don't even look or notice another guy with no clothes on. Hey, Adrian, what do you reckon?" Shayne said. "If you don't, Rocky, we will tackle you and pull your clothes off and chuck you in. Nah, only kiddin'."

"That's right. There is nothing wrong with mates getting nude. There's nothing sexual or gay about it. Just freedom," Adrian said. "But if Rocky has a concern about a guy his age swimming nude with guys your age, that's understandable. I'll sure be in it, and I think Rocky will too. He knows we are all mates and that there is nothing to it to suggest any perverted or devious attitudes," Adrian said. "After all, if Rocky was the coach of a football team, and he was in the change room when the guys were showering or changing, same deal. Rocky, these guys are your mates. They completely trust you, and you trust them. They want you to join in their deal. Be in it, chief; it's okay."

"Okay, then. I suppose I'm thinking what other people might say and not what I really think. I have sometimes let what others might say dictate to me how to feel and how to react to a situation in the past. You guys are right. You got me; I'm in," Rocky said. "After all, it's not full light; it's in the dark and in the water."

"Ah yeah, but, Rocky, we want to do the same thing at our beach. That will be full sunlight. Careful of sunburn. Don't rub the sunscreen in too long or too hard," Tony said, his devious mind working overtime once again.

"Ha-ha," Rocky said, laughing. "I'll have to think about that one, bud."

"Now, how about some music, fellas? I need some foot tapping and some moves," Adrian said. "Who's in charge of the music?"

"I'll get the stereo organized and some disks," Piet said. "Will we set it up outside, or are you cool in here?"

"In here is sweet," Adrian said. "Let's clear a space so we can move a little. How about I show you some moves, just basic ones?"

"Yeah, that's prime. I'll put on this dance mix; it's awesome," Piet said.

The music played, and Adrian performed a couple of dance moves, and the guys followed. When Adrian was happy with the guys' moves, he moved on to a few more. He did this a few times until he was happy that the guys were reasonably comfortable with them. He then went over them briefly once more. Rocky controlled the disk player under Adrian's instructions, replaying certain parts of the chosen song.

"Okay, guys, let's put that all together. I'll do it a couple of times; then it's your turn. Now watch closely," Adrian said. He indicated to start the music, and he put all the dance segments together and performed a dance routine to the entire song. The guys watched intently, moving about to some of the moves, itching to have a go.

"Two lines—five that side, arms outstretched sideways, fingertips touching the fingers of the guy on each side, and five opposite, spread the same way, lines facing each other," Adrian instructed. "Okay, music, Rocky, please."

The guys performed the routine a couple of times. A couple of them fell or tripped occasionally, but overall, they did well.

"That's it, guys, you have learned your first dance routine that you can practice repeatedly over the next few days. Then I will look at it again, and see how you are doing with it," Adrian said.

The guys were very excited at their newly learned skill.

"How long have you been dancing, man?" Nick asked.

"Well, I started tap dancing when I was about six," Adrian said.

"You tap dance? Man, that's unreal. I always love watching tap dancing. That's awesome," Adam said.

"Yeah, I started tap dancing and did it for about three years. Then I did some break dancing, then hip-hop and modern dancing. I do it all now, sometimes incorporating some of the styles in one routine. Most people don't realize that there is a story to my dance, but in my head, there is nearly always a story."

"That's awesome that you kept going when you were being bullied and bashed and messed with," Haydon said. "I betcha you're rapt you kept going?"

"It was bad; it was hard, trying to hide my dancing and trying to hide being upset at being messed with, but I am pumped that I made it through that."

"What kind of moves did you do in the taxi when you stripped?" Tony asked.

"Don't really know. Don't even remember doing it," Adrian said, realizing what was coming next.

"Can you show us some moves that you would use, just like Manpower?" Tony asked.

"Don't know about that. Strippers usually strip for members of the opposite sex, but hey, Tony, I'm not a stripper. Apparently, I just take my clothes off when I dance after a few jays and a couple of drinks. No, I wouldn't say that I was a stripper. It's more art, I'd say," Adrian said.

"That's okay. Sorry, didn't mean that you were a stripper. I just wondered what moves you would use," Tony said.

"I'll put it together but only down to my jocks." Adrian said. "I'll have to put my clothes on again, and can these lights be turned down low or most switched off with one left on—on one side of the barn?" Adrian asked, giving a wink to Rocky.

"Yeah, how about all lights off and that reading light over there left on," Piet said, "like this." He turned the lights off, leaving the table light on, which cast a very soft light across the cleared area used for a dance floor earlier.

"Yeah, that's cool. Pick some music while I put my clothes on again," Adrian said. "I'll get Rocky to turn one light off at a time." He moved over to Rocky and whispered, "Turn one light off at a time when I click my fingers like this. Don't tell them; I will go free-willy when the table light is on, I will slowly undo my pants and pull them down quick. That should give the gay perverts a thrill."

"Yeah, cool, mate, but don't get it caught in the zipper. I'm not up for easing your schlong out of a fly zipper, buddy," Rocky said.

"Good point. I'll leave the fly undone and pretend to undo it slowly. They won't notice, I don't think."

Adrian put on his singlet, shirt, and tie, loosely around his neck. He removed his shorts and jocks and slipped on his jeans and then his socks. He looked around and got a hat belonging to one of the guys to complete his costume. "I'll leave my shoes off; they are a pain to get off when you are dancing. Right, I'm ready. How about the music? Got it sorted yet?"

"Yeah, ready when you are," Piet said.

"Just play a few verses so I can get the feel for it," Adrian said. "Rocky, get ready to turn the lights off, one by one, as I told you."

The music played as Adrian moved to the center of the floor and began dancing around. He slowly removed his left sock without breaking his routine and threw it to the audience. Then his right sock. He clicked his fingers, and one light went out. He danced for a few seconds and then slowly removed his tie and threw it to the guys. He then slowly unbuttoned his shirt and slowly removed it, hurling it into the audience. A click of his fingers resulted in another light being turned off. He danced a bit more; then, as the music became louder and faster, he gripped his singlet and, with a brutal force, ripped it off and threw the torn singlet to the guys. He clicked his fingers. Rocky turned another light off, leaving just one light and the table light, which was in the distance, turned on.

Adrian slowly undid his belt, throwing it also. Then, in time with the music, in one flawless move, he jumped up and performed a somersault, somehow removing the hat and giving it a kick on his way down, propelling it toward the audience. That left just his jeans, and, the guys thought, his jocks. He stopped dancing and started to gyrate, undoing and doing up the waist button of his jeans a few times, lowering the waist band down and then up again, teasing the guys as he did.

Adrian then clicked his fingers. Rocky turned the last light off, leaving only the table lamp glowing in the distance, which cast a very low level of light across Adrian's body. He again performed a somersault, somehow undoing his waist button, and as he landed, he jumped up, pushing his jeans to the floor. Then he jumped out of them, revealing a totally naked body. The guys didn't realize immediately that Adrian was nude. He continued for a few seconds—spinning around, another somersault, a few more step moves—and then, out of his hand came a red scarf printed with white sculls, which he draped over his midsection.

"Hey, you totally stripped," Decles said.

"Yeah, your jocks came off too," Aiden said.

"Yeah, dudes, fooled you all, you faggots," Adrian said. "Did you enjoy that, you deviates? You can turn the lights on now, Rocky."

As Rocky turned the lights on, he asked, "Where did you get the scarf?"

"Oh, I had it in my pocket. I pulled it out and held it in my closed fist, but I forgot which pocket. Nearly messed up big time."

"Did you free-willy?" Adam asked.

"Yeah, bud, just to do the complete thing. Just thought of it at the last minute. I saw one of the scarves you guys wore to the theater over there, so I just put it together. Don't know whose scarf it is, but it won't smell too much. My old fella is pretty clean."

"That was totally wicked. Awesome," Piet said. "You really are a talent."

Adrian was still standing in front of them with the red scarf barely covering his hips and pelvis. "Someone throw me the shorts, please," Adrian said, as he teased by lowering his scarf a little. As the shorts were thrown to him, he let the scarf drop to the floor as he caught the shorts and put them on.

"Hell, you move quick, man," Haydon said. "You just let that scarf drop, caught your shorts, and had 'em on in five seconds flat."

"Didn't you see enough, dude?" Adrian said as he undid the rip cord and started to drop them again. "You don't notice when I am naked 'cause there is no hair there. If you don't see any patch of bushy pubes, it doesn't register—just an old trick I learned by accident. Also, it's a case of now you see it, now you don't. I'm rapt with that routine; it turned out awesome. I must remember that one, just for art's sake, but guys, don't get too excited."

"Let's chill outside by the pool. Do you reckon we can have another drink now, Rocky?" Piet asked.

"Don't know about that. You guys better get this drinking habit out of your system. You don't want to go down that track again," Rocky said.

"It's cool, Rocky. We're not pissed; we are only having weak ones, relaxing. We know what you meant when you told us that a few quiet drinks spaced out don't hurt. It's just the binge drinking, just to get wasted, that was the problem. We learned our lessons. We don't want to do that again," Aiden said. "Anyway, we've only had two."

"Only teasing guys. Come in, suckers," Rocky said.

Aiden, Jacob, and Adam poured the drinks, making Rocky's and Adrian's a bit stronger than the rest. Piet and Decles took the stereo outside and set up a few lights around the pool. Nick, Shayne, and Jay set up some chairs and a small table on the lawn at the far end of the pool. Rocky, Adrian, and Haydon got the biscuits, cheese, salami, and dip and set them up on the table in the center of the chairs, which were placed in a circle.

The group settled into enjoying the drinks and snacks, chatting about their day, their night, the dancing, their new skateboards, and looking for Mitch's star. It went on for thirty to forty minutes, with their chosen music playing in the background. Discussion then progressed to their plans for the youth center and then onto planning a musical and dance performance.

"Hell, you guys are going to be busy. You got school and homework and your sports. You all work a couple of afternoons or nights a week. And now you'll be building skate jumps, a stage, bike and walking tracks. You have water sports to organize, helping other kids, and your band—don't let your band go, fellas. When are you going to find time?" Rocky said.

"That's sorted, Splinta. When you live there, you can give us a hand with our homework and assignments. We will put time in after school, after work, weekends, and our school holidays. You can help us design the jumps, tracks, and stage and show us how to build them. There are ten of us, and the other kids we get can help too. If we all get into it when we can, it won't take that long," Aiden said.

"We can all go there to do our homework after dark, just like a class at school. We can help each other, and you, the old master brain, can help us, and we will get it done in no time—just like a dad helping with homework, just like other kids have. Never had that feeling, you know, a dad to help with homework," Piet said.

"You guys got it worked out, haven't you? No doubt about you boys," Rocky said.

"You're not getting away from us, Splinta. We want to spend all the time that we can there. It will be our base. You won't mind, will ya, Rocky?" Adam said.

"No, mate, I won't mind. I suppose it will keep you off the streets and out of trouble," Rocky answered.

Rocky turned to Adrian. "You see, mate? This is what I was telling you before—how these guys have changed, how they think, and plan ahead, and how well adjusted they have become. You can see the difference; you remember what they were like. They have become true champions."

"No, Rock Daddy, you are the champ. You are the one who did it for us, man. You gave us a reason to live," Aiden said.

"Hey, Rock Daddy, you were going to tell us about your sickness and your memory loss," Piet reminded Rocky. "We had our girl talk."

"Oh, can we leave it for another time, fellas? It is a bit depressing for me, and we are having an awesome time tonight. I don't really feel like going there and getting depressed. I still have trouble talking about it. I hope you will understand. I know I promised, and I hate going back on a promise, but it is a bit scary and yucky for me still. How about we save it, maybe, for when we are at the van park sometime?"

"Yeah, that's cool," Piet said. "Plenty of time."

The group then continued their discussions on plans for the van park. After a few minutes, Adam said, "How about our swim. Who's for it?"

Everyone's hand went skyward, including Adrian's.

"Hang on a minute, guys. You have had a few drinks. Remember the dangers of swimming after drinking?" Rocky said.

"Oh, always the practical one, always the rules," Nick said.

"Cut it out, Nick," Aiden said. "Don't be rude to the big guy."

"It's okay, dude," Rocky said. "I don't take offense at things like that."

"Yeah, I know, but he shouldn't say it like that."

"Yeah, you're right, Aiden," Nick said. "Sorry, Rocky, I didn't mean anything bad."

"That's cool. I know you didn't say it to be offensive. It's okay, really. Okay, a sobriety test."

"A *what* test?" Jay asked. "What's sobriety mean?"

"It means if you are sober, you know, not drunk," Piet said.

"Okay, all stand up in a line and face me. Put your left foot in front of your right foot, touching, making a line with your two feet. Now, arms out straight to your sides, like this. Now, bring them out in front of you, like this," Rocky said, demonstrating. "Now, the pressure is on. Anyone who falls doesn't go for a swim, okay? Now, close your eyes. I'll count to ten and see how you go."

All of them swayed a bit, tensing either their left or right calf muscles to keep themselves upright. On ten, Rocky said, "Okay, guys, open your eyes. How did you do?" All of them thought that they failed because they swayed about quite a bit.

"You all passed. You see, if you were pissed, you wouldn't be able to tense those muscles to correct your swaying or the falling feeling. It is impossible to stay upright, perfectly still, with that test. The test is to see if your brain can tell your muscles to flex to correct your swaying."

"Well, Rocky, we worked out before that we are going skinny-dipping, but instead of just taking our shorts and underwear off and jumping in, we will do it to music, one at a time. We are going to stand on the edge of the pool and move to the music, slowly strip, and then jump or dive in. That means you two guys too," Declan said.

"You guys seem to have a fascination with stripping and nudity. You are almost obsessed with it," Rocky said. "What's your deal?"

"Aw, Rocky, we're not obsessed. We do it all the time. It's just the feeling of being natural, feeling freedom. There is no embarrassment, no hang-ups. We don't worry about being nude or seeing each other naked. You know that," Piet said. "Clothes restrict our movement. We like our jewels hanging free. That's all. You know, we have done a lot of things with nothing on, even skateboard. Come on, Rocky. You're the same, but you don't go nude in front of others; that's the only difference. Hang loose, dude," Aiden said.

"Sorry, don't get upset, mate. I didn't mean anything by it. I just wondered, that's all." Rocky said.

"That's cool, Rocky. We know you don't mean anything against it," Piet said.

"You can't see much in this light anyway. We are not doing it to see each other, just to have the feeling of being unrestricted by clothes. Anyway, as soon as you hit the cold water, they shrivel up, go wrinkly, and almost disappear. You'll see—we even got a game worked out. It will keep everyone busy, so you won't have time to look at anyone anyway," Aiden said.

"Oh, that sounds bad. When you guys work out a game, it gets a bit random," Rocky said, still stressed about what was going down. "I'm going to sit out. As I told, I don't think it is appropriate that a guy my age should be swimming naked with boys your age. I don't think I should swim nude at any time. I hope you are cool with that. I'll just sit over there and have a quiet smoke and drink while you guys enjoy your swim and unwind a bit."

"I'll join ya, Rocky," Adrian said. "I probably should let them go without me. Like you say, it is probably not appropriate for me too, even though I love a good skinny-dip."

Everyone splashed and swam around for a while, and then Piet got the two beach balls into play. They formed two teams of five, throwing the balls from one end to the other. The rules were simple—just throw the balls. One team split with three on one end, two on the other end; the other team of five was in the middle. The team who held the end positions had to throw the balls to each end, trying to keep the balls from the team in the middle. When the middle guys had the two balls, the teams changed positions. However, there was a twist. The boys named it the streak. If a ball went out of the pool, the guy who touched it last had to get out of the pool on the opposite side or end to where the ball stopped, run around to pick up the ball, and then run around to the opposite side again to reenter the pool where he got out. Still, there was another twist. The guy who picked up the ball had to run with it holding it above his head with both hands.

The game was so simple, but it provided a lot of fun, a lot of laughter and cheering, and a few grazes on butts, arms, and legs. After about forty minutes, the game came to an end, with participants exhausted.

"That was totally awesome," Nick said. "We gotta do that again soon."

"That really is a good game, fellas. You guys did well, thinking that one up," Rocky said.

After a few minutes of swimming and mucking about in the pool, everyone got out, grabbed a towel, and went in search of their shorts.

"You guys sure know how to have fun," Rocky said. "You guys better keep that game in your heads. You can use it when you have other young guys over at the youth center—but with clothes on."

"Yeah, but when we have chicks over, they can do it nude. How wicked will that be?" Haydon said, drawing yahoos and cheers from some of the guys.

"Yeah, that game was wicked," Adrian said, still smiling at Haydon's wish. "So simple but so much fun."

The guys settled down, lounging in the chairs or lying on the grass that surrounded the pool. Piet said quietly, "Rocky, I think that calls for another bourbon, don't you think?"

"Yeah, buddy, I tend to agree with you. What do you think, Adrian? Need another bourbon? Do you think these guys could have another drink?" Rocky asked.

"Oh, no. They can't have a drink. They're too young. They're only minors," Adrian said, laughing.

"Rack off," Pieter said. "Don't you start that *minors* shit again."

"What do you mean, 'don't start that shit again'?" Adrian asked.

"That minors crap. Rocky said that last week. I hate being a minor and you oldies making decisions for us," Pieter said.

"Hey, dude, only joking, Piet. I didn't know that you felt so strongly about it. You really are a fiery little dude, hey bud. Yeah, sure, it's cool by me if you have another drink. Really sucked you in. I think you guys have earned another drink. How awesome is it—chillin' out under the stars with good guys for company? Yeah, you gotta have another drink on a night like this."

Pieter, Aiden, and Declan got the drinks, while Adam, Haydon, and Nick topped up the snacks. "I'm sorry about the *minor's* crap, I thought Rocky, or someone must have told you about it." Pieter said, thinking that Adrian knew about his issue of being a minor.

Pieter continued. "Ah, got you, Adrian, sucked in big time. Hey man, only gagging ya."

Aiden delivered Rocky's drink to him, and Adam, Nick, and Haydon waited on Adrian and Rocky with the food plates.

Adrian got up from his chair as Pieter walked away. Like a flash, Adrian rushed up behind Pieter and dacked him and then lightly wrestled Pieter onto the grass. Pieter burst into laughter, rolling around the grass, laughing uncontrollably and wrestling with Adrian. They both got up and embraced each other to acknowledge each other's jokes. Pieter then paraded around the grass with his shorts around his ankles for a while, saying, "If this is what you want, I'll leave them down for you. I got no shame."

It took quite a time for the laughter and yahooing from everyone to subside, with Pieter pulling up his shorts, and Pieter and Adrian walking back to the group with an arm around each other's shoulders, laughing and joking as they went.

Idle conversations took place on how they could develop the areas for chilling at the van park, how they could clean and fill the pool, and planning some tracks and pathways with flares along the sides to the beach and the jetty in the creek.

"That place is going to be awesome when we finish with it," Pieter said.

"Yeah, it is going to rock. Rocky, can we repair and do up a couple of dongers, so we can have a pad for chillin' and sleepovers?" Aiden asked. "I want to move in, really, to be near my Rock Daddy, but like you said, I should really stay at home with Mum and the kids and stay over sometimes."

"Yeah, guys, we will eventually repair, paint, and furnish all of the cabins and buildings. You will be able to stay for sleepovers. I guess eventually, when you leave school and find work, you would be able to live onsite. Really, if a couple of you guys lived onsite, it would provide better security. But guys, I must insist that I have full permission from your mums until you are eighteen," Rocky said.

He turned to Adrian and said, "Hey, mate, you should see this place. It is awesome—some of the things that we can do with it. I'll have to arrange an inspection for you soon. I guess in the morning before you take your lady for your romantic afternoon and sunset picnic. I suppose we better organize keys for all you guys too, so that you can have access to all areas. Thinking about it, probably a gate key each and a key safe located somewhere convenient. If you all had a key to the gate and a key to the key safe, you can then get a key for whatever building or gate, use it, and put it back when you are finished. We better look at that tomorrow and look at 'my' railway carriages."

"Are there railway carriages there too?" Adrian asked.

"Yeah, Adrian, that's where Rocky is going to live. Since his wife had her operation a year ago and has effectively thrown the wheel-chair away,

Rocky, his wife, and his two sons will move in here. She has not seen much of Rocky lately, with his work commitments, and helping us, he is looking forward to settling down with his new job here with his family. We appreciate the fact that Mrs. Scott has allowed Rocky to spend so much time helping us. Now, we can see her more often, she is really a great lady, we will all get on so well together." Aiden said.

"Cool. I love railway carriages too," Adrian said.

"Ha-ha, I beat you to them, but you never know. I won't live forever, so if you are around, someone will have to take over when I go."

"Don't talk like that," Piet said. "You can't die for years, Rock Daddy. All legends live forever."

"Thanks, champ. No, I'm not going to cark it just yet. Been there, done that. Not good, no future in that. I'm going to be around for another forty more years, just to spook everyone."

"When do we pick up our gear from the theater, Rocky?" Declan asked.

"We better plan our day now, I guess," Rocky said. "The stage guy will be there from ten onward. Do you guys want to sleep in tomorrow, or should we get up early and go down to the van park, look around, and plan a few things?"

Most were cool with getting up early and checking out their park, beach, and jetty.

"How about we do that? The first up tomorrow wakes everyone up. We have a quick breakfast and go down to the park," Rocky suggested. "Are you okay with that Adrian? And can you take your car as well and take a few of these guys?"

"Yeah, that's cool, looking forward to seeing this place. You'll have to take me home first, so I can pick up my car," Adrian said. "Then we can go to the theater and collect the band equipment."

"Okay, guys, that's settled," Rocky said. He went to a cooler, got two bottles from it, and placed them on the table. "Guys, as promised, a nightcap. Can someone rustle up twelve shot glasses? You all must have a try of each one, just the smallest sip. There is a good port and a bottle of rum liqueur. You can decide which one you would like a shot glass of after you have tried both." Rocky poured the port first. The guys tried it, washed their glasses, and then tried the rum liqueur. The guys made their decisions, and Rocky put a piece of ice in each glass and poured their selected drink.

"Now, just sip it slowly, and enjoy it. Don't scull it; you won't really enjoy it that way."

Discussion turned to the skateboards that the Cleator Social Club gave them. "Those skateboards are awesome, guys," Adrian said. "I hope you aren't going to use them."

"Probably only once or twice, just to say that I have ridden it, but I want to keep mine like new," Aiden said.

The other guys followed suit with the opinion that they would keep theirs like new also.

"Hey, Adrian, you didn't get one. Did you want one for yourself?" Aiden said.

"Yeah, mate, but that's cool. You guys deserved yours, and I came to the group late."

"No way, man. I'll ask the guys," Aiden said. "As chairman, I would like to suggest that we give the extra skateboard to Adrian. He's as much in this group as the rest of us, and he's an awesome guy. He was there for us at the wharf that night and afterward. And he's teaching us to dance. I would like you all to vote on it. If you agree, put your hand up. If you don't, leave it down. Majority rules."

All the guys put their hands up—all except one. "Don't you agree that Adrian can have the skateboard, Rocky?" Aiden asked.

"Oh sure, mate. I thought the vote was for the guys and not me," Rocky said.

"Rocky, how many times you gotta be told that you are one of us, man?" Aiden said. "And don't you forget it."

"Sorry, mate. Yeah, I agree. I won't forget that I am one of the gang," Rocky said, as he put his hand up.

"That's settled, then. Adrian, we all agree, even Rocky, that the twelfth skateboard is yours," Aiden said.

"Hey, thanks, Aiden. Thanks, guys. I will treasure it, and I too will keep it like new," Adrian said.

"Now, while we are in meeting mode, we need to decide what we are going to do with the prize money," Aiden said. "There are two lots of a thousand dollars in prize money. The band can either keep it for themselves or put it in the bank and use it to fix up the park and buy music equipment or lighting or sports equipment."

"No, I think we would get better value if we put it in the foundation money, even if we say that the two thousand is allocated to sound equipment," Piet said.

"Let's vote on it now. Hands up if you want to bank the money into the funds," Aiden said. Everyone indicated their agreement. "Everyone agrees that the money gets banked into the foundations' bank account."

"Rocky, how much money did we get from the rock concert?" Jay asked.

"Good question. George told me that they got just over sixteen thousand dollars from door tickets and leftover cash from the sponsors and donations. Apparently, this year was the best yet, so you guys should get just over eight thousand dollars. How about that!" Rocky said. "I'll get the check on Monday or Tuesday. A few of you guys need to come with me to collect it. The paper and television stations want to get some pictures, along with the high school captains getting their check."

"How did you handle the paper, radio, and TV interviews, guys?" Adrian asked.

"Oh, cool, I think," Haydon said.

"Yeah, we went okay," Aiden said. "Got sick of saying the same thing over and over, though."

"Um, they were persistent, weren't they?" Adrian said.

"Yeah, sure were. Couldn't get away from them," Declan said.

"It is good for us, though," Aiden said. "Everyone out there will sure know about us by next weekend."

Rocky nodded. "Hell yeah, everyone will know about you, but that can only be a good thing. Just think how easy it will be to get donations and help from businesses. Everyone wants to get with successful people. You may not know it, but you guys are now successful and famous. I am going to see a couple of counselors I know well from the Takerny Shire Council next week to get their support. Their budget is coming up soon, and they like to support worthwhile causes in the community. They spend lots of money on donations, so I intend to get some for the foundation. When that happens, the sky is the limit."

"You better get your autograph hands in tune," Adrian said. "Because you guys will be signing them soon and pushing the chicky babes out of your way."

"So, Rocky, that means with the two-thousand-dollar prize money, the two hundred in tips you gave us, and over eight thousand dollars, we will have over ten thousand dollars in the bank!" Jay, the treasurer, said.

"Yeah, that's right, dude," Rocky said.

"Wow, man, that's real money," Jay said.

"Yeah, Jay, it's real money—a real lot of money," Rocky said. "Anyway, guys, it's way past midnight, and you dudes are tired. How about we go to bed, so we can get up at sunrise?"

"Yeah, good idea, chief," Adrian said. "It's been a really awesome day and night."

"I can't stop thinking—there is no way we would be sitting here talking and chilling and thinking about all this money and all the good things that we have done if it wasn't for the big guy," Piet said, as he walked over to Rocky. "Get up, big guy, my Rock Daddy. I want to thank you for believing in us and staying with us and showing us how to live better. Thanks, dude."

Piet took Rocky's right hand with his right hand and hugged Rocky with his left arm. Tears flowed from Piet's eyes and he then said, "I love you so much as a mate, Rock Daddy. Thanks," Piet blubbered.

Tears ran down Rocky's cheeks as he let go of Piet's hand and put both of his arms around Pieter's shoulders. "You know, dude, I love you too, all of you. I feel great to have been able to pick you guys up, offer a helping hand and guide you all through life's maze. I am proud of you all."

As Pieter moved to Rocky's side, all the other guys did the same, hugged their champ, and thanked him for getting their lives moving upward and achieving so much.

Adrian walked over to Rocky and said, "Rocky, I am really proud to call you a mate also. I have seen what you have done for these guys and the other kids before them. You don't know this, but you remember young Michael, Kai, and Liam—those three twelve-year-old boys you helped a few years ago? Michael is my cousin. You knew that the twins, Kai and Liam, are related to Michael, didn't you? They aren't related to me directly, but I know them just as well as I know Michael. Michael is nearly the same age as these guys—the three of them are—and he is doing well since you helped him. He moved away with the two others to be fostered by a relative of theirs. You didn't know that, did you? He keeps in touch, and he often talks about you. I am planning to get him to visit me later this year. I know that he would love to see you again, and I know that you would love to see him too. Now, mate, thanks for helping Michael, for helping the twins, and for helping these guys here. And mate, thanks for what you have done for me." Tears ran down Adrian's cheeks, and he hugged Rocky.

Rocky said, "I can't talk much. I am crying my eyes out too, guys. Buddy, I had no idea that Mick was your cousin. I knew Kai and Liam were Mick's cousins, but I had no idea you knew them."

"Mick, that's right; you called him Mick. You know, you were the only person who ever called him that, the only person who could call him that. How did you do that?" Adrian said.

"That was funny. He would get hell angry when someone else called him Mick, for obvious reasons. He related it to a part of the female body. I got away with it in the beginning to teach him anger management, but I also used to say it in a different tone than other people, and I used it as a kind of pet name, just me and him. It then became a habit, I guess," Rocky said. "I would hell love to see him again and the other kids as well. I suppose I wouldn't recognize them; kids grow quickly at that age. Thank you all, guys. When you do good, feel good, and laugh and enjoy yourselves, I feel totally awesome."

"Group hug," Aiden said. "Look at us—hell, we are sooks. Yeah, Rocky, I know you said it's always okay for blokes to get teary-eyed, especially when it is for happiness."

As the group hug fell into a heap of bodies on the ground, a few of them noticed a flash in the sky.

"What the heck was that?" Adam yelled.

"Beats the shit out of me," Aiden said. "Can't be lightning—the stars are out."

"Must have been a shooting star. Make a wish, everyone, just in case it was. Don't tell anyone what your wish is," Rocky said.

"I haven't heard that for a long time, Rocky," Adrian said.

"What's that?" Pieter asked.

"Oh, old school. When you saw a falling or shooting star, you made a wish, that's all," Adrian said.

"That's cool, man. I see them all the time," Piet said. "Me and Aiden see them a lot when we just sit outside and look up at the stars and talk to Mitch. We always say it is Mitch, sending us a message that he agrees. So, that flash before was Mitch, agreeing with what everyone said and joining in the group hug."

"Yeah, he is with us all the time. We miss him a lot, Rocky. It really isn't fair. That poor bastard had to lose his life just to wake us up," Aiden said, bursting into tears once again.

Rocky rushed over to comfort Aiden as his crying got louder and uncontrollable, just as he had done many times in the past six months. "Come on, calm down, big guy. Yeah, it's not fair, but you gotta be strong, mate. He has gone, but you still remember him and the good times with him. That's awesome. You will always remember him for the rest of your life. Come on, dude. You have all had an emotional two weeks, and today you are all drained. That's normal. You can only take so much emotion; then you crack. That's the way it goes, but guys, it only goes to prove that you are mere humans. That's what is so awesome about all of you. You are all back to living normal lives. Now, I think we'd better sort out the mattresses, and get some sleep. Another big day tomorrow, you lucky dudes."

The guys got into the task of putting the mattresses and pillows on the floor. They decided that all the mattresses should be placed side by side and end to end to form a large square. Then they threw the sheets and covers onto the gigantic bed. They also decided to sleep across the mattresses, so no one would fall between them. Faces and hands washed, teeth cleaned, and all into bed. Good night wishes all around; then giggles, jumping, and wrestling, as the guys expelled the last ounce of energy they possessed.

"Get your leg off me, you faggot," one said.

"Oh, come on. You know you want me," another joked.

"Good night, darling," someone else said, laughing.

"Oh, who dropped their guts?"

"Rocky, Aiden's spanking the monkey."

"No, I'm not. Don't tell lies. Anyway, what if I am? You do it all the time."

"Yeah, every guy does it."

Someone let out an almighty loud fart.

"You dirty prick. You stink."

"Ah, stuff that. Your butt smells like a goanna crawled up there and died."

"Rocky, can you smell that one? Good one. Hey, I'm proud of that one," Adam said.

"Yeah, mate, you stink. You better sit on the toilet and give birth, mate, and flush it at birth," Rocky said, laughing. Rocky thought, *it's just a group of young guys being happy, doing harmless things that guys their age do when they are together.*

"Hey, guys, if anyone has a wet dream or wakes up with a morning bone, just keep it to yourself. Remember, all of you are free-willy," Adrian said. "Just remember that there is a guy sleeping on either side of you."

"Good one, dude," Rocky said. "Remember, too, if you spread your legs apart, there could be a lot of kidneys and no steak."

"Yeah, I'll sleep nude," Jacob said. "Anyone who wants to sleep natural, do it now."

"Oh, guys. Maybe not tonight. That's fine in the privacy of your bedrooms, but not here, when there is a large group of guys. You can sleep one night with your boxers or shorts on," Rocky said. "Now, guys, get some sleep. Big day tomorrow. Sweet dreams all of you."

Very soon, Rocky noticed faint snoring coming from all the guys, and he too drifted off to sleep, thinking how lucky he was to be mates with so many guys who were so happy with their lots in life.

CHAPTER 14

**My world is awesome for me; leave me in it …
unless you can prove that yours is better.**

As the first sun's rays peeped over the horizon and through the windows of the barn, Rocky awoke and noticed a few motionless bodies surrounding him were beginning to stir. He glanced at his watch; it was nearly a quarter to six. The bodies moved and sat up, hands rubbing eyes, arms stretching, and a few primal noises coming from a couple of the stretching bodies. Rocky's head told him that he needed a coffee and a smoke, and his bladder told him it needed emptying. As he got up off the mattress, stepping between the sleeping and waking bodies like an obstacle course, he noticed that a few of the guys had similar messages from their bladders.

The toilet in the barn was working overtime, with a few waiting their turn.

Rocky leaned down and whispered in Pieter's ear. "Is it okay to take a piss in the backyard?"

"It's cool," Pieter said. "I need to go too, so I'll go outside as well."

"Where ya goin', Piet and Rocky?" Aiden asked as they approached the door to the barn.

"Dingo's breakfast," Rocky replied.

"Dingo's breakfast? What's that?" Aiden asked.

"Aw, a stretch, a piss, and a good look around," Rocky replied.

The barn erupted in laughter and applause.

Aiden said, "Good one, Rocky. They never stop coming, do they?"

"No, mate. Plenty more where that came from." Rocky rushed out the door, holding his crotch so as not to let it flow.

As the two guys stood behind the barn, relieving their bladders, Pieter said, "You know, Rocky, I gotta keep pinching myself to see if this is real—you know, all these things that have happened to us lately."

"Yeah, mate, it certainly is different to what you guys were used to. I am just so happy you and the others listened, thought, and followed. Now that you have made it, you can all be proud. The future for you all is awesome, if you keep the attitudes that you have and make the right choices. But never slack off. It's easy to fall back into your old habits and lose all that you have achieved. If ever you see any of these guys slipping back, give 'em a good kick in the butt for me. No, I don't mean that; just talk to them like I used to talk to you. Like I say, 'Remember the good times with a passion, but never forget the bad times. Learn from them and move on.' You know what that means by now. I have told you all often enough."

Bladders emptied, the two moved to the chairs near the pool.

"Rocky, that is so true. You know, when we were the bad guys of the town, we thought what we were doing was so cool, and we thought we felt good. Now we are living a clean life and know how wrong we were 'cause nothin' beats what we got now."

"Yeah, mate, you now realize that by doing good things with your life and for yourselves that your mind becomes healthy, your bodies get healthy, and your heart becomes healthy, which makes you feel good about enjoying other people's company."

"What are you two up to?" Adrian said as he surfaced and joined them, lighting a cigarette for himself and one for Rocky.

"Why don't you two give that away? It's bad for you," Pieter said.

"Yeah, I must try, now that there is a change in my life," Rocky answered. "Adrian, we were just talking about changing attitudes, choices, and enjoying life and other people being around."

"Oh, that's cool. I could see you two were in a deep conversation. Wondered what was going down," Adrian said. "Aiden is making us a coffee. He reckons that you need one really bad by now."

"Thanks, that's awesome. Now, Piet, here's another saying I made up to help me understand what's going on: 'My world is awesome for me. Leave me in it … unless you can prove yours is better.' Do you understand what I mean by that?"

"No, not really, Rocky," Piet said.

"*My world is awesome for me*—I love the way I live my life, and I am happy with the life choices that I have made."

"Yep, got that."

"*Leave me in it*—piss off and leave me alone; don't try to change my life."

"Oh, yeah, got that."

"*Unless you can prove that yours is better*—show me that what you do, how you live your life, how you are trying to change my life to the same as yours is better than how I think and live."

"That's wicked, Rocky," Pieter said "That's so true. You gotta be strong enough that what you do and think and say is right for you and not worry about what others think or do or say. That's a good thought to remember when dickheads try to get into our heads and try to make us change and join in their ways."

"Hell yeah; that's sweet. You know exactly what I am saying," Rocky said. "I'm not saying that I am right, but no one has been able to show me that I am wrong. Like you guys—things I told you, showed you, and taught you have succeeded and produced the awesome young men that you are today, ready to tackle the world and tackle any obstacles or temptations put in front of you. Some things probably didn't work too well, but overall, it has worked for all of you … and me. That's good enough for me. No one can ever tell me or show me that what I do and talk about with you guys or other teenage guys is wrong. They can just get out of my face and stuff with someone else."

"Hey, settle down, old man, settle down," Adrian said. "Hell, you get worked up, man."

"Yeah, I do, but it really annoys me up when people tell me what I do is not normal and that I can never change the attitudes of adolescents to change their lives. Get out; I have done it. I do it. As I said last night, what's normal? Surely helping other people, no matter how old or young they are, who have problems and confusion in their lives must be normal. Like I say, my life is awesome for me. Get out of my face now and leave me in it, unless you can prove that yours is better," Rocky said, still sounding angry.

'Well said, Rocky," Pieter said. "We all can learn a lot from you when you get stirred up. You are so strong in your beliefs. No one can bump you off course or make you give in."

"Oh, thanks, Aiden," Rocky said, as Aiden delivered the coffees. "I need this. Hey, buddy, can I flog another smoke from you? I'll pay you back later. Mine are inside," Rocky said to Adrian.

"Sure, old man, I can see the fire in your eyes and the stress in your face. You better have one," Adrian said.

"Thanks, mate, you're awesome," Rocky said. "That's one awesome coffee, Aiden; thanks, buddy. Oy, mate, what's this 'old man' talk? I notice you have started calling me 'old man' lately. Not so much of the 'old,' hey?"

"Sorry, man, I don't mean that you are old. A lot of guys call their dad's 'old man.' I've never had anyone I could call 'old man' that way. If you don't like it, I won't say it again. I'm sorry."

"Oh, that's cool. Not you too? I didn't realize that you too had no father. What the hell goes on in this world? I'm sorry, Adrian. It's cool if you want to call me that."

"Mine is a bit different. My dad was killed in a mining accident when I was five. They never found his body. He is buried somewhere hundreds of feet underground, and it was too dangerous to excavate to find him."

"Buddy, I am so sorry. I never knew that. Isn't it amazing that everyone, at some stage in their life, has secrets or personal tragedies, but it never shows? You just keep it close to your heart and move on. It's cool by me if you want to call me your 'old man,' Adrian." Rocky put his arm around Adrian's shoulders and hugged him tightly.

"I'll start getting breakfast ready soon. What are we doing today?" Aiden asked.

"We're taking Rocky's and my cars to the van park for a look around," Adrian said. "Then we'll pick up the band gear from the theater."

"Can we make some rough plans on what we want to build at the center?" Pieter asked. "We got the rock fest out of the way."

"Yeah, sure," Rocky agreed. "We will check out every building and see what's there, what we can use. We gotta look for a place to put a key safe, a space for group meetings, a chill-out area, the beach, the jetty, a sleepover place, a band practice area—the list is long, but we will just look around and see what can be used. We also gotta look at a place where Cleator's can move the timber and building materials so we can sort it and stack it neatly."

"Hell, we are going to be busy," Aiden said.

"Yep, we won't be in a rush, though. We might take a notebook and make notes, so we can refer to it later and see how things fall into place. Probably should start with a bit of a clear-up, mowing, clearing bush tracks, and cleaning up the shelters on the beach and the jetty first. Cleator's will take care of the building restorations for us from time to time."

"That's a good plan," Adrian said. "Don't forget that I want to take Christy there for a picnic and a talk."

"That's cool," Rocky said. "Want a hand with breakfast, Aiden?"

"Yeah, if you want. I'll cook the bacon and snags if you want to cook the eggs. I love watching you break eggs with one hand; it's wicked." "I'll help too," Adrian said.

"I'll get the plates, knives, and forks and things," Pieter said.

The breakfast team got stuck into the task and worked their butts off, preparing the food. A few other guys surfaced and put a couple of tables together and placed twelve chairs around in readiness for the food.

"Okay, guys, it's ready!" Aiden yelled to the rest of them, banging a metal plate with a metal spoon.

The food went down well, the discussions were about the experiences of the day and night before, remembering some of the things that happened, the bands' performances, the prize money, the money given by the organizers, Adrian's dance show, and the conga line and dance competition. They agreed that this weekend would stay in their memories for a very long time. Discussions then turned to the youth center plans, the things that they would build or do, and what activities could be used when other troubled kids came to visit. Rocky and Adrian let them go, looking at each other from time to time, showing approval for the points raised and spoken about.

"Hey, just remembered. I must get my wish-in-a-bottle down. The wish I have in it is now happening. Anyone else thought about their wish lately or need to change theirs?" Rocky said.

A couple of the boys indicated that they should update theirs or had forgotten what they had in their bottles. "What's the wish-in-a-bottle?" Adrian asked.

"Look up there on that shelf. See that row of bottles? Each one belongs to each of us, Rocky too, and there is a wish, goal, or message in them," Piet answered. "When we get the wish or want to change our goal, we get it down and change it. Mitch's is there too. No one has opened it since he died. It will sit there until some special time; we haven't decided when, either the twelve-month anniversary or his eighteenth birthday." "It's something we started a while ago to help these guys with their emotions or goals. They have been changed a few times; they have achieved many milestones in the past. Mine has happened, so I have to think of another wish or goal, get it down, and change it," Rocky said. "Let's clean up, wash our faces or freshen up in the pool, and get over to the park."

Everyone got up and did his little bit to collect the plates and cutlery, put away the sauces, and wash and wipe up. Even the garden furniture was set up around the pool and covered area very neatly. Not one of them was lazy or stood around while others got the tasks done. When the chores were completed, each of them jumped into the pool and bobbed or jumped around or swam a few lengths. Then they coaxed Adrian and Rocky to join them.

"This water is wicked," Jay said. "It wakes me up big time."

After about ten minutes or so, the group made their way to the Youth Center.

Tony got out at the entrance to open the gate and quickly got back in Rocky's car. As they rounded the first bend of the track, they saw a large banner stretched across the road between two trees.

WELCOME, YOUNG GUNS, TO THE TEEN-MORPH YOUTH CENTER

"That's awesome," Haydon said. "That sign is wicked. Do you think Mr. Cleator put that up?"

"I'd say so," Rocky replied. "Isn't that great?"

"Yeah, cool," Aiden said. "Makes you feel sort of important. Makes you feel part of it."

Both vehicles pulled up in the car park at the first railway carriages, and discussion about the banner took place between the groups from both vehicles.

"Oy, Rocky, look at this arrow," Jacob said. "It has words on a sign on it.

START YOUR JOURNEY HERE.
FOLLOW THE ARROWS.

The guys ran over to see what Jacob was talking about.

"Do you think George put it there? There must be a course to follow," Adrian said.

"Yeah, I guess so," Rocky replied. "Let's follow the direction and see where we end up."

The direction on the sign took the group to the amenities block. The building was rundown and in need of some repairs, a cleanup, and a coat of paint; otherwise, everything worked. At one end was a note and a map of the van park; at the other end was some used outdoor furniture and barbecue grills and gas bottles.

Hi, welcome, guys. Follow the arrows that are numbered to 25 and use the map so you can see where you are in relation to the overall caravan park area. The furniture, barbecue grills, and so forth are for you to clean up at your leisure and use as you see fit. Now, find arrow 2 and follow it to the next step.

The group found arrows 2, 3, 4, and 5, which took them to the shed building that housed the workshop. Aiden found the key that opened the door to the shed, and the guys went inside, taking in all the machinery and tools.

"Are we able to use these tools, Rocky?" Aiden asked.

"Yeah, mate. It will still be used by some of the men at Cleator's, but I am now in charge of this, and it's available for each of us to use."

'That's awesome," Pieter said.

"Look, here's the note!" Haydon yelled, as he walked out of the shed and looked around the corner. "And heaps of mowers, brush cutters, and golf buggy-type things."

Haydon read the note.

> Guys, this is the storage shed and workshop. The mowers and brush cutters are for your use to clear the park and maintain the area for the future. They have been checked and serviced and are ready to go. The buggies are also for your use, but Mr. Scott will need to instruct each of you on their correct use. This is a Workplace Health and Safety requirement.

"Rocky, what's Workplace Health and Safety?" Adam asked.

'Good question, buddy. It's a set of government regulations that provide a safe and healthy workplace for everyone. I'll instruct you in the use of every piece of machinery or equipment before you use it, just so you know how to use it safely and how to stop it or turn it off in case of emergency. We'll cover each one as we start to use each piece of equipment."

The group continued from the shed along the bitumen roadway to the next arrow pointing to another shed. Aiden looked at the map and told everyone that it was the boat shed. As he opened the door, they noticed that it contained two dinghies on trailers with outboards, several canoes, oars of all sizes, life jackets, and more buggies.

The note told them:

> Everything in the boat shed is also for your use. The dinghies on trailers are only to be towed by the petrol-driven buggies. The rest are rechargeable electric-driven buggies.

The arrows then took them to the jetty on the creek, past some picnic shelters, through another car park, through a gate, and onto the beach. The walk south along the beach took them past another two shelters, through another gate back into the park, along an overgrown track to a very large hall-type building. They found the key, opened the building, and entered. It had the appearance of a large hall or possibly an old dormitory-type accommodation. It contained fifteen to twenty single beds, four double beds, bedside tables and lamps, lounges, tables and chairs, ward-robes, cupboards, and heaps more furniture, including fridges, freezers, and washing machines, all checked and working.

The next stage took the guys back onto the beach and then back into the park and to another building with a faded sign that read:

> ## COMMUNITY BUILDING

This building contained TVs, VCRs, stereos, desks, computers, and lockers. The journey then took them along an overgrown path, past the railway carriages, across the main entrance road, and into the pool area, with two gazebos stacked high with outdoor furniture. It then lead them back to the main car park where the walk had started.

"How about that, guys?" Rocky asked.

"That's awesome," Jay said. "Is all that stuff really for us to use?"

"Sure is, mate. All that stuff is obviously secondhand. I would say it was used by the fellas who lived here during the last construction and stored away. It's all been checked and serviced, ready to go. How much money does that save us, guys?" Rocky said.

"That's wicked," Adrian said. "That is so cool. I'm so glad I met up with you guys and that you let me into your gang. That's awesome. And, Rocky, did you notice that there are two sets of railway carriages? I can't wait to help you guys clean up and set up this place."

"Oy, Adrian, you'll piss yourself you are so excited. Settle, petal," Rocky said, laughing. "No, I didn't notice two lots of carriages."

"There are these here, and we passed another lot over there, near the workshop shed, behind those trees. I might get one yet, hey, Rocky?" Adrian said.

"Well, you possibly will, if you want to. We will have to look inside and see what all you guys want to use them for."

"Did you see the donger-type buildings?" Piet said. "There must be at least four around the place."

"Yeah, I did notice some," Rocky said. "We had better plan a whole day soon to look at everything and plan what will be used for what, but we'd better get to the theater and pick up the gear. Before we do, let's work out where Cleator's can put the building stuff for us to use. I saw an area outside the boundary opposite the shed and workshop that might be a good spot. We will need to organize another gate, so we can have access to it. Let's look at that map, Aiden. Yeah, the road to the boat shed goes right past it so we might drive down there and take a look."

They parked their cars and walked over to the fence adjacent to the area.

"Yeah, this will be good. It's away from everything, and the workshop is just over there, across the roadway. All we need is a gate to get access to it. What do ya say?" Adrian said.

"It's cool by me. Hands up, guys, if you agree. You guys gotta decide on most of this stuff, not just me and Adrian," Rocky said.

They all agreed.

"That's decided, then," Aiden said. "Rocky will tell George during the week."

"Now, Secretary Pieter, have you made enough notes in your book about this place to hold some meetings and decide what will be used for what?" Rocky asked.

"Yeah, Rocky. I think I got enough info. I'll keep the plan and notes from Mr. Cleator together with the book, so we can talk about it at a meeting some day this week," Pieter said.

"Aiden, you are chairman. Work out with your committee a date, place, and time for a meeting and to start planning this place. The sooner you start the better. I'll talk to George tomorrow or Tuesday and find out the finer details. I want to check out the carriages and those dongers over there, so I can put forward some thoughts on what I want to use. The rest will be for you dudes. Adrian, when are you home this week?" Rocky asked.

"I'm back at work tomorrow and back home on Friday afternoon," Adrian said, "and then back to work the following Monday and home Thursday. That's Easter long weekend. I got five days off."

"That's awesome. I forgot about the long weekend coming up. That gives us four days, guys, and then you got the week off on holidays. Cool," Rocky said. "Who's going away for the Easter weekend or the school holidays?"

None of them planned to go away. They never went away on holidays for several reasons. As they told Rocky, there was nowhere to go, their mums couldn't afford it, or they were just bored and staying home.

"Well, guys, you won't be bored this time. You now have somewhere to go, you have plenty to do, and it's all for your benefit. I'll be finished with the taxi after this week too, so that will be wicked," Rocky said.

The group walked to the carriages nearest the car park and surveyed the area and the interiors. The surrounding area was a bit overgrown and untidy, but with a little bit of work, it could be transformed into a very comfortable residence. The donger closest to the carriages and car park was divided into two rooms that had been used as accommodations, big enough to hold three to four beds in each room.

"Can I suggest that this donger be used as office space on one end and a meeting room the other end?" Rocky said. "Your very own boardroom, guys. Don't decide now; just make a note in your book, Pieter."

The group walked over to the other set of three carriages and found them in a similar condition as the others.

"This is awesome, Rocky," Adrian said. "These would be wicked to chill out in. I could live in one of these, no probs."

"Yeah, they're awesome," Pieter said.

"I can see why you guys want to live in train carriages. This is sick," Aiden said.

"Maybe we can set these up for the nights that we have a sleepover on weekends and holidays," Haydon suggested.

"Talk about it at your next meeting," Rocky said. "Just check with Adrian and see if he wants to be at your meetings. If not, find out what points he wants brought to the meeting. Now, we better get to the theater and get the gear."

"Hi, fellas, how's things?" the stage manager asked as the guys entered the backstage area. "Hope you enjoyed yourselves last night."

"Yeah, we sure did, thanks. We had an awesome time. It will stay in our heads for a long time," Pieter answered.

"Rick, these are the DVDs I promised you of the band competition. George said it was okay for you to have a set," the stage manager said, as the guys busied themselves carting the band gear to the cars.

"Is George here?" Rocky asked.

"Yeah, he is in the function room. I think the front entrance is open; if not, come back here, and I will get you in from this end."

After the cars were packed, the guys came back onstage and looked over the empty theater, revisiting the experience they'd had the day before.

"Sure, feels different, hey guys?" Aiden said. "Pretty quiet and lonely and empty, hey?"

"Yeah, but if you concentrate and listen hard, you can still hear the music and crowd," Jay said.

"You were always a bit bent, Jay," Rocky said. "Can you really hear the music in your head?"

"Yeah, Rocky, you can imagine it if you really try. Yeah, I'm bent, but I let my imagination take me away a lot; it makes me feel good."

"That's cool, dude," Rocky said. "Nothing wrong with having an imagination. That's where dreams are born. Okay, guys, let's go find George."

The front entrance was open. George and a few other people were busy packing up decorations and other items into cartons for storage for next year's event.

"Hi, George," Rocky said. "How are you doing this morning?"

"Oh, hi, Rick. I'm good. How about you, and how about these guys? Did you have a good time last night?"

"Yeah, great, thanks, Mr. Cleator," Aiden said. "Can we help you pack up this stuff?"

"Oh, Aiden, fellas, that's very thoughtful of you," George said.

In the matter of moments, the guys had everything packed up, with George and Bob instructing which cartons contained what.

"Thanks, boys," George said. "We appreciate your help."

"Mr. Cleator," Aiden said, "we all want to thank you very much for the things that you have done for us and for the old caravan park. We were there this morning, and it's awesome. And thank you for letting us come to the party last night. We had a great time, and we will remember it for a long time. Thanks, Mr. Cleator."

"That's okay, boys. It is a pleasure to reward you boys for what you have achieved. You all deserve it, and I am proud that I can help Mr. Scott and you boys realize your dreams and goals. I know I have made the right decision just by how you came in here and put this gear away. That shows Mr. Watson and me the character you boys have," George told them. "Well done, boys."

"George, as Aiden said, we went to the park this morning. Thank you for all the furniture and equipment you had there for the guys. They are over the moon," Rocky said.

"You're welcome, Rick. That gear was stored onsite from the last construction gang. I planned to sell it some time ago but never got around to it. Really, you don't get much if you sell it, but if you go to buy that stuff, it costs a fortune. Now I know it will be put to good use."

"Well, that's true. Thanks heaps, George. It is really appreciated."

"Now, Rick, can you come to see me on Tuesday? I will have the check for you, and there are a few things that I need to go through with you. Oh, have you decided when you want to start work for Cleator's and which building you want to use for your new home?" George asked.

"Yeah, George, I'm finishing with the taxis next weekend, and I can start straight away, if that suits," Rick answered. "The lads are keen to start work on the youth center as soon as possible. They have the long weekend and their weeklong school holidays straight after. I'm thinking of using the railway carriages closest to the car park to live in, and the guys are thinking of using the first donger for their office and boardroom. They are going to hold a meeting or two this week and nut a few things out. They probably will want to camp onsite over the weekend and their holidays, if that is okay."

"Sure. Rick, it's okay. You don't have to ask or tell me. The site is yours and the boys to use as you see fit," George said. "Let me know if you decide to use the carriages, and I will get some building staff to remodel them and spruce them up so that you can move in. And the office and boardroom idea is great. Also, think where we can build a double carport. I have two older vehicles that are not being used that I would like to put onsite for you to put to good use."

"How about I let you know when I see you on Tuesday?" Rick said.

"That's fine, Rick. Now, before you go, I know Bob wants to speak with you about a few challenges he has at school," George said.

"All right, George. I'll see you on Tuesday."

Bob motioned to Rick to move away from the guys, and Rick walked over to where Bob was standing and said, "How's things, Bob? You guys sure put on a good show yesterday and last night."

"Yes, it did go well, Rick, didn't it? Makes it all worthwhile, seeing young people enjoy themselves and do well," Bob said. "Rick, I have two boys that I would like you to help me with. We at school cannot seem to get anywhere with them."

"Sure, Bob, what's the problem?" Rick said.

"I know that you are a long way from being set up, but we are worried about them. Both are acting out of character. I apologize for not giving you time to establish yourself in your new role. One boy you already know—Dillon. He doesn't want to cooperate with anyone; he seems to have a problem that he won't talk about. He has asked to see you and spend time with you, but he hasn't been able to get hold of you."

"Yeah, I know Dillon. I had a word with him that day I met you at the school. I did notice that he was a bit distant and that his attitude had changed since I last saw him. I did mean to catch up with him. I guess all that has happened with the rock fest and the youth center has kept me out of circulation a bit."

"I told him that, and I told him that I would talk to you about him when I saw you next. The other boy, Matt, also was a diligent student. Lately, he has caused a lot of trouble and is beginning to harm himself. The teachers, counselors, and chaplain have not been able to get any information from him or get through to him. I would like you to talk to him and see what the problem is and how we can help him."

"Okay, Bob. I will call you and come to the school this week, if you wish, and see each of them, one at a time, of course. Do they know each other or get on well together?"

"Don't know, really," Bob answered.

"I'll find out that when I talk to them. I'll mention each of their names during general discussions about these guys, and it will be okay. Now, Bob, I don't know how you operate with these issues. I find that I get quicker and better responses by telling them that anything they tell me remains confidential, unless they give their permission to pass on information or, of course, if there is serious criminal activity involved, especially any activity that is dangerous or causes harm to them. I find that the trust is a great tool in achieving the desired or positive outcome."

"Yes, that's okay. We don't need to know personal details. All we seek are kids who behave, achieve to their abilities, and who feel good about themselves. Kids who do their best, really."

"All right, Bob. I'll give you a call tomorrow or Tuesday and make a time. I do need you or one of your staff to be present at the beginning, to introduce me to them and them to me. That breaks the ice and lets them know that the meeting is sanctioned by your school. I think we better let their parents or guardians know that I will be talking to their boys and that we have the kids' welfare at heart."

"Okay, guys, we better get this gear over to Piet's and let Adrian get to see Christy," Rocky said. "I'll see you on Tuesday, George, and I'll phone you soon, Bob."

"Yes, Rick, about midmorning would be best, if you can make it then," George said.

"Rick, I'll await your call. Look after your boys; I would like to see all you boys just before parade tomorrow, maybe in my office or at the steps to the stage. Prepare yourselves because I want to introduce you onstage to the entire school population as the Teen-Morph Foundation and talk briefly to the students and teachers about your achievements. You might like to come, Rick, as well. The kids know you and some of the staff know you as well," Bob said.

"Sure, Bob," Rick said. "I'll certainly try to be there at about a quarter to nine."

"That's good. We are planning a more formal introduction second week back from holidays, where you all, including George, will be introduced to the school, and we'll let the students know more about what Teen-Morph is all about. I'll see you boys before parade. Oh, by the way, congratulations on what you have done and what you have achieved. I am very proud of all of you; you are a credit to the school. Good luck with your future endeavors. I know that this stage of your journey has just begun, and I know with Mr. Scott by your side, you will go a long way. Good to meet you too, Adrian. I would like to talk with you further about your life, how you handled being teased, ridiculed, and bullied, and about your dance abilities."

"Thanks, Mr. Watson, it's great to meet you too, sir, I will look forward to seeing you soon."

"Now, now, Adrian, please call me Bob, and please forget about the *sir*," Bob said.

"Okay, Bob, I'll see you in a week or two," Adrian said.

Goodbyes were exchanged; the guys climbed into the two cars and made their way to Piet's barn.

"Gee, Mr. Watson sounds a lot different outside of the school," Declan said. "He's almost human."

"Yeah, he is different," Jay said. "I've never heard him say so much without being mean."

"Yeah, notice that he doesn't root us up the butt lately?" Aiden said. "Do you think it's because we don't muck up any more, Rocky?"

"Yeah, bud. People who used to finger you will talk to you much more pleasantly now that you have climbed that mountain and made it to the top with your changed attitudes and achievements. You will notice people like to be near pleasant, successful people who have made something of their lives. You must all agree that what I have been telling you about attitudes has worked for you all."

"I'd better be off and pick up Christy and take her back to the park for a quiet talk and picnic. I'll get these keys back to you before I leave for work in the morning," Adrian said. "Thanks for an awesome weekend, you guys, and for letting me be your mate. It has been wicked. I will see you next weekend; meanwhile, have an awesome week."

The guys all shook Adrian's hand and patted his shoulder or hugged him as they said their goodbyes.

"Have a great afternoon and picnic, buddy." Rocky said. "Adrian, I hope everything goes well for you with Christy." Rocky winked. "See ya Friday or Saturday, mate."

"I'll see ya or give ya a call," Adrian said as he left.

"Now, Rocky, we better plan our week," Aiden said.

The guys wanted to travel back to the youth center one last time for the weekend to experience the atmosphere and tranquility and have their first meeting at their newly acquired meeting place. As they pulled up, each lad raced over toward their office/boardroom area, sat in a circle, and excitedly began their meeting.

"Get your notebook, Pieter, and take some notes. Do you want to hold a short meeting and make it official?" Rocky asked.

"Yeah, suppose we better," Aiden said. "Let's set up a couple of tables beside the pool and sit around that."

"Okay, meeting opened. We will hear the minutes from the last meeting." Aiden said, reading from the flowchart he had made for himself from the first meeting.

Pieter read the minutes and moved that they be accepted.

Then came the business from the minutes and then the treasurer's report.

Jacob told the group they had $200 in the bank and two checks of $1,000 each, the prize money from the rock fest. "And we have a big check of about eight thousand dollars to come," he said. "Rocky will pick that up from Mr. Cleator on Tuesday, so we will have probably just over ten thousand dollars."

The guys began clapping and cheering upon being reminded of how much money the group had. The meeting continued with discussions and agreement on the area for the building material, which buildings would be used for the office and boardroom, and the railway carriages used for Rocky's living quarters, with the second group of carriages used for Adrian to stay in when he wasn't away for work and for sleepovers for the lads.

Rocky said, "I think I might get a couple of Staffy dogs, just to roam around and protect the park."

"That sounds cool, man. I've always wanted a Staffy, but we can't have a dog where we live," Declan blurted out.

"All in favor of setting up the other carriages for our sleepovers and for Adrian when he stays in town?" Aiden asked. All agreed.

"Can we build a barbecue and covered area for chillin' out?" Adam asked. "That would be cool."

"As long as you invite me too," Rocky said.

"Yeah, sure, Rock Daddy, 'course you can come over. You better come over, mate," Haydon said.

"With a barbecue and patio," Aiden said.

Discussions continued about where the key safe should be placed and the location of the car port and mention of the vehicles.

"What's that about? Has Mr. Cleator got some cars for us to drive around?" Adam asked.

"Seems like it. I'll probably find out about it on Tuesday. He must have to Utes available cause he wants to build a carport for two cars," Rocky said. "Looking at this map, I think it would be good here, between my carriages and the office block." Rocky pointed to the spot on the map. "We can change that path, so it joins up to the path to the office block. That way, it's all together near the car park. I might even build a carport on this other end for my cars," Rocky continued.

"Do we all agree that the carport goes where Rocky suggested and we put the key safe in the carport?" Aiden asked and got everyone's agreement.

"Does anyone have anything else to talk about or to decide on?" asked Aiden.

"Yeah, what are we going to do next weekend? Are we going to start clearing up somewhere?" Jacob asked.

"Yeah, Rocky. Can we start some work this week and get ready to work over the Easter weekend and our holidays?" Aiden asked.

"Can't see why not. Have a think about what you want to do, and I suggest we have another meeting on Tuesday or Wednesday night, after I have seen George and have the check," Rocky suggested.

"Can we stay there over Easter?" Nick asked.

"And for our holidays?" Tony added.

"That sounds cool. We can work part of the day, muck around on the beach, and chill out at night," Shayne said. "Can we, Rocky? Can we? That will be so cool."

"Where are you going to sleep? We probably won't have any buildings ready by then," Rocky said.

"Ah, we saw some large tents in the boat shed. It would be wicked to camp out and have a campfire at night, just like you told us about months ago. That sounded wicked when you told us about camping and campfires. That would be totally cool," Declan said.

"I can't see any harm in that, but you'd better clear it with your mums," Rocky advised.

"That'll be cool. They won't mind. We might even be able to get some mums over one afternoon and have a barbecue and show 'em around," Pieter said.

"That's a great idea, guys. Have a think about it and decide at your next meeting. Probably Easter Sunday afternoon would be a good idea. Your mums can bring you the Easter goodies that the Easter Bunny leaves for you," Rocky teased.

"Oh, Rocky, get real. The Easter Bunny? What are you on about?" Adam asked.

"That's cool. My mum always gives me Easter eggs at Easter. All your mums do, even yours, Adam," Aiden said.

"Yeah, I know, only gagging ya," Adam said. "It would be awesome to have a barbecue, a tour around the park, and get some eggs."

"Anything else to talk about?" Aiden asked.

"If everyone else is finished, I've got a couple of things," Rocky said. "First, keys. All you guys need a gate key. All gates are keyed alike, and you will need a key to the key safe," Rocky said.

"What's 'keyed alike' mean, Rocky?" Haydon asked.

"Means every gate has a padlock that has one key that opens all of them, so that means you only need one key to unlock all gates."

"How many gates are there?" Pieter asked.

Aiden counted. "Counting on the map, there are seven—main gate, two on the creek end, and four along the beach."

"Also, each of you should have a key to the key safe," Rocky said. "That way, each of you will only need two keys; the rest we will keep in the key safe."

"Where do we get keys?" Haydon asked.

"I noticed a key-cutting machine and a lot of key blanks in the workshop," Rocky said.

"Oh, I saw all of those straight keys hanging up and wondered how they would work in a lock without any notch things on them," Aiden said.

"They are blanks. You put them in a cutting machine with the key you want to copy and cut a new one. Tell ya what—first thing we do next weekend is cut keys. I'll show each of you how to do it, and you can each cut your own keys," Rocky said. "I might get a key safe during the week and put it temporarily on the office block, and when the checkbook arrives, you can pay me back."

"Anything else, Rocky?" Aiden asked.

"Yeah, Mr. Watson spoke to me before and told me that he has two lads that he wants help with at school. I'm going to talk to each of them next week. You guys want to help other kids; you got your first two takers," Rocky said.

"That's cool, Rocky. Who are they?" Adam asked.

"Before I tell you, are you sure you want to help other kids? You gotta remember that you might end up helping kids that you might not get on with all that well. Seeing that you guys are such a tight group, I think you should remain that group, but at the same time, allow other kids in at times to help. No fighting; no pushing them away. I'm sure that you can stay as you are while spending time with others. Sure, they can stay overnight occasionally; it's up to you. If you find someone who would be an asset to your group in helping others, learning new skills, let it happen. I just want you to know that I am there to help you with other guys."

"Yeah, that's cool, Rocky. I think we all know what you are saying," Pieter said.

"Who are they?" Haydon asked.

"Tell you in a minute. Another thing you need to remember is that any information you get must remain confidential. You can talk about it among yourselves or with me but no one else. And only talk about them when you are formulating a plan to help, not just for the gossip value. At times, I will have information that I might not be able to tell you, and you must respect that and understand why," Rocky said. "Now that we got that straight, the first boy is Dillon. You remember, he was at Bob's office last week. The second is Matt. Apparently he is injuring himself," Rocky told them.

"Yeah, I've seen Matt cutting himself and banging his fingers at woodwork. He's crazy, man," Jacob said.

"Now, fellas, remember—kids do things that may seem crazy, but there is always a reason. Something is happening in his life that is not right. Remember you guys did a lot of crazy things too until I came along, got you off that tram and onto another, and took you away from the shit that caused your problems. Give him some space, some respect, and we, together, will find out what is going wrong in his life and help him with whatever it is. Each of you will pick up on just a little clue, and when we put them all together, the causes will come out."

"I don't think that we have to vote on that. After all, that's what we said we wanted to do—help other guys; that's what got us the park," Aiden said. "Whatever Rocky decides, we will work together and see if we can help Dillon and Matt. Now, if there is nothin' else, the meeting is closed until Tuesday or Wednesday night."

"Hey, dude, you did well, holding the meeting. You all did well; you really are very level-headed and very fast learners. Congratulations, guys—you awesome Young Guns," Rocky said.

"Okay, who's for a swim? That sunshine is wicked on our bodies. Wicked," Pieter said.

After some time, swimming at the beach, everyone got together for a chat about the events of the best weekend the guys had experienced. Fond discussion took place about the skateboards, the rock festival, and the chance to play live onstage in front of an audience. Discussion moved onto their dinner experience, the happiness on their mothers' faces at being out together for a formal event, the dancing, and the dance routine that Adrian had performed and had taught them to compete in that impromptu dance competition.

Talk then turned to the chill sessions around Pieter's pool, the skinny-dip, and the game they invented, the quiet drinks and food, and the chats that took place.

The guys then went on to talk about the events of today, the trip to the park, the discoveries on the walk through the park, finding equipment and furniture, the buildings onsite, planning on building their dream—the dream of a place of their own. They continued their discussions onto how they could set aside areas for activities that could be used in their mission to help other guys at risk of getting into trouble, planning their campout over their school holiday, and their future sleepovers. Excitement was at a fever pitch as each of the ten Young Guns spoke and remembered their awesome weekend.

"This adrenaline rush sure is better than any trip I've had on booze and drugs, Rocky," Aiden said.

"Yeah, Rocky, you were right when you said a long time ago that there are better highs in life when you're clean than from doing that shit we used to do," Haydon said.

Jacob chimed in, "Yeah, this mate here, Rocky, told us that one day it would all happen. I didn't believe him but went along with you other guys to see if it could happen, and, yep, it did."

Pieter said, "How did you know, Rocky? How did you know that this would happen?"

"Well, guys, I believe that if you can dream it, you can achieve it," Rocky began. "I had a dream, a goal for you guys, that you deserved a better life than what you had. You were alone, together, but each of you in your own world was alone, with no mentor, no one to look to, and no one to show you an alternative. Each of you needed some hope, some direction, and, I guess, some brotherly or fatherly love. That love, hope, and belief in yourselves was sadly missing. I was able to make my dream become your dream, and you guys made your dream come true. In no way did I ever think it would ever be this good. I hoped it would, but I never imagined how it could be achieved. Luckily for you, you all stopped and listened to this old tool and tried what he was suggesting. Obviously, what I was telling you made some sense to you, or you would not have followed."

"We really gave you heaps back then. Why did you keep on to us, Rocky?" Jay asked.

"I had many times when I could have walked away from the crap you all gave me," Rocky said. "I'd go home, thinking, *Stuff you guys, stuff you all. I don't need this.* Then I would pour myself a bourbon or two or even many more, and I'd chill and think of each of you, most times with tears in my eyes at the thought of where you were headed. Then I would come around and think, *someone needs to help these young lives.* I used to tell myself, 'You gotta keep going. You can't leave them on the scrap heap to rot. Get back in there and fight on.' I could see the potential in each of you. You each have your own personalities, your own mannerisms, but each of you, as far as I was concerned, had the potential to win, and, stuff me, now that you are the winners I imagined, you can't imagine how that makes me feel to see the champions you all are."

"You poor bastard. We are sorry for putting that shit on you, making you suffer so much because we were such pricks," Tony said.

"Yeah, sorry, Rocky, but we are so stoked that you kept at us to change," Aiden said.

"Hey, Rocky, we are not the champions; you are, dude," Pieter said.

"Hey, no way, man. You guys are the champions. You are the ones who started the race with nothing but hate, ignorance, and disrespect and ran the obstacle course to cross the finish line as champs," Rocky said. "You could probably say that I was the coach who provided the advice, offering alternative thoughts and the perseverance to allow you to change your attitudes to everything that got you where you are today. Well done, fellas. How about a group hug to celebrate our championship?"

The ten Teen-Morph Young Guns broke out of their group hug and burst into that now familiar tune, singing, "We are the champions of *our* world," as the sun set over the mountains behind the youth center camp.

Printed in the United States
By Bookmasters